THE GUILD CODEX: SPELLBOUND / SIX

DRUID VICES
AND A VODKA

ANNETTE MARIE

Druid Vices and a Vodka
The Guild Codex: Spellbound / Book Six

Dark Owl Fantasy Inc.
PO Box 88106, Rabbit Hill Post Office
Edmonton, AB, Canada T6R 0M5
www.darkowlfantasy.com

Cover Copyright © 2019 by Annette Ahner
Cover and Book Interior by Midnight Whimsy Designs
www.midnightwhimsydesigns.com

Editing by Elizabeth Darkley
arrowheadediting.wordpress.com

ISBN 978-1-988153-40-7

MORE BOOKS BY ANNETTE MARIE

STEEL & STONE UNIVERSE

Steel & Stone Series

Chase the Dark
Bind the Soul
Yield the Night
Reap the Shadows
Unleash the Storm
Steel & Stone

Spell Weaver Trilogy

The Night Realm
The Shadow Weave
The Blood Curse

OTHER WORKS

Red Winter Trilogy

Red Winter
Dark Tempest
Immortal Fire

THE GUILD CODEX

CLASSES OF MAGIC

Spiritalis
Psychica
Arcana
Demonica
Elementaria

MYTHIC

A person with magical ability

MPD / MAGIPOL

The organization that regulates mythics and their activities

ROGUE

A mythic living in violation of MPD laws

DRUID VICES
AND A VODKA

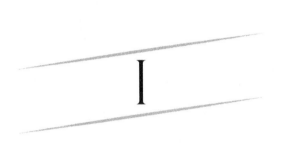

I

"'**FROM THE BEST-SELLING AUTHOR** of *The Devil She Loved*,'" Aaron read dramatically, "'comes *Her Demon's Heart*—'"

"Aaron—"

"'—a *scandalous* new romance with—'"

"Aaron!" I growled, grabbing at my phone.

He held the device higher, electric blue eyes dancing with mirth. "'Will Angela win her soul back from the demon who holds it, or'"—he cracked up, swallowed, and finished in a choked gargle—"'or will he claim *her heart* as well?'"

I took one more swipe for my phone, almost fell on the bar between us, then dropped back onto my heels. Folding my arms, I glowered at him. Lucky for me, the two dozen patrons in the Crow and Hammer weren't paying attention to Aaron's enthusiastic narration. Though the pub had quieted after the dinner rush an hour ago, it was busy for a Wednesday night.

"Is *this* what you like to read?" Cackling, he dropped back onto his stool. "I thought you were more into thrillers and detective stories and stuff."

"It's just a stupid ad."

He arched a skeptical eyebrow and sipped his rum and coke. "I mean, you can read what you want, Tori, but—"

"I wasn't looking for romance novels." I plucked my phone out of his hand and closed the app displaying the unwanted ad. "I was just—just doing some Googling earlier, okay?"

The amusement in his eyes dimmed, but he hitched his smile back into place. "You won't find anything like that on Google. 'Demon' searches will just get you loads of movies, video games, and *scandalous* romances."

"And blogs by crazy people," I muttered, jamming my phone in my pocket.

Trying a regular ol' internet search had been dumb, but I'd had no idea where to start. How did a not-very-mythical girl like me research demonic artifacts? The closest thing to a mythic Wikipedia—a Mythipedia, if you will—was the MPD's outdated website. What did that even leave?

I'd learned one thing, at least: use an ad-blocker. Whatever advertising tech-juju had decided I was into fictional escapades with sexy devil men was hella determined. Not that some of the novels didn't look intriguing, but the topic lacked appeal right now.

Noting Aaron's lingering smirk, I asked irritably, "Shouldn't you be working?"

"We're done. Everyone is just bullshitting now."

I looked past him. Clustered around several tables was a group that included not only the familiar faces of my fellow guildeds, but also six members of Odin's Eye. I knew Mario, a demon contractor, but the others—three more tough-looking men and two equally tough women—were recent acquaintances. Chatting with the Crow and Hammer mythics, they lazily packed up their array of papers and maps.

Leaning one hip on the bar, I let my gaze wander to the dimmest corner of the pub. My mouth quirked up and I laughed softly.

Aaron followed my gaze. "Subtle, aren't they?"

Tucked in the private little corner, Kai and Izzah had their chairs pulled close. Ostensibly working—exactly two papers sat on their table—they were deep in conversation. His arm rested on the back of her chair, and she was leaning into his side as he spoke.

Yeah, super subtle.

Noticing our attention, Kai pulled away from Izzah. They slid out from behind their table, grabbed their papers, and headed over. I hid my glee as the beautiful hydromage settled onto the stool beside Aaron, her thick black hair sweeping down her back and her russet skin tinged with an almost indiscernible flush. Her cocoa-brown eyes sparkled with delight.

His companion absorbing most of his attention, Kai took the stool on her other side. A tiny smile lingered on his lips— and, oh my, that hint of flirtatious amusement on the normally serious electramage was devastating. My heart gave a sympathetic flutter as Izzah's blush deepened.

Resisting the urge to fist-pump triumphantly, I calmly asked, "How'd the meeting go?"

"Well," Izzah drawled in her throaty accent, which I'd recently learned was Malaysian, "we pooled the results from our surveillance missions over the past week."

"The results were a resounding 'nothing,'" Kai added.

I pulled a rocks glass from under the counter and scooped ice into it. "And that's a bad thing?"

Izzah propped her chin on her hand, elbow braced on the bar. "Criminal activity has dropped off a cliff-*lah*. We can't even *find* rogues, let alone catch them. It's abnormal."

"I think Red Rum could be making a comeback," Aaron mused, "but we haven't found any evidence."

"Like I said, there's no way Red Rum is involved." Kai tilted his head in a silent request and I obligingly doubled the amount of rum I was pouring into the glass. "Between losing ships in September and MPD crackdowns after that, they've had a tough winter. I think they've pulled out entirely."

"*Aiyoh*, such a shame," Izzah sighed with mock sympathy.

I topped Kai's drink off with fizzy cola and slid it to him. "If they're gone, who's left?

"That's what we're trying to figure out," Aaron answered. "The Odin's Eye officers are convinced the power landscape is shifting, and they think the absence of crime is related. I don't know about that, but I'd sure like to know who the kingpins are and who's gone off to a new playground."

Izzah pulled Kai's drink out of his hand and took a long sip. "I know one rogue who may have left the arena entirely—that or someone finally killed him-*lo*."

A spike of nervous energy hit my gut. "Which rogue is that?"

"The Ghost."

"Oh," I said vaguely. No sense in confirming that, yes, the notorious rogue known as the Ghost, a wanted criminal so mysterious no one knew his name, face, or class, had indeed left Vancouver for good. That would prompt a whole bunch of awkward questions like, "How do you know that?" and "Why have you been protecting the identity of a dangerous felon?"

"*Wah*, now that's a bounty I'd love to claim." Her eyes brightened as she passed Kai's drink back to him. "Have you two ever thought about making a go at it?"

"Pass," Aaron replied casually. "Waste of time."

No truer words. "Elusive" was Zak's middle name. The guy could literally become invisible with a bit of fae magic.

A clatter of chairs interrupted our conversation. The six Odin's Eye mythics had climbed to their feet. Calling farewells, they headed for the door.

"*Chup*, that's my cue," Izzah said, sliding off her stool. Her gaze found Kai and softened in a distinctly sultry fashion. "I'll see you later, *leng chai*."

Sweeping her hair off her shoulders, she glided away in a weightless, sashaying walk. I watched her go, grinning like an idiot. *See you later?* See you later *in bed*, more like.

Okay, no, I shouldn't jump to conclusions. Their obvious attraction aside, Kai was technically unavailable. That's the whole reason they'd been cozied up in a corner, under the cover of a joint-guild job, instead of cozied up together in a more private, and horizontal, location.

Hmm. I was maybe too invested in their sex life. Was that weird?

As the last Odin's Eye mythics left with a jingle of the bell, Kai gulped half his rum and coke. "I don't like it."

"Don't like what?" I demanded, my mind still on him, Izzah, and whether I could machinate a properly romantic evening for them without either realizing what I was up to.

"How quiet everything has been since New Year's. Something is brewing, but I can't imagine what."

I shrugged. "How bad can a crime respite really be? I've had more than enough excitement lately."

Glimpsing an approaching customer from the corner of my eye, I switched on my professional Bartender of Awesomeness smile and turned to ask what I could get them.

A pair of ocean-blue eyes peeked up at me through dark-rimmed glasses. Robin Page, our guild's one and only demon contractor, stood three long steps away, twisting the hem of her black sweater in her hands. Her brunette hair was tied in a ponytail so short it stuck off the back of her head, loose strands framing her heart-shaped face.

My mouth hung open, my question forgotten. She was at the guild so rarely that seeing her was a shock.

"Hi Tori," she began in a soft, shy alto. "How are … you … to … night …"

She shrank in on herself with each stuttering word. I blinked and glanced sideways. Kai and Aaron had spotted her as well—and they were giving her the coldest stares I'd ever seen them direct at a fellow guild member, including several assholes who routinely deserved punches to the throat.

"Good … good to see … you," Robin whispered, backing away. With a frightened look at the two mages, she practically ran to the stairs.

As she rushed up the steps, I whirled on my friends. "What *the hell*, guys? I know razzing new people is a thing around here, but she—"

"She's trouble," Kai interrupted.

"*Her*? You almost made her cry just now."

Aaron shook his head. "You've seen what her demon can do. There's no way she's as easily intimidated as she appears. We don't know anything specific, but we've heard things."

"Such as?"

He frowned at his drink, the last mouthfuls diluted by melting ice cubes. "The Crow and Hammer tends to collect misfits. Some of our members are former rogues who've turned their lives around. Darius is usually a good judge of character, but not every mythic who gets a second chance here changes their ways."

Now that he mentioned it, what did I know about Robin? Not much, and a lot of it was kind of suspicious. "So you're saying …"

"She's too new to trust," Kai said bluntly. "Believe us on this one, Tori."

I mulled that over, then untied my apron. "I'm taking a break. Holler if anyone needs me."

They nodded. Tossing my apron on the back counter, I cut around the bar to the stairs. On the second-floor landing, I paused in the open doorway that led into the communal work area, packed with long tables, shared computers, whiteboards and corkboards, and a screen with a scrolling list of bounties and jobs from the MPD website. I'd spent a fair number of hours up here with the guys, working on college assignments while they planned their next job.

Now that I was training regularly, I was probably ready to join them on their less dangerous jobs—assuming they wanted my help—but the recent calm in the city had left the Crow and Hammer's bounty hunters out of work. Same for Odin's Eye, which was why our guilds had joined forces to unravel the mysterious ceasefire among rogues.

Ten members were scattered throughout the room, all working alone except for a group of four at the far end: Liam, the weaselly telekinetic; Julian, a new apprentice sorcerer and our youngest member; and Alyssa, a banana-haired apprentice a couple of years older.

They were sitting at a table with Ezra, who'd come up here to avoid the Odin's Eye team—or more specifically, to avoid Mario, their demon contractor. A wise precaution for an illegal demon mage.

He was pointing at a laptop screen, and I could tell from his slow gestures and his gaze, shifting from person to person, that he was explaining something. I could almost hear his soothing voice as he patiently talked the younger mythics through whatever they were working on. A magnetic pull tugged me toward him, luring me to his side.

His head turned, and his eyes met mine from across the long room.

I flashed him a smile and waved cheerily, then hurried up the next flight of stairs. Jaw clenched, I leaned against the wall and breathed deep.

Damn it.

Since Christmas, I'd dedicated every waking hour outside work and school to researching the demonic amulet. Seeing as I'd stolen it from a demon and used it—once—to interrupt another demon's contract, I didn't have much to go on.

As soon as I got home tonight, I would pull out the stack of books and printouts hidden under my bed—Demonica jobs and bounties from the MPD archives; books I'd borrowed from Arcana Historia, a guild with a semi-private library; histories of summoning; studies on demons—and spend an hour or two paging through them, exactly as I'd been doing for weeks. So far, I'd found nothing.

And I was almost out of time.

Ezra's demon had promised to wait until the full moon on January 21—only five nights away. If I didn't have answers by then ... I wasn't sure what would happen, but I was willing to bet it'd be messy.

Pushing off the wall, I straightened my spine. Ezra thought he was doomed. Aaron and Kai thought he was doomed. Somehow, all three of them were continuing on with their lives like usual, as though Ezra's remaining days couldn't be counted in months. That wasn't good enough for me. I wasn't giving up.

Desperate times called for desperate measures.

Robin hadn't been in the workroom, which meant she was up here. Turning away from the guild leadership offices, I tiptoed down a narrow hall. No, I didn't need to tiptoe, but it seemed appropriate since, technically, I had zero business being up here.

Most of the guild's magic-usage rooms were in the basement—the alchemy lab, the sparring room, and a spell-testing bomb shelter sorta hole thing—but the Arcana Atrium was the exception. A white sign hanging on its door read, "Arcana In Progress," and scribbled underneath was, "So keep out, losers!" I recognized Ramsey's handwriting.

Raising my hand to knock, I froze at an almost inaudible murmur.

"... not happening."

Was that Robin's voice? Canting my head, I saw that the door wasn't latched, the gap allowing sound to leak out.

"Forget it," she continued, her words too quiet and muffled for me to make out everything. "You can't ... *smelling* ... would I explain ..."

Smelling? Had I heard that right?

"We'll have to ... right time. You'll get ... to ... mages eventually."

Mages? What mages was she talking about? Eyes narrowing, I seized the handle and whipped the door open, revealing a largish room crowded with stuff. A permanent circle, aligned beneath a square skylight, had been etched into the dark floor, which was made of a smooth material that shone like glass. Cupboards, bookshelves, and a worktable, all well-worn and bursting with their contents, lined the walls.

Perched a stool, Robin was facing a newish grimoire, open on the scuffed worktable—and beside her was her demon. He stood like a lifeless statue, his softly glowing eyes the color of bubbling lava. He didn't so much as twitch at my appearance, staring blankly at the opposite wall, his arms hanging at his side.

Robin made up for her demon's lack of response by whirling on her stool with a frightened squeak. Her wide eyes goggled at me from behind her glasses, one hand pressed to the side of her face.

"T-Tori," she stammered. "Um. Just a moment, please?"

She shifted her hand, and I spotted the cell phone she held.

"I'm sorry," she said to her phone. "Can I call you back? Thank you. Bye." Lowering her phone, she rubbed her sternum. "You startled me."

"Sorry." I only half heard her, my stare fixed on her demon. This was my first up-close look at him. "Who were you talking to?"

She hesitated, taken aback by my nosy question. "Amalia."

Her blond friend she'd joined the guild with? If Robin was an absentee member, I didn't know how to describe Amalia.

I took a cautious step closer to her demon, amazed at his slight stature. To be fair, he was no pushover. A couple inches taller than me, the demon was all muscle—hard, ropey muscle that suggested agility as much as strength. Compared to the other demons I'd seen, however, he was a shrimp.

My gaze traveled from the small horns poking out of his messy black hair and across his disconcertingly human face to the mixture of light armor and dark fabric he wore. Not that he wore much. Most of his reddish-brown skin was exposed.

"Do you dress him?" I asked curiously, studying the metal plate over his heart, the center etched with a strange symbol. "Or did he come fully accessorized?"

She peeked between me and the demon. "He—he came that way. Um. Can I help you with anything?"

"Yeah." I leaned sideways to get a better look at the demon's midriff. "Damn, girl."

"P-pardon me?"

I pointed. "You can see this, right? I know he's a demon and all, but *those abs*. They might be the most demony thing about him. No man has abs that perfect."

When Robin didn't respond, I glanced over. She was cringing on her seat, her blush so intense her face was glowing as red as her demon's eyes.

"I can't put clothing on him," she babbled, hands twisting together. "Extra clothes can't go into the infernus with him. But—but it's fine. He's a d-demon, not a ... not a ... *man*," she finished in a strained whisper.

I arched an eyebrow. I hadn't been suggesting she dress him—I'd merely been wondering if she enjoyed the view—but apparently, her demon being half naked and totally ripped made her uncomfortable for some reason.

Planting my hands on my hips, I gave the unmoving demon one more swift assessment, this time comparing his eyes to

Ezra's when they glowed with demonic power. Before being bound inside a human body, had Eterran looked like this, or was he more like the winged demon who'd stalked us on Halloween?

"Why've you got him out, anyway?" I asked.

"I …" She patted one cheek as though to make her blush fade faster. "I've been looking into … the magical properties of … demon blood."

That sounded unsavory. With a thoughtful "hmm," I parked my butt on the table beside her, happy to put the girl between me and the demon. Great bod or not, he gave me the heebie-jeebies.

"So … I want to ask you something."

"Something *else*," she muttered under her breath, a hint of an annoyed bite in her voice.

"Yep." I squashed my final doubts and jumped right in. "Do you know anything about demonic artifacts?"

"You mean objects used for summoning and contracting, like the infernus?"

I glanced at the silver pendant hanging around her neck. "I mean an artifact made *with* demon magic. Made *by* demons. Is that a thing?"

Asking her was a risk, but neither Ezra nor I had much to lose. I had to ask *someone*, and I'd rather take a chance on a guild member, however new and possibly untrustworthy, than a complete stranger.

Robin absorbed my question, her expression serious. "Why do you ask?"

"Just some research I'm doing for a job."

"Oh." Another hesitation, then she turned to her demon. She rapped her knuckles against the square plate over his heart.

"This is a demonic artifact. It has magical properties, but I don't know more than that. Summoned demons might carry artifacts, but once contracted, they can't use them or create new ones."

Her demon's armor was magical? Interesting, but not helpful. "Any idea who might know something about these sorts of artifacts?"

"Short of discussing it with a demon, I don't know how anyone could learn much …"

"Do people do that? Have conversations with a demon?"

"Well, summoners talk to demons before making a contract with them, but … even if someone has studied it, finding Demonica experts is difficult." Her brow wrinkled, and she sighed like she also knew how it felt to run into dead ends at every turn. "Summoners aren't common, and experienced, knowledgeable ones are even more scarce."

Frustration burned through me. How was I supposed to learn anything about the amulet, then? The MPD's database listed only one active summoner in the greater Vancouver area, and he was currently in custody—on charges I didn't have clearance to see. Even if I could talk to him, why would he tell me anything?

My hands clenched as I fought back a wave of anxiety. Ezra's life depended on me, and I was getting nowhere.

Robin cleared her throat. "I'm also researching more obscure facets of Demonica. Not about that, specifically, but …" She fidgeted with the hem of her sweater. "There's a mythic … a retired summoner. He's an infernus maker now. I heard he's a collector of esoteric Demonica knowledge. I was planning to go speak with him but I …"

As she trailed off into a mumble, I caught the words, "go by myself."

"Can I come along?" I asked immediately. A *retired* summoner—that was exactly the sort of approachable Demonica mythic I needed. "We can both see if he knows anything about our ... research topics."

Her blue eyes warmed. "That sounds good. You work most evenings, don't you? When's your next day off?"

"Saturday," I answered promptly, then silently swore. Saturday was only two nights from the full moon. That was cutting it way too close.

Robin was already nodding. "Okay. Let's meet here at seven."

Would it look suspicious if I tried to rush things? Damn it! "Seven it is."

Her face brightened with a smile. I squinted at her open, obvious pleasure at having a research buddy and wondered what on earth Aaron and Kai thought this girl was up to. She didn't have a deceptive bone in her teeny, five-foot-nothing body.

I sighed. "Robin? Can I offer some advice?"

Her brow furrowed. "Yes?"

"When someone butts in on you and starts asking questions you'd rather not answer, 'get the hell out, you nosy asshat' is a good response. You should try it."

She blinked. "Oh."

"See you on Saturday." With a final glance at her demon, who hadn't even blinked during our conversation, I left her to whatever weird "magic blood properties" thing she'd been up to before I burst in.

At the stairs, I paused with one hand on the railing, reconsidering my new plans with the odd demon contractor. She seemed so harmless … but that demon definitely wasn't. Even if it didn't make sense to me, I knew better than to disregard a warning from Aaron and Kai.

With a shake of my head, I continued downward. Her infernus-maker lead was all I had, and I wasn't backing out now. I'd just be careful.

After all, what sort of dangerous secrets could a girl like Robin be hiding, really?

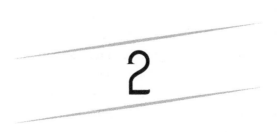

2

WITH MY MIND on a hundred different things and my gaze on my feet, I trotted down the stairs. I was so lost in thought that when another pair of shoes appeared in my line of sight, I didn't react.

Until I ran right into the sturdy body attached to those shoes.

Strong hands caught my elbows, steadying me, and a mouthwatering scent teased my nose. I looked up into mismatched eyes, one warm brown like melted chocolate, the other pale as ice with a dark ring around the iris.

"Ezra!" I gasped. Should I have pulled away from him? Yes. Did I? Hell no.

His hands slid down my arms. Even with my sweater between his palms and my skin, I shivered, fighting the urge to plaster myself against him. Did this man have any idea what he did to me with a casual touch?

He smiled that soft smile of his. "Has Odin's Eye left? Am I clear to go downstairs?"

Yeah, he had no clue.

"You're good," I replied, only slightly breathless. "I was coming to get you. I need your help."

"With what?"

"Making Kai blush over his super-crush on Izzah."

Ezra laughed. "We'll make it happen."

I grinned, battling the renewed urge to touch him as my heart did painful flip-flops against my ribs.

It'd been like this for weeks. I wanted to touch him, hold him, drag him straight into my bed. But he'd asked me to be his friend, so I was pretending as hard as I could that we'd never shared an earthshaking kiss. He was pretending too. Neither of us had mentioned it since Christmas, and I suspected that was the only reason he wasn't avoiding me.

Luckily, I had lots of practice pretending I wasn't wildly attracted to him. The bigger problem was the way my throat closed with panicky anguish whenever I got near him. *That* reaction was more difficult to hide, but I'd been doing a damn good job anyway. The last thing Ezra needed was me tearing up every time he walked into a room.

Still grinning, I caught his hand and tugged him across the landing. He'd asked to be friends, but holding hands was the one thing I couldn't resist—and he didn't seem to mind either.

We got halfway down the stairs before I realized the noise level in the pub had risen. Ezra slowed, his fingers tightening around mine. Had the Odin's Eye team returned?

Cameron wheeled around the corner at the bottom of the stairs and charged up them. Ezra and I pressed into the wall to avoid getting run over.

"Oi!" I yelled. "Where's the fire?"

"You won't *believe* who just came in!" he called over his shoulder. "It's *Shane Davila!* I'm getting Cearra!"

As he vanished into the second-floor workroom, I frowned. "Shane Davila? I think I know that name."

"He's a bounty hunter," Ezra supplied. "Pretty famous. He was at the Sinclair Christmas party."

"Oh, I remember! Wait—he was at the Christmas party? Why didn't anyone point him out? I didn't notice a bounty hunter."

"He's hard to spot in a crowd. Come on, let's go see."

In the pub, everyone was clustered in a tight group, and I spotted Aaron's telltale copper hair. He was enthusiastically shaking the hand of a man in his forties. Next to Aaron's well-muscled, six-foot-one build, the new arrival looked laughably short and frail, with a slight potbelly on his wiry frame and a perfectly spherical, bald head. Round spectacles gave him the air of a grumpy middle manager.

No wonder I hadn't noticed him at the Christmas party. I'd probably mistaken him for some rich dude's valet. Face scrunched in disbelief, I circled the group and dropped onto Aaron's vacated stool. Only Kai had remained seated, his phone in one hand and the other elbow propped on the bar.

"So that's the famous bounty hunter Aaron admires?" I asked dubiously as Ezra settled onto the stool beside me. "Not what I was expecting."

"Don't let his appearance fool you," Kai warned. "Shane Davila is a genius. He's a modern-day, mythic Sherlock Holmes."

"Does he have the magic power of deduction?" I asked as Shane patiently shook hands with each Crow and Hammer admirer, a worn briefcase clutched under his other arm. Completing his odd getup was a pair of black leather gloves.

"Just about. He's a psychometric. He can read an object's past by touching it."

"Huh? *Read* an object's *past*? How does that work?"

"Mr. Davila!" Appearing from the kitchen, Ramsey had joined the group and was shaking the bounty hunter's hand with both of his. "It's an honor to meet you!"

Returning from the upper level in a rush, Cameron and Cearra squeezed into the group too, and Shane nearly vanished beneath the press.

"Guys!" Aaron waved his arms. "Give Shane a little space here. You're gonna crush the guy."

The mythics backed up and Shane reappeared.

He cleared his throat. "Thank you, Aaron. A drink, perhaps?"

As the others goggled at the realization that Aaron and the famous bounty hunter were on a first-name basis, I hopped off my stool and hurried around the bar. I was properly in position when Aaron and Shane reached the counter. Shane set his briefcase on the floor.

"Rum and coke, please," Aaron ordered. "Shane, what would you like?"

"Vodka, straight."

My eyebrows rose. Not quite as sissy as he looked. I grabbed a rocks glass and a small tumbler.

"Shane, you remember Kai and Ezra, right? We didn't get much of a chance to talk at Christmas."

I grumbled silently as Shane shook hands with the other two mages. So they'd gotten to meet the bounty hunter, but not me? I'd been with them most of the night. Must've been bad timing on my part.

"You were in Europe before this, weren't you?" Aaron asked, leaning against the bar. "On a special MPD case?"

"Yes. It was an interesting one. I wish I could tell you the story, but it's classified."

"That's no fun," Aaron complained, amused rather than annoyed.

Ezra listened with interest, but Kai's attention was on his phone, that little smile back on his lips. I'd bet my paycheck he was texting Izzah.

"Bounties are my livelihood," Shane replied good-naturedly. "I can't go around revealing my cases or methods. The MPD is always too interested in what I'm up to next."

I considered the vodka in my well, then decided this guy was important enough for the good stuff. I ducked into the kitchen to see what was in the fridge. Quality vodka needed to be chilled.

"How about a hint on your current case?" Aaron was asking as I returned with a frosty bottle. "My dad said you're in Vancouver for a big bounty."

As I filled the small tumbler, Shane smiled mysteriously.

"Perhaps I can do better than a hint," he said. "I have some investigative work to complete before I'm ready for the tag, and I could use a skilled combat mythic as an escort. Would you be interested, Aaron?"

Aaron's eyes widened. "Damn right I'm interested! It'd be a privilege to work with you."

"Perfect. I'm still working out the details, but I'll be in touch in the next few days."

I slid the mythic his drink. "It's on the house. Enjoy."

"Thank you, Miss …"

"Dawson, but call me Tori." I canted an exasperated look at Aaron. "Thanks for introducing me."

He winced. "Oh shit, sorry! I didn't realize you hadn't met. Shane, Tori was at our Christmas party too, but you might have missed her."

"I remember you." Shane picked up the tumbler and sniffed its contents. "However, we didn't have a chance to speak."

He remembered me? Must've been my dress. I'd looked smokin'.

"So, what's the job?" Aaron asked eagerly. "I know Vancouver inside and out, so I might be able to steer you in the right direction."

Shane lifted his glass to his lips, took a sip, and rolled it in his mouth before swallowing. "Are you familiar with the Ghost?"

I froze halfway through pouring rum into the rocks glass. Aaron's expression blanked and Kai's gaze snapped from his phone to Shane. Only Ezra's poker face didn't flicker.

"Uh … reasonably familiar." Aaron couldn't quite suppress the cautious note in his voice. "Every bounty hunter from here to Seattle knows about the Ghost, but it's always a dead end."

"Some interesting information has come to my attention, and I'd like to see where it takes me."

Realizing I'd filled Aaron's glass halfway with rum, I set the liquor bottle aside and topped his drink with cola. Here's hoping he wouldn't choke on his first sip.

"Tagging the Ghost would be wild," he told Shane, "but recent evidence suggests he's left the Vancouver area. There haven't been any sightings of him in months."

"Deeply entrenched rogues don't lightly abandon their territories," the bounty hunter said confidently. "I have several leads to follow. If you're comfortable tackling a DOA bounty like this one, I'd like to have you on board."

"I—of course. Not an issue at all. I have no problem with …" As Aaron hurriedly assured the famous bounty hunter that he wasn't intimidated by any rogue, Ezra murmured quietly, "Kai? What's wrong?"

I looked over. Kai sat rigid on his stool, staring at his phone. His face had paled, his jaw so tight a vein throbbed in his cheek.

He stood, almost toppling his stool. "I need to go."

"Kai?" I began anxiously. "What—"

He was already striding away. Ezra was off his seat, a step behind Kai as the electramage made a beeline for the door.

"Excuse me, Shane." Aaron hardly spared the bounty hunter a glance as he rushed after his friends.

I gritted my teeth. My shift wasn't over for hours, meaning I was stuck here. If it was urgent, they'd tell me … right? I yanked my phone out of my pocket and hammered out a message: *What the hell is going on? Is Kai okay?*

"Miss Dawson?" Shane murmured.

"Call me Tori," I muttered distractedly as I sent the question to our group chat. "Would you like anything else? Appetizer? Dinner?"

"Perhaps I could ask you a few questions."

My gaze froze on my phone, the chat abandoned except for my lonely question. Raising my head, I looked into Shane's gray-brown eyes behind those icky round glasses. "What sort of questions?"

"You're a witch, correct? Discovered as a mythic last August?"

"Yeah, that's right."

"And you've worked at the Crow and Hammer for eight months?"

Nervous anger flitted through me. "That's public info, dude. You don't need to ask me."

"Has anyone from the Crow and Hammer ever investigated the Ghost before?"

Even if I'd been born yesterday, I would've recognized that for the trick question it was. "What do the MPD records say?"

"The Crow and Hammer has never officially investigated the Ghost, but last summer—June and July, specifically—several members made urgent inquiries to other guilds and MPD offices regarding the Ghost and his suspected whereabouts."

Shit. The Crow and Hammer had made urgent inquiries because the Ghost had kidnapped me.

"I was just a bartender back then," I told him.

"Even Darius King was asking interesting questions," Shane continued as though I hadn't spoken. "The Crow and Hammer seemed very keen on the Ghost, but they never logged anything in the system."

"Maybe they never got anywhere so there was nothing to log."

"Perhaps," he agreed neutrally, taking a long sip of his vodka. "Around the same time, the MPD questioned several Crow and Hammer members, including Aaron, Kai, and Ezra, concerning a case that involved the disappearance of a teen girl."

I returned the rum bottle to my well and said flatly, "Did they."

"You were questioned as well, according to the records, but you were … just a bartender back then?"

"Yeah, I was," I snapped. "You read the report, right? So you can screw right off with your bullshit questions."

He sipped his vodka and didn't budge from his seat. "The human suspects in that case claimed that the red-haired woman who used an illegal artifact to question them was allied with the Ghost."

"Oh damn." I laid the sarcasm on thick as I glared at him. "Then that must've been me, because there couldn't *possibly* be more than one red-haired woman in the greater Vancouver area."

"A red-haired woman in the company of Aaron, Kai, and Ezra?"

Ignoring the panicked racing of my heart, I planted my hands on the bar and leaned forward, putting myself eye to eye with the bounty hunter. "A little pointer, Shane. You won't be the first asshole with an agenda I've thrown out of my bar, and you won't be the last."

Shane didn't flinch at my arctic glare. Without breaking eye contact, he lifted his briefcase onto the bar and popped it open. Plastic rustled as he reached inside it.

He closed his briefcase and set a clear plastic bag on top of it. "Evidence" was stamped across it in red, and shielded inside was a pair of women's runners with an ugly black stain discoloring the sides.

My face went cold, the blood draining from my head, but I couldn't stop my visceral reaction to the sight of those shoes.

"These," Shane murmured, "belong to you."

It wasn't a question, and I didn't bother denying it. My shoes. I remembered staggering up a flight of stairs, drunk from dragon blood exposure. I remembered kicking those runners away as I stripped off my clothes to get in the shower.

I'd left my shoes behind. I'd forgotten them in Zak's bathroom, in his private upper-floor suite, in his farmhouse in the hidden valley that was his only refuge.

"Miss Dawson," the bounty hunter said quietly, "let's talk about where you were last summer from June thirtieth to July fourteenth."

He was a psychometric, able to read an object's past with a touch. What had he learned from my shoes? How much did he know? Knees weak, I took a stumbling step backward—and thumped against someone. A hand closed around my shoulder, squeezing gently, and a familiar voice spoke above my head.

"What an honor to have a renowned bounty hunter in my guild. A pleasure to encounter you again, Shane."

The evidence bag was already back in Shane's briefcase as he rose to his feet, gaining a few precious inches of height as he looked up at the man beside me.

"Darius," Shane said coldly. "I would say the pleasure is all yours."

"Oh, most certainly." Darius settled his arm over my shoulders. "What brings you to my humble bar?"

"I asked the Sinclair boy if he was available to assist me on a case, though perhaps I should've considered how much your influence may have corrupted him over the years."

"I prefer to think my influence is all to the positive."

"I doubt that very much." Shane slid his briefcase off the counter. "I hope you're enjoying retirement, Darius. You're very lucky it's here and not in a prison cell."

"I do enjoy my creature comforts." A mocking, steely note slid into Darius's voice. "But luck has nothing to do with it, Mr. Davila. Have fun with your case."

Dismissed, just like that. I squashed my grin.

Shane picked up his glass, tossed back the last of his vodka, and replaced the tumbler on the counter. His gaze turned to me, and with a faint smile, he crossed the pub. The bell jingled as the door closed behind him.

I let out a shaky breath and tipped my head back to bring the guild master into view. His gray eyes were bright with amusement as he looked down at me.

"So ... Shane doesn't like you," I guessed.

Dropping his arm from my shoulders, Darius scooped up Shane's glass and added it to my stack of used dishes. "Not at all."

"How come?"

Deep satisfaction flashed over his face, and he rubbed his short salt-and-pepper beard as though to erase the expression. "I belong to a small and very exclusive club that Shane would likely call The Ones Who Got Away."

I arched an eyebrow. "Are you admitting to being a rogue?"

"Roguish, maybe," he replied with a wink. "Now, Tori, I believe Clara is heading out in a few minutes. Why don't you call it a night and let her drive you home?"

"But my shift isn't over."

"Ramsey and I will cover for you. I would hate for any impolitely persistent individuals to inconvenience you on your way home."

Ah. Now we were on the same page. "You got it."

I packed up my things, and ten minutes later, Clara was dropping me off outside my place. I waved as she drove away, her sedan's taillights retreating up the quiet street. Anxiously tugging my coat shut against the frigid January wind, I hurried through the gate and into the backyard. I unlocked the outer door, then the second door that led into my basement apartment.

"Twiggy?" I called as I descended the stairs. "I'm home!"

I paused a few steps from the bottom to squint at my phone. Ezra had responded to my anxious questions with a message that the three of them were home and nothing crazy had happened. Shortly after, Aaron had confirmed that Kai was locked in his room and didn't want to talk to anyone. Aaron and Ezra would keep an eye on the electramage and update me in the morning.

My thumbs hovered over the keyboard, then I stuck my phone in my pocket without sending a reply. I would provide an update in the morning as well. No sense in adding to their stress—and a famous bounty hunter connecting me to a wanted rogue was definitely cause for stress.

Lower lip caught between my teeth, I kicked my boots off and dropped my purse on the little table beside the stairs. As my head spun with questions about Shane and how the hell he'd gotten hold of my old shoes, I hurried into my living room.

"Twiggy?" I called again. "Where are y—"

I stopped dead.

The green faery was right there, but I could see why he hadn't answered me. Bands of shadow pinned his small frame to the sofa, and his huge green eyes were wide with terror. On the cushion beside him, Hoshi's serpentine body was bound with the same dark, semi-transparent restraints, the tip of her tail thrashing in agitation.

A huge black eagle perched on the back of the sofa above her prisoners, glaring at me with vibrant emerald eyes. Shadows rippled off her feathers like wisps of inky smoke, and her deadly talons were embedded in the cushions.

I stared at the eagle, my heart careening with a suffocating blend of alarm, anticipation, and cold dread. "Lallakai?"

3

LADY OF SHADOW. The Night Eagle. Zak's familiar. I hadn't seen the fae in months, but if she was here, that meant …

I spun in a wild circle. "Zak?"

The enigmatic druid didn't appear with a sweep of his long black coat. My apartment was silent.

"Zak?" I called. "You here?"

Lallakai snapped her beak, and I gave her a squinty look. Was she here *alone*? No way. She and Zak were never far apart.

I pointed at my two fae friends. "Would you mind letting them go?"

Another beak clack. The shadowy bindings on Twiggy and Hoshi dissolved, and the two fae leaped off the sofa. Twiggy skidded behind me and grabbed my legs, hiding from Lallakai's glare. Hoshi circled me, her long body undulating weightlessly, and settled with her small chin on my shoulder and her tail looped around my waist.

"Is Zak here?" I muttered to them.

A flash of dark red in my mind—Hoshi's telepathic reply. Twiggy confirmed her response with a trembling, "No, the Night Eagle c-came alone."

The cold dread in my gut deepened.

Lallakai unfurled her wings. They spread wider than the length of my sofa, elegant feathers sweeping across the cushions. The shadows swirling around her deepened and she launched off her perch. Darkness rippled across her, obscuring her form as she landed on the floor three long paces away. The shadows dissipated.

My mouth hung open.

Gone was the eagle. In her place was … a woman.

Let's be clear right now: I like dudes. Always have, always will. But my obsession with manly muscles aside, I'd never before seen an embodiment of sensual femininity like this—and I was getting one hell of an eyeful.

Tall, elegant, sexy. Her unfairly curvaceous figure was perfectly proportioned: shapely hips narrowing to a petite waist, flat stomach, full bosom, and long, lean legs. All those womanly attributes were unblushingly displayed by an outfit that, while made of beautiful black silk with bold green accents, was more or less a bikini top and a long skirt with equally long slits that ran all the way up to her hips.

Above her swan-like neck was an oval face with crystalline eyes that watched me from beneath slim, graceful eyebrows. Her full lips were distractingly red, her nose exactly perfect for her cheekbones. Knee-length black hair in loose waves drifted around her in a nonexistent breeze.

I scanned the fae's alabaster skin from her bare feet back to her face. Holy freakin' shit. Zak was totally banging his familiar. How could he not? I wasn't judging, but damn was I glad I hadn't slept with him. Not that I'd ever considered it. At least, not seriously.

Anyway.

Gulping back my shock, I cleared my throat. "Hello, Lallakai."

"Victoria Dawson, human of the Crow and Hammer guild."

Even her voice was ridiculously sensual, all purring and throaty. No human woman could compete with that.

"Where is Zak?" I asked.

The beautiful fae woman glided forward, her hair swirling around her like it couldn't decide if gravity was a thing. Halting in front of me, she gazed down into my face with solemn tranquility, three inches taller than my five foot seven.

Hoshi hissed softly.

Lallakai's pupil-less eyes turned to the sylph. Poor little Hoshi held her ground for about five seconds, then her nerve broke. She dove away and shimmered out of sight. I couldn't blame her.

Twiggy tightened his hold on my legs, but I knew it wasn't bravery. He was too petrified to move.

The Lady of Shadow refocused on me, and I could feel her attention like a tangible weight. Power sweetened the air, the room too dim, the shadows too deep.

She brushed smooth fingers across my jaw. "What do you think of my druid, Victoria Dawson?"

I ignored her touch with effort. "In what way?"

"You are drawn to him." She leaned in, her honey-sweet breath on my lips. "As are all who know him, fae and human. It is his gift, his curse."

"He's my friend."

"Your *friend*," she whispered. "Though he is a dark druid? Though he treats with foul beasts, flaunts your laws, and kills when he sees fit?"

"I know all that about him already. I'm not a fan of murdering people, generally speaking, but he isn't a bad guy."

She studied me, twirling a lock of endless raven hair around her finger. "What would you do for my druid? Would you fight for him? Would you break human laws or take human lives?"

"That depends." My muscles tensed. "Is Zak in trouble? I thought you and him were off building huts in the wilderness or something."

Early last September, Zak had bid me farewell. His enemies had been getting dangerously close, so he'd shut down his farm and gone into hiding, druid-style. He hadn't even taken a phone with him.

Lallakai combed her fingers gently into my hair in a way that was either maternal or loverlike, and it extra freaked me out that I couldn't tell which. Talk about mixed signals.

Her gleaming eyes stared into mine. "I must know, Victoria. Can my druid trust you?"

"Of course he can trust me. I've kept his secrets this whole time, haven't I?"

"His secrets, yes, but can I entrust you with his life?"

I was two seconds away from shaking answers out of her. "What's going on, Lallakai?"

"My druid is in grave danger. He needs aid that I cannot give him." She abruptly swept away from me, her hair flowing behind her in gossamer strands. "The news reached us but days ago. We were far from here, having wandered the lands of human and fae for many months."

"What news?" I demanded, confused.

"News of ... home."

"You mean Zak's farm?"

She faced me again, her expression oddly blank. "My druid's territory, left to the witch to safeguard in his absence, was violated. An enemy breached its protections and ..."

"And what?"

"And laid it to ruin—or so we were told."

Cold horror swept through me.

"My druid was *enraged* that someone would dare befoul his treasured land. He was inflamed with fury. I could not soothe his raging heart."

That sounded bad.

"He wanted only to return and discover the truth. With haste and without caution, he rushed to secure the fastest route home. We were waylaid at the crossroads—a place of fae power—and he was taken by bounty hunters. They think him a suspicious, unregistered druid. They do not know his identity."

My hands tightened into fists and I sucked in air through my nose. Zak, the elusive and untouchable Ghost, had been captured? I would have said it was impossible, except I couldn't imagine any other reason Lallakai would be here otherwise.

If bounty hunters had him, and if they figured out who they held prisoner ...

A faint crease marred Lallakai's perfect forehead. "The hunters are taking him to the city, where they will surrender him to the MPD. That cannot happen."

I agreed one hundred percent. If he ended up in MagiPol custody, that would be it for him. But that meant …

"Hold up. You're here because you want me to save him?" My eyes narrowed. "Me. The sort-of-witch human. You expect *me* to rescue Zak from *bounty hunters*?"

I tried to imagine rescuing Zak from the six Odin's Eye mythics who'd been at the bar earlier. I couldn't picture it at all—and I was pretty sure whatever team had managed to capture Zak would be even tougher.

Lallakai swept close again, getting way up in my personal space. Her hands caught mine, cool fingers gripping tightly. "You are his friend. You said this. You are drawn to him."

"I wouldn't say I'm *drawn* to—"

"When you look upon him, you see not a dark druid. Who else could I beg for aid, Victoria? Who would risk anything for him? Only you and I—but I cannot save him."

I gulped, a squirmy feeling in my chest. Zak didn't have friends. He might have allies, but none he could trust while in such terrible danger. Lallakai was right: it was me or no one.

Shit.

"In that case …" I inched back from her uncomfortable closeness and tugged my hands free. "How long until the bounty hunters turn him over to MagiPol?"

"One day, perhaps two. The location of his capture is remote, but they can travel quickly."

That was *so* not enough time to plan and execute a rescue mission. "We have to get him away from them before they reach the city. Are they part of a Vancouver guild? Do you know the guild's name?"

The slightest twitch tarnished her expression, gone in an instant. "He was not captured here. This is not the city where he will be taken."

"Huh? Then where are they taking him?"
"Los Angeles."
"Oh." I cringed. "Well, that complicates things."

I PACED BACK AND FORTH in front of the stairs that descended into my apartment. Bad, bad, bad. This was bad. And stupid. I should not even be considering a jaunt down south.

Zak was in *California*. Lallakai hadn't been kidding when she said they'd wandered far. Twelve hundred miles, no big deal.

I rubbed my sweaty palms on my pants. I had less than a week to figure out the demon amulet before Eterran's deadline, but Zak had *a day or two* before he disappeared into MPD lockup, and once that happened, they'd figure out his identity. Shane Davila was already putting the pieces together, and I wondered if Zak's farm being "laid to ruin" had anything to do with Shane getting his psychic hands on my old shoes.

As for who had done the laying of the ruin, I had my suspicions. Varvara, the nasty old sorceress who'd kidnapped one of Zak's teen wards, had struck me as the vengeful type—and she'd been furious with the druid for stealing Nadine back. Varvara was the reason he'd shut his farm down and gone into hiding.

A quiet knock sounded on the door at the top of the stairs, then it clacked open. A moment of rustling, then Kai descended with near-silent steps. I rushed to intercept him as he reached the fake hardwood floor.

"Tori." His dark eyes slashed across me as he unzipped his leather biker jacket. "What—"

"Are you alone?" I asked urgently. "Do Aaron and Ezra know where you are?"

"No." He touched my elbow, stilling my anxious fidgeting. "What's going on, Tori?"

I gauged his level of calm. When it came to sneaky dealings, Kai was my go-to man, and this issue required maximum discretion. Also, he didn't dislike Zak as much as Aaron did, which was a huge plus.

"Don't freak, okay?" I took his wrist, then hesitated. "And, um, keep a clear head—if you can."

His forehead wrinkled with confusion. Deciding to get it over with, I pulled him into the main room.

Lallakai, still in her womanly form, sat on a stool at my breakfast bar, her long legs crossed at the knee and hands resting demurely in her lap. Her not-so-modest outfit exposed miles of soft, porcelain skin, and her silky hair was draped around her.

Kai jerked to an abrupt stop, his mouth hanging open.

I coughed. "Kai, this is Zak's familiar, Lallakai. She—"

"Consort," she corrected, her sultry voice caressing the word.

"Er, right. This is Zak's consort, Lalla—"

"No, child." Her lips curved up. "He is *my* consort."

I shivered at the layers of possessiveness in those two words. "This is Lallakai. She and Zak have a thing."

Kai didn't respond, and I looked over to find him staring at the fae, eyes glazed. I pinched his arm and he started.

"Zak needs help," I told him, putting some bite in my voice. "According to Lallakai, I'm basically his only hope. That's why I called you."

He pulled himself together. "I see. What kind of help does he need?"

"A bounty hunting guild captured him—in California."

"*California?*"

"They haven't figured out who he is, but once they dump him at a MagiPol precinct, someone will."

"I see." He scanned my face. "And you're planning to go to California and break him free from this guild before he ends up in MPD custody?"

"Um, well, I'm thinking about it."

He nodded—then, inexplicably, pushed up his jacket sleeves. "Is there any chance you're going to come quietly?"

I blinked. "Come quietly where?"

"Back to the house."

"But I just called you here—"

"And I'm glad you did, because going to California to pick a fight with a bounty hunting guild is suicide. If you aren't outright killed, you'll end up tagged, bagged, and dumped at the MPD right alongside Zak. Any guild that can capture him will flatten you."

I folded my arms, glaring furiously. "I called you for help, not so you could veto the whole idea before you even hear the details."

"The details won't change anything."

"But Zak is—"

"—a rogue who actively engages in criminal activity." He squeezed my upper arms. "He wasn't framed or set up. You're thinking of him as a friend you need to rescue from danger, but what you're planning is the equivalent of springing a convict from prison."

"But …" I bit my lip. "If you went to prison, I'd try to spring you."

He laughed softly. "I appreciate the thought, Tori, but I really hope you wouldn't. If I ever go to prison, I'll have earned it—just like Zak."

My eyes stung and I blinked quickly. I couldn't just abandon Zak, but …

"You are so eager to surrender *your* freedom, mage?"

Kai and I jumped. Lallakai stood at his shoulder, but I hadn't seen her leave her stool. She leaned close to him, smiling a sweet little smile that raised my hackles. My nose filled with the alluring scent of a wildflower glade on a cool night. She and the electramage were the same height, their eyes locked.

"Forsake my druid," she purred, "and you will join him in the iron confines of the MPD."

"Why is that?" he asked cautiously.

"Secrets, mage." She brushed a fingertip down the side of his temple. "So many secrets kept safe in my druid's mind. So many secrets for the MPD to pry from him once they realize his identity."

Kai stiffened.

"Is it not a crime to shield a rogue from justice? Is it not a crime to pretend a human is a witch?" Her emerald gaze drifted to me. "Is it not a crime to give a lost child into a rogue's care?"

Oh … right. I had sort of done that, hadn't I? After we'd rescued Nadine from Varvara, all she'd wanted was to go back to Zak's farm with him. At least now she was reunited with relatives in England.

"Should they tear these truths from my druid, what will become of you, mage, and your beloved Victoria? What of your guild, entangled in your law-breaking as well?"

A faint crackle ran across Kai's skin. "Back up."

Her coy smile widening, Lallakai stepped away from the electramage.

He scrutinized her coldly. "Would I be wrong to suspect that, if we fail to save Zak, you'll make certain the MPD hears all about our involvement with him?"

"I seek only to shield us from such a disaster."

"Sure you do," he muttered. "How was Zak captured?"

"We were approaching a crossroads. My druid planned to call for a fae to carry him north, but these guild hunters had set an ambush intended for another rogue. By unlucky chance, we sprang their trap instead."

"Even walking into a trap, I'm surprised he couldn't escape."

"Their expected quarry was also a user of fae power. The hunters possessed magic that drove me away." She blinked slowly, but the motion couldn't hide the feral, dangerous fury building in her breathtaking eyes. "They took him, and I could not stop them."

"Then what?"

"I attempted to reach him, and I heard the hunters as they conversed. They planned to wait three days for their true target to appear, then they would return to their home city and hand over their prisoners. That was nearly two days past."

Leaving us around twenty-four hours to find and extricate Zak—assuming Kai didn't truss me up, throw me over the back of his bike, and drive me straight to Aaron's house instead.

Kai arched a disbelieving eyebrow at Lallakai. "And there wasn't a single person between here and California who could help him?"

She stroked her fingertips down my face instead of his. "None who would not learn of my druid's quandary and see naught but an opportunity to profit."

I stepped closer to Kai. "Hands to yourself, bird lady."

"There are fae who would help him without question," she added as though there was nothing at all weird about the touchy-feely petting thing she kept doing, "but none who could pierce their accursed magic barrier."

"Abjuration sorcery," Kai murmured. "It's the only thing that can reliably interrupt fae magic."

"The dragon lord could annihilate them," she added, "but he will not answer my call."

My fingers drifted to my wrist, where Echo had once placed his mark, but I'd used up my favor from the dragon months ago. Did I mention his "help" had nearly gotten me killed in about ten different ways?

"Depending on what guild has him and how good they are, freeing Zak could be impossible," Kai said. "That's not even taking the timeline into consideration. Plus, Shane Davila is on the Ghost's case, and I don't want to know how much he's already figured out."

I winced. "Yeah, speaking of that ... he knows Zak kidnapped me for two weeks. He tried interrogating me after you left the bar."

Swearing under his breath, Kai stared moodily at the floor, then refocused on me. "Rescuing Zak is a huge risk. The MPD already tried to connect you to him, and now Shane is doing the same. If you're caught freeing him from a guild, you're looking at jail time or worse, depending on how violently this guild protects their catch."

I swallowed hard.

"However, if we leave him to MagiPol and he talks, you'll end up in an MPD cell for sure. Aaron, Ezra, and I will get fined at best or arrested at worst. And ..." His jaw tightened. "And I really don't want anyone taking a close look at our past activities. Ezra's records can pass muster at a glance, but it wouldn't take much to reveal they're all forgeries."

All forgeries? I'd suspected Ezra's records, which didn't extend beyond the past six years, weren't completely legit, but I hadn't realized *everything* was fake.

I twisted my hands together. "If we can save Zak, we can ask him for help. Ezra's time is running out. I know you and Aaron did years of research, but Zak knows things we don't. He has resources we don't."

It was something that'd been in the back of my thoughts since Christmas. Zak knew all sorts of scary dark magic things. He could steer me in the right direction for researching the demon amulet, but before now, I'd had no clue where he was or how to contact him.

"That's a long shot, Tori."

"Saving either of them is a long shot, but we need to try." I breathed deeply. "Will you help me?"

His dark eyes moved from me to Lallakai. He studied the fae, who gazed back at him without expression, waiting for his decision.

A slow minute passed, then he asked resignedly, "Where is the guild taking him?"

My heart swelled and I blinked away silly tears before he noticed. "Los Angeles."

He jerked like I'd smacked him. "LA?"

"Yeah. Is that a problem?"

He hesitated, then pulled his phone out of his pocket. "It's fine."

I watched nervously as he brought up his contacts list. "Are you calling Aaron?"

"No. I won't ask Aaron and Ezra to help with this, and you shouldn't either. Let them keep their hands clean." He gave me a long look, his expression unreadable. "We won't be heroes this time, Tori. We'll be the bad guys. We're breaking a fugitive out of rightful custody for selfish reasons."

"I've always thought you were a bad boy at heart, Kai."

A dark, dangerous smile flickered across his lips. "You have no idea." He scrolled through his contacts list. "We don't have much time, so we need to move fast. Get your combat gear together, plus a change of clothes. Nothing that can identify you."

I nodded earnestly.

"I need to make a few calls, and I have to pack my gear too. I'll meet you back here in an hour." He stuffed his cell in his pocket. "Give me your phone."

I obediently passed it to him. "What do you need it for?"

"I'm going to leave it at our house. I'll get Aaron and Ezra to stay home tomorrow as well." He swung toward Lallakai. "You wait here too. I have more questions about these bounty hunters."

Her emerald eyes flashed at his command, but she dipped her chin.

Confused, I followed him to the stairs. "Kai? Why are you leaving my phone at Aaron's? I might need it for, you know, calling people. Navigating in LA. That sort of thing."

"Two reasons." He zipped his coat and started up the stairs. "One, your phone can't go to LA, because then anyone who tracked your phone would know you went to LA. And two, Aaron and Ezra will be our alibis. Your phone needs to be where we're pretending to be."

Anxiety unfurled in my chest as we reached the back landing. "We won't march in there and announce our names and citizenship. Two random, unidentified mythics are going to spring a random, unidentified druid from a guild's custody. How could anyone possibly tie that to us?"

"Better safe than sorry. We aren't taking any chances." He pulled on his shoes and tugged his keys out of his pocket. "No phones. No names. No credit cards, passports, or paper trails that can prove we ever left the city."

My eyes widened. "No passports? How will we get to LA?"

"I'm calling in a favor." He pulled open the door, letting an icy breeze inside. "How familiar are you with international smuggling?"

"S-smuggling?" I stammered.

That dangerous smile returned. "Like I said, we're the bad guys this time, Tori."

With no more explanation than that, he strode into the night.

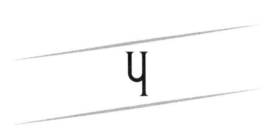

4

I STEPPED OUT OF THE CAB and straightened. An icy winter wind whipped down the narrow highway, and it was so dark I could only see what the vehicle's headlights illuminated—namely, a small but cute sign on a wooden fence that read "Ladner Bed & Breakfast." Peeking through the treed front yard was the roof of a house.

Kai passed the driver some cash, pulled his backpack out of the car, and shut the door. The cab accelerated away, taillights glowing.

"So … we're going to get some sleep now?" I asked, attempting to stifle a yawn and a shiver at the same time. I failed at both, shuddering my way through a long yawn.

"The B&B is the drop-off point. Walking off into an open field would draw too much attention." He slung his nondescript black backpack, which contained our gear, a laptop, and a change of clothes each, over his shoulder. "It's a twenty-minute walk to our real destination."

"Which is what? What's even out here?" I had no idea where we were. All I knew was that the cab had driven us straight out of the suburbs, across—or rather, under the Fraser River, and through several miles of empty farmland.

"To our plane." He pulled a cell phone from his pocket—a cheap burner that couldn't be linked to us—and turned on its camera flash to light our way. "Let's go."

I had a million questions, but he set a grueling pace and I had no spare breath for talking. Our footsteps crunched in a chilly silence, his light the only illumination. It was four in the morning and the world slept—except us.

Zak was gonna owe me big time for all this missed sleep.

We followed the unlit two-lane road, bordered by more farms, for ten minutes before turning onto another equally rural road. We seemed to be well outside city limits—so imagine my surprise when we passed a bus stop. Brow scrunched as I puffed after Kai, I squinted ahead. Lights glowed from an unseen point on the horizon.

Five minutes later, his flashlight illuminated a sign featuring a small airplane. "Turn left," it read, "and come fly with us!"

"Huh," I muttered. "There's an airport here?"

Unfortunately for my frozen ears, Kai didn't take the next left as the sign instructed. Striding past a large gray building, he switched off his flashlight and turned, leading me into a maze of blocky buildings, hangars, and parking lots.

When it seemed like we'd passed every single building, he cut around one. A chain-link fence blocked our path, "No Trespassing" and "Emergency Lane" signs all over it. On the other side was a wide stretch of pavement, then the glowing lights of a runway.

Kai boosted me over the fence, then jumped it after me. Moving more cautiously, he skulked to the edge of the building and peered around it.

Basking in the airway's lights, a handful of dinky little planes with nose propellers were parked in neat rows, and positioned off to one side like their aloof big brother was a significantly larger plane. Though it was no commercial passenger jet, it had two big propellers on the wings, five windows along the side, and a far more impressive presence.

Lights gleamed through its windows, and a door near the tail, which swung down to form a short staircase, was open and waiting.

Kai broke into a swift walk and I rushed after him, eyes wide. Nothing moved on the tarmac, the whole place abandoned as far as I could see. Unhesitatingly, he strode to the lit-up plane.

A silhouette appeared in the doorway. A short Asian man wearing a headset hurried down the steps. He waved at us to keep moving, and Kai nodded as he climbed the steps. I followed him on board.

It wasn't exactly glamorous. Heavy-duty mesh straps strained over a stack of unmarked cardboard boxes in the tail of the plane, and six basic seats filled the rest of the interior. Kai dropped into the rearmost seat and put his backpack on the floor, so I took the spot beside him. The center aisle running between us was so narrow it was like sitting together on a sofa.

"Cool," I whispered to Kai, rubbing my frozen hands and considering whether I wanted to unzip my leather jacket. It was warmer in here than outside, but not by much. "So this is a smuggling plane? What's that stuff back there?"

Kai cast me a flinty look. "Tori, I know you're insatiably curious, but this isn't the time or place. Around people like this, questions can get you killed."

"Oh."

I gazed around as a few clunks and clatters sounded from outside, then leaned toward him.

"Okay, no questions," I whispered. "But how did you arrange this so fast? And how do you know smugglers? And—"

"Tori," he growled.

"—does this have anything to do with—"

"I'll answer your questions," he hissed through gritted teeth, "after we're off the plane and in *private*."

I glanced around the empty plane. "This isn't private?"

"No."

Grumbling, I sat back in my seat. Kai was good at everything—so it seemed, anyway—and I wasn't surprised he'd had an immediate solution for flying to California on super short notice and without leaving a paper trail. But I suspected this "favor" predated his membership at the Crow and Hammer.

As in, dated back to when he'd been involved with his family, who happened to run a notorious international crime syndicate.

The pilot climbed on board, pulled the door up, and latched it. Without a word to his passengers, he strode up the narrow aisle and into the cockpit. Once inside, he pulled a curtain across the doorway.

"Friendly guy," I whispered.

Kai shook his head warningly.

The plane engines rumbled to life, vibrating my seat in a way I really didn't like. I stretched my legs out, trying to relax. "How long is the flight?"

"It's three hours on a commercial airliner," he murmured, pulling out his burner phone. "But it'll take a little over five hours on this one."

Could be worse. "What about the trip home? Are we flying with smugglers again?"

"That'll depend on whether there's a guild chasing us."

As I watched him tap on the phone, a niggling feeling like I'd forgotten something burrowed into the back of my brain. "Five hours puts our arrival at around ten a.m. That'll give us less than a day to—" I cut myself off, squinting toward the cockpit, but the dull roar of the engines was too loud for the pilot to hear us. "Less than a day to find the bounty team that has Zak, plan our strategy, and perform a daring rescue operation."

"And escape the city with him."

The immensity of *impossible* we had to overcome to make this work dragged at my limbs. We didn't even have Lallakai as backup. Maybe we could've smuggled her on board with us, but after sharing all the information she had about the bounty hunters, she'd taken off—literally soaring through my apartment ceiling like a ghost. She hadn't admitted it, but I figured flying twelve hundred miles in two days had exhausted her.

"Were Ezra and Aaron suspicious?" I asked. "When you told them we were going on a sudden trip and needed an alibi?"

"Aaron complained that he was being left out of the fun, then complained some more that I wouldn't tell him what kind of fun we were planning without him. He isn't sure whether this is personal to me or personal to you, so I don't think he's guessed who we're off to rescue."

"And Ezra?"

"He didn't say much. He's been quiet lately … since Christmas."

"Oh." My gaze dropped to my lap. "He's seemed mostly like himself to me."

"He's been trying to keep things normal for you." Kai stared at the blank screen of his phone. "He never wanted you to know. Now that you do … it's hard on him."

My hands tightened. "You all hid it from me."

"Ezra's choice." Dark eyes flicked to mine, shadowed with pain. "I would've chosen the same. You'll grieve for him either way, but losing him suddenly is far preferable to months of dread and helplessness."

The jittery urgency I'd been battling since Christmas collapsed my lungs. He was right that this was more difficult, but if I hadn't learned the truth ahead of time, I wouldn't have had the chance to alter the trajectory of Ezra's fate.

Watching Kai's profile, the tension in his jaw and the wrinkle of misery between his eyebrows, I reached across the aisle and gripped his wrist. "We're going to save him."

"It isn't possible."

"We'll make it possible."

He slouched in his seat, avoiding my fierce stare, unwilling to crush my hope. Soon, he would be able to hope too. If I could combine the demon amulet with Zak's knowledge of dark magic, we would find a way.

I peered out my window, unable to see much besides a big, boring hangar. Kai navigated an app on his phone, and for a second, I wondered if he was texting Izzah, but that would have defeated the purpose of leaving our regular phones behind. Hopefully, we didn't get any emergency calls while we were—

I jerked upright. "Oh shit! I totally forgot!"

"Forgot what?" he asked, alarmed.

"You got a message or something at the pub." Guilt hoarsened my voice. "You were upset and I never asked what was wrong. I'm so sorry."

"Oh." He relaxed again. "You had other things to worry about."

"That's no excuse. What happened? Do you want to talk about it?"

"No."

My eyes narrowed. "That sounds like an 'I totally need to talk about something but only if you pry it out of me' sort of no."

"That was a normal no. The 'don't pester me' kind."

"Hmm. I'm pretty sure not."

"Then you're pretty wrong."

I rolled my eyes. "Okay, fine, but you do realize you're stuck in this chair, right beside mine, for the next five hours."

His lips thinned. "Is that a threat?"

"Nooooo. But I have a sudden urge to recite my favorite song lyrics while describing my personal interpretation of every verse—"

He heaved a sigh.

"Okay, fine," I grumbled. "I won't torture you, but I wish you'd tell me things. You know I'll keep your secrets, right?"

His startled gaze darted to me; he recognized those words as ones he'd said to me months ago. He slowly lowered his phone.

"It was a text message. It said, 'This game is over.'"

A shivery chill ran through me. "What the hell does that mean? Who'd send you something like that?"

"It was a warning from my family. They've noticed I'm spending too much time with Izzah."

Oh boy. Not good. "How could they know? You've only been seeing her at the guild."

He shook his head tiredly, as though his family knowing intimate details of his life was no surprise.

"What are you going to do?" I asked.

"Stop talking to Izzah."

"But—"

"I have no choice." Anger roughened his tone. "I shouldn't have been talking to her in the first place. My family doesn't bluff, and if I ignore their warning, they'll take action. I won't get her killed, Tori."

With no counterargument in mind, all I could do was sit in silence as he glared at the empty seat in front of him. He'd broken ties with his family at seventeen, but he couldn't escape his arranged marriage to a woman his family had chosen for him at birth. His family's threats were the reason he'd dumped Izzah three years ago, and she had no clue.

Now he would ghost her again, and that would be it for them. She wouldn't give him a third chance.

Exhaling forcefully, I curled my fingers around his inner elbow and held tight in silent comfort. He leaned his head back and closed his eyes. We didn't speak as the plane rolled onto the taxiway. It aligned with the dark runway, sat for a moment, then accelerated with a roar. The runway lights flew past, and we lifted into the air. I watched out the window as the ground swept away, leaving the city behind.

Zak, captured by bounty hunters.

Ezra, doomed to lose his mind and soul to his demon.

Kai, trapped under the uncaring thumb of his powerful family.

And I wasn't sure I could save any of them.

I ENJOYED only the briefest glimpse of Los Angeles before Kai closed all the window covers. My meager impression: huge. Like … *huge*. Anonymous gray buildings sprawled from horizon to horizon, the structures made grayer by a hazy blanket of smog.

With the view hidden behind plastic covers, the plane's descent was boring and uneventful. We disembarked inside a shadowy hangar, where Kai directed me to the driver's seat of a gunmetal gray sedan. The keys sat in the ignition, waiting for us. He got in the passenger side, provided quick directions, and the next thing I knew, I was driving through a security gate and out onto a road.

We'd just been smuggled into the USA. So cool.

"That was crazy!" I gushed, squinting against the ridiculously bright sunlight. Los Angeles wasn't particularly inspiring—not yet—but the sky was gorgeous. Huge and empty and breathtaking, the endless blue dotted with fluffy cotton-tip clouds. "And you never even *spoke* to the pilot!"

"I arranged everything in advance." He slid his laptop out of his bag. "Keep following this road until you see the freeway overpass. You can't miss it."

Nodding, I changed into the center lane behind a fancy little Porsche. Strip malls slid past, not too different from Vancouver. Except more palm trees. *Way* more palm trees.

I flipped on the air conditioning. LA's January sun wasn't blazing hot, but I was already cooking. "What next?"

"Depending on where the bounty hunters are coming from, we either have a very long drive east, southeast, or north to intercept them." His fingers flew across his laptop keyboard. "And that's the first thing we need to find out."

"I know you looked up a bunch of their guild members," I said, not pointing out how his hard work during our flight had made me feel lazy. All I'd done was try to nap. "But they won't just *tell us* where the bounty team is."

Lallakai had helped us pinpoint the right guild, but she couldn't describe the location of the "crossroads" well enough for us to pick it off a map.

An unpleasant face appeared on Kai's screen—buzzed hair, sunken eyes, and a square jaw. He was an abjuration sorcerer from the bounty hunting guild, and according to his MPD stats and records, he'd claimed bounties for seven black witches and one druid in the last three years. He was one of the mythics Kai had zeroed in on during his research.

"Let's see if this sorcerer is susceptible to a bit of social engineering." He plugged his cell into his laptop, clicked around some more, then entered the sorcerer's number. "And if not, this program will give me the location of his phone. Keep quiet, okay?"

"You got it."

Kai hit the call button and the phone rang on speaker.

"Hartley," an impatient male voice answered.

"Hey, yeah," Kai drawled, deepening his voice. "Is this Leon Hartley?"

"Yeah."

"Owner of a Mustang Shelby GT350, license plate 2FBT124?"

"Yeah, that's me," Leon replied warily. "What—"

"Where did you last park your vehicle?" Kai interrupted in that slow tone, his syllables heavier than usual and an unfamiliar roughness touching the first sounds of each word. He rubbed his sleeve across the cell's mic to create distortion, then glanced at me and exclaimed to no one, "Yeah, yeah, I'm calling him!"

"Who is this?" Leon demanded. "My car is parked in my garage, so if you—"

"Look, dude, I'm just doing my job." Kai peered at the program running on his laptop. "When we're called in for a tow, we gotta tow it, so—"

"You can't tow my car from my *garage*. Where are you? If that's my car, someone stole it and I'm calling the cops."

"We got the report on an abandoned vehicle three days ago," Kai bluffed. "You didn't notice your car was stolen in—"

"I was out of town!" Leon barked. "I just got back. Now tell me where my car is."

I went rigid, my hands spasming on the steering wheel.

Kai's eyes widened. "You just got back?"

"From a business trip, yeah. I got in two hours ago, so I didn't know my car was gone. I'm reporting the theft, so tell me where—and don't you dare freakin' tow it."

Kai's jaw tightened. "Fine, man. I'll leave it till this afternoon. Do what you gotta do. It's parked behind the Palm Springs High School."

"Palm Springs?" Leon swore. "Damn punk teenagers! I'm dealing with it. Don't touch my car."

The line went dead.

Kai lowered his phone. I swallowed hard, my gaze darting between him and the road.

"The sorcerer is back in town," he said quietly. "The tracking software confirmed it."

"Two hours … Is that enough time to turn in their catch to the MPD?"

"More than enough."

Silence stretched between us.

"They must've caught their original target and left early," I mumbled. "They beat us here and probably already turned Zak over."

"He's in MPD custody now," Kai agreed.

I stared straight ahead, scarcely seeing the other vehicles on the road. We'd gotten here as fast as we could—but we were too late. It was only a matter of time before MagiPol figured out who they were holding. The Ghost was mysterious, with little known about his true identity, but MagiPol wasn't the FBI. They had far better tools—like telethesians, telepaths, psychometrics, and who knew what other sorts of mythics—to help them unravel a criminal's secrets.

And once they unraveled his secrets, they'd unravel ours next.

"Now what?" I whispered, my knuckles white as I gripped the wheel. "If MagiPol finds out about us through him … and if they investigate Ezra …"

Kai closed his laptop. "We're already here. How far are you willing to go?"

I pulled my attention off the traffic to glance at him. "Are you asking if we're bad enough to bust a rogue out of mythic jail?"

"That's exactly what I'm asking."

Well, shit.

5

"**THIS WON'T WORK,**" I muttered under my breath, my back pressed to the alley wall. "It *definitely* won't work."

Beside me, Kai pulled on a black ski mask, the knitted fabric covering every inch of his head except for two eye holes and a slit over his mouth.

I tugged mine down over my face, making sure all my hair was tucked up inside. "We look like cartoon burglars."

"Better to attract attention than have anyone from MagiPol see our faces." Kai adjusted a buckle on his black combat vest. "I'm just hoping they don't have any telethesians on staff. Shaking a tail will be tricky."

"Telethesians can track people by their brainwaves or something, right?"

"More like a psychic scent trail, but yes."

I fidgeted with the straps of the heavy backpack on my shoulders. I was wearing it so Kai could go all Bruce Lee without a bulky bag restricting his movements. "How do you lose a telethesian?"

"I know a few tricks. They're all inconvenient." He passed me a pair of thin leather gloves before donning his own. "You ready for this?"

"Yeah. No. I don't know." I concentrated on breathing as I slid the gloves on. "We're about to break into an MPD office and spring a rogue from prison."

"This isn't a regular office. This is the largest precinct on the west coast."

"Oh god. This is a terrible idea." Wilting against the wall, I peered at his covered face suspiciously. "Is it just me, or are you not nearly freaked out enough about what we're doing?"

He snorted.

"Kai."

"What?"

"What're you hiding?"

"I'm not hiding anything."

I folded my arms and waited.

Slipping past me, he headed toward the bright, sunny street at the end of the alley. A stealth infiltration in broad daylight, but we had no choice; we had to get Zak out of there before the agents took a close look at their new detainee.

Kai peeked around the corner, then ducked back and repeated, "I'm not hiding anything. It's just that I've never gone up against the MPD head-on like this, and I'm kind of enjoying it."

My mouth hung open behind my ski mask. "Huh?"

He checked around the corner again. "The goal is always to avoid drawing MagiPol's attention. This is the opposite."

I dragged my jaw back up to where it belonged. "Oh."

"A lone agent just crossed the street." Another peek. "He went into the restaurant. Let's move."

He darted out of the alley and I followed on his heels, painfully aware of my "look, I'm up to no good!" ski mask. Kai zipped between parked cars, homing in on the small building across from the precinct. "Restaurant" was a stretch; it was a colorful burger joint with bright murals of food spray-painted over the sides and enough floor space for three two-person tables.

Dinky it might be, but we'd spied on a dozen people who'd exited the MagiPol building, entered the gaudy shack, and returned to the office with a to-go bag five minutes later. The precinct was single-handedly keeping the place in business.

Our unlucky target had already disappeared inside. We zoomed past the small parking lot, getting as close to the door as possible, and ducked behind a car.

"Ready?" Kai whispered.

I nodded bravely. Yes. Totally. No doubts here, oh no.

One minute dragged past, then two. My nerves wound tighter, adrenaline pumping.

The burger joint's door jangled loudly as it swung open. A man stepped out—Hispanic, average height, reasonably fit, dress shirt and slacks, rocking a wicked law-enforcement mustache. He crossed the sidewalk, heading for the street.

Kai sprang from our hiding spot, and I was right behind him, my hand clenched around a small object, its leather tie looped over my wrist. The agent looked up at the sound of our steps, saw two masked strangers charging him, and stumbled back in shock.

Going from a sprint to a low kick with perfect grace, Kai swept the agent's legs out from under him. As the man pitched over backward, Kai caught his shoulders so he wouldn't split his skull on the sidewalk.

I jumped on the guy's chest, ramming all the air out of his lungs, and slapped my ruby crystal against his face. "*Ori decidas!*"

The man slumped bonelessly. Kai heaved him up, a hand clamped over the agent's mouth. I snatched up his dropped food bag while holding the artifact to his cheek.

Kai dragged our victim behind the restaurant and into the shadowy gap beside the dumpster. The man grunted and squealed unintelligible words against Kai's hand, his eyes showing white all the way around.

I glanced at the street, waiting for the outcry. We'd just abducted a man in broad daylight.

And it had worked?

"Hurry up," Kai whispered.

Right. Keeping my fall spell pressed to the guy's face, I lifted my other hand, the tie for a second crystal looped around my wrist. I laid it on his forehead. "*Ori ostende tuum pectus.*"

The poisonous-green crystal shimmered and the man's face went eerily blank, his eyes staring at nothing. I shuddered, remembering what it had felt like to be under the interrogation spell's power. I really hated this spell.

Kai lifted his hand off the man's mouth. The agent blinked slowly.

"Are you an MPD agent?" I asked in a firm whisper.

"Yes. I'm an auditor," he droned. "I've worked here for eight years and I don't like it much but I'm hoping to finally get promoted to—"

"Were any rogues booked today?" I interrupted, remembering the black-magic artifact's side effect:

unrestrained babbling as you spilled your heart out to your questioner.

"They booked six rogues since my shift started. We don't usually have that many in one morning, so Annie was talking about that part, but what had everyone gossiping were the two druids. I've only ever seen one druid before, and today a guild dropped off two. Everyone is talking about it. And then we heard that—"

"What do you know about the two druids?"

"Only what Enrique told me. He said one is the Sand Druid, wanted for selling fake fae artifacts on the black market, but Enrique said he isn't a very good druid and maybe he's actually a witch faking it, but we don't know yet if—"

"What about the other druid?"

"Enrique said he hasn't been identified yet, but everyone is curious because he hasn't said a word and we can't find any record of him and—"

"Where are the druids?"

"In the holding cells. The Sand Druid is in regular holding but they put the unknown druid in solitary because we don't know if he's dangerous or just unregistered but Enrique said he has a dangerous look about him so—"

"Where are the holding cells?" I asked as Kai shifted impatiently beside me.

"In the basement. They're much nicer here than the ones at the precinct in San Diego, where I used to—"

"What's the best way to get into the holding cells?"

Glazed eyes staring, the agent described the various routes to the basement. I asked him about security, safeguards, and possible traps, and he blurted everything and more. Damn, no wonder this spell was illegal. I felt bad for the guy, knowing that, while he babbled on without a care, on the inside he was screaming at himself to shut up—but no amount of internal resistance would dull the magic's compulsion. I knew from personal experience.

"Is that everything?" I whispered to Kai, palming the agent's ID card.

He nodded. "We need to get moving."

I pulled my gun from the built-in holster on my belt. The agent's hazy eyes widened with muted terror.

"It's okay," I said reassuringly. "It's just a sleep potion."

"Don't talk to him," Kai growled. "Just shoot him."

I aimed at the agent's chest, the barrel wavering left and right. "But it's going to really hurt at point-blank range Where should I—"

"Just do it!"

I cringed. "Sorry, dude."

The CO_2 canister popped as I pulled the trigger, and the shot splatted over the agent's chest, soaking through his shirt. Pain rippled over his face before it went slack. Hoo boy, that was gonna leave a bruise.

Shoving my gun back into its holster, I snatched up my spent artifacts, stuffed them in my belt pouches, and jumped to my feet. Kai waved at me to follow as he started out from behind the dumpster.

"Wait!" I darted back, snatched up the guy's food bag, and tucked it beside his limp arm. Rushing to Kai, I whispered, "He deserves his burger after all that."

Kai's silent pause was full of commentary he didn't say aloud.

Together, we faced the street and the building on the other side. It resembled a warehouse more than an office building—

and it was hella big. Two overhead doors, large enough for cube vans to drive through with room to spare, dwarfed a single person-sized entrance with a metal door. Long horizontal windows ran along the uppermost level, too high to be used as an illicit point of entry.

It wasn't a glamorous building, but it was strategic. Surrounded by parking lots on three sides and a street on the fourth, the location wasn't conducive to stealthy breaking and entering. Discounting the handful of fire exits, we had two choices: the front doors or the back doors.

Guess which one we were using.

We wheeled around the corner and into the largest of the three parking lots around the precinct, ignoring the security cameras mounted high on the walls—we weren't worrying about those ones. Two more overhead doors faced the lot. Unloading rogues in public was a definite no-go, so when guilds arrived with criminals to book, they unloaded their catches in the privacy of the building's interior.

Kai and I raced to the small access door beside the large ones. Pulling ahead of him, I slapped our stolen ID card against the nearby black panel. A light blinked green and the latch clicked loudly.

Too easy? That's what we would've thought, but as our poor informant had explained, magical security created a big, ugly pit of complications. What sort of complications, I wasn't sure, but he'd started a story about one precinct implementing arcane security, only to have all the agents who weren't sorcerers accidentally lock themselves in or out of rooms all day long.

So, MagiPol relied on mundane tech—which, with an electramage on my team, was better than I could've hoped for.

Putting my shoulder against the metal, I cautiously cracked the door open.

Inside was a concrete pad slab large enough for four vehicles to park and open all their doors. A glass wall on my left, reinforced with metal, revealed the intake area—a desk at one end and some uncomfortable seating opposite.

Two obvious challenges awaited us: the two men behind the desk, and the fact that the wall behind them was also glass. Beyond it was the precinct bullpen—dozens of desks, cubicles, and offices bustling with agents and analysts hard at work. Or hard at slacking. Either way, it was a terrifying number of eyeballs that could spot us.

Steeling myself, I leaped through the door and slapped my stolen ID to the next door's panel. As I burst into the intake area, the two agents looked up and saw my gun aimed at them. I pulled the trigger twice—and the lights went out.

Two dull thuds sounded as the mythics collapsed forward onto their shared desk. Beyond the glass wall, muffled voices exclaimed in shock, and the solid darkness broke as spots of light flared—agents turning on their phone flashlights.

"Keep moving."

I almost jumped out of my skin at Kai's whisper right beside me. Scarcely able to see where I was going, I homed in on the three lights glowing on the far wall—the call buttons for a freight elevator and the security panel for the door to the stairwell. Both must be on separate circuits from the one Kai had fried to take out the lights.

With another tap of our stolen ID, we were away from the glass wall and unconscious booking agents. Kai flicked on the light attached to his vest, the muted glow just enough to guide us down the stairs. We trotted to the bottom, every sound echoing, and I pressed the ID to the pad beside the door.

A red light blinked.

"Shit," I muttered. "That analyst doesn't have clearance down here? He didn't say that."

Kai touched two fingers to the panel and a spark erupted. The red and green lights flickered wildly. He puffed a breath, shoulders tense. Another spark, brighter this time—and the lock clicked.

"You did it!" I whispered gleefully.

He flung the door open. I launched out first, gun clutched in both hands.

The lights down here must have been on a different circuit too, because the room was brightly illuminated. A security desk blocked our way forward, and two agents sat behind it, staring at their computer monitors. Their heads snapped up as I flew into the room, gun waving.

"Don't move!" I commanded.

Kai was right behind me, one hand already thrust out, and electricity burst over both men simultaneously. Discorporate ignition of his magic—*without* a switch. Kai was a serious badass.

As the two men crumpled, I fired a shot of sleep potion into each of them. They went limp.

Kai swung his hand toward the security camera in the corner. A crackle rushed across its metal body and smoke boiled out of it. He jumped the desk and crouched between the agents, then rose again with a new ID card and a fat set of keys.

Behind the desk was a heavy-duty door. With a touch of the card, the light blinked green. He opened the door.

A long hall stretched away, the concrete floor and walls painted a plain white that had faded over the years. On one side were open doors to interrogation rooms, currently empty. Across from them were two long stretches of bars: the group holding cells for short-term inmates.

At our appearance, the dozen mythics—eight men in one cell, four women in the other—stirred to alertness. I could feel their eyes on us as Kai zapped two more cameras. We sped to the end of the hall, where four more doors on heavy sliding tracks waited. The solitary holding cells.

Our informant hadn't known which cell the mysterious druid was in, so Kai and I split up to peer through the tinted, barred windows. The first one was empty. I checked the second one on my side—empty too—then Kai and I swung toward the final door.

I pressed my nose to the glass.

A man sat on the bench-like bed attached to the wall, the only furniture in the cell aside from a steel toilet in the corner. His arms were folded, back against the cinder blocks, tense and glaring at the blank wall across from him. The tinted window was too dim to see more than that—a privacy thing for inmates?—but I recognized that tall, fit, menacing build easily.

We'd found the Ghost.

6

I NODDED TO KAI and he shook out the keys. Only a few matched the bright, shiny steel of the bolt, and Kai slid one into the keyhole. It turned with a loud clack. I grabbed the door and slid it open with a dramatic flourish.

Zak looked up—and a lash of fear hit me so hard I almost stepped back.

He hadn't changed much in the four months since I'd last seen him. His dark hair had grown long enough to look shaggy—except, being an Adonis-level hunk, he just looked tousled and extra sexy. His jaw was dark with stubble, suggesting he'd gone several days without a razor. Lallakai's feather tattoos were missing from his muscular arms, bared by his sleeveless shirt, but the druid tattoos on his inner forearms were dark and bold, the intricate circles filled with colorful fae runes.

His appearance wasn't what had triggered cold adrenaline in my veins—even with the scuffs, scrapes, splattered blood, and generous coating of dust that adorned him. No, it was his green eyes. They weren't bright and inhuman with Lallakai's power.

They were dark and inhuman with blood-chilling hatred.

Frozen in the doorway, I didn't move as he glanced up and down me as though deciding how best to skin me alive, no recognition in his expression. Then I remembered.

"Oh!" I grabbed the bottom of my ski mask and pushed it up to reveal my face. "I'm Luke Skywalker. I'm here to rescue you."

He blinked, shock dousing the fiery loathing in his eyes. He blinked again—and his mouth fell open in a very non-deadly-rogue way. "*Tori?*"

"No names," Kai barked from behind me. "Let's move."

Zak pushed to his feet, and I noticed the heavy cuffs chaining his wrists together, the wide bands carved with hundreds of runes. Pulling my mask back into place, I zipped out the door and followed Kai down the hall, Zak right behind me.

A low whistle brought me up short. The mythics in the two large holding cells were crowded against the bars, watching us pass.

"You gonna let us out too?" one asked in a slow drawl.

"Yeah," Kai said, striding past. "Wait a minute while we get ready."

The convicts exchanged confused looks.

"Is he serious?" a woman muttered to her cellmate as we reentered the security vestibule where the two guards were out cold behind the desk.

Kai rifled through the keys and slid several off the ring—ones that matched the bolts on the large holding cells. He tossed me the leftovers and I sorted through them for a handcuffy-looking one. According to our informant, Zak's cuffs were anti-magic artifacts—meaning we needed them off him ASAP.

As I searched, I flicked a glance at the druid standing in front of me, waiting to be freed. "Hey, so, long time no see. How've you been?"

"What the hell are you doing here?"

"Glad to hear you're enjoying your SoCal vacay." I pulled his hands toward me and tried to insert a small key. "Weather's nice, isn't it?"

"Do you have a plan for getting out of this building?"

I shot him an irritated look. "Bet our plan is better than yours was when you got your dumb ass tagged by a guild."

"You don't have a plan, do you?"

I jammed another ill-fitting key in his cuffs.

"Getting in is always easier than getting out," Kai said, rolling his shoulders. The electrical sockets near him sparked ominously. "We're making a run for it. Fast and hard, straight for the exit."

Zak's cold green eyes slashed to the mage. "Do you really think that will be enough?"

Kai stepped back into the hallway and tossed the keys into the holding cells. The rogues shouted in surprise and delight, scuffing on the floor for the keys.

"A little chaos can go a long way." Rejoining us, he pulled throwing stars from his pocket, holding them between his fingers so that his fists bristled with short, sharp blades. "Get those cuffs off him."

"I'm working on it." I slid a third key into his cuffs as a metal clang echoed from the hall—the rogues opening the holding cell. "We—"

The door to the stairwell flew open.

A group of agents burst in, all urgency and tension, but whatever they were all worked up about, the sight of two masked intruders and an inmate standing where the guards should've been didn't match. Their expressions went blank with disbelief, and for a single heartbeat, no one moved.

Kai flung a fistful of bladed stars into the group. Cries of pain rang out—then lightning burst from Kai's outstretched hand. Three agents collapsed in convulsions.

I released the key ring and yanked out my paintball gun. My first shot hit a guy in the chest, splattering yellow potion everywhere. As he fell, the woman behind him dove through the open door and into the stairwell. I fired two more shots, emptying my clip. The last one just missed her as she shot up the stairs.

An agent in her forties cast her arms out. A gust of wind straight out of a tornado struck me and Kai. We flew backward and slammed into the wall. The air punched out of my lungs and I barely hung on to my gun as I slid down to the floor.

A shrieking alarm erupted from a small speaker beside the fried security camera. The aeromage and another agent, the last two standing, ducked into the stairwell—hiding on either side of the doorway, meaning we'd have to walk between them to get out. Waiting for the elevator wasn't an option, and I hadn't seen any other exits.

Kai slapped his hand against an electrical outlet and white light blazed up his arm. The lights flickered wildly. I popped the magazine out of my gun, stuffed it in my pocket, and fumbled for a new one. A cautious rogue stuck his head through the thick security door to check what was happening.

Crouched behind the desk between the two unconscious desk agents, Zak twisted the key in his remaining handcuff, the first already hanging open. The bulky cuffs dropped off him. He tossed the keys aside and slowly curled his fingers into fists, an almost exhilarated expression passing over his face.

Footsteps thudded down the stairs, loud enough that the alarm couldn't hide their approach. A stream of agents filled the landing as they lined up around the door, preparing to charge us.

We were so screwed.

Kai pulled his hand off the socket and clenched his fist, vibrating with the amount of electricity he'd absorbed. With the ski mask covering his face, I couldn't guess his expression, but if it was anything like mine, then "stark terror" would be pretty accurate.

Zak turned his left arm over, baring his druid tattoos to the ceiling. He ran two fingers from his wrist up to the chartreuse rune emblazoned in the topmost circle. As the alarm blared, his lips moved with words I couldn't hear.

The rune lit with a faint glow. It rippled, then turned to liquid light that dribbled off his arm in radiant droplets. They splashed onto the floor and sank into the solid concrete.

Breathing fast, I jammed the new magazine in my paintball gun and prepared to attempt the impossible. On the plus side, the MPD agents would probably try to capture us rather than kill us. Maybe.

The ground quivered under my feet.

I looked down in alarm. Another quiver. A shivering rumble.

A crack appeared in the floor. Another zigzagging line split the concrete, jolting the desk. A shudder traveled through the ground and into my legs, vibrating my teeth—then the earth heaved. The floor shattered, bits of concrete shooting into the air.

Dark, twisting vines thrust out of the ground, lengthening by the second. The desk flipped as a vine thicker than my arm uncurled beneath it. The computer monitors smashed on the floor, and the desk splintered into pieces, crushed between engorged plants.

I shrieked as the floor fissured between my feet. A vine a foot in diameter unfurled, shoving me into the wall as it stretched upward.

Zak vaulted over the remains of the desk and charged for the stairwell.

I tore free from the vine as it thickened, the flexible stem bulging with quarter-sized bumps. Inch-long thorns with glistening black tips sprouted from the nubs.

Kai grabbed my hand and sprinted after Zak. Darting around a vine, the druid rammed his shoulder into a panicking agent. The man crashed into a thorny plant and loosed a scream I could hear over the blaring alarm, shattering concrete, and groaning earth.

Zak shot past the remaining agents, who were too busy fleeing or helping their comrades to stop him. Ever-thickening vines pushed upward, climbing the stairs or ripping straight through them. I chased the druid up the steps, stumbling and clutching the railing as the whole building rocked.

The stairs split open, a vine thrusting through them. I sprang over the widening gap with a desperate cry. I stumbled on the landing and Kai caught my elbow, steadying me. We raced for the main level.

Zak was already through the door, but I doubted he'd face any resistance. The precinct was in chaos—alarms blaring and people screaming. The cubicles were collapsing, the floor was quaking, and chasms were erupting everywhere. As I burst out of the stairwell, a five-foot section of the floor caved in and a swarm of vines spewed out like writhing tentacles.

I sprinted after Zak as he flew past the booking desk, the glass wall behind it in pieces. He shoved through the first door, and I caught up as he slammed through the second and out into the parking lot. I grabbed his arm and pulled him to the right, Kai behind us. We sprinted alongside the building toward the street.

Glass shattered overhead. Shards rained down, disintegrating into sparkling dust on impact. Above us, vines surged out of the second-floor windows, seeking sunlight. A hunk of dislodged concrete slammed down on a parked car, caving the roof in.

We bolted across the street and into the mouth of the alley where Kai and I had waited for an unlucky agent to ambush at the burger joint. The restaurant staff was standing on the street corner, gaping upward.

Just before the alley could cut off our view, I stopped and turned, pulling off my ski mask.

The ground groaned and trembled as the precinct shook under the onslaught. Agents were fleeing out the doors in droves, and a handful of unagenty rogues dashed across the parking lot for safety. Debris pummeled the street as the walls split and the ceiling ripped open.

As we watched, the writhing plants slowed, then stiffened. The quaking violence quieted, broken only by bits of falling debris and shifting rubble. A twisted sculpture of dark green vines and black thorns rose from the precinct's roof like a hideous crown.

Reaching out blindly, I closed one hand around Kai's wrist and the other around the druid's.

"Zak," I whispered hoarsely, "what did you do?"

He tilted his other hand up, glancing at the empty circle on his forearm. "The fae who gave me that magic wasn't very specific about its effects."

Kai swore quietly. "How will MagiPol explain this to the public? Conspiracy theorists will go nuts."

Disbelieving humans crept closer, their phones out and video recording. Sirens wailed in the distance.

"Holy shit," I whimpered.

Zak tugged his wrist from my hand. "Do you have a vehicle?"

"This way." Tugging his mask off, Kai turned his back on the disquieting sight. "We should hurry."

He broke into a jog and I hastened after him, Zak trailing behind me. My head was spinning, and as the adrenaline faded, cold dread grew in its place. Were the people in there okay? Had the agents survived the unleashing of the vines and the collapse of the ceiling?

"Zak," I muttered over my shoulder, "don't you think that was overkill?"

"I told you I didn't know the spell was that destructive."

"Then you shouldn't have used it." I glanced back at him, furious and scared and relieved all at once. "Maybe I should start calling you pea-brain instead of dickhead. How could you—"

I ran into Kai's back.

Bouncing off with a gasp, I flailed for balance. Zak caught me by the waist and heaved me upright. Winded, I opened my mouth to berate Kai for stopping so suddenly.

We'd reached the far end of the alley. Our borrowed car waited on the adjoining street for our triumphant getaway, but it wouldn't be going anywhere—not with two big black SUVs parked inches from its front and back bumpers, trapping it in place.

Four Asian men, dressed in identical black suits with reflective sunglasses, stood on the sidewalk in front of the SUVs. The one beside the nearer vehicle opened the back door and held it wide in invitation, accompanying the motion with a polite bow.

Kai, standing rigidly, didn't seem to breathe. I looked from him to the waiting men to Zak, whose eyes had gone flat and scary again.

The man at the SUV door held his bow, waiting. No one moved. The tension was so thick I could taste it.

The second stranger bowed as well. "Yamada-*dono, onegaishimasu.*"

I got two things out of that: the name Yamada and that the language was Japanese. Icy alarm splintered through my veins.

At the man's words, Kai's rigidity broke. His shoulders slumped, the fight going out of him, his air of defeat palpable.

No. No, Kai didn't give up. He *never* gave up.

"Tori, go back to the airfield and wait in the hangar with the plane. When the pilot returns, tell him I said to take you home."

His tone was as emotionless, as hopeless, as his body language. Between my confusion and concern, it took a moment for his instructions to register.

My eyes widened. "Kai—"

The man bowed again. "Yamada-*dono, tomodachi to go-sanka kudasai.*"

"*Nani?*" Kai stiffened, his spine straightening. "*Karera wa kankei nai de.*"

The man bowed even deeper. "*Onegaishimasu.*"

A long pulse of silence. Kai's hands tightened into fists, then he turned his back on the men. His dark eyes met mine, his face a mask I couldn't read—a mask I scarcely recognized.

"I'm sorry, Tori. I'm afraid you have to come with me."

"Come with you where?"

Terror flashed in his eyes, there and gone in an instant. He faced the waiting men again, his jaw tight.

"To see my family."

I SAT BETWEEN Kai and Zak, my elbows bumping theirs as the SUV rolled smoothly through the LA streets. I barely noticed the buildings or the bumper-to-bumper traffic that filled the four lanes.

"Kai," I hissed. "What did you mean, *your family?*"

Zak folded his arms. "Our chances were better with the MPD."

"Shut up, Zak. Kai, what's going on?"

He stared determinedly at the front seats, where the driver and his identically dressed co-pilot sat. The second SUV followed behind us, keeping close in the heavy afternoon traffic.

"I didn't think we'd be here long enough for them to notice," he said, his voice low and terse. "I'm sorry."

He was gripping his knees, his knuckles white. I remembered how, months ago, we'd accidentally run into a few members of his family at an illegal auction. During the encounter, he'd clamped me tight against his side—so tight I'd had sore spots the next day from his fingers.

"Kai …" I gauged his tension, then swallowed my questions, aware that the men in the front could hear our every word.

The SUV continued to creep through traffic, and I grimaced at the gridlock. It was only, what, two in the afternoon? I'd noticed a lot of congestion on our way into downtown LA, but I'd thought that was the lunch rush. Did the city's rush hour last all day?

"Tori," Kai said tonelessly after ten minutes of anxious silence. "We're passing through Hollywood now."

Forgetting my apprehension, I leaned across him to peer out the window, but there wasn't much to see. The four-lane freeway was bordered by a wall on one side and a scrubby bank on the other, but as we came around a bend, a distant green hill peeked out from between buildings. For a few seconds, I could see the huge white letters near the crest before the road curved again and I lost sight of the famous sign.

As the terrain grew hillier, low green plant life contrasting with yellow patches of dead grass, the traffic began to thin. I watched the palm trees fly past as we picked up speed.

When the buildings disappeared, replaced by hills, I mumbled worriedly, "Are we leaving the city?"

"Hm?" Kai glanced at me distractedly. "No, we're entering the San Fernando Valley. We'll be in North Hollywood in a minute."

"How do you know that?"

"I lived here for eight years."

Say *what?* He used to *live* here? Talk about things I would've liked to know before now.

The driver eventually exited the freeway, only to join another, this one bordered by walls on both sides. The road went on ... and on ... and on. I couldn't believe the endless lines of traffic and the monotonous glimpses of rooftops stretching as far as I could see. I'd never felt like a small-town bumpkin before, but this place was blowing my mind. How could a single metropolis be this big? Where did it end?

When green hills started to outnumber buildings, we left the freeway entirely. The exit ramp curved around, and the next thing I knew, the driver was braking hard, bringing the vehicle's speed down to a crawl. Huge mature trees shaded the road for all of two hundred yards, where it met a grand wooden arch that spanned the street. "Hidden Hills" was written across it in wrought-iron letters.

A gatehouse with a red-and-white-striped arm blocked our way, but as the SUV approached, the arm lifted. The two vehicles passed through.

Inside the gated community, the quiet road wound past white fences and big, healthy trees. Instead of desert scrub, everything was green and manicured. Huge mansions sprawled across expansive properties. Tennis courts, pools, grand gardens, fountains. We even drove by a small pasture with grazing horses.

The properties grew grander and grander until, abruptly, they ended. The road continued, the arid terrain taking over again. The SUV accelerated up a lazy hill, and I leaned forward, inexplicably tense as we crested the slope.

The land dipped down again, and nestled in its own private depression between hills was a property like none I'd seen in LA.

Transported straight from Japan, the estate lounged within a surrounding wall topped with a clay-tile roof. Sloping roofs with curling eaves formed a maze of structures around green gardens, stone courtyards, and ponds that sparkled in the afternoon sun. My immediate impression was of serene, perfectly balanced beauty.

The road wound down to the entrance, where large gates were propped open. Inside, the road branched, leading to different parts of the estate, but we didn't go far. The SUVs halted in the center of a stone courtyard, and Kai unbuckled his seat belt. He was out the door before I had mine undone, and Zak exited on the other side.

I scrambled out, my gaze darting from the traditional architecture to a garden peeking out from behind a two-story building.

Kai strode away, leaving the suited goons behind. Gulping, I jogged after him, and Zak paced beside me. Kai ascended the steps of the largest building. The huge double doors parted before he reached them, opened by men in Japanese clothes. They bowed as Kai passed.

He led the way through a huge but empty room. A mural in black ink, depicting towering mountains amidst artful clouds, spanned the golden walls. A set of sliding doors waited, and again they opened before we reached them.

Another large, barren room waited, but this one ended in a platform raised one step above the floor. Kai stopped before the vacant platform. Zak and I followed, and the two men who'd opened the doors bowed, stepped out of the room, and closed the doors.

I peered around at the paneled walls. The mural continued into this room, and as much as I didn't want to be impressed, it was beautiful.

Two steps in front of us, Kai stood silently, so I copied him—for about two minutes. Then I leaned toward Zak and whispered as quietly as I could, "What are we waiting for?"

"To be granted an audience, I assume."

"With who?"

A panel of the wall on our left slid open. Six men in dark Japanese clothing walked in, their loose, pleated pants swishing. Six women in somber kimonos with their hair pulled into simple buns followed them. They lined up facing each other, men on the left and women on the right, and sank into kneeling positions on the floor, forming an aisle that led to the platform.

Another panel slid open. A woman in a plain kimono knelt just inside, bowing low. An old man walked onto the platform and lowered himself onto the flat cushion in its middle. The woman rose, stepped through the doorway, knelt again, and slid it closed.

At the old man's arrival, the twelve others bowed low, holding the subservient poses as he settled himself.

"*Kiritsu*," he murmured in a gravelly voice.

The dozen subordinates straightened, hands in their laps, waiting in docile silence. They didn't even look curious, just blankly disinterested.

A long moment passed.

The old man's mouth twitched slightly, disturbing his thin silver beard. "You will show no respect to your grandfather, Kaisuke?"

His English was flawless, only a hint of an accent lightening his syllables.

"When I lived here," Kai replied coolly, "you never once let me forget that I'm not *Nihon-jin*. Why should I observe your customs?"

"*Sō desu ka? Mā.*" He studied his grandson, the length of the room between them. "Eight years since you last set foot here, Kaisuke, and you have learned nothing. When I was informed of your return, so soon after receiving your final warning, I dared to hope that you had come to abase yourself before me, beg my forgiveness, and at last accept your duties with humble grace."

A long pause. "But as ever, you disappoint me. For years you have acted with impunity, shaming yourself beyond reparation. You do not deserve to be treated as a son of this family, or as a man."

The Yamada leader turned his dark stare to the line of women. "Makiko."

"*Hai, Oyabun?*" the young lady closest to us answered, her eyes demurely downcast.

"You were promised to Kaisuke at his birth, but such an abject failure is not worthy of a woman of your stature. Instead, I now give him to you. If you deem him to have any value, marry him. If you find him lacking, as I suspect you will, he will be your eager servant from now until you determine that he is your equal in merit, purpose, and honor."

The man's attention shifted back to Kai, crushing in its arctic authority. "He will obey your every command. Should he fail to submit to your slightest whim, send word immediately."

"*Hai, Oyabun.*"

"His restoration is in your hands. Ensure I do not hear a whisper of his name until you return to present him as your dutiful husband." He rose to his feet with a final, cutting glance at Kai. "I can no longer allow my love for your mother to soften my heart. Do not test my mercy again, Kaisuke."

He strode to the panel, and it slid open for him. He vanished through it. Not once had he looked at me or Zak. The instant he was gone, the dozen witnesses rose to their feet and filed out.

All except one.

The young woman turned, her eyes no longer downcast and submissive. Her dark stare blazed as it fixed on Kai, her beautiful face carved from ice. "Kaisuke."

Kai didn't move, his back to me. "Makiko."

Her frigid mask fractured, intense emotion rippling over her features before she recovered. "You lost the right to address me that way eight years ago."

"*Mōshiwake gozaimasen*," Kai said softly, "Miura-*sama*."

She raised her chin, stretching her body taller, but it did little to increase her stature. She was several inches shorter than me and several more inches shorter than Kai.

"Well, Kaisuke. The *oyabun* has given you to me to do with as I please. Starting now, your transformation from shameful runaway to respectable Yamada heir begins."

I BLINKED AT THE SUN, wondering how its golden light had lost all warmth over the last couple hours.

Zak stood beside me, arms folded as he leaned against the black SUV. Several goons in suits waited around, eerily quiet—small talk was not a thing here—and more men and women in traditional garb moved about in a busy sort of way.

"I don't understand what happened," I whispered.

"We laid eyes on the Yamada *oyabun* and lived to tell the tale." He shrugged. "A better outcome than I expected."

"*Oyabun*?" I repeated in a mumble.

"The head of the head family. The Yamadas are like the mafia. One family in charge, and dozens of lesser families under their command. Most people call them all Yamadas, but that's not accurate."

"How do you know so much about them?"

He angled his face toward the sun, eyes closed. "I've dealt with them on and off over the years. They're a dominant player in the Vancouver black markets."

"Oh." I rubbed my face. "So, what the hell was going on in that room? Kai's grandfather *gave* him to that woman?"

"You can't figure it out yourself?"

I shot him a glare.

"The woman is his fiancée, right?" Zak didn't open his eyes. "The *oyabun* is bringing Kai into line by humiliating him. He made Kai subservient to a woman—to his future wife. For a traditional family like the Yamadas, that's the ultimate emasculation."

"How will that change anything? Kai won't obey her. Once we're back in Vancouver, he'll ditch them again."

The druid cracked an eye open. "You aren't familiar with the Yamadas, are you?"

"You know that already."

"I thought you might've learned something while I was gone. The *oyabun* doesn't need to make obvious threats. Kai knows what'll happen if he disobeys. See?"

He tilted his head and I looked in that direction. Makiko was gliding down the main building's front steps, and she'd replaced her kimono with skintight leather pants and a sleeveless black top, its collar snugged tight around her throat.

A thick belt circled her narrow hips, and two odd silver rods hung from it, swinging with her steps.

Kai followed her, carrying two suitcases, and I could only assume they belonged to Makiko.

My hands curled into fists, but I choked back my fury. I needed to keep it together—at least until I could get Kai alone and find out how much we should be panicking.

He glanced at me, and the warning in his tight expression reinforced my restraint. Setting the suitcases down, he opened the hatch on the SUV and loaded his fiancée's luggage into the back.

"Kaisuke, ride with me," Makiko ordered. "Your friends can take the other vehicle."

Kai shut the hatch with a bang. "*Hai*, Miura-*sama*."

"English, Kaisuke. The *oyabun* doesn't deem you worthy of Japanese."

"Yes, Miura-*sama*."

She cast an icy stare at the nearby men, as though daring them to comment—and it was a good thing she was looking elsewhere, because Zak had to grab my arm as I lunged for her. Breathing hard through my nose, I let Zak pull me toward the second vehicle.

Kai stood obediently beside Makiko as she gave instructions to the driver. Slim Japanese men surrounded them, some in suits and some in traditional clothing, and I was struck hard by how much Kai stood out. Taller than any of them, his complexion far more Caucasian than Japanese, and his features such a unique blend of his two heritages that he didn't closely resemble either.

I slung his backpack off my shoulders. I'd been carrying it around since we'd left the precinct, and Makiko must've assumed it was mine. Otherwise, I was betting she would've confiscated it, snooped through his things, then thrown it all in the garbage, just to make Kai feel worse. Setting the backpack on the floor in front of my seat, I climbed into the vehicle.

Zak shut my door, though not out of chivalry; he was making sure I couldn't punch Makiko. He circled around the SUV and settled into the seat beside me.

"What were you saying?" I demanded as soon as he'd closed his door. "About Kai having to obey that woman?"

"Think about it, Tori. You don't need me to explain."

My stomach turned to a hard, sick lump. "If he doesn't do what she says, she'll tell his grandfather. And his grandfather will …"

He would threaten the people Kai loved, the same way his family had threatened to kill Izzah when she and Kai first dated. Except … what had his grandfather said? *Do not test my mercy again.* That almost sounded like—

"It wouldn't be the first time the Yamadas have assassinated a family member who became a liability," Zak murmured.

I stared out the window, horror rolling through me as Kai got into the SUV. Two men headed toward our vehicle—the driver and a spare goon.

"Frankly," he added, "I'm surprised they let him off the hook for this long. Maybe his friendship with Aaron played a role in that. The Sinclairs are powerful enough to inconvenience the Yamadas."

"You sound really choked up about this," I growled.

He leaned back in his seat. "Kai knew this was coming. You can never truly leave a family like this one."

"Yeah, but—"

"He's alive." His sharp stare pinned me in place. "There are far worse things, and far worse people to control your life."

That flat, frozen hatred burned in his eyes again, and my heart drummed in my throat, a voice in the back of my head whimpering fearfully.

The driver's door opened, saving me from answering. The goons got in, started the engine, and pulled behind the other SUV as it drove through the front gate. I could just make out the shadow of Kai's head through the tinted window.

Far worse things ... but that didn't mean this wasn't Kai's worst nightmare.

8

I WAS BACK ON A PLANE—or more accurately, a jet. And it was a whole different beast from the one we'd flown on this morning.

The sofa—yes, *sofa*—I was slouched on was upholstered in supple white leather. The ceiling was a smooth arch paneled with more leather and gentle yellow lights, uncluttered by overhead compartments. To my left, four plush armchairs sat around a floating tabletop attached to the wall. Across from me was another sofa, and on my right was an elegant little bar, wine glasses clinking gently with the occasional rumble of turbulence. I was pretty sure I'd glimpsed a full bedroom at the back, partially obscured by a privacy partition.

This was one of the Yamadas' private jets, and we were on a direct flight back to Vancouver.

Kai and Makiko sat on the sofa across from me and Zak. She held a slim, shiny tablet, a small crease of concentration between her brows and her thin legs crossed at the knee.

"A lot has changed since you left," she murmured, her quiet tone a stark contrast to her snapping commands from earlier. "My family has expanded operations significantly in the Vancouver region, and in Seattle as well. Our standing with the *oyabun* has increased proportionately."

Kai said nothing.

"My father transitioned to semi-retirement four years ago, and I've stepped into his role—with his guidance." She glanced at her fiancé, a hint of hope in her eyes, as though he might praise her accomplishment.

"Yes, Miura-*sama*," he said after a moment.

Her lips squeezed together—not angrily, but to suppress her reaction. "If you'd stayed in the family, you would already be head of our Vancouver operations. I can't place you in a senior role immediately, but we can move you up from a junior position quickly."

"Yes, Miura-*sama*."

She leaned toward him. "If you commit to your role, I think my father would name you his successor in as little as three years."

My eyebrows rose. Wasn't *she* the current successor? Why did it sound like she wanted Kai to usurp her position?

"Yes, Miura-*sama*," he repeated.

Makiko's knuckles turned white as she gripped her tablet. She opened her mouth—then glanced at me and Zak. She coughed delicately and tapped on her screen.

"For now, you can shadow me and get reacquainted with everything," she went on, her tone cool and businesslike. "With the preparations we're making, my schedule will be hectic. Are you aware of the recent developments following Red Rum's withdrawal?"

A flicker in his expressionless face, but he said nothing.

I, unfortunately, did not have Kai's impulse control. "Do you mean the lack of crime? Did you give all your thugs a holiday or something?"

She scoffed, annoyed that I'd responded instead of Kai. "*We* haven't altered our operations. We drove out the last dregs of Red Rum at the end of December, and with the disappearance of the Ghost, it's grown unusually quiet."

Zak, who'd so far been trying to nap upright in his seat, cracked his green eyes open.

"The Ghost?" I repeated warily. "What does he have to do with anything?"

"His habit of inconveniencing larger organizations gave other lone wolves the idea that they could defy us, but without him, they've tucked their tails between their legs. Either way, he isn't a concern anymore—or won't be shortly."

All-too-familiar dread rekindled in my gut. "Meaning what?"

"I suppose you haven't seen the update." She tapped on her tablet, then handed it to Kai.

He read something on the screen, his eyes zipping back and forth. A muscle jumped in his cheek, his posture rigid. He held the tablet out to me.

I could feel Zak's attention as I took the device. An email from noreply@mpdalerts.com, sent at 1:36 p.m., waited to be read.

Subject: Vancouver Area Bounty Update for "The Ghost"

Following an anonymous tip, a high-priority bounty for the Vancouver-based rogue known as the Ghost has been updated. To view the additional 178 charges, please see the full bounty listing.

The new bounty sum is $1,220,000, payable upon positive identification.

Please note that the Ghost's mythic class has been added, pending confirmation:

Di-mythic – Spiritalis, druid; Arcana, alchemist.

This rogue is considered highly dangerous and the bounty is classified as Dead or Alive—proceed with utmost caution. See the listing for more information.

Sincerely,

Susan Manley
Administrative Manager – Bounties
Northern West Coast Region
MPD

My mouth hung open. I blinked as though that might change the words.

"The Ghost has always been too evasive for the MPD to link him to many crimes," Makiko remarked. "But with a bounty of one-point-two million, he'll be too busy dodging elite bounty hunters to cause us trouble."

"One-point-two *million?*" Zak blurted.

Her eyebrows arched. "Rather impressive, isn't it? It won't take long before he's caught or killed."

I stared at the email, unable to look away from one line. *Di-mythic – Spiritalis, druid; Arcana, alchemist.*

How? How could MagiPol know that? Who had told them? Who even knew? The Crow and Hammer team from last summer had figured out he was a druid—while he was abducting me—but with my capture and everything else, they'd never reported it to anyone. And they hadn't known anything about his Arcana gift.

The mystery of Zak's class was part of what made his reputation so terrifying—and it protected his identity.

My gaze darted to his bare arms, druid tattoos plainly visible. The email had gone out shortly before we broke into the precinct to rescue him, but the timing had to be a coincidence. No one there had a clue who they'd been holding—though that one group of agents *had* come rushing downstairs all in a tizzy … yet they hadn't seemed to be expecting intruders. Had they just seen the alert and been on their way to check out their mysterious druid captive?

I hastily handed the tablet back to Makiko, not wanting Zak to glimpse the email. His reaction to the unveiling of his class wouldn't be pretty.

Makiko's attention slid between me and the druid in a way that made me distinctly nervous, then she turned back to Kai. "Do you have a preference between a room at my father's house, or a private apartment in—"

My temper, stretched thin by too much stress and too little sleep, snapped. "Don't act like you care about what he wants."

Kai shot me a "be quiet" glare, which I ignored.

"What's your plan here, Makiko?" I sneered at her. "You were a complete bitch to him back in LA."

"You have nothing to do with this." She set her tablet on the seat beside her. "And the moment we land, you'll have nothing more to do with Kaisuke. Ever."

I lunged off my seat, but Zak yanked me back down. I almost jumped up again, so strong was my desire to shove her out a tiny airplane window and wave goodbye as she fell thirty thousand feet.

"Tori," Kai said quietly, "this isn't the time."

"Why not? We've got nothing else to do." My hands balled into fists, fingernails cutting into my palms. "Let's chat about how she thinks she can treat you like her damn servant and—"

"*Tori*," he snapped. "Drop it."

My teeth clacked together. I glowered at him from across the aisle. "How can you expect me to sit here and pretend nothing is wrong?"

"Wrong?" Makiko placed a hand on Kai's arm. "This is where he belongs."

My vision went red. I was vaguely aware of Zak gripping my shoulder, holding me in place. "What do you know about where he belongs? You don't know a damn thing about him!"

"What do *you* know?" she shot back, her face hardening. "I bet Kaisuke has never told you a thing about his life outside that ridiculous guild. Did he tell you he grew up with *my* family? That I was his best friend—his *only* friend—for his entire childhood?"

My fury sputtered like a flame in the wind. Suddenly uncertain, I looked between her and Kai.

"I was one year old when I was betrothed to Kaisuke. My father risked our family's reputation to unite our bloodline with the *oyabun*'s *hâfu* grandson." She turned to Kai, her lips pressed thin. "We welcomed you and your mother. We shielded you. We built you up and supported you when your relatives tried to tear you down."

Kai's jaw tightened.

"They hated you." Her fingers bit into his arm. "But I dedicated everything I had to your success. After all we'd been through, after all I'd done—and all my family had done—you still ran away without a single word or even a *goodbye*."

Her voice broke on the last word, a tremor vibrating her small frame. Shoving off the sofa, she strode to the cabin partition and stopped.

She didn't look back, her voice steady but her shoulders quivering. "But you can't ignore me or your proper place in the family any longer. Say your goodbyes to your friends now, because they don't belong in your life anymore. They never did."

She disappeared into the bedroom at the back, and the door thudded shut.

Kai let out a slow breath, the same tremor in his exhalation as Makiko had tried to hide. Pushing off the sofa, I crossed the aisle, dropped down beside him, and curled up against his side, hugging his arm to my body.

"She's letting me off too easy," he whispered.

"Because you left your family?"

"Because I ran away like a coward. I didn't even have the courage to tell her I was leaving, and I've been running from her and them and everything ever since."

I rested my head on his shoulder. "Or maybe it took all you had to leave."

His fingers tightened around mine.

Zak watched us, his gaze shadowed. Kicking his boots off, he laid across the sofa and pillowed his head on a cushion.

"Sometimes," he murmured, eyes closing, "the only way to keep moving forward is to never look back."

Kai breathed deeply to steady himself. I relaxed against his side, exhaustion weighing me down. My stamina had run out several crises ago, and Kai was pale and hollow-eyed. Zak didn't look much better. He put his arm over his face to block out the light.

I stifled a yawn. "So ... what's the plan when we arrive in Vancouver?"

Kai looked down at our linked fingers. "For now, I do whatever Makiko says."

My stomach twisted with anxious denial, but I didn't argue. There'd be time for arguing, after I got in an emergency meeting with Aaron and Ezra.

"You have more urgent concerns," Kai added, lowering his voice. "As long as Shane Davila is in town, you'll need to watch your steps carefully."

Zak lifted his arm enough to peer at us. "Shane Davila? The bounty hunter?"

A rustle from the other side of the archway drew my attention. I glimpsed the sleeve of a uniformed flight attendant peeking out from behind the divider and cleared my throat.

"Did you hear how Shane is in Vancouver because he thinks he has a strong lead on the Ghost?" I asked airily. "He even came to the Crow and Hammer, asking weird questions about last summer. But I was on vacation in the mountains, remember?"

Zak dropped his arm to his side, head turning toward me, scary intensity gathering in his green eyes.

"I remember that," Kai replied, as casual as me. "You had a nice trip, didn't you?"

"It was great," I lied. "Shane mentioned going to the mountains too. He brought back a souvenir from the same place I visited."

Zak's eyes widened.

"Now he's hanging around Vancouver," Kai murmured. "I bet he's watching things very closely."

"Especially with that MPD update. It said …" Swallowing nervously, I shot Zak a warning look. "An anonymous tip identified the Ghost as a di-mythic druid and alchemist."

I expected him to shoot up in horrified disbelief, but instead, he went eerily still. His eyes lost focus, his expression blanking and his breathing slowing. The only sign of his tension was the abrupt clenching of his fists.

"I don't know how they found out," I mumbled. "Who could have told them?"

Zak's gaze snapped to Kai. He mouthed a silent word: *mages.*

"No way! They didn't!"

Kai's hand squeezed mine and I bit my tongue. Teeth gritted, I glared at Zak. Aaron, Ezra, and Kai knew Zak was a druid alchemist but they would never report that to the MPD—not even anonymously.

Zak met my glower, then closed his eyes, covered his face with his arm, and said nothing more.

9

IT WAS ALMOST ELEVEN P.M. by the time the black sedan parked at the curb, mature trees lining the opposite side of the familiar residential street. The pavement shone from recent rainfall, reflecting the cheery glow from the windows of Aaron's cute cottage-style house.

Slumped in the backseat between Kai and Zak, I dredged up remnants of energy from a deeply buried reservoir. Between Lallakai's surprise visit, two flights, a rescue mission, a vine-monster attack, an abduction, a family reunion, and an MPD bombshell, I didn't have much gas left in the tank. Napping through most of the flight home hadn't really helped.

Kai pushed his door open. A damp, wintry breeze blew across me, chilling my neck above the collar of my leather jacket. The rest of my gear was in the backpack at my feet.

Zak cast me an unreadable look, then climbed out the other door. He'd barely said a word on the drive from the airport, his silence borderline hostile. As Makiko exited from the passenger seat, I hauled my weary butt out of the car, dragging the backpack with me.

Light brightened as the house's front door opened. Aaron's familiar silhouette leaned on the jamb, observing the new arrivals. We hadn't been able to warn him that we were back, or what had happened while we were gone. Kai had ditched our burner phone in LA to better cover our tracks—especially since Zak's vine-monster spell meant the precinct incident would make international mythic news.

Part of me hoped Aaron would keep his cool when he found out what was going on, but another part really wanted him to explode. A few fireballs to Makiko's face would make me feel so much better.

She pushed to the front of our small group and strode up the walkway. Aaron watched her approach, then stepped back. She marched through the door, stopped to remove her tall leather boots, then resumed her bold entrance.

Kai didn't bother to take his shoes off, but he lived here, so whatever. I left mine on too, just in case I needed to kick a certain someone in her pretty little kneecaps. We all piled into the living room, and my gaze swept hungrily across the space, searching.

Ezra stood in front of the sofa, his feet set and hands hanging loose at his sides in readiness. His gaze flicked across Kai and Makiko before giving me a swift once-over, checking that I was unharmed.

Aaron retreated to Ezra's side, the pair of mages facing Kai and Makiko, and I was reminded of a different tense encounter in this room, where Aaron and Ezra had also faced off with Kai and a suspicious stranger.

I glanced around, realizing Zak hadn't come inside with us.

"Kaisuke," Makiko commanded sharply. "Get your things. You have five minutes."

I rolled my eyes. Why politely remove her boots if she was going to act like *that* as soon as she was inside?

Aaron's cautious expression hardened. "Who are you?"

"Makiko Miura. You would be Aaron Sinclair." His name came out of her mouth in a sneer, and I wondered if she blamed him for Kai's defection from his family—and her life.

Aaron's disbelieving stare shot from her to Kai and back. "Makiko?"

"Kaisuke is coming with me. You may say goodbye if you'd like. You will not see him again."

Aaron's hands formed instant fists and sparks leaped from his fingers.

Kai stepped around Makiko, crossed to his best friend, and grasped his shoulder. "Miura-*sama*, may I handle this, please?"

Her lips thinned. Pivoting on her heel, she strode back to the entryway—which put her two steps away from me. I considered joining Kai, who was speaking to Aaron and Ezra in a rapid murmur, then tossed Kai's backpack onto the recliner, regretting my decision to pack up my artifacts so I wouldn't lose any on the jet. Getting the Queen out now would be like announcing my intent to attack.

"You knew him eight years ago," I told Makiko quietly. "But you don't know him now."

She ignored me.

"*What?*" Aaron yelled. "That's bullshit! No way in hell are you—"

Kai cut him off, his voice a low, urgent rumble.

I stepped closer to her. "You have no idea what he wants, what he cares about, or what he's like."

Her breath rushed between her lips, then she pushed her shoulders back. "That's what you're failing to understand. What he wants and what he cares about are selfish distractions. The interests of our families must always take priority."

"Why should he do a damn thing they want when they treat him like—"

She leaned toward me. "A Yamada heir who puts himself first has no place in the family. I will make Kaisuke valuable to his family, *indispensable* to them, not only because that's what's best for me and my family, but because that's the only way he can survive."

Whirling away from me, she raised her voice. "Kaisuke, I've changed my mind. If you want anything from this house, I'll send someone to get it. We're leaving."

Aaron's head snapped around. "If you think you can just—"

"Now, Kaisuke!"

Kai muttered one more thing to Aaron, then squeezed Ezra's shoulder. Three best friends, as close as brothers. They'd fought together, grown together, suffered and survived together.

Now Aaron and Ezra had to watch Kai walk away from them, and not even Ezra could hide the pain on his face.

Kai plucked his phone off the end table, where it waited beside mine—our tech alibis—

then strode over to me and Makiko. He swept me off my feet in a hug, his cheek pressed to mine.

"I'm counting on you, Tori," he whispered. "Keep them under control. Keep them safe."

I clamped my arms around him. "This isn't over."

He gripped me harder, his forehead dropping to my shoulder. "Please, Tori."

My eyes stung, and I sucked in a trembling breath. He held on a moment longer, then released me. I dashed my hand across my wet eyes as he stepped past me. Makiko zipped up her boots, and she and Kai walked out of the house. The screen door banged shut behind them.

I stared across the room at Aaron and Ezra, our shared anguish reverberating in the space between us.

Aaron's expression crumpled—then he bared his teeth. "No. No fucking way."

Flames rippled over his fingers, singeing his sweater's sleeves. He stormed forward, furious strides eating up the room.

Heart cramming itself into my throat, I stepped into his path. "Aaron, please wait—"

"No, Tori." His eyes sparked like blue fire. "Kai is letting this happen—but I won't."

My mouth opened, but panic threaded through my grief and helplessness. I didn't try to stop him as he swept past me. He hit the front door at a jog.

"Makiko!" he roared.

Ezra grabbed my hand, racing for the door after Aaron. We ran out onto the steps as Aaron reached the bottom, fire blazing over his clenched fists.

Kai had already disappeared into the car, and only Makiko, standing beside the open passenger door, turned to face the oncoming pyromage. A silver rod from her belt was in her hand, and with a flick of her wrist, she snapped it sideways.

The rod opened into a gleaming metal fan, each featherlike panel inscribed with runes.

"*Hyah!*" she shouted ferociously, sweeping it sideways through the air.

Dirt and leaves blew skyward. The howling gust lifted Aaron off the ground and flung him across the yard. He smashed into me and Ezra, knocking us backward. We crumpled in a heap on the front stoop.

A car door slammed. The engine revved.

"*No!*" Aaron snarled, shoving himself up.

The black sedan accelerated up the street. Its taillights flashed around the corner, then it was gone.

Ezra's arms were around me, one hand shielding the back of my head from an impact with the stoop. Aaron's heavy weight lifted off us. As I slowly sat up, he strode down the steps, breathing hard. I blinked sluggishly in the silence, not quite able to believe it.

Kai was gone. He'd left. He'd gone with Makiko, allowing her to steal him away from us.

"You're a dramatic bunch."

My head jerked toward the voice that had rumbled from the shadows. Zak leaned against the house beside the living room window, one side of his face lit by the interior lights.

"What—" Aaron gasped. "*You!* What the hell are you doing here?"

I pretended not to notice how the air around Ezra chilled warningly. Pushing to my feet, I dusted my clothes off.

"I thought you'd left," I told the druid.

"Am I supposed to walk home?"

My teeth clenched. "Could you not be an asshole for once? This all happened because Kai and I went to LA to save *you*."

"Kai went to LA?" Aaron tore his glare off the druid. "That's the seat of Yamada power!"

My shoulders slumped and I wrapped my arms around myself. "I didn't know that. He didn't tell me. He said it was fine …"

Ezra placed his hand on the small of my back, his gentle touch grounding me against a tide of guilt and regret. As tears welled in my eyes and spilled down my cheeks, Aaron pulled me into his arms, the same way Kai had moments ago. Ezra shifted closer, standing right behind me, offering silent support.

"It's not your fault." Aaron cradled me against his chest as I sniffed back tears. "Kai never told you anything about—

An electronic ring jolted through me.

Aaron and I broke apart, and he shoved his hand in his pocket. He yanked out his phone, the screen lit with an incoming call.

He slapped the phone to his face. "Kai, are you—" He broke off, forehead scrunching. "Oh, Shane. Sorry, I … Look, I'm in the middle of someth—" Another pause, and I could vaguely hear a male voice speaking rapidly. Aaron's eyes widened. "They're *under attack*? What does that even … Shit. Okay, I'll be ready in fifteen minutes … Fine, ten minutes."

He ended the call with a curse. "That was Shane. A group of rogues is laying siege to the Pandora Knights guild—"

"What?" I gasped.

"—and it's a goddamn warzone. Shane's on his way to pick me up so we can get over there."

"He's on his way?" My panicked stare jumped to the extremely wanted rogue standing in plain sight. "But—but—but this is a *really* bad time!"

Zak pushed off the wall. "I wasn't planning to stick around anyway."

"Oh yeah?" I stepped away from Aaron and Ezra as the druid walked onto the lawn. "I'm still waiting for you to thank us for saving your ungrateful ass."

"I didn't ask you to save me."

A high-pitched hiss escaped my clenched teeth. I stomped up to him and stopped almost on his toes. "Well, we *did* save you, and now you owe us. And I'm calling in my favor immediately."

He tilted his head back, gazing at the dark sky. "I agree that I owe you, but it'll have to wait. I have more important things to worry about than Kai's family drama."

"Too freaking bad." I grabbed the front of his shirt and yanked hard, trying to force him to look at me. "Zak!"

He pushed me backward. "Get out of the way."

"Out of the way of what?" I growled, tightening my grip on his shirt. "You—"

"Tori, *move*—"

Wind blasted over us.

Debris flew everywhere, my hair whipped across my face—and something boomed like a parachute catching the wind. A solid force slammed me into Zak. The world spun, I was being crushed around the middle, the wind was roaring in my ears—

And the ground disappeared from beneath my feet.

Monstrous black wings, dusted with blue and purple stars, swept down, propelling us higher. Shimmering galaxies swirled in waves, and it took my bewildered brain a moment to recognize the shape.

A dragon.

The huge winged reptile soared upward. Below us, Aaron and Ezra were specks, their pale faces tilted upward as the dragon carried me into the night sky.

10

"ECHO!" ZAK SHOUTED over the roaring wind. "You weren't supposed to bring her!"

I gasped for breath, crushed against Zak, the dragon's huge clawed hand encircling us both. The air was so cold it hurt.

"That doesn't mean—I know, but take her back!"

Another sweep of giant wings. The city lights, far below, shimmered and rippled, losing solidity as though we were underwater—a terrifying distortion I remembered from my one and only dragon flight before this.

"Z-z-zak," I chattered. "What the h-hell is g-g-going on?"

He started to speak but the wind whipped his words away. Leaning close, he put his mouth to my ear, his breath hot on my chilled skin. "I called him to take me home, and since you were standing with me, he decided you were coming too."

"B-b-but—"

"He won't go back. You're coming along for the ride now."

The world eddied and shimmered around us, obscuring my view of the ground and warping the passage of time. I had no idea if seconds or hours were passing, aware only of the icy wind and Zak's body heat. That, and the crushing grip of the dragon's foot, but like hell I was going to ask Echo to loosen his hold on the shrimpy, wingless humans. Echo was enough of a dickhead to take that as permission to drop us. He and Zak were a matched pair of dickish jerks.

My stomach swooped as the dragon began to descend. His shimmering black wings surged up and down in a sedate rhythm, and the rippling world began to steady.

The darkness resolved into a star-dusted sky, the waxing moon peeking out from behind thin clouds. Its silvery light reflected off snow-capped mountains, the white peaks seeming to glow. They jutted into the sky all around us, stretching as far as I could see.

Echo soared over a ridge, then tilted his wings to sweep into a dark valley. I squeezed my eyes shut, unable to watch as the ground rushed toward us. Our plummet abruptly slowed, the wind whipping over me, then a jolt and a thud as we landed.

I cracked my eyes open.

Echo lowered me and Zak, and my feet met wonderfully solid ground. His thick, scaled digits uncurled and I staggered backward, limbs numb. Zak caught my arms and pulled me upright.

Echo's huge body, luminescent with soft swirls of blue and purple light, cast an eerie glow over the thin dusting of snow, but neither the snow nor the darkness could hide the charred, lifeless earth that surrounded us.

Zak's hands tightened, squeezing hard.

A soft whoosh of wings much smaller than the dragon's broke the silence. A black eagle glided out of the darkness on outspread wings. Shadows spiraled around Lallakai as she swept to Zak's side, and her human form appeared, her bare feet touching down with soundless grace.

"My druid," she breathed throatily, enveloping Zak in a tight embrace

I stepped back, pulling away from his hands. Lallakai purred delightedly at her consort's return, her full bosom pressed against his arm and a hand splayed against his chest. Her crystalline eyes cut across me, her gaze lacking either gratitude or warmth.

Zak didn't seem to notice her. He was staring into the distance, his face tight.

I turned. The gentle hill slanted down toward the base of the valley where the house, gardens, and stable formed the three points of a sprawling triangle beside the winding creek.

The house was a crumbling, blackened ruin. The barn was a burnt shell. The garden was gone—along with every tree, every plant, every blade of grass. Everything was black, scorched ... dead.

With the scuff of slow steps, Zak walked past me. I wasn't sure he saw me any more than he'd noticed Lallakai's arrival. Her expression sobered as she followed him, a respectful two steps behind. Despite his sleeveless shirt, he seemed unaware of the cold as he trekked down the slope toward the ruins of his home.

I watched him go, my heart aching.

Light erupted in a colorful swirl behind me. Wisps of mist and magic circled the massive dragon crouched on the hillside.

The rippling distortion spread outward, then sucked back in, and with a shower of azure sparks, it disappeared.

Echo turned his midnight eyes on me, his smooth, androgynous features as indecipherable as his reptilian face had been. Exotic robes draped his slim humanoid frame, and his raven hair, streaked with blue and purple, hung over his shoulder in a thin braid that fell to his waist. Black wings, shimmering with stars, rose off his back and a long dragon tail rested on the ground behind him.

In my totally unbiased opinion, he was way more beautiful than Lallakai.

"Brazen one," he said softly, the words accented by his otherworldly voice. "We meet again."

"Hi," I mumbled. "Why did you bring me here? I don't think Zak wants company."

The dragon fae studied me. "Come, human child."

"Where?"

He glided into motion, following Zak's footprints in the snow. The druid wasn't moving quickly. He was only halfway to the house's wreckage.

I fell into step beside the wyldfae, scarcely able to comprehend his existence. Rows of tiny horns in the same pattern as on his reptilian head poked out of his hair. His ears looked just like Legolas's.

His eyes turned to me, and I forgot all about make-believe elves and movie makeup tricks. His stare pulled me in, black holes of mystery, unearthly wisdom, and unfathomable power. Fear tingled in my fingers and toes. As we drew nearer to Zak and Lallakai, I rubbed my hands together to banish the feeling. Was it the cold? An icy wind was blowing through the valley in half-hearted spurts, tugging at my hair.

I'd thought Zak was heading toward the burnt-out husk of his house, but he angled in a different direction. With ever-slowing steps, he approached the barn.

Ten paces away, he stopped. Lallakai waited behind him, her hands folded patiently in front of her. For a full minute, he stood there, then he forced himself forward again. He walked to the wide threshold, the shattered door lying on the floor inside. He placed a hand against the charred frame, his head bowed. He didn't enter. Just reaching the building had taken all his resolve.

Deep, icy horror crystalized inside me. The barn. His horses. They weren't … they couldn't be … inside?

A memory, soft and brightly lit like a pleasant dream: Zak striding into the green pasture beneath the cheerful summer sun, whistling for his horses. Their perked ears and bouncy trots as they came to greet him. His gentle hands patting their shoulders and stroking their noses as he carefully checked each horse's health before leading one to the barn to be groomed and saddled.

My throat closed and my eyes burned. One palm on the doorframe, head and shoulders bent with grief, Zak stood motionless. Steeling myself, I took a step toward him.

Cool hands touched my shoulders, halting me. Echo's breath stirred my hair.

"To your eyes, he stands alone." He leaned down, his head above my shoulder, silky strands of his hair brushing against my cheek. "Do you wish to see what my eyes can reveal?"

His hands left my shoulders, and he lay them gently over my eyes, blocking my vision. Shivers ran over my skin and dizziness engulfed my head. My eyes felt inexplicably cool, as though a breeze was blowing across them. He spread his slender fingers, forming two triangular windows through which I could gaze straight ahead.

A pale mist that hadn't existed moments before draped the valley. It drifted serenely, immune to the fitful wind. The remains of the barn were there but not, a dark structure almost dense enough to be solid. Half a dozen large shapes, heaped on the ground inside, were far darker.

Zak stood before the ethereal building. I could see him … but I hardly recognized him at all.

Shadows spilled out of him like heavy smoke overflowing from an incense burner. Charcoal flames danced across the ground, and pale sparks shot through the strange mist, sharp and agitated. The fae runes on his inner arms glowed with power, and he—he glowed too. A soft, effervescent light radiated through his skin, shimmering like ripples on a sunlit pond.

"Do you see it?" Echo breathed in my ear. "His power, his allure. Sweet, intoxicating. It draws us. Humans possess but a touch. Witches, a taste. Druids … a feast."

I shivered.

Zak still hadn't moved, but the darkness spilling from him was thickening. It writhed, flashes and sparks erupting like tiny bolts of lightning in inky clouds. His body's ethereal glow brightened.

"They come. Called to his power. Called by his pain."

As though the dragon's words had lifted a veil, I could see them—shapes drawing closer. Shadows, silhouettes, glittering forms that made no sense to my human brain.

Black wolves with glowing red eyes came first—his vargs. A white panther, its two tails lashing in agitation. Tiny pixies, their gossamer wings fluttering. Strange reptiles, wreathed in shade, crawling on the ground. Tall, thin beings with long, dragging arms and gray skin—the darkfae who'd tried to kill him in the forest last summer. A shaggy creature, similar to a bear, lumbering upright on two legs. Two shimmery silver sylphs, twins to Hoshi, undulating weightlessly as they nervously approached.

I couldn't breathe as creatures of fantasy and nightmare emerged from the darkness.

A huge stag, his coat unblemished ivory, his golden antlers rising high above his head in an impossible tangle, picked his way across the ground. With each press of his golden hooves, grass sprang from the ravaged earth. The plants shot upward, leaves sprouting, flowers blooming. A strip of summer meadow marked the buck's path out of the forest.

The fae, light and dark, ugly and beautiful, gathered around the grieving druid, but none approached him—and in the empty space between them and Zak was Lallakai.

The Lady of Shadow, the Night Eagle. Phantom wings arched off her back and inky power swirled around her feet, mixing with the darkness flowing out of Zak. She stood with her hands on her curved hips, her chin tilted up in confident challenge, daring the other fae to approach *her* druid. *Her* consort.

"Echo," I whispered, "what is Zak's relationship with Lallakai?"

"She is his guardian, his guide, his keeper. For a long time, as time passes for humans, she has nurtured him. A druid as potent as he, as seductive to the fae who hunger for a feast, would have perished long ago without a protector so powerful and dedicated."

The darkness, the light, the shivering power rolling off Zak deepened. My limbs tingled, the magic in the air sparking off my skin. The gathering fae shifted restlessly.

"She will own him until his last day."

Lallakai swept her hand out, dragging it through the druid's thickening power. Raising her fingers to her lips, she licked them as though they were coated in sweet wine.

Green eyes burning in her flawless face, she turned to Zak as he bowed beneath his grief, lost in whatever dark hell he'd spiraled into—a hell so deep he was calling the fae of the forest to him. The darkness spilling out of him continued to deepen, the sizzling flashes inside it growing more violent.

He was inflamed with fury. I could not soothe his raging heart.

But had she tried?

She slid closer to him. The other fae drifted nearer. Zak was disappearing in the haze.

My heart thumped loudly in my ears.

I pushed Echo's hands off my face and launched down the slope. The cool magic infusing my eyes held, and I could see the gathered fae scattering out of my path. I charged through them and into the empty ring around Zak, guarded by Lallakai.

She was watching him, lust on her face. She didn't see me until I was almost on them.

"Zak!"

He jerked upright, half turning—and I collided with him, my arms locking around his head and pulling his face into my shoulder. He almost fell but righted himself, grabbing my waist.

"Zak," I gasped, holding him so fiercely I couldn't breathe. "Zak, it's okay to cry."

His fingers bit into my sides.

"I'll cry too." My voice wavered. Tears stung my eyes. "You're not alone. I'm with you."

He sucked in a trembling breath—and he buckled.

I held him tightly as he sank to his knees, his shoulders shaking silently. Kneeling with him, I held his face to my shoulder, shielding him with my arms, hiding him from the fae and their watching eyes. And I cried too.

I wept for the innocent lives he'd treasured so deeply, for the unconditional love he'd lost. His horses had never demanded anything of him. Had never tried to use him. Could never have betrayed him. He'd loved them as he couldn't love another person. Trusted them because he couldn't trust anyone else.

And someone had taken that from him.

A step away, Lallakai stood frozen, gaping down at her druid, clutched in my arms, his hands fisted around my jacket, his rage drowned in anguish. My borrowed fae vision, now fading, revealed that the shadows surrounding him were dissipating.

Fury twisted her face. Teeth bared, she reached for me, her fingers curled.

With a sweep of starry wings, Echo landed beside her. His hand settled lightly on hers, halting her reach—her pointed nail inches from my face. Her blazing eyes shot to his.

"His grief is human," Echo murmured. "You are not."

She hissed softly—and he smiled, revealing his carnivorous teeth. A ripple distorted the air as immense power rolled out from him. It sizzled over me, buzzing across every nerve in my body.

Lallakai faced the dragon, breathing hard, then pulled her hand free. She whirled, hair sweeping out, and took three steps away. Now it was the dragon standing guard over the druid, his back to us, wings spread like a curtain, hiding us from the hungry stares of the gathered fae.

Closing my eyes, I rested my cheek on Zak's hair. The hard ground under my knees didn't matter. The cold wind didn't matter. The terrifying fae all around us didn't matter.

I would hold him for as long as he needed me.

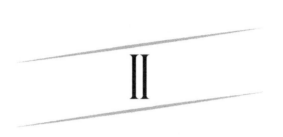

II

ZAK AND I SAT TOGETHER against the side of the barn, out of the wind. Night lay heavy across the mountains, no hint of dawn on the horizon. I stared up at the waxing moon, only a few days from full.

Like me, Zak's head was tilted back, his dull green eyes on the stars. His hand, warm and calloused, was tucked between both of mine.

"Did all the fae leave?" I asked quietly. Lallakai and Echo had wandered off, but I couldn't tell if the others remained. My eyes were back to normal.

"Lallakai chased them off. How did you know they were there?"

"Echo gave me fae x-ray vision for a few minutes. It was wild. You glow like a nuclear experiment gone wrong."

He huffed. "Makes it hard for witches and druids to blend in with the crowd, doesn't it?"

"What do humans look like?"

"Most don't have visible energy. Mythics can have an aura, but it's different."

"Can *you* see auras?"

"No, but Lallakai can."

I rested my head against the wall. "Is that how you knew I wasn't a diviner? Way back when we first met?"

"In part. I also had a contact of mine dig up every scrap of information on you, legal and illegal, that's ever existed. There's no mythic anything in your background."

"I'm first in a new line of humawitch."

A corner of his mouth lifted. "Is that what you're calling it?"

"I don't like witchuman as much."

"Didn't I tell you that you're a real witch? You don't need a special term."

"I know, but I don't feel like a witch. Fae sort of pay attention to me sometimes, I guess, but we don't have a special connection. Besides, I'm kind of dabbling in everything. I have the Queen of Spades, and the crystals you gave me—"

"That you stole."

"—and these cool brass knuckles. Wait until you see them. I've been learning to use offensive and defensive alchemy, too. I have my own paintball gun now. The guys gave it to me for Christmas."

"Hmm. Maybe 'witch' is too limiting, then. You're on your way to becoming a jack of all classes."

"No." I grinned. "I'll be the Jack of *Spades*. Get it? Because SPADE stands for Spiritalis, Psychica, Arcana, Demonica, and Elementaria."

"I know the acronym, Tori," he said dryly. "Usually, only advanced combat mythics excel in wielding multiple classes."

"I'm just that awesome."

His gaze turned to me. "Yeah."

My cheeks heated. I pushed myself up out of my slouch and leaned back again, letting his hand slip from mine. He returned his attention to the sky, the moonlight softening the haggard lines around his mouth.

"You said you want to call in your favor right away," he murmured.

"I was just angry. You don't owe me anything."

"But there's something you need."

My stomach twisted. "Ezra ... he's running out of time."

"Don't demon mages last the better part of a decade? He's young yet to be—"

"He's been a demon mage since he was fourteen."

A long, disbelieving pause. "Who would turn a kid into a demon mage?"

"I don't know, but Ezra's had his demon for almost ten years now, and his demon is getting stronger. He's starting to lose control, and he may only have a few months."

Silence slid between us.

"Tori." Zak's rumbling voice was unusually gentle. "Any form of demon contract is for life. They only ever end with a death."

"I know that, but ..." I gulped. "I found this amulet. It— well, it belonged to a demon, and it has the power to interrupt a demon contract. I used it to stop a demon from killing me. The amulet freed the demon, and it turned on its contractor."

His eyes widened. "The artifact belonged to a demon?"

"I need to know how the amulet works and whether it can be used to separate Ezra and his demon, but I can't find any information on demonic magic or artifacts. That's what I need your help with."

"An artifact with power like that …" He rubbed his mouth, fingers rasping over dark stubble. "Could it be sorcery? If it is demon magic, I don't know whether information on it would even exist. Interrupting a demon contract … but would that work on a demon mage? The simplest way to find out would be to test it on a demon mage, but where would you find another one?"

"I've gotten the impression they're rare."

"Extremely, yeah. The important question might not be whether the amulet can separate the demon from the mage, but whether they can survive it. How tightly bound are the demon and its host?"

"I don't care if the demon dies."

"Demons are hardy. It's Ezra you should be worried about. An otherworldly creature has been possessing him for ten years. How much has it changed him?"

Cold that had nothing to do with the frigid January air pierced me. "He's stronger and faster than a human."

"And he can endure injuries that would kill a regular man. He kept fighting with a sword wound that should've had him down in minutes."

Zak was referring to that terrifying battle to save Nadine last summer. Aaron's sword flashing downward. Ezra falling. He'd fought until the very end, and only collapsed from blood loss after it was all over.

I hugged myself. "Ezra is doomed anyway, so I have to try. But I can't just *give* him the amulet, not without knowing what will happen." Especially since Eterran wanted it so badly. The demon's desire for it had triggered all my alarm bells.

"I'll see what I can dig up on demonic amulets, but I don't think it will be much. What about demon mage contracts? What do you know about them?"

"Me? Uh …"

"Have you done *any* research? If you want to save Ezra, you should be learning everything you can about demon mages."

Déjà vu jolted through me. Darius's somber gray eyes, his chilling instruction: *Ask Ezra to teach you everything he knows about demon mages.*

"Aaron and Kai already researched—" I began.

"Them," Zak interrupted with a dismissive scoff. "*Maybe* Kai would've tapped into illicit sources, but his experience is with crime—the black market, smuggling, forgeries, embezzlement, blackmail, racketeering. Neither mage has a clue how deep the webs of dark magic run."

A hint of energy revived his green eyes as he sat forward. "Real summoners are like druids. They don't write how-to books or do interviews with scholars or volunteer as MPD consultants. All their knowledge is passed from master to apprentice, and they jealously, violently protect it."

"So how am I supposed to learn about it, then?"

"The hard way." He tapped my knee in emphasis. "The guidebooks MagiPol created are the beginner's version of Demonica. You need an expert level education in it if you want any chance of figuring out the amulet and saving Ezra."

Didn't that just sound impossible. "Will you help me?"

"I pay my debts." He pushed to his feet. "But it'll have to wait. I have something I need to do first."

Feeling oddly nervous, I scrambled up too. "What's that?"

Flat, frigid hatred flared in his eyes as his gaze swept from the barn to the house. "I'm going to kill the bitch who did this."

I was still gaping as he stalked away. "Wait. You know who did this?"

"She might as well have carved her name in Morgan's body."

"*Morgan—*"

Without breaking stride, Zak whistled softly. A few paces away, the air shimmered and a fae appeared—an albino panther with yellow eyes and two tails, their furred tips glowing with faint power.

Zak crouched, his hand extended toward the feline. "Niari."

The panther slunk to him, head low and tails drooping. It pushed its forehead into his chest and he stroked its thick fur.

A ping in my memory—that panther poised over me, fangs bared, while the blond and bossy witch Morgan stood nearby. *Tori, meet Niari, my familiar.*

"I would've guessed who did this even without a witness, but Varvara wasn't as thorough as she could've been." He rubbed Niari's ears, then added in a whisper, "Morgan died quickly."

"Is ... is she here? Should we ..." I couldn't finish the sentence.

"MPD agents took her body."

So Shane wasn't the only one who'd found the valley after Zak's farm had been destroyed. "Varvara did this?"

I wasn't surprised. The dark sorceress was a hell of a piece of work. Between kidnapping her enemies' daughter to raise as an apprentice, almost killing Kai and Aaron when we'd tried to save Nadine from her clutches, and sending her minions after Zak and forcing him into hiding, Varvara was one of my least favorite people on the planet.

With a final caress for the panther, Zak rose. "She wants one of two things—for me to disappear forever, never to trouble her again, or for me to reveal myself in a blind fury, making it nice and easy to get rid of me for good."

"Well, the first one definitely isn't an option," I said warily. "But neither is the second."

"The second is exactly what I intend to do."

"But—"

He looked over his shoulder, his rage burning deep. "Her mistake is thinking she can kill me. I ran from her once. This time, I'll destroy her."

My throat bobbed in a failed attempt to swallow. He continued walking, and it took me a moment to get my numb legs moving. I pulled my jacket sleeves over my frozen hands.

"Okay ..." I trotted to his side. "What next?"

"Next, I figure out what she and those MPD bastards didn't steal." His jaw tightened. "I left things here. I thought they would be safe ..."

He trailed off, then extended his stride until I needed to jog to keep up.

First, he checked the former alchemy garden. All that remained was burnt earth and a few charred fenceposts. A hole in the ground revealed a metal case, empty except for dirt and snow. Zak gazed at the uncovered cache, then turned away and kept walking.

"What was in there?" I asked worriedly.

"Dangerous artifacts I didn't have time to get rid of. And Harry."

"Harry? The talking skull?" My eyes widened. "What if Varvara or the MPD got him, and *he* told them you're a di-mythic?"

"He wouldn't betray my secrets. We have an agreement." He frowned. "I'll have to recover him at some point."

"You sure he didn't betray you?" I persisted as we headed toward the house. "He wouldn't have been happy about being buried for months."

Zak kicked the porch steps to ensure they were sturdy before stepping onto them. "I have a different idea of where the MPD's anonymous tip came from."

"Aaron, Kai, and Ezra didn't blow your secret," I said angrily. "They would never do that, especially since you know about Ezra. Why would they take that chance?"

"I know."

"Then who do you think tipped off the MPD?" I demanded. When he continued into the house without explaining, I muttered under my breath, "Fine, be mysterious."

Going through the house was depressing. Everything was burnt beyond recognition and it smelled like rot and mold. What had survived had been searched, either by Varvara or the MPD, and their efforts had left a trail of disturbed debris and missing objects.

Including my shoes, wherever those had ended up before Shane got his mitts on them. I was surprised they hadn't been thrown out months ago, but maybe Morgan had been planning to clean them and add them to the farm's stash of spare clothing. Waste not, want not.

Zak had to jump a collapsed section of stairs to reach the second level. I wasn't the complete wuss I'd been before, but I didn't trust my newfound athleticism *that* much. I waited at the bottom.

He returned a few minutes later, shaking his head. "I didn't leave much up there, but it's all gone."

We exited the wreckage. Zak surveyed the valley, all death and soot except for one meandering strip of summer greenery where the white stag with golden antlers had walked, then headed toward the line of winter-bare trees and snow-covered evergreens at the far edge of the meadow.

With a flash of dark wings, Lallakai swept out of the sky in her eagle form. Clutched in her talons was a black bundle, and as she dove, she dropped it for Zak to catch. Shadows swirling out from her wings, the eagle transformed midway through her landing and touched down on light human feet, her hair sweeping out behind her.

Straightening, she turned her bright eyes on me—and loathing was written all over her face. I gave her a catty smile, because why not? Her full red lips thinned.

Zak knelt to set the bundle on the ground. Whatever it was, it was wrapped in heavy black plastic and thoroughly duct-taped. Dirt coated most of it, as though it had been buried.

"My druid," Lallakai purred. "This is all that remains of your hidden caches in the farther reaches of the valley."

"Did you dig that up all by yourself?" I asked, pretending to be impressed.

She shot me an ice-beam glare.

Hmm. Maybe I shouldn't antagonize the scary darkfae?

Zak ripped the tape off, pulled out a backpack, and unzipped it. As he dug around inside, the telltale clink of glass suggested alchemic contents. He fished out a bundle of leather and unrolled it to reveal a long black coat. He slid his bare arms into the sleeves, then withdrew a handful of colorful crystals on long ties and dropped them over his head, the artifacts resting on his chest.

Lastly, he lifted out a belt. That went around his waist, the sides lined with potion vials. He clipped several fist-sized bottles with leather holders onto the belt as well, then zipped his bag and slung it over one shoulder.

He looked almost like himself again, just less groomed than usual. With a pleased smile, Lallakai reached for his shoulders. Her hands fogged into dark mist and sank into him.

He stepped backward, and her hands reappeared, misty with shadow.

"Not now, Lallakai," he said, turning away. "I don't want you in my head right now."

She dropped her arms, her hands solidifying. An expression twisted her face, one I easily recognized: the jilted, furious humiliation of a rejected woman. Except she wasn't really a woman—she was a fae.

A fae with a temper who'd just noticed I was watching her.

The emotion melted off her face. She sauntered toward me, hips swaying. I thrust out my jaw, unwilling to let her intimidate me. I wasn't scared. Nope. No way. But I really wished I had at least one artifact with me. Too bad my dumbass self had stored them all in Kai's backpack, then left said backpack on the recliner in Aaron's living room.

She stopped so close I could taste sweetness in the air. Her cool fingers stroked my cheek as she whispered softly, "Do you think you can win him from me, pathetic girl?"

"Weren't you the one telling me how I had such a *special* bond with him?" I retorted. That'd been back when she wanted something from me, and I wasn't all that surprised her attitude had changed with Zak's return.

Her pointed nails pricked my face. "He belongs to me in ways you cannot conceive."

Zak, who'd already walked away, glanced over his shoulder. Seeing us, he stopped.

"Lallakai, don't—" he began sharply.

She stepped back from me. With a pretty little smile, she threw her hands up. Shadows swirled out from her arms and blurred into feathered wings. The rest of her body rippled and shimmered. The eagle took form. Her wing smacked into my head, almost knocking me over as she soared away.

Flying past me, she banked sharply—and shot at Zak. His eyes widened in the instant before the huge eagle swept into him. Her body sank into his, disappearing, and shadows spilled off him like pooling fog.

He staggered backward, his shocked eyes inhumanly bright with fae power. A low sound of pain caught in his throat as he regained his balance.

I rushed to his side. "Zak? Are you—"

"I'm fine," he snapped, breathing harder than normal. "Lallakai is just in a mood."

He strode away, and I followed with my teeth gritted. Whatever the hell had just happened, "fine" didn't seem like the appropriate word. He'd told her not to possess him, and she'd done it anyway—and not in a nice, gentle way either.

As we drew closer to the woods, I realized the destruction that had ravaged the farm ended in an unnaturally perfect line at the forest's boundary. The snow-dusted leaf litter crunched loudly as we walked into the dappled moonlight under the canopy of branches.

A glimpse of shadow out of the corner of my eye.

From between the trees, a shaggy black varg ghosted closer, its red eyes fixed on Zak. On our other side, a second varg kept pace. Farther out, a third trotted along, its nose to the ground.

With the faintest crinkle of disturbed leaves, a fourth one cut out of the undergrowth and swerved toward Zak. He rested his hand on its shoulders, fingers curling into its fur, and it paced beside him for a few steps before veering back into the brush.

I knew the moment Zak had reached his intended destination. I didn't need to ask. There was no mistaking that this was his goal.

The fir tree wouldn't have been particularly remarkable among the hundreds of others if not for the charred black fissure that split the broad trunk from roots to crown. It was large—so broad that Zak and I together couldn't have stretched our arms all the way around the trunk—but it would grow no larger. Deep inside the long crevasse gouged into the trunk, the scorched heartwood glowed faintly; it was still burning deep inside.

"That bitch," he hissed.

He laid both palms against the bark, then leaned forward until his forehead touched it. Eyes closed, he murmured too softly for me to hear. The waxy needles of the surrounding coniferous trees rustled in the breeze, the sound rising and falling.

Under Zak's hands, the bark blurred. Slowly, he sank his hands into the tree, then his forearms. Still murmuring unknown words, he opened his eyes and pulled. The bark rippled, deformed. He drew it toward himself.

As familiar shapes formed inside the distortion, part of the tree separated from the trunk. Cradling it against his chest, he sank to his knees.

I crept closer, staring.

A child lay in his lap. Supporting her with one arm, he gently combed dull green hair the texture of straw away from her face. Her huge eyes, almost the same color as Twiggy's but flat and empty, were half lidded and unfocused. Thin legs, the color of bark, sprawled limply on the forest floor.

Her petite hand fluttered up and he caught it, placing it over his heart.

"You ... returned," she whispered in the high voice of a young girl.

"I did," he murmured. "But I came too late."

"I could not ... protect it ..."

"You did everything you could."

"She is powerful." A trembling breath. "Be wary, druid."

"I will make her pay, Marara, I promise."

She smiled weakly, eyelids flickering. "Druid ... she took your first treasure, but she ... did not think to search ... for a second. I hid it ... deep enough."

He combed her hair back again. "You're amazing, Marara."

"Take it now, druid. I waited ... for your return, but I am ... so tired."

He looked up. "Tori."

Throat so tight I couldn't even swallow, I crossed to his side and knelt. He lifted the frail woodland fae from his lap into mine. I held her small, inhuman body, her skin the texture of wind-worn bark.

"Stay with her," he murmured. "I'll be quick."

I nodded, too numb to ask where he was going as he rose and faced the tree. Again, he pressed his hands to the bark. His arms sunk into the shimmering surface, then he stepped into the tree and disappeared.

My jaw fell open so hard it popped.

"You ... are human ..."

I dragged my stare down to the fae. She gazed at me with a glimmer of curiosity.

"A human … but you have known fae. You … have been marked."

My forehead scrunched. "Marked?"

"As a … friend of fae."

"Do you mean my familiar mark?"

"I see that, too. But the mark of friendship … is different. It means … you are safe … to approach." She smiled faintly. "Humans are silly. We write messages to each other upon them, and they … suspect nothing."

I blinked dumbly.

"Are you … a friend of the druid?"

"Yes," I said softly.

"That … is good. He needs … a … friend." Her eyes drifted closed. "I am so tired … He must … hurry."

"Zak, she said to hurry!"

He didn't reappear. A soft, trembling breath slid from her. Her slight frame seemed to deflate.

"Zak!" I yelled.

The bark twenty-five feet up the tree blurred. Zak's head and torso appeared, and he pushed out of the trunk. The instant he came free, he dropped. Shadowy wings lifted off his arms and spread wide, slowing his fall. He landed with a thud, and as the wings sank back over his arms, he hurried to us.

"Marara," he said, kneeling beside her.

"Did you … recover it?"

"Yes, I have it."

"I will sleep now."

"Yes." He cupped her cheek. "I'll feed your roots one last time."

"That … would be … a sweet gift."

He scooped her off my lap and laid her against her tree's roots. She rested her head against the burnt fissure, tangled hair catching on the bark.

Reaching around his back, he slid a knife from his belt and nudged his sleeve up. He ran the knife across his wrist, just below the lowermost circle tattoo. Blood spilled off his arm, splattering on the tree roots beside the fae.

She sighed. "Thank you, druid."

"Sleep well, Marara."

He held his bleeding wrist above the roots. Another deep exhalation slid from her … and she didn't inhale again. Her diminutive body sank against the roots, limbs stiffening and the rough texture of her skin growing more pronounced.

As her body hardened like the bark it so resembled, he whispered, "And thank you."

Tucking the knife away, he pressed his thumb into the bleeding cut and straightened. Together, he and I watched her body slowly merge with her tree. After a few minutes, I could just make out her shape among the roots, her slumbering face a round hump with the faintest indents for eyes.

"Tori," he said heavily. "Could you grab that?"

I looked around. A square of purple fabric lay on the thin dusting of snow where he'd landed after leaping from the tree. I picked it up, its weight surprising me. Not that it was heavy, just heftier than I'd expected for a folded cloth small enough to sit on my palm.

"What is this?" I asked.

He gazed tiredly at the woodland fae and her tree, then straightened his shoulders. "The Carapace of Valdurna."

12

RETURNING TO VANCOUVER via dragonflight was fast but just as uncomfortable as the first time, the icy wind burning my face and numbing my limbs. It was a relief to be back among city lights, but I wasn't a fan of the exhaust fumes or the prevailing stench of garbage.

I looked to the left. Looked to the right. Scowled and planted my hands on my hips. "Zak."

"What, Tori?"

"Where the hell are we?"

"The Eastside."

I made a face at the druid's back as we walked. His hood was up again, and he'd added black leather gloves to complete his villain outfit.

"Let me rephrase: Why are we in the Eastside and not, say, at my house? Or Aaron's house?" I kicked a beer bottle off the sidewalk. "Or, you know, somewhere *not* unpleasant."

When it came to unpleasant neighborhoods, the Eastside was an award winner. A mix of commercial, industrial, and scarily rundown apartment buildings bordered the streets, their walls tagged with ugly graffiti. It was so late—or so early—that there was no traffic. Only the annoyingly frigid winter wind rustling garbage broke the silence.

"If you want to go home," Zak replied, "call a cab."

"Oh, let me just grab my phone and do that right now." I slapped my hips, my pockets empty—or almost empty. But no phone. That was at Aaron's house, along with my artifacts. "Why don't you lend me your phone? Oh wait, you don't have one either."

"Temper, temper."

I gritted my teeth. "I've only had a few hours of sleep in the last *two days*. I'm tired."

"And cranky."

"Damn right," I snarled. Extending my stride, I fell into step beside him so I could glare more effectively. "Why didn't you have Echo drop us off at Aaron's house?"

Shadows filled his hood, masking his face. "Because I have things to do here."

"Like what?"

"Like finding where Varvara is hiding."

"What makes you think she's in Vancouver? She could be anywhere."

"Unless I'm very wrong, she's been consolidating her influence here since I left." He paused at a dark intersection, two streetlamps broken and the windows of the featureless buildings boarded up. "You and the Miura woman talked about a lull in crime."

I followed him across the road, ignoring the crosswalk's "don't walk" light. We were so bad. "Yeah, the lull has all the guilds stumped."

"It isn't a mystery—not to rogues. The Yamadas know what's going on. Miura said they're making preparations."

"Preparations for what?"

"A power shift. They want to take control of the underground network. Varvara is planning to do the same, and she wants me out of the picture before she makes her move. That's why she passed information about me to the MPD."

"*She* did that? Are you sure?"

"She destroyed my farm to lure me back, then leaked those details to increase my bounty and whet the appetites of bounty hunters. She's counting on someone catching me before I catch her."

"It wouldn't've been difficult to figure out you're a druid and an alchemist from her battle with you last summer, but what about the hundred and something new charges against you? Where'd they come from?"

"My grimoire." He drew to a halt, staring straight ahead. "That's what I left in Marara's tree. Most of it is written in code, but I didn't bother to code my records of artifacts I've acquired, traded, or destroyed."

I stood beside him, nerves churning. "She gave that information to the MPD? And they used it to tie you to new crimes?"

"I didn't think she would find the tree. One fir in an entire valley? Even if she knew to look for dryads, there are hundreds." His hood shifted as he shook his head in frustration. "Now Marara is dead and that bitch has my grimoire. If she cracks my code and gets anything else from it …"

He swept into motion. Rushing after him, I shoved my cold hands in my pockets. My fingers brushed against silky fabric, and I pulled out the folded square of purple he'd retrieved from the dryad tree.

"Why am I carrying this again?" I asked, nose scrunched as I prodded it.

"Do *not* unfold that."

I weighed it on my palm. "The Carapace of Valdurna ... Didn't you offer to trade this to that nasty darkfae, the Rat thing?"

"Yes, but I knew he wouldn't accept it. The point was to start the negotiations off with something impressive and valuable."

"How valuable are we talking?"

He tapped a gloved finger against the square on my palm. "The only thing more priceless than this, and with a more treacherous power, is probably your demonic artifact."

"Oh." I hadn't thought about the value of the demon amulet. All I cared about was whether it could save Ezra. "What does the Carapace do?"

"It's a fae-created artifact that makes you invincible."

I tripped on nothing. Catching myself, I gasped, "I'm sorry, did you say *invincible*?"

"If you're wearing that, you can't die, even if you're mortally wounded. No magic can affect you and no weapon can touch you."

If you were *wearing* it? I cocked my head, trying to imagine what it would look like unfolded.

"Is it a cap?" I asked, flipping it over.

"A cap?"

"Or a glove? A sock? The only other 'wearable' thing I can think of that would fold up this small are panties." I shot him an arch look. "That's why you aren't using this artifact right now, isn't it? You don't want to wear the Invincibility Panties."

He made a disgusted noise.

"No one would *see* that you were wearing them."

"Powerful magic," he said loudly, "comes at a commensurate cost. The Carapace's price is too high for me."

"What's the price?"

"All of my magic."

I stopped dead. He took two more steps, then paused. He touched his inner arm through his sleeve.

"It consumes all magic within and around it. All the magic fae have gifted me would be erased. My artifacts would be wiped clean. My potions would be rendered useless. All my inherent Spiritalis and Arcana magic would be drained, and though that would eventually recover, the rest would be gone forever."

He waved at me to get moving again. "The cost to fae is even greater, since they have far more magic to lose. The Carapace is powerful, dangerous, and an artifact I would only use if I were about to die."

"And you're making me carry it because …"

"Because I can feel its magic and it sets my teeth on edge."

I grimaced and shoved it back in my pocket. "Where'd you get it?"

"I stole it."

"From the Wolfsbane Druid," I murmured. "Your master."

He kept walking. "Yes."

"Did you kill your master?"

"Yes."

"Why?"

"Because I wanted to."

I rolled my eyes at his "end of conversation" tone. As he rounded a corner, I trotted a few steps to keep up. "Zak?"

"What now?

"Where the hell are we going?"

"I'm checking locations where I can usually find rogue informants, but they've all been abandoned so far." His voice went a little raspier. "Varvara's been very thorough."

I dusted my hands together. "Well, guess you'll have to come back another time. We can go home now."

"If you want to go, then go."

"And what, walk through the worst neighborhood in the city, by myself, in the middle of the night, without a single artifact for defense?"

He glanced at me, and I imagined him frowning in his shadowy hood. "I'll send a varg with you."

"Your *vargs* are here? How? Echo only carried the two of us."

"My vargs," he said, taking another corner—this time into a very dark alley, "have finally found some mythics, so I can spare one to make sure you get home safely."

And miss out on the fun now that he was going to question someone? I folded my arms. "Nah, I'll stick around."

He growled under his breath.

I peered around Zak at the overflowing dumpsters and drifts of garbage. The air reeked of moldy food and piss. "This is gross."

He swung his arm out to block my path and I walked into it. "Wait here. I'm known for operating alone. You'll be a distraction."

I rolled my eyes again. "Fine."

He strode deeper into the alley. I watched him go, counting down in my head. When he was almost out of sight, I tiptoed after him. Yeah, he'd told me to stay out of it, but I could at least sneak in close enough to watch.

The alley was unusually long and full of the garbage from the businesses that backed onto it. No lights broke up the darkness, and I had to rely on distant streetlamps and murky light pollution to find my way. The wind calmed as I moved deeper, but the stench worsened. Yuck.

I heard the rogues before I spotted them. Male voices rumbled in low conversation, occasionally joined by a croaky female voice. I stole behind a dumpster and peeked out.

Four men and a woman, smoking and talking, were huddled in a doorway with a single bulb. Scarcely any light leaked from the dim alcove. Dressed in dark clothes, they had the ratty appearance of trashy people who just didn't care. Two men were big and heavyset, and the larger of the pair had a tattoo on the back of his shaved head. Of the other two, one was average height and one was short. The woman was middle-aged, crack-addict thin, and clutching a jacket that was far too flimsy for the winter chill.

"… almost got roasted," the big man was grumbling.

"That's why I bailed," the smallest man said, twitching his cig uneasily. "Knew better than to take on mages."

The woman huddled deeper in her oversized coat. "But if it works—"

"It ain't gonna work. MagiPol will crush this whole thing." The small man flicked his cigarette into the alley, a glowing speck in the darkness. "But maybe she'll take the Yamadas down with her, and then there'll be no one left but us."

They laughed, the sound an unnerving mix of hope, fear, and bitterness.

I glanced past them, not seeing Zak. That could mean only one thing: it was time for one of the Ghost's patented dramatic entrances.

Almost on cue, the conversing rogues fell silent. They peered nervously into the shadows, elbowing each other as though hoping someone else would speak. I had no idea what they'd detected, but they already looked scared.

With a swirl of shadow, the Ghost materialized from nothing.

Coat sweeping out, hood full of shadows, dressed head to toe in black. Not even his backpack, slung over one shoulder, could detract from his aura of "holy shit, this dude is *bad*."

I almost snorted aloud.

The rogues froze like rabbits, gawking in disbelief. The big guy tried to shrink behind his slightly less massive counterpart.

"Gh-Gh-Ghost," the woman stammered.

I clapped a hand over my mouth, stifling a laugh. Jeez. They were nearly peeing themselves. Zak had done an excellent job beefing up his reputation to terror-inducing levels.

"I just got back into town," he rumbled, "and it seems I've missed some interesting developments. Which of you volunteers to bring me up to speed?"

They exchanged horrified looks, as though he'd asked them to donate their kidneys. And then they bolted.

Two ran farther down the alley while two charged straight toward my hiding spot. I ducked deeper into the shadows, and they rocketed right past me without a glance. The fifth rogue, the short one, flung open the door behind him and dove into the building.

Zak didn't bother chasing the runaways. He strode forward and disappeared through the door after the short guy.

I glanced around, then skittered to the doorway and stepped through it. Inside was a foul, reeking stairwell, bare bulbs lighting the stained steps. Clattering sounds echoed from somewhere above, and I trotted up the stairs in pursuit.

Four stories later, I peeked through a half-open door that led onto the rooftop. The building was much wider than it was long, the rough concrete covered in a layer of grit.

Dead ahead, the unlucky rogue was backing fearfully across the roof. Zak leisurely advanced, a hint of shadow clinging to his legs with each slow step.

"I-I don't know nothing," the man stammered. "I'm just scraping by. You know how it is—"

"That didn't sound like 'nothing' you were discussing a moment ago. Let's start with that."

"I didn't touch your territory, Ghost, I swear. It was all that psycho sorceress. She—"

"We're going to talk about her too."

The man's mouth trembled. "You—you won't be around long, not with that new bounty. You're a dead man." The rogue straightened his spine, gaining confidence. "Or should I say, a dead druid? Are you even a druid or is that MagiPol bullshit?"

"What do you think?"

With quiet snarls, two vargs appeared on either side of him, white teeth flashing against their black coats and red eyes gleaming with hunger.

Paling, the rogue retreated in a frightened scramble. The vargs prowled after him, and the man halted with his heels at the rooftop's edge.

Zak ambled after his fae minions. "Tell me what you bailed on and what you think won't work."

"I d-don't know nothing—"

Stepping between the vargs, Zak seized the front of the man's jacket and pushed him closer to the edge—then shoved him off.

The rogue squealed as he pitched over backward. Yellow light spiraled off Zak's wrist and the wire-like magic snaked around the falling man's torso. He jerked to a halt, his feet still on the ledge but the rest of his body tilted at a forty-five-degree angle over the street four stories below.

Zak gripped the end of the magical rope, literally holding the man's life in his hand.

"Please," he gasped. "Please don't. Please—"

"Let's try one more time. Tell me what the sorceress is planning."

The rogue's whole face trembled with terror. "Pandora Knights. The guild. She promised us revenge on them. They mess up rogues so bad when they catch us. She—she got a bunch of guys together and gave them a plan and convinced them to attack the guild."

"Did you see this yourself?"

"N-no. She only talked to a few people and they did the rest, but it was—it was definitely her."

"And you didn't participate?"

"I knew the Pandora Knights would wreck them. I w-was right. All they did was destroy the guild's building."

"Hm."

"That's all I know. Just what I heard from—"

Zak opened his hand. The magical rope slid across his palm and the man dropped with a terrified shriek. Closing his hand again, Zak brought the rogue up short. Now hanging almost parallel to the ground, his boots scraping the rooftop edge for purchase, the rogue whimpered.

"Since when do independent rogues take suggestions from a sorceress?" Zak asked conversationally.

"Since you left," the man blurted. "You were gone, Red Rum screwed up so bad they had to give up their holdings, and the Yamadas were throwing their weight around. They were taking over everything, but this sorceress, she came along and started interfering with the Yamadas' plans and kept some of us out of MagiPol cells. She was better than the Yamadas, so we just went with it."

A long pause. "And?"

"And she was offering good perks to anyone who wanted to work for her." The rogue was near sobbing, head jerking as he looked from the shadowy Ghost and his two fae wolves to the lethal drop below him. "Most independents and small rogue guilds went to her. She's got some sort of big plan, but I know better than to g-get involved in that kind of shit."

"I see. And where is the sorceress now?"

A whine of terror. "I don't know. She only meets with a few people at a time and always somewhere different. That's all I know, I swear."

"Are you sure?" Zak let another few inches of slack slide through his hand.

"That's it! That's it, that's it, I swear. I don't know anything more. Please, please let me—"

"Last chance."

"I don't know! Please, Ghost, please don't—I don't know anything else, I was staying out of it, I didn't want any trouble. Please … *please* have mercy."

As the rogue trailed off into trembling whispers, Zak's shoulders relaxed. I let out the breath I'd been holding, then straightened out of my tense crouch. Mission accomplished. Pretty sure, anyway. We at least knew why the rogue crime rate had dropped, but I had a lot more questions about Varvara's big-picture scheme.

Zak pulled on the rope, lifting the rogue, and the man's face went slack with relief.

"Ghost," he stammered, sniffling like a child. "Thank y—"

Zak flicked his hand and the golden rope vanished.

Horror splashed across the rogue's face—and he plummeted out of view. His scream rang out, sharp with terror. Falling. Receding. Then the most awful sound I'd ever heard. A sound so terrible it would be burned into my memory forever.

I could still hear it, even after silence had fallen.

Turning, Zak pushed his hood off and reached down to pat a varg. His bright green gaze caught on me, standing frozen in the dark doorway.

He frowned. "I told you to wait in the alley."

My legs wobbled. I braced my hand on the doorjamb and whispered, "You dropped him."

His frown deepened.

"You *killed* him."

"He'd have run straight to Varvara with the news that I'm here and hunting her."

"He told you what he knew." I swallowed hard. "He was so afraid."

Zak's gaze flicked across my face, and his frown shifted to a scowl. "What were you expecting, Tori? I didn't come back to enact justice or some noble shit like that. I'm here to *kill Varvara*. I don't give a f—"

"You couldn't find a way that didn't involve killing that man?" I demanded, my voice shrill, words trembling in my throat. "I thought you were just scaring him, not—not—you didn't have to—"

He swept toward me. I stumbled back, my mouth dry.

He stopped in the doorway, a foot of space between us. "I warned you before, but it seems you weren't listening. Don't get the wrong idea about me."

I forced my gaze to his. "You destroy black magic. You rescue homeless teens. You save baby dragons."

He started down the stairs.

"You saved *me!*"

His unfaltering footsteps receded as he left me on the landing, breathing hard and fighting for composure. He was dangerous, but he wasn't a bad guy. The good he did outweighed the violence.

That's what I'd told myself. That's what I'd believed all these months. That's why I'd forgiven him for the cruel things he'd done to me. Was I wrong? Was I a naïve fool?

Or had Varvara's atrocities tipped the scales of his morality?

The fierce druid warrior I'd so admired was inside him somewhere, but his heart had been torn open. He'd lost everything—his farm, his horses, his allies, his safe haven, his grimoire of condemning secrets. If he didn't stop Varvara soon, she would destroy what little he had left—but how far would he go to stop her?

Gasping back my shivers, I shoved off the doorframe and dashed down the stairs, oblivious to the stench, the stains, the graffiti. I slammed through the door at the bottom and rushed out into the dark alley.

The stretch of asphalt was empty.

Panting silently, I waited on the stoop, unable to believe he'd abandon me here. He was coming back. He'd be right back, sweeping dramatically from the darkness in a swirl of shadows, annoyed at me for delaying him.

The seconds stretched into a minute.

My nerves prickled. I looked toward the dumpsters.

Ruby eyes above a dark snout looked back at me. The varg, sitting in the shadows, flicked its ears forward and back, then its muzzle ridged in a warning snarl.

I drew in the deepest breath I could and held it until my heartbeat filled my ears. Letting it out, I stepped off the stoop. As I passed, the varg slunk after me, trailing ten feet behind. I glanced back every few steps, hoping its master would appear.

When I reached the main road and stepped under the glow of a streetlamp, the varg faded from view—but I could feel its watchful eyes. It would follow me until I was safe.

I checked the street signs to get my bearings, then wrapped my arms around myself, bent my head, and strode toward safety—the warm, bright safety I desperately needed right now.

13

I STOOD BENEATH THE TRELLIS that spanned Aaron's front walk. The house was dark, its windows devoid of the warm lights that would've welcomed me back.

Makiko had taken Kai, then Shane Davila had demanded Aaron's help with the Pandora Knights attack and investigation. Ezra must've gone with Aaron. It made sense. I'd been whisked away via dragon, so Ezra wouldn't have stayed home alone.

My three mages weren't here.

I bit the inside of my cheek, fighting a wave of emotion. This was nothing I couldn't handle. It was just a night alone. I was used to dealing with crap on my own. I was used to shitty people doing shitty things, even if I'd never witnessed a murder before.

Pressing both hands to my face, my fingers and cheeks equally numb from the cold, I let out a harsh breath. Stay here or go home? Did I want to walk another thirty minutes, or did I want to sit in the empty house? I was used to being home alone, but hanging around the house without the guys would feel so … hollow.

A quiet clack.

I dropped my hands, my gaze darting to the house. The front door opened. A silhouette appeared in the dark threshold, followed by a soft, familiar voice that I needed to hear so badly I ached for it.

"Tori."

I was running. I didn't remember moving, but I was running, and then I was flying up the steps and throwing myself into Ezra. His arms closed around me, squeezing tight.

Enfolded in his arms, the rigid tension inside me released. I slumped against him, hoping he wouldn't notice the tremble in my limbs. My heart ached, wrung out from so much conflict and so little rest. He held me for a long minute—though not nearly long enough to suit me—then drew me inside the house and shut the door. When he flicked on the hall light, I flinched against the brightness.

He gazed at me with mismatched eyes, somber and serious—*actually* serious, not his deadpan-humor version. His hair was rumpled and tired lines edged his mouth. "Tori, are you okay?"

I nodded wearily. "I'm fine."

His fingers tugged on my coat zipper. I blinked confusedly as he unzipped it, pushed the jacket off my shoulders, and tossed it into the closet. He scanned me—double-checking I was unhurt—then brushed his thumb against my cheek.

"What do you need?"

Those might've been the best four words I'd heard this year. Closing my eyes, I weighed my options.

"Shower," I answered firmly. "Definitely a shower first."

"Straight downstairs, then." He softened the order with a smile. "I'll bring you clothes and a towel."

The hot shower warmed my frozen bones, and I spent a ridiculously long time standing under the million-and-one jets, basking in the heat. When I was too tired to keep upright, I exited the shower to find two fluffy towels and a stack of folded clothes on the counter. After scrunching the water from my hair and twisting it into a damp bun, I donned a tank top and snug-fitting yoga pants. He'd brought me a sweater as well, but I carried it instead, too overheated to put it on yet.

On the main floor, I discovered Ezra in the kitchen, his back to me as he fiddled with something on the counter. He ushered me into the living room and onto the sofa, then flipped a thick, fuzzy blanket over my lap. Retrieving a pillow from upstairs, he tucked it beside me.

I snuggled into my cushy nest—definitely no need for that sweater now—and waited as he clattered in the kitchen. A moment later, he returned with a steaming mug.

"For me?" I wrapped my hands around the mug, my mouth instantly watering at the aroma of chocolate. Clean and warm, bundled in a blanket, with hot chocolate, lights holding back the darkness, and—

He sank onto the sofa, the cushions dipping with his weight.

—and Ezra beside me, steady and strong. This. This was what I'd needed. Exactly this.

My lower lip trembled. I blew on my hot chocolate to hide it. "Is Aaron still out with Shane?"

"Yes. The Pandora Knights are chasing down rogues, and Shane is dragging Aaron all over downtown to question everyone involved."

"I figured you'd be with him."

He caught the edge of the blanket as it slid off my shoulder and readjusted it. "We didn't know when you'd be back, or if you needed help."

"You stayed to wait for me," I mumbled. He'd waited all night. He must've been checking out the window—how else would he have known I was standing there on the front walk like a lost puppy?

"I got the better end of the deal," he said with quiet amusement. "Aaron's been texting me and he isn't too happy with Shane's priorities."

I lifted my mug to my lips, blew one more time, and took a long sip. The chocolaty heat flowed down to my stomach and warmed me from the inside out. With a shuddering breath, I leaned forward and set the mug on the coffee table.

"Is it too hot?" Ezra asked. "I can add some milk to—Tori? What—"

He broke off as I climbed into his lap. I curled up against his chest, arms around his neck, face pressed to his shoulder. He wrapped his arms around me, and I closed my eyes with a sigh. This, too, was what I needed.

Maybe this was something I needed every night. To be in his arms. To be safe and warm and protected.

The thought surprised me. I'd spent half my life molding myself into the most independent person I could be—a woman who didn't need anyone to take care of her—but somewhere along this crazy mythic road with the guys, I'd learned that it was okay to be weak and scared. Sometimes, it was okay to let someone you trusted shield you.

I tucked my face against the side of Ezra's neck, thinking of Zak out there in the Eastside alleys, walking among garbage and rogues, alone and grieving. Terrifying victims into giving up the information he wanted. Maybe hurting them. Maybe killing them.

And with no one to stop him.

I DRIFTED ON THE EDGE of sleep, drowsy thoughts worming into my exhausted brain as I gradually came awake. Faint light leaked through my eyelids, which meant morning had arrived. That, or some jerk had turned on a light.

Warmth suffused me, and I was so comfortable I couldn't imagine ever moving again. Why were mornings like heaven, but it was impossible to get comfy when you were trying to fall asleep at night? So dumb. But I was comfy now, cocooned between cushions on one side and ... uhhh ...

My fingers twitched, the pads of each fingertip pressing against warm, bare skin—and my eyes flew open.

I stared. Gulped. Commanded myself to keep it together.

So, it turned out I'd fallen asleep on the sofa. And I wasn't the only one. Ezra was stretched across the sofa too, and I was half on top of him, snugged between him and the back cushions. My cheek on his chest. His arms around me. I had one leg flung over his thighs and one hand ...

In my sleep, I'd slid one hand under his shirt, my palm resting on his stomach.

I blinked a few times. His head was pillowed on the armrest, and he was breathing slow and deep, each inhalation lifting me slightly. His impossibly mouthwatering scent, his soap or cologne or whatever, clouded my head.

Well … guess I'd just go with this.

Resettling, I let myself appreciate the moment. Wrapped in Ezra's arms as he slept. Warmth, strength. And good god, his body was all hard, heavy muscle. Despite my best intentions, I couldn't stop my fingers from drifting. How many times had I daydreamed about touching him? How many times had I relived our kiss under the mistletoe?

My fingertips met a ridge of texture very different from his smooth skin and uber-fit mage muscles.

Ezra inhaled sleepily. "Tori … that tickles."

Oh shit. My cheeks heated. Feeling him up in his sleep. Nicely done, Tori.

Since he'd already busted me as a perv, I rubbed my fingertips across the ridge, realizing what it was. A scar. One of the three scars that ran diagonally from his right hip to his center, petering out just below his sternum. I traced it downward—then tickled my fingernails over his side.

He started, arms constricting so suddenly air whooshed out of my lungs.

"You're ticklish?" I wheezed.

"I said that," he grumbled, grabbing my hand through his shirt before I could move my fingers again.

Grinning wickedly, I tipped my head back to bring his face into view. "I am *so* glad I know that now."

He peered at me warily. "With great power comes great responsibility, Tori."

"Are you suggesting I don't abuse this new information?" My grin widened and I tried to wiggle my fingers free. "Fat chance."

He tightened his hold on my hand. "Let me guess. You aren't ticklish."

"Not—one—little—bit," I sang cheerily.

His mouth twisted in a way that was dangerously close to sulky—and my heart flipped. How could a *sulk* be sexy? I was hopeless.

"I don't know if I should take your word for that," he muttered. "Honesty would be tactically unsound."

"True, but luckily, I don't need to lie." I arched an eyebrow, my chin resting on his chest. "But if you don't believe me, you can always find out for yourself."

His expression didn't change, but something flickered in his eyes. Something that made my heart do that flippy thing again.

"However," I warned dramatically, "if you want to tickle me, you'll have to let go of my hand. And if you do that …"

He pressed my hand into his side, and I relaxed my arm, hoping to lull him into a false sense of security. He rolled his mismatched eyes, seeing right through that.

Laughing, I nestled against his side more comfortably. "I'm beat. What time is it?"

"Not sure. I'd check my phone, but it's in my pocket and I need a free hand to get it." His other arm was pinned under me. He wasn't getting it free without tossing me right off the sofa.

I smirked. "Guess you'll have to trust me."

"Guess so."

Releasing my hand, he reached down. I was considering whether I could, in good conscience, tickle him after daring him to trust me, when he tilted his hips sideways to get at his back pocket. The shift of his body against mine threw all thoughts out of my head.

He settled down again and checked his phone's screen. "It's just after nine. Aaron sent a message thirty minutes ago. He thinks Shane will be done soon."

"They're *still* working?" I yawned widely. "Poor Aaron."

Ezra reached above his head to put his phone on the end table, his stomach tautening with the motion. My fingers reflexively pressed into his side—and his mysterious scars.

"Ezra, what happened to you?"

His breath caught, muscles going rigid. I'd asked without thinking, and I almost took the question back—but if I didn't ask, would he ever tell me? His past wasn't something I could ignore, especially since his secrets could make all the difference in his future ... and whether he'd live to see it.

Brushing my fingers across a scar, I murmured, "You've been a demon mage for over nine years, which means you were fourteen when ... that's really young."

His expression had gone poker-face blank, tension still gripping him. I gauged his reaction, then pillowed my cheek on his chest.

"It's okay," I said softly, withdrawing my hand from under his shirt. "Forget I asked."

He pulled me closer, and I released a slow breath, burying my disappointment that he still wouldn't—or couldn't—tell me the whole story. My eyes closed, my thoughts drifting to other dilemmas and worries.

"The scars are from another demon mage."

My eyes popped wide. His words were a dry whisper, his normally silk-smooth voice hoarse.

"I was fifteen, and I'd been a demon mage for a year. She was fourteen, and she'd had her demon for three months. Sometimes ... some people aren't ..." He stopped to breathe. "The first year is the hardest. The demon tests you constantly, but it's worse than just the mental attacks. Your own emotions ..."

I lifted my head. Ezra was staring at the ceiling, ghosts in his eyes.

"It isn't natural," he whispered, "sharing your body ... sharing your mind. Sometimes, I don't know which thoughts are mine and which are his. When I'm angry or afraid, it feels like I'm drowning, like I'm disappearing. It feels like my emotions aren't my own anymore. They reflect off him, and everything starts spiraling and I can't stop it ..."

My hand closed around his upper arm, gripping hard.

"You've seen it ... the cold and dark. It happens when I start losing control of my emotions. That's when Eterran tries to take over—or sometimes, he pushes me back from the brink to save us both."

His fingers tangled in the hem of my tank top. "That's what we're all afraid of. If the demon takes over, we can fight back— retake control. But if we lose ourselves ... if our emotions overwhelm us and we disappear and all that's left is the fear and the rage ..."

He trailed off, and all I could do was hold him as desperately as he was clutching me, as though the closer we were, the less terrifying his words would be.

"She'd had her demon for three months," he whispered, "and she couldn't handle it. Either her demon or her emotions, or both. I was trying to help, but what the hell did I know back then? One night, she ... she was crying, afraid they would kill her because her control was so poor. I was trying to reassure her, but her fear was getting worse and worse, that awful feedback loop, and she ... went berserk."

"Her demon took over?" I murmured hesitantly.

"No. The human mind isn't the only one that gets messed up. She and her demon went mad together. Rage and fear and power and magic, all unleashed without reason or restraint."

"That's what you meant when you said you would lose your mind to your demon?"

"It's how all demon mages go. Eterran might survive it, but I won't." His hand slid gently up my back and into my hair. "I knew what was happening, but I thought I could save her. Maybe I could restrain her, or knock her unconscious, or do something to snap her out of it, but when I tried, she ... ripped me open. I only survived because Eterran healed my injuries. He couldn't fix my eye properly."

When he said nothing else, I asked softly, "What happened to her?"

"I couldn't do anything. I was fighting Eterran, trying to get up because they were coming to kill her ..."

He trailed off again, and I didn't ask for more. I could guess what had happened—I'd seen it already. Ezra had begun to lose consciousness, which allowed Eterran to take over and heal his injuries. And they, whoever "they" were, had killed the female demon mage.

Now I knew who the girl in his hidden photo was—the blond girl with her arm around a young and unscarred Ezra, the Oregon Coast Range spread out behind them. At only fifteen years old, he'd tried to save her, and instead, he'd watched her die.

Her fate was his. In her, he'd witnessed the madness and violence that would be the last experience of his life. Aaron and Kai had promised to end his life before that happened, and I finally understood how they could make such a terrible, merciful promise.

I opened my mouth—but I couldn't speak. I couldn't promise that we would save him, but determination burned through me, scorching my bones with its intensity.

I would not fail him.

Unable to say anything, I brushed my fingers across his cheek, trailing them down to the soft scruff that edged his jaw. Then I smiled and asked brightly, "How about some breakfast?"

For a heartbeat, it didn't look like he could respond, the despair dark in his gaze. He inhaled, and as he let the breath out, his soft smile returned. "Only if you're cooking."

"Deal." I sat up, and for one wonderfully torturous moment, I was straddling him, my hips pressed into his, a hand braced on his chest. But I kept moving, swinging off the sofa and straightening.

Leaving him in mid-stretch, I locked myself in the bathroom. Aaron's house had one of those old, weird layouts that didn't have an upper floor bathroom, which was normally inconvenient but worked in my favor this morning. It gave me a quick escape where I could compose myself.

I took care of business, brushed my teeth—yes, I had a toothbrush here—and gave my curls one helpless look before giving up. No fixing that mess without a lot of water and hair product.

My hazel eyes stared at me from the mirror. Zak had promised to look into demonic artifacts. Robin was sharing her lead on rare Demonica knowledge. And I had the demon amulet. Between the three of us, we would figure it out. We had to.

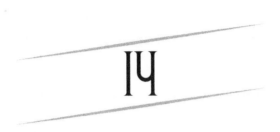

SPEAKING OF KAI, I mused as I pushed the bathroom door open, the fourth musketeer in our quartet needed saving too. Maybe not quite as urgently, but I wasn't abandoning him in Makiko's loving care. One night was already too long. He belonged with us, and we would get him back.

Humming thoughtfully, I passed the empty living room and started up the stairs. Makiko and I were due to exchange some words. Or fists. A good ol' catfight could accomplish quite a lot under the right circumstances—though the way she'd flung Aaron across the yard with a single blast of aero magic concerned me. So maybe I wouldn't punch her, but I should probably go for my leather combat pants today, just in case.

Still considering what wardrobe options I had stored in Ezra's closet, I pushed his bedroom door open and walked in.

He stood in front of his dresser, halfway into a shirt. His jeans were undone, barely clinging to his hips, the black waistband of his dark gray boxers sitting just above them.

My brain short-circuited, all thoughts disappearing in a wave of hot longing. I jerked my gaze off his midriff and up to his face. With his shirt partway down his mouthwatering abs and one hand holding the fabric, he watched me ogling him, a hint of bashfulness in his expression.

And that, somehow, was even hotter.

Heat flushed through me, and I wanted so badly to take another step. One more. Then I would be close enough to touch him. To peel his shirt off and run my hands all over his beautiful body. To give his jeans the little nudge they needed to get the hell out of my way.

Shiiiiiit.

I gulped hard, choking back the dirty thoughts. Geez, I was awful. He'd asked me for one thing and one thing only: to be his friend. It wasn't even a difficult request. All I had to do was *not* jump him. Was that so hard?

Well, yes. But I would restrain myself anyway.

"Sorry," I said, embarrassingly breathless. "Should've knocked. I'll come back."

I turned for the door, mentally congratulating myself. Yeah. Being a good friend, no matter how much I secretly wanted to—

A warm hand closed on my wrist. Ezra tugged me backward and I swung toward him, brow scrunching with confusion, ready to ask what was wrong.

He pulled me into him—and then his mouth was on mine.

For an instant, I couldn't believe it. I couldn't believe his hands were gripping my arms, our bodies pressed together, our lips locked. Except it was definitely, absolutely happening and *holy freaking shit*.

A wild gasp rushed through me. My arms were around his neck in an instant, my fingers sinking into his hair. His mouth pressed into mine, hot and urgent. I parted my lips, and the first touch of his tongue sent me reeling. I pushed into him, deepening the kiss, demanding more.

He jerked back with a sharp breath. Wide eyes flashed across my face with horror.

"Shit," he said, almost as breathless as me. "I'm sorry. I just— I shouldn't have—"

I seized his hair as he tried to back away from me. "Don't you dare."

He blinked. "I—"

"Don't make me explain all the reasons you don't need to stop."

"But—"

Dragging his head down, I stretched up as far as I could, our lips tauntingly close. "Stop *thinking* for once, Ezra. I want you. Kiss me, damn it!"

He stared at me. I glared at him, still trying to get his head down that last inch but unable to budge his stupid superhuman strength. His lips twitched—and he laughed, soft, husky, and so unexpected that the sound lit my core on fire.

Then he kissed me again.

As I kissed him back just as fiercely, his arms slid around me, his hand cupping the back of my head to pull me up to his mouth. I ran my hands down his sides and under his shirt. My palms pressed against his warm skin. Yes. *Finally*. I dragged my hands up his abs, his muscles tensing in delicious response to my touch. Lifting his shirt with my arms, I moaned against his mouth as I traced his hard pecs.

A low sound in his throat answered me. He pushed into me so hard I stumbled back a step. My back bumped the wall beside the dresser—and he grabbed my thighs, heaving me up with easy strength. His warm weight pinned me against the wall, and my legs clamped around his waist, my core pressed against him. I couldn't breathe from need.

I tore my mouth away, desperate for air, and he ran his mouth along the side of my neck. Tangling my hands in his messy curls, I guided his head down. He boosted me up higher, his mouth sliding to the low neckline of my tank top, the thin fabric clinging to my breasts.

My shirt was really, *really* in the way right now. So was his. So were all our clothes.

"Ezra," I began.

He lifted his head. His mismatched eyes burned with hot, desperate need that had been building for weeks. Maybe months. Maybe since the day we'd met, since that first smile, that first laugh.

Concealing dangerous secrets and unwilling to become intimate with anyone, he'd never hinted that he was attracted to me. Certain that he'd reject any advance and distracted by Aaron, I'd never admitted my crazy lust for him either. As the months of denial carried us along, our relationship growing ever closer, the fire had slowly heated. And now the inferno was consuming me.

Forgetting what I'd been about to say, I caught his mouth and kissed him with all the pent-up need I'd denied, with all the desperate urgency I was trying to conceal. His mouth devoured mine, taking everything, wanting more. His tongue slid across mine. His hands clutched my legs, his torso crushing me into the wall.

I tore my mouth away a second time. "Ezra," I gasped. "The bed is over there."

Hazy, hungry eyes raked across my face, then he stepped back from the wall. Sliding down him, I got my feet back on the floor, grabbed his shirt, and pulled it over his head. He released me just long enough to free his arms from the fabric, then his hands were on my waist, sliding under my top, fingers gliding over my skin.

Plastering myself against his hard chest, I pushed him backward, steering him across the room. He moved with me, hands exploring, mouth locked on mine while I greedily traced every inch of his skin. As we stumbled toward the bed, my fingers found the waistband of his boxers, and I slid my hand across the fabric, taking advantage of those undone jeans.

Spinning us, he leaned me back over the bed. I fell onto it, aching, burning, needing him. Standing between my knees, he paused, his gaze roving over every curve of my body, drinking in the sight of me lying across his bed, damn near ready to beg.

He put a knee on the mattress between my thighs. Ran his hand up my leg to my hip. Leaned down.

The front screen door banged loudly.

"Ezra?" Aaron called, hoarse with exhaustion. "You up?"

Ezra's eyes went wide. We stared at each other for a long heartbeat—then we both lurched off his bed. As I grabbed his shirt off the floor, he did up the fly of his jeans—with difficulty, the sight making my breath catch. I handed him his shirt and he pulled it on.

Aaron's voice echoed up the stairs. "Ezra?"

Ezra brushed his fingers across the back of my hand, then rushed out of the room. His footsteps thudded down the stairs.

"Aaron, how did it go?"

"It was a nightmare. Any word from Tori?"

"She turned up around four. She'll be down in a minute. She's just changing."

Oh, right. I still hadn't changed. I dug into the closet, searching through my stash of clothes. Stripping naked—Ezra's door was still open, but oh well—I dressed in cotton pants, a tank top, and an oversized sweater. I'd change into leather if or when we were ready to kick some ass. Grabbing a pair of socks, I hurried down the stairs.

"Where did that prick take Tori last night?" Aaron asked, his voice coming from the living room.

"I don't know yet. She fell asleep on the sofa before she could tell me, and we only woke up a few minutes ago." Ezra yawned. "She seems okay, but disturbed about something."

I breezed into the room, but my carefree attitude faltered at the sight of Aaron. He was slumped in the middle of the sofa, his face pale, haggard, and smudged with soot. Sharpie, safely in its sheath, lay across the coffee table, and his combat gear was dusted with ash and dirt. The stench of smoke clung to him.

"Holy shit, Aaron." I hastened to the sofa and sat beside him. "Did Shane take you for a stroll through hell?"

"Seemed like it," he muttered, head resting against the cushions and eyes closed. "The Pandora Knights' guild was leveled. It was all on fire. Bodies ... the Pandora mages didn't hold back. Those idiot rogues paid a heavy price for ... whatever they were trying to do."

Ezra perched on the edge of the recliner, elbows braced on his knees. "Any casualties from the Pandora Knights?"

"Some injuries. No deaths. They're tough as shit. Still, they lost their headquarters and everything in it. All their gear, training equipment, personal belongings … They're pissed." He rubbed a hand over his face, leaving streaky fingerprints in the soot. "It's been dead quiet around here for weeks, then out of nowhere, this. I don't get it."

"What does Shane think?" Ezra asked.

"Who the hell knows? The guy is a steel trap when it comes to information. He said he's here for the Ghost's bounty, so I can't even guess why he's so interested in this attack. He was all over the scene, then he dragged me across downtown, chasing clues and rogues."

Heaving a sigh, he sat up and opened his eyes. "But enough of that. Tori, are you okay? Where did that dragon take you?"

"We visited Zak's farm—or what's left of it. You remember Varvara, right? She obliterated it, stole all his stuff, and killed the person he'd left to watch over it, his horses, and at least one fae he had a relationship with. And she's using his grimoire to leak information about him to MagiPol."

Aaron scratched at the five o'clock shadow roughening his jaw. "Where is he now?"

"Downtown somewhere, hunting Varvara." I unrolled my socks and tugged one on my foot. "I think I have an idea why Shane is so keen on the attack against the Pandora Knights. One person connects everything."

Aaron's brow crinkled. "Who?"

"Zak." I pulled on my other sock. "The crime lull, the rogue attack, Varvara, even the Yamada activity in Vancouver are all connected to Zak."

Aaron and Ezra leaned forward, watching me intently.

"You said before that the power landscape is shifting. Red Rum was driven out, and Zak went into hiding. That left a big gap in the Scary People of Vancouver group, and the Yamadas—or, I guess, the Miuras, since it's Makiko's family running things here—began a takeover. But then Varvara got involved."

"Varvara is involved?"

"She lured all the little guys over to her side. That's why the rogues and rogue guilds got so quiet. She was taking control of them. According to the guy Zak questioned last night, Varvara was behind the Pandora Knights attack."

"Shit," Aaron muttered.

"Why?" Ezra looked between us. "What's the point in attacking a guild?"

I grimaced. "That part I'm not sure about, but Varvara's got to have some sort of evil plan. Evil plans are her thing. Considering she spent fifteen years secretly raising an abducted kid to be her apprentice, we've got to assume it's both nasty and sneaky."

"Hmm." Aaron gazed thoughtfully at his sword, then his face twisted. "Damn it! We need Kai. He understands this stuff."

I nodded fervently. "Yes, Kai. We need a plan for him."

Aaron flopped back onto the sofa.

I waited a moment. "Aaron?"

"I'm not sure we can make a plan."

"What? Why not? We can't just *leave* him—"

He slanted his head toward me, still limp with exhaustion. "I don't want to leave him either, but we can't protect him from an international crime syndicate. Whatever we might attempt will only make things worse for him."

Disbelieving fury bubbled up in me but I choked it back. "If Kai got away from them once, he can do it again. We just have to—"

"But he didn't get away," Aaron corrected heavily. "He never confronted them, or even told them he was done. He just stopped going home, and they allowed it. I have no idea why, and neither does Kai. He didn't expect it to last more than a few months, but his family decided that if he was going to ignore them, then they'd ignore him too—with a few exceptions."

"What exceptions?"

"If he tries to date anyone, mainly, or if he interferes in their business. We found out about the second one when we tagged a Yamada associate without realizing who the guy was."

My forehead scrunched anxiously. "What happened?"

"Kai vanished one night on his way home." His voice went oddly flat. "I found him on the front lawn the next morning, unconscious with his left arm and left hand broken in six places."

Ezra's face lost all expression, the air around him chilling.

Aaron stared broodingly at his clenched fists. "All the freedom Kai had was freedom they allowed him, and they've taken it away. I'm not sure there's anything we can do."

"We have to do *something*."

"I know, but we can't just rush in with magic blazing. We need to be cautious."

I sighed miserably. "Those are words I never expected to hear from you."

"I have to be the responsible one since Kai isn't here to do it."

"Wait." Ezra gazed between us, extra serious. "If you're Kai now, is Tori you? Or am I you and Tori's me? Or—"

"Please don't torture my poor brain." Aaron pushed off the sofa. "I need to shower and get some sleep."

"Do you want to eat?" Ezra asked.

"Too tired. Save me something to warm up in a few hours."

As he headed downstairs to the shower, my eyes met Ezra's—and we both quickly looked away. A blush warmed my cheeks and I bit my lower lip. Talk about bad timing for an impromptu make-out session.

I glanced at the front window. Pale sunlight streaked through the drapes, marking a new day—and bringing me that much closer to my deadline with Eterran.

Ezra. Kai. Zak. Too many dudes in distress and not enough time—or enough power—to save them. They needed a superwoman, and it was becoming all too clear I wasn't up for the task.

15

PERCHED ON MY SPARE STOOL behind the bar, I stared at my laptop, the MPD's hideous white website filling the screen, open to a list of cold Demonica bounties. My thoughts churned nonstop and anxiety bubbled in my stomach.

No word from Zak.

No word from Kai.

Only three more nights until the full moon, at which point I would be having words with Eterran, whether I wanted them or not.

My conversation with Ezra spun through my head—a heartbreaking tale of two teenage demon mages. He'd learned control. She hadn't, and they'd killed her. It was the most messed-up thing I'd ever heard. As much as I wanted to know what sick bastards would turn fourteen-year-olds into demon mages, it was Ezra's other comments I couldn't shake.

It feels like I'm drowning, like I'm disappearing.

All that's left is the fear and the rage.
Eterran might survive it, but I won't.

Only once had I seen Ezra really lose control of his emotions. It had been at Aaron's house, during Zak's first visit. I'd been hysterical and screaming, and Ezra had shattered the doorframe.

That was why Aaron and Kai were so protective of Ezra. That was why his fear and anger were so dangerous. It wasn't just an opportunity for Eterran to slip into the driver's seat. It was so much worse than that. Eterran seemed logical, even reasonable, but the emotional feedback loop Ezra had described, that breakdown of all control that could ensnare both demon and mage …

"Hellooo? Tori?"

I jolted, my gaze snapping up.

Sin stood at the bar across from me, her eyebrows pinched with concern. "You okay?"

I smiled wanly as I shook off my apprehension. Her new hair color was still a shock—a silvery purple-gray that set off her fair complexion, the dramatic look accentuated by smoky makeup.

She looked enigmatic and gorgeous, but the timing of her makeover worried me. I hadn't seen any of her bright tops or swirly skirts lately either. Her sweater today was long and very black, paired with warm black leggings and knee-high boots I'd never seen before.

She slid onto a stool. "What's going on?"

I almost said "nothing" but changed my mind. "I can't get into it."

"Hmm." She propped her chin on her hand. "Got anything to do with this crowd tonight?"

I glanced around. The pub was hopping. Not unusual for a Friday evening, but last night's attack on the Pandora Knights had brought over half the guild out. Everyone was chatting, but the gossip was underlaid with unease. Rogues combining forces to attack a guild was unheard of.

Adding to the crowd was the Odin's Eye team who'd been working with our guys to solve the mystery of the crime lull. Izzah and Aaron sat at the head of a cluster of tables, collecting notes on what everyone had learned since the Pandora Knights assault.

It looked all wrong without Kai there, cool and competent and smart.

Sin leaned sideways, putting her face in my line of sight. "You're spacing out again."

"Sorry."

"*Sorry?* What, no sassy comeback? Are you feeling under the weather? Do you need a vitality potion?"

Not unless Zak made it for me. Every other vitality potion I'd tried had tasted like ass.

"I'm just tired. It's been a long couple of days." I'd fallen asleep again after breakfast, but even sleeping until three hadn't cured my fatigue. Shaking off my self-absorbed lethargy, I focused on her. "What about you? Are you okay?"

"Of course. I'm fine."

I frowned helplessly. Should I outright ask if she'd changed her appearance in response to the events over Christmas? Leaning across the bar, I lowered my voice. "I mean, how are you, really? Sleeping all right and stuff?"

Her gaze dropped. She tugged on a lock of silvery hair. "For the most part, yeah. I've been okay. Aaron's been checking up on me too."

He had? As far as I could tell, her crush on him had gone nowhere since our return from the academy—though, as Aaron's ex-girlfriend, I wasn't in a position to ask either of them about it.

"If you want to talk, I'm here." I smiled encouragingly. "Anytime, just say the word."

"Thanks, Tori. And I'm here for you too, you know. You can tell me what happened with Ezra."

My mouth fell open. "What? Who said anything happened?"

She nodded as though I'd confirmed her suspicions. "Did you tell him how you feel?" She pursed her lips, painted a deep red to go with her new look. "You kissed him, didn't you?"

My eyes bugged out.

Another nod as she fought back a grin. "When did it happen?"

I considered lying until my tongue turned black, then muttered, "That stupid pixie mistletoe got us at the Christmas party."

"Oh my god! I had no clue. What …" The excited light in her eyes died as she looked around the Ezra-less pub. He was upstairs, staying out of sight while the Odin's Eye mythics were in the guild. "You two aren't dating, are you?"

"No." I drew in a deep breath. "He wants to be friends. I think."

"You think?"

"That's what he said. He might … but however he feels, he doesn't want to be more than friends." Aside from, you know, that super-hot make-out session this morning.

"I'm sorry," Sin said softly.

I drooped. "Yeah."

"Well, at least—"

Huffing angrily, Sabrina stormed up to the bar, yanked out a stool, and dropped into it. "Do you mind if I join you?"

"Uh ..." I began.

She slammed her purse down on the counter. "I am *so sick* of Rose!"

Sin and I looked past her. At the other end of the pub, the elderly diviner was leaning over a table where Lyndon, Bryce, Taye, and Gwen were drinking. She thrust a pale crystal ball under Lyndon's nose, speaking emphatically.

"She just won't shut up," Sabrina growled, raking her fingers through her neatly styled blond bob. "Apparently, she did an *amazing* séance for Robin Page a few weeks ago, and she keeps going on and on about how she's a true mouthpiece of the fates, unlike some *young and inexperienced* diviners."

I composed my expression into one of sympathy. "That's just rude."

"She's way out of line," Sin agreed supportively.

"Thank you." Sabrina's indignation melted and her features softened into her usual good-natured cheer. "I'm so sorry for butting in. What did I interrupt?"

Damn, was this girl ever in a bad mood for more than five minutes? I should take notes.

"Nothing," I answered at the same time Sin said, "Boy troubles."

"Whose boy troubles?"

"Sin's," I said, while Sin replied, "Tori's."

Sabrina's forehead wrinkled in confusion. "Both of you? ... Same boy?"

"No," we answered simultaneously.

"Oh," Sabrina breathed. "That's good. It'd be awful if you were in love with Ezra too, Sin."

My jaw dropped for the second time. "Are *you* in love with Ezra?"

"Of course not," she said serenely. "You are."

I didn't know what to say. I had nothing. Brain. Buzzing. Blankly.

Sabrina's small smile faded as she studied my face. "Doesn't she know?" she asked Sin.

"I think she's surprised that you know," Sin replied dryly.

"Oh." Sabrina dipped her hand into her bag and pulled out a bundle of silk. Unraveling it, she revealed the black and gold tarot deck. "Don't you remember, Tori? Your last reading? The most unexpected card ..."

Pressing her fingers to the top card, she slid it off and flipped it over.

My stomach dropped. The Devil. A horned beast, holding a man and a woman in chains, and I could see Ezra and me so clearly in that illustration. I even had a name for the demon now.

"Temptation," Sabrina declared. "Infatuation. Addiction. You're in love with Ezra."

"I—I'm not ... not in ..." I tried to compose myself. "I'm just ... He's ..." I shrank on my stool, my shoulders curling inward. "I don't know."

"Tori ..." Sabrina touched the deck again, then flipped the card. A naked couple was passionately entwined across its face, the name at the bottom declaring The Lovers. "Falling in love is always a little scary, but you have to make yourself vulnerable. Otherwise, how can you open your heart to him?"

"But ..."

"Do you remember your very first reading? The Six of Cups? The reversed Hermit? The Eight of Swords? And—" She flipped the next card on her deck. "The Knight of Swords. Your past and your fears are still holding you back."

I stared at the illustration of an armored knight on the card. "How do you remember all that?"

"I'm a diviner," she answered simply. "Tori, have you told him how you feel?"

"No."

She touched the deck one more time, and my heart dropped. Somehow, I knew what the next card would be. It had appeared in my first reading and stalked me ever since, warning me again and again of what was coming.

She flipped the card, revealing the grim reaper and his bloody scythe. Death. The card of transformation ... of irreversible endings.

"I think you need to tell him soon," she whispered.

Staring at that relentless Death card, I wanted to throw up. What was I doing here, working my regular shift, earning my pointless paycheck, while Ezra's life trickled away? I had days left before the full moon. I didn't know anything yet. I needed to—

"Sorry to interrupt, ladies." Kaveri stepped into the gap between Sabrina and Sin. "Tori, could I get a bourbini?"

"Sure," I replied automatically.

As I reached below the counter for a cocktail glass, the young witch leaned a slim hip against the bar. "What do you three think of it all?"

"All of what?" Sin asked politely.

"The attacks. Did you see the footage from the LA precinct yesterday?" She shook her head. "A guild-run film studio had to take credit for it, pretending it was a publicity stunt, but rumors are running wild. And now the Pandora Knights? It's scary."

I busied myself pouring bourbon into a shaker, pointedly keeping my mouth shut.

"But they aren't connected," Sin said. "What does an LA precinct have to do with a Vancouver guild?"

"I don't know, but it's way too much of a coincidence. And when you add in the news that the Ghost is a druid, well …"

"How is *he* connected to anything?" Sin demanded in frustration.

"Those Odin's Eye men are saying a druid attacked the MagiPol building," Sabrina mused uneasily. "One of them checked the precinct's logs. Two druids were booked only a few hours before."

"Of course it was a druid." Kaveri sniffed. "A witch would know better than to accept magic that powerful from a fae."

Assuming a fae would *offer* a witch something that powerful, which I doubted.

"Hey, Kaveri," I said abruptly as I added half an ounce of liqueur to the bourbon, peach bitters, and ice. "I've never understood—what's the difference between a witch and a druid?"

"Order and chaos."

"Uh … could you be any more specific?"

She tucked a lock of long brown hair behind her ear. "Most people will tell you the only difference is power. They'll say a druid is just like a witch but with all the Spiritalis dials turned up to ten. They can sense energies more easily, see fae and fae magic better, connect with fae more directly, and so on."

"But that isn't correct?" I guessed as I strained her drink into the cocktail glass and added a sprig of mint.

"It is, but there are varying power levels in every class. Thank you," she added as I passed her drink over. "What truly separates us isn't how much power we have but how we use it. Witches restore order to the natural world through ritual. In the same way Arcana users build spells to channel arcane energies, we use rituals to channel and shape the energies of the natural world."

She took a long sip. "Druids skip the ritual and go straight to direct manipulation of energies. They can do it because they're more powerful, but without the structure of a ritual, it's like trying to hold water in your bare hands. They create chaos rather than reduce it."

I remembered the wild, violent magic spilling out of Zak while he'd been lost in grief. Yeah, I could see where Kaveri was coming from.

"Their interactions with fae are the same," she added. "We use ritual to formalize the exchange of favors and magic. It makes everything simple and straightforward. Whereas druids just … allow fae all over them."

Or maybe druids didn't allow it so much as they couldn't stop fae from coming for the "feast," as Echo had put it. The Rat darkfae Zak had attempted to bargain with last fall had straight up *licked* him. He was a tasty little druid morsel, and without a powerful protector like Lallakai, he'd be exposed to every nasty fae who wanted a bite.

She will own him until his last day, Echo had told me. Or had he been warning me?

With a clatter, the Odin's Eye/Crow and Hammer meeting broke up. Mythics stood, stretching and talking. Aaron, still in deep discussion with Andrew, headed upstairs while Izzah scooted off her chair and strode to the bar.

She smiled tightly as she joined our small group. "*Eh*, Tori, have you talked to Kai today?"

I froze. "Uh ... no. Did you ask Aaron?"

Her cocoa eyes clouded. "He said Kai had a family emergency." She glanced at the other women, who were pretending not to listen—badly—then leaned closer. "Is he okay, Tori?"

I opened my mouth, then closed it. "Can I get you something to drink, Izzah?"

Her eyes narrowed. "I want answers-*lah*, not a drink. You're hiding something. You and Aaron both."

I flinched. "Let me get you a drink first, then we can talk about Kai." Vaguely. *Really* vaguely.

"A martini, please," she said, stiff and angry.

"You got it."

Deciding to spoil her—since I couldn't give her real answers—I turned to the shelves of high-quality liquor. Behind me, the pub bell jingled. Odin's Eye mythics on their way out, I assumed as I browsed my options. Where was the stuff I'd given Shane Davila? Oh wait, that was in the fridge. Duh. Should I use gin instead? Hmm ...

The back of my neck prickled, and I frowned. My ears buzzed in the sudden silence.

The pub had gone dead quiet. I could hear my breath catch in my throat as my adrenaline spiked. A bottle of gin in my hand, I whirled around.

The pub hadn't suddenly emptied, nor had a magical force teleported me into a silent dimension. Everyone was exactly where they'd been, scattered around tables or standing in clusters. Sin, Sabrina, Kaveri, and Izzah were still gathered beside my station.

They were all there, silent and spellbound by the man standing two steps away, waiting for me to notice him.

Not a mere man.

A druid.

A rogue druid.

A rogue druid by the name of Zak—and he was standing inside my guild *in plain freaking sight!*

16

THE BOTTLE OF GIN slipped out of my numb fingers, hit the floor, and shattered.

Expensive liquid splashed all over my jeans, and my shock broke. Fury and fear and disbelief and *oh-my-god-how-moronic-is-he?* rushed through my head in a dizzying wave, and my mouth was moving before my brain could catch up.

"You are the dumbest dickhead on the entire planet!"

My furious exclamation rang through the silent pub. His green eyes—human-green, not fae-power iridescent-green—flashed angrily.

Sin, Sabrina, Kaveri, and Izzah turned their heads in perfect unison, mouths hanging open as they looked from me to the rogue and back again. Shock had silenced them, but they were recovering quickly—and wild curiosity was igniting in their expressions.

At least it wasn't horror or fear. They didn't know he was a rogue. Or a druid. Or a murderer.

Since I'd last seen him, Zak had shaved off his untidy scruff and gotten a haircut. His dark locks were barely an inch long on top and even shorter on the sides—not that the short style detracted from his ridiculously striking face. If anything, it highlighted his amazing cheekbones and gorgeous eyes, framed by luscious lashes.

I cleared my throat loudly, mentally scrambling. "What are you doing here?"

His mouth thinned and I realized I should've invited him somewhere private to talk. Oops.

He stepped closer to the bar, and the four women on his side of the barrier drew awed breaths. The way his unfairly handsome face combined with his black clothes, villainous coat, and leather gloves was too perfect, and he was oozing bad-boy pheromones so strong the girls were nearly drooling.

"You're a difficult woman to contact," Zak said in a low, raspy rumble. The female foursome beside him swooned. "Would you mind?"

He held out a shiny new cell phone. I took it, since he was offering it, but once it was in my hand, I stared from the device to him and back, painfully aware that everyone in the pub was watching our every move.

A muscle in his cheek twitched. "Despite what you may think, I don't know your number by heart."

Oh. *Oooh.* I woke the screen. His contacts, already open, contained exactly zero phone numbers. Did he buy—or steal—this phone just to contact me? I might've been very slightly flattered.

Okay, I was flattered. Also nervous about why he wanted to talk to me so badly.

I added my number, then tossed the phone back to him. He caught it and pushed his coat aside to slip it into his back pocket.

"You're an alchemist?" Sin blurted loudly. She tactlessly pointed at his waist. "That's an alchemy combat belt."

His cold stare swung to her as he let his long coat fall back into place. She went silent, mouth gaping lamely as her crippling shyness in the face of any hot man took over. Turning his back on the bar, he strode toward the door.

Seriously? He'd just invaded my guild, demanded my phone number, flaunted his edgy man-beauty everywhere, and now he was leaving without another word? Did he *want* to make his visit as memorable as possible?

"Hold on," I called irately. Planting my hands on the bar top, I vaulted over it. "You're going to call me as soon as you're outside, so we might as well talk now."

He halted. The instant I reached him, he was moving again. I walked beside him, heading for the safety—or at least the privacy—of the street.

"What the actual hell are *you* doing here?"

Aaron's furious shout rang through the bar. Stumbling in surprise, I looked back. The pyromage was halfway down the stairs from the upper level, his teeth bared. Andrew and Girard stood behind him, their eyebrows raised in question.

"Hey Aaron," I said with forced calm. "We're stepping outside for a chat. You should join us."

His jaw clenched, visible from across the bar. "I'd love to have a little *chat*."

Great. This was going to be so much fun.

He stormed down the stairs and strode aggressively to my other side. He and Zak glowered at each other over the top of my head, and I almost face-palmed. Sure, guys. Go ahead. Make a scene. Why not?

"Idiots," I said in a sugary whisper, putting a hand on each of their shoulders and squeezing hard as I smiled for my audience. "Please move your testosterone-crippled asses outside *right now*."

Their glares singed me, then they marched to the exit, side by side. Zak's slightly longer stride won out, and he shoved through the door first, Aaron right behind him. I followed them outside, rolling my eyes so hard they blistered in their sockets.

"What's wrong with you, barging into our guild?" Aaron snarled the moment the door shut. "With your face showing, no less?"

"Was I supposed to come in with a hood and mask?" Zak snapped. "You were the ones broadcasting your reactions to the whole guild. If you and Tori had an ounce of brainpower between you—"

"Why are you here, Zak?" I interrupted, folding my arms—partly for sass and partly because it was freakin' cold out.

"I don't have any of your phone numbers, or secure access to the MPD database to get your numbers. This was the only way to talk to you, and it couldn't wait." His gaze cut across us. "Where is Kai?"

"Kai?" I repeated. "I have no idea. Makiko took him away, remember?"

"So he's with her?"

"We think so."

"Can you contact him?"

"He isn't responding to messages," Aaron said flatly. "I don't know if he's seeing them."

Dread built in my chest like cold liquid compressing my lungs. "Why are you asking, Zak?"

"I've been gathering information about Varvara and her plans. The Pandora Knights are the highest-grossing bounty guild in the city. She got them out of the way first so they couldn't interfere with her next move."

I almost asked him how many people he'd killed to get that information, but I really didn't want to know.

"What's her next move?" Aaron demanded.

"To consolidate her new power in Vancouver, she needs to eliminate her competition."

My heart stuttered. "You mean the Yamadas, don't you? That rogue guy said the Yamadas were taking over, and Varvara showed up to oppose them. That's why you want to know where Kai is?"

"She's going after the Yamadas' presence here in the city next—probably tonight while the Pandora Knights incident has everyone distracted. I want to head her off. Where can I find the Miuras?"

Aaron swore. "I need to get my keys."

"If you know where they are, just tell me."

"No way." Aaron put a hand on the door, his blue eyes blazing. "If you didn't need information, would you even have warned us that Kai is in danger?"

He pushed into the guild, letting a wave of conservation out into the quiet street. The door thumped shut behind him.

Zak leaned against the wall. "Next time I show up somewhere unexpected, Tori, try not to act like I'm a specter returned from the dead."

"Don't worry. I'll just tell my guild you're my ex-boyfriend and I dumped you for being an egotistical dickhead."

"Nice try, but you haven't been part of the mythic community long enough to have a mythic ex. Unless you want them to think you were cheating on Aaron."

"Huh." I thought for a moment. "Then I'll tell them you're in love with me and you've been stalking me like a total creeper."

"I'm sure that will get a great reaction."

I grimaced. "The women would probably ask me why I'm not all for it."

"All for what?"

"All for the hot alchemist trying to get in my pants."

"When have I tried to get in your pants?"

"We're talking about my cover story, not real life, Zak."

He grunted irritably.

"By the way." I stuffed a hand in my pocket, feeling for the square of fabric. "You took off last night before I could give you the Cara—"

The guild door swung open. Aaron marched out, his jacket over his arm, sheathed sword slung over his shoulder, and keys in his hand. Zak gave his head a slight shake and I reluctantly left the Carapace in my pocket.

Ezra followed Aaron through the door, carrying his pole-arm—and my combat gear. I grinned as he passed me my belt and badass leather jacket. Too bad I wasn't wearing my matching leather pants—too hot for a long shift behind the bar—but good enough.

As I buckled on my belt, I realized I was forgetting something. "Uh, one sec, guys."

I stuck my head back into the pub. Chatter circled the room, the gossip engine revving hard. Several people looked around at my reappearance, including the four girls still at the bar.

"Hey, Cooper," I shouted.

More conversations broke off, gazes swinging toward me. I scanned the mythics for a familiar greasy head.

"Cooper!"

"What?" came the reluctant response from the back corner.

I spotted him tucked at a table between Cameron and Cearra. "Cover the rest of my shift."

"Huh? No way. It's Friday night and—"

"Just do it!" I bellowed.

"Tori—" he began in a whine.

I stepped outside and shut the door firmly. Turning to the three men, I shrugged. "Okay, we're good to go."

SIX MINUTES LATER, Aaron pulled his SUV up to the curb of a downtown street, the streetlamps glowing and a handful of cars zooming past. Though it was Friday night, it was a cold, dark, windy Friday night, and this was the business sector of downtown. Almost everyone had gone home for the weekend.

I looked around, then leaned over the center console. "Uh, Aaron? Why are you stopping?"

He cut the engine and pulled the keys out of the ignition. "We're here."

"This is, like, twelve blocks from the guild."

"Yep."

From the passenger seat, Zak scrutinized Aaron. "You sure about this, Sinclair?"

Ignoring him, Aaron directed his words at me. "Remember what I said about that time we tagged a Yamada associate and Kai disappeared for a night? After that, I made sure I'd know where to look if he went missing again."

Nodding, I threw my door open. "Let's go get him."

We climbed out and gathered on the sidewalk, facing a towering skyscraper with one curved end, like a closed-in U. It was sleek, elegant, and all windows, the flawless glass reflecting the surrounding lights.

Beside me, Ezra craned his neck back. "It's completely dark."

I blinked. At least a few windows glowed in all the surrounding buildings except this one.

"Zak," I muttered, fishing a hair tie out of my pocket. "What exactly is Varvara's plan?"

"All I know is she's targeting Yamada holdings next."

"What's *our* plan?" Ezra asked.

Aaron rubbed the back of his neck. "Go inside. Get to the top floors. Find Kai."

Zak snorted.

"Got a better idea, asshole?"

The druid reached for the hood of his long coat. As he pulled it over his head, dark wings swept out of nothing, and a feathered body followed. The huge eagle collided with Zak's back, and her wings furled around him as she melted into his body.

Aaron made a harsh noise. "That's freakin' creepy."

Zak strode toward the tower's main doors.

"Let's go," I muttered, trotting after him as I pulled my curls into a high ponytail and looped the hair tie tight around it. Unobstructed visibility over fashion.

Aaron and Ezra followed as we boldly approached the building, passing an industrial but sort of pretty water feature that bordered the broad sidewalk. Zak reached the glass doors, grabbed a handle, and pulled. It opened without resistance.

The four of us entered a grand concourse, the ceiling three times the height of the doors. Upscale shops, closed for the night, faced a wide swath of shiny tiled floor, and an understated security desk sat in the middle of the space. The only illumination came from the street, shining through the endless windows.

"Is it supposed to be abandoned?" I asked, my quiet voice echoing.

"Not sure," Aaron muttered.

Zak approached a bank of elevator doors lining a short hall and jabbed the call button. Nothing happened. No light to indicate an elevator had been summoned. No dings or glowing numbers to show what floor the elevators were on and how long we needed to wait for one to return to ground level.

Aaron crossed to a door with a small sign that marked the stairwell. "Guess we're taking the stairs."

This building was over thirty stories tall. He didn't actually think I could climb thirty flights in one go, did he? Because I did not have buns of steel, unlike these guys.

Opening the door, Aaron peered inside. "Shit. The lights are off in here too. Is the power out?"

"Guess we can't take the stairs either," I said brightly. "What a shame."

Aaron flicked on the light attached to his protective vest and grinned at me. I grumbled under my breath.

Ezra turned on his light as well, then tugged up the tops of his steel-reinforced bad-guy-smasher gloves. "You can do it, Tori."

"I'm pretty sure I can't," I muttered, reluctantly following them into the dark, echoing stairwell.

To no one's surprise, twenty-six flights proved me right.

"I ... am ... going ... to ... die," I panted with each agonizing step. "Just ... *die*."

"One more flight to go," Ezra assured me, two steps behind, his light illuminating the endless mountain of concrete stairs waiting for me.

"You've been saying that for ten flights now!" I accused between gasps.

"It's true. There's one more to go. And then one more, and probably one more after that. At least."

I rolled my eyes.

"Hurry up, you two!" Aaron called in a low voice from the floor above us. "The impatient asshole is already on the thirtieth floor."

My thigh muscles screamed in protest as I dragged my foot up another step, lungs heaving, limbs trembling, stomach threatening to chuck up my dinner. Tears of pain and frustration stung my eyes as I tried to make my abused muscles move faster. A two-minute breather, please. A thirty-second breather. Something. Anything.

But we didn't have time for that.

Clutching the railing, I forced myself to the next landing and faced another flight. Oh god. Stairs. Who invented these torture devices? I could've kept up okay on flat ground—probably—but you could only repeat the same motion so many times before your muscles were all, "Screw this shit," and quit entirely.

Ezra caught my wrist, tugging me back as I lifted a trembling leg onto the first step.

"Tori," he said, "let me help."

"I can do it," I groaned, grabbing the railing to pull myself onto the step.

He tugged me back again and I slumped against him. Wrapping an arm around my waist, he put his mouth against my ear and whispered, "We won't tell them. You can have a few minutes to breathe."

I squeezed my eyes shut, furious and ashamed that I couldn't keep up. "Okay."

Pulling his pole-arm off his magnetic baldric, he crouched in front of me, and I hauled my exhausted body onto his back. Hooking his arms under my legs, he jogged up the stairs. I clutched his shoulders, grumbling about his impossible strength and stamina.

Five flights later, when Aaron's and Zak's voices echoed around the next bend in the stairwell, Ezra let me slide off his back. He swung his pole-arm over his shoulder, the metal clamping to his baldric, and continued upward.

The short break had done wonders for my poor legs, and I was barely limping as I puffed up the last flight. Zak and Aaron waited beside a door with a large "32" painted on the white wall beside it. The druid had pushed his hood back, and I was pleased to see perspiration shining on his face and Aaron's. Thirty flights hadn't been a breeze for them either.

"Why this floor?" I asked as I joined them, Ezra beside me. "Not the top?"

Aaron pointed at the door. A tall, skinny window interrupted the steel face, just wide enough to see if there was a person on the other side. His vest light shone across the pane.

Red droplets ran down the glass, a bloody handprint smearing the gory splatter.

17

"HOLY SHIT," I WHISPERED.

"Varvara—or her pawns—beat us here," Zak rumbled, cool and businesslike. "There are three floors left—this one, and the next two. We should split up and search them."

"No," Aaron countered immediately. "We have no idea what we're up against. The Miuras and their people could attack us too. We're safer together."

"We should start at the top," Ezra suggested. "Kai and Makiko are probably on the penthouse level, and if Varvara hasn't made it up there yet, we can warn them."

"Right." Aaron nodded. "Let's go."

He shot up the stairs at a quick jog, and Zak followed. Ezra grabbed my hand and pulled me with him as we sprinted up the final two flights. My legs were on fire by the time we reached the top—and found the door hanging open, one hinge broken. Deep scratches marred the steel as though someone, or something, had smashed its way inside.

Aaron drew Sharpie, the long blade coming free of its sheath with a slithering sound. Ezra pulled his pole-arm off his back, and I unholstered my paintball gun, loaded with sleep potions.

Zak drew his hood up again, then pushed his coat open so it wouldn't impede access to his belt, test-tube-shaped vials circling his hips. He stepped into the dark corridor. Aaron went in second, his vest light flashing across the walls. More deep scratches tore through the beige paint.

Spotting a panel of light switches, I flipped them up and down, but nothing happened. No power. Finding Kai could take a while—unless I could speed up the process.

I reached into my belt's large back pouch, my fingers brushing across a gently ridged surface. *Hoshi?*

Her dormant form uncoiled in a burst of silvery scales. The bluish sylph floated out of my belt, her huge pink eyes turning from me to Zak. She spiraled around me, her odd little antennae bobbing.

The men watched as I patted her nose. "Hoshi, can you look around and see if Kai is somewhere on this level?"

As I spoke, I pictured what I meant in my mind—Kai's face, the building, and an imaginary little scene where the sylph led him back to me. She nuzzled my hand, replaying some of my images along with flashes of color and patterns I didn't understand. Whatever they meant, they gave me a positive vibe.

Her tail squeezed around my waist and she pushed her cool nose into my cheek. Another image flickered inside my head: Zak's face, but with Lallakai's features overlaid on his. The sylph couldn't communicate with words, but I felt her meaning: *Be careful.*

She slid her tail away, then launched down the corridor in a flowing ribbon of silver.

Zak watched her go, then glanced back at me. "Interesting."

"What?" I asked nervously, Hoshi's warning crowding my thoughts.

"She won't talk to me anymore."

Based on the sylph's telepathic vision, I suspected it wasn't the *druid* she didn't want to interact with.

We continued down the corridor, Zak in the lead, Aaron behind him, Ezra and I bringing up the rear. The soft carpet absorbed our footsteps, the simple walls interrupted by blank doors. The quiet was unnerving, and I huddled closer than necessary to Ezra's side. His head turned, his senses attuned not only to sight and sound but also to the minute shift of air around us.

"Maybe there's no one here," I whispered, gripping my paintball gun. "What if—"

A distant boom shook the floor. The overhead lights sparked and flickered weakly before going dark again.

Aaron launched into a sprint, shoving past Zak. The druid rushed after him, and I belatedly pushed my tired legs into motion. With Ezra following, I chased the two guys down the corridor. Aaron whipped around the corner, out of sight, and Zak disappeared after him.

Aaron shouted wordlessly, a sound of shock.

Ezra and I flew around the corner and I came up short, my eyes widening. Aaron and Zak had stopped just ahead of us, but even the two tall, broad-shouldered men, standing side by side, couldn't block my view of what waited beyond them.

The hall had widened, resembling a posh hotel with numbered doors and oil paintings decorating the walls—where they hadn't been torn off. The source of the damage stood in the middle of the corridor, so out of place I could barely wrap my head around it.

Welded steel formed the rough shape of a four-legged animal. Blocky head with no features except for a large mouth full of crude teeth. Heavy legs with clawed feet. Gears for joints. Spikes running down its back. And the entire thing was covered in runes that glowed pale red, almost pink.

The steampunk wolf opened its mechanical mouth—and green liquid spouted from its metal gullet.

Aaron and Zak dove aside, and Ezra grabbed me around the waist as he leaped clear. The jet of fluid shot twenty feet down the center of the hall and splashed across the floor. The rug bubbled, reeking white steam roiling off it.

"Caustic poison," Zak barked. "It'll eat right through your weapons."

And, obviously, our poor human flesh.

The mechanical creature launched at Zak with thundering steps. He jumped across the bubbling line of potion to Aaron's side of the hall, and the clanking wolf whirled after him.

Flames erupted across Aaron's arms and shot down his blade. He whipped Sharpie in an arc and the blade swung into the canine's hollow snout with an ear-splitting clang. Fire exploded down the sword, washing over the steel body. The thing didn't even slow, its lumbering steps backed by several hundred pounds of momentum.

"Shit!" Aaron dodged sideways. "Are these Varvara's specialty or something? I remember them from last time—they don't like to die."

Last time? The memory popped into my panicked brain: suits of armor coming to life in Varvara's garden; Aaron and Ezra hacking at the metal bodies, unable to stop the enchanted armor.

"What is it?" I squealed from behind Ezra. "Should I shoot it?"

"It's a golem." Scarlet light swirled off Zak's right hand and a curved saber took form in his grip. "Don't waste your ammo."

As the thing charged, he swung his saber down. It sliced through the golem's steel muzzle, but the unstoppable monstrosity bowled into him, oblivious to the new split in its face.

Zak rolled clear, shot to his feet, and struck its neck again. His fae blade ripped through the steel. The golem pivoted, its head hanging on its half-severed neck—but it didn't seem to notice.

Clanking steps vibrated the floor.

A second wolfish golem stomped around the corner, mouth gaping. What looked horribly like blood dripped from its triangular teeth. It charged like a steel bull, forcing Zak and Aaron to press into the wall to avoid it.

Ezra shot forward. With a gust of wind to propel him, he leaped over the nearer golem, landed between the two, and slammed the butt of his pole-arm down on the one's half-severed head. Its head tore off with a hideous shriek of metal, and Ezra smashed the other end of his pole-arm in the second one's side. It jolted from the impact, its side dented in—but the dent did no more to stop it than decapitation had stopped the other golem.

Zak rammed his saber into the neck hole of the headless golem and sliced upward. It lunged into him, almost crushing him against the wall.

"Zak!" Aaron yelled as he dodged around the second one. "How do we kill these things?"

He and Ezra slammed their weapons into their golem from either side. It pivoted with far too much speed for a clumsy hunk of metal, its teeth snapping for Aaron's thigh. Ezra thrust his pole-arm into its mouth to save Aaron's leg. Steel teeth crunched down on his weapon and tore it from his grasp.

"There's an animation array somewhere inside it." A yellow wire—the same spell Zak had used to dangle a rogue off a building—spiraled out of his hand and wrapped around his golem's legs, halting its charge. It strained against the binding. "You have to destroy it!"

"I'm a mage," Aaron snarled, evading another charge. "Why the hell would I know what an animation array looks like?"

"Or you can just wait. The magic only lasts ten or twelve minutes in combat."

"Not helpful!"

Alone at the edge of the fight, I slammed my paintball gun into its holster. Useless. What else did I have? I shuffled through my pouches as Ezra ducked away, weaponless, and Aaron held Sharpie defensively, its blade useless against the steel-bodied golem. Zak was doing only slightly better, his golem immobilized as he sank his saber into a geared joint, disabling its foreleg.

Aaron's golem swung its huge head, Ezra's pole-arm stuck in its mouth, and rammed the pyromage off his feet. As it jumped on him, Ezra drove his steel-reinforced fist into the heavy brute, adding a blast of wind to knock it off its feet.

It slid half a foot with scarcely a wobble. Even Ezra's demonic strength wasn't enough, and he didn't have a proper weapon—

But I did. I had the perfect weapon for him.

I whipped my brass knuckles out of their pouch, drew my arm back, and shouted, "Ezra!"

He looked toward me, and I flung the brass knuckles. All my practice tossing potion balls finally paid off—the artifact flew in a beautiful arc and he caught it out of the air.

"Punch the golem again!" I yelled. "The incantation is *ori amplifico!*"

He shoved the brass knuckles on his hand as Aaron twisted, a clawed steel foot almost landing on him. The golem's paw hit the floor, cracking the concrete under the rug. Aaron was trapped, about to be crushed.

Air whooshed down the corridor.

"*Ori amplifico!*" Ezra shouted, wind forming around his hand, muscles bulging in his arm. His fist slammed into the golem's shoulder. The air boomed in a bone-breaking concussion. Steel split wide open under the impact and the golem crashed down on its side, almost crushing Aaron's ankle.

Its legs screeched against the floor, but its metal joints were too inflexible. It couldn't get up.

"Ezra, Zak, over here!" I rushed forward, pulling out my Queen of Spades. "Aaron, time to make it hot!"

"I can't *melt* them, Tori!" he shouted in exasperation, scrambling to his feet.

"You can make it hot enough to mess up the spell arrays, though!" I grabbed Zak's sleeve and dragged him away from his mechanical opponent. He snapped his golden spell away, and the golem staggered awkwardly on three working legs. The other golem was still waving its feet like a mindless robot. One foot caught on the floor and its body rocked.

Aaron raised his switch, pointing the blade at the ceiling. "Ready?"

I thrust the Queen of Spades out, Zak and Ezra safely behind me. "Ready!"

The metallic scent of ozone stung my nose. Shimmers of superheated air rippled over Aaron's sword, faint blue flames licking up the steel as it glowed.

He swung his sword down. A wall of blue and white fire exploded across the golems—and straight toward us.

"*Ori repercutio!*" I cried.

The air rippled and the fire rebounded into the golems. The inferno collided with itself, white sparks flying, the walls scorching black, the carpet igniting. The flames swirled wildly, heat blasting me, then shrank.

The golems reappeared. The one Ezra had knocked over, its split side glowing red from heat, no longer moved. The radiant markings over its body had disappeared. But the other, its extremities steaming with heat, creaked in an awkward half circle, its gaping neck hole pointed at Aaron.

A loud pop echoed from inside its body. I heard the splash of liquid, then sizzling. Steam poured out of the golem's joints, and a horrible burnt stench assaulted my nose.

The golem's glowing runes faded to darkness, and it went still.

Aaron lowered his sword. His half-melted vest barely clung to him, and his shirt was no more than a few blackened shreds.

"I hate golems," Zak muttered.

"Me too," I volunteered.

"Same here," Ezra agreed. "Aaron, did my pole-arm survive?"

Aaron tilted his head, then kicked at the golem's jaw. "Nope. Fused to its teeth." He peeled off the remains of his vest one-handed, then lifted his leather baldric off. It was blackened and the top had burned away. "Damn."

Ezra tossed me the brass knuckles. "Thanks, Tori."

"No problem."

Zak leaned over the unmoving golem, sniffing at the lingering odor. "What *is* that? Another potion?"

"It's blood."

Zak glanced questioningly at Aaron.

The pyromage shrugged. "Burning shit is my area of expertise. That smells like burnt blood. Mostly."

"Blood as part of a golem array?" Zak muttered. "That doesn't make any sense."

"Can we worry about it later?" I tucked the Queen of Spades and the brass knuckles back into their pouches. "I'd like to get the hell away from here in case more golems show up to—"

With a pale flash, Hoshi swept right through the nearest wall. As she whirled around me, an image filled my head: Kai, blood running down his face, skin smudged with soot, the flickering light of flames washing over him.

"Holy crap!" I yelped. "Lead the way, Hoshi!"

She zoomed ahead of me and I charged after her, leaving the guys in the dust.

"Tori!" Aaron sprinted after me. "Did Hoshi find Kai?"

"Yeah, and we need to hurry!"

I was so focused on running, so frantic to get to Kai, that I didn't immediately notice the building heat. When Hoshi stopped in front of a door with a push bar, I kept running—my brain too slow to realize Aaron was shouting at me to stop.

I rammed the door open—and fire exploded all around me.

Aaron tackled me to the floor, arms banded over me, body and magic shielding me from the heat. The wave of flames burst through the doorway in a roaring maelstrom before subsiding.

He pushed onto his hands and knees above me, and I raised my head.

Beyond the door was a huge, smoke-hazed room that occupied the curved end of the U-shaped floor. Windows filled the double-height walls, and probably offered a spectacular view of the harbor when the room wasn't filled with smoke. Fires burned across the remains of the furniture.

A silhouette appeared in the smoke, moving closer. A handkerchief was tied over his nose and mouth to filter the smoke.

"Who the hell are you?" he demanded in a deep voice.

Aaron shoved upward, unarmed—he must've dropped his sword so he wouldn't impale me. Fire rippled up his arms, and the other mythic lifted his hands in response, flames leaping from the floor to his palms.

Still sprawled on my stomach, I yanked out my paintball gun and pulled the trigger.

Yellow potion splattered across the mage's upper chest and neck. Shock widened his eyes, and he toppled backward, hitting the floor with a thud.

From the smoke behind him, three more silhouettes appeared—three strangers. Three enemies. I scrambled up, Aaron in front of me, Hoshi hovering above my head, Zak and Ezra crowding in the doorway behind me.

The air crackled.

Throwing stars flew out of the haze, firelight flickering over their shining edges. They struck the three rogues, and sizzling white power leaped out of the smoke, a branch of electricity slamming into each man. They convulsed from the shock and dropped to their knees with cries of pain.

The smoke swirled. Wind whipped through the room, bending the flames sideways and lifting the choking haze.

Makiko strode across the burning carpet, the fires in her path snuffing out before she reached them. She held a shiny metal fan in each hand, angled elegantly. Kai followed a step behind her, his face exactly as Hoshi had shown me, his clothes torn and splattered with blood, one sleeve charred off his arm.

Makiko's glare locked on the three rogues, on their knees from Kai's electric shock—but not for long. They were already recovering, fury and pain twisting their faces.

She stretched her arms out, then slashed with her fans. A rippling hiss of air.

The three rogues jerked, their heads snapping backward, then they pitched over, blood gushing from their sliced necks. They writhed helplessly, their blood sizzling on the carpet.

I stared, my lungs locked. She had ... she had slit their throats with *air*? I hereby retracted all thoughts I'd ever had of fighting the petite aeromage.

"*There* you are, Kai," Aaron announced, his voice carrying over the crackling flames. "We were looking for you."

Kai's eyes narrowed. "Why are you here?"

"Saving your ass."

"Gee, thanks."

"We do not require help," Makiko snapped. "We—"

Kai strode past her to Aaron. They clasped arms, then Kai and Ezra did the same. Lastly, the electramage caught me around the waist with his uninjured arm and pulled me against his side.

"Not what I meant when I said keep them under control, Tori," he muttered in my ear.

"Who's leading the attack?" Zak demanded impatiently. "Is Varvara here?"

Kai pulled away from me. "Varvara? The sorceress?"

"Who's leading the attack?" Zak asked again.

"No idea, but there aren't many mythic intruders left. Those *things*, on the other hand—"

The floor vibrated with heavy steps. A clanging racket grew louder—metal footsteps drawing closer.

"—are impossible to stop."

"Watch it!" Zak yelled.

Too late—a jet of green liquid shot out of the smoke, straight for us.

Makiko flicked her fan at the same time Ezra thrust out his hand. The double gust of wind blew the potion back at its source. It splashed across a new golem, drenching its head and back. The liquid bubbled, toxic steam pouring off it as it dissolved the golem's steel body.

With clanking steps, two more canine golems stomped out of the thickening smoke.

"Let's go!" Kai said sharply.

Hoshi swirled around my head, then flew back into the corridor we'd just left. Makiko went first, Kai behind her. The rest of us rushed into the wide hallway, and we sped back to the stairwell.

"Kai," Aaron called as we streamed down the stairs one by one. "Are there civilians in the building?"

"No," he answered, half a flight ahead of us. "It's mostly offices, closed for the night. We evacuated everyone else when the attack began."

"Our security alerted us before the rogues got far into the building," Makiko added. "Kai and I came back to look for any of our people who might have been left behind."

"And we ran into the golems," he finished. "My magic wasn't much use, and Makiko's was only slightly more effective."

"Well," I panted, my knees like jelly as I pounded downward, "the golems probably aren't too quick on the stairs, assuming they can follow us."

All of us were panting hard by the time we hit the last flight. Makiko jogged down, Kai a step behind her. I was almost keeping up, Aaron and Ezra trailing after me. Zak brought up the rear.

Reaching the landing first, Makiko shoved the door open. It swung wide at the same time a popping, sizzling sound erupted.

Wind gusted from Makiko's hands as fire blasted through the doorway. Orange flames boiled through the threshold as she held back the inferno, the heat thickening the air in the stairwell. Fire splattered the floor around her like burning oil, clinging to every surface it touched.

The flames began to die—and a steel head burst through the flickering orange.

The canine golem leaped through Makiko's magic and slammed into her. She flew backward, throwing her arms out to break her fall—but the stairs were too close. I sprang toward her, reaching desperately.

She landed on the steps with the sickening thud of bone against concrete.

"Makiko!" Kai cried hoarsely.

I crouched beside her, swearing under my breath. She wasn't moving, eyes closed, mouth slack. A trickle of blood ran along the dusty gray step under her head.

Kai crouched on her other side—and Aaron leaped over us. He landed with a thump in front of the golem as it opened its jaws, its front teeth broken like it'd recently lost a fistfight. As fire spouted from its throat, he extended his hand—and the orange flames died to nothing. Dark liquid that smelled vaguely of gasoline splattered all over him, the floor, and my legs, but Aaron had put out the fire.

That didn't do a thing to stop the golem, though.

Ezra and Zak sprang over us too, yellow magic glowing up the druid's arm. His wire spell shot out from his hand and tangled around the golem's legs.

"Get out of the stairwell!" he shouted.

Kai reached for Makiko. Before I could stop him—his arm was burned and bleeding—Ezra was there. He carefully lifted Makiko and sped toward the exit. I followed on Kai's heels, and we bolted into the open concourse.

Zak jogged after us a moment later, the yellow glow fading from his hand. The golem thundered after him.

Kai swore viciously. "That's the same one that roasted my arm half an hour ago. I can't believe it's still going."

"It isn't the same one." Zak ran to us, outpacing the golem. "They don't last that long. Let's get out of here."

"It has the same broken teeth," Kai barked angrily. "And we can't leave that thing to chase us out onto a public street."

"It isn't the same golem, not if you fought it thirty minutes ago. Golem magic—"

"Argue later!" I roared as the golem clattered after us at a full charge, burning liquid dripping from its steel jaws like nightmare drool. "It's coming!"

Teeth bared, Zak slid to a stop and whirled. Black wings lifted off his arms, and Lallakai's eagle form pulled out of his body. She shot upward with one sweep of her broad wings. Emerald eyes shining like backlit gemstones, she slashed her wings down a second time.

Darkness condensed out of nowhere and formed a tight orb around the golem. Its glowing runes shone dimly through the dense shadows as it continued its charge, unaffected. Zak didn't move as the golem barreled toward him.

The shadows deepened. The thunder of the golem's steps slowed. Slowed even more. The light of the runes dimmed.

Like a toy with dying batteries, the golem took a final clattering step, moving no faster than a snail. The final whisper of magic in its runes died, and the shadows lifted. The golem stood still and silent, its animation magic gone. Its toothy muzzle was less than three feet from Zak.

Lallakai drifted downward and sank into the druid's body once again.

"Shit," Aaron muttered. "Why didn't you bring the fae out before now?"

Zak rolled his shoulders. "She needs more room to work with than—"

"This chat can wait until later too," I growled irritably, knowing any exchange of words between the pyromage and druid was guaranteed to turn into an argument. "Kai, how is Makiko?"

Standing beside Ezra, Kai was holding her arm, his fingers pressed to her wrist. "Her pulse is steady, but she needs a healer as quickly as possible."

"Sanjana was at the guild when we left," I said, immediately recalling the hot toddy I'd made her earlier that night. "She'd just settled for a good long session with her textbooks, so she should still be there."

Kai nodded. "Let's go."

He and Ezra headed for the door. I looked between Aaron and Zak, who were—surprise, surprise—glaring at each other, and figured I'd better head off the explosion. Stepping between them, I took their elbows and steered them toward the exit.

Back to the guild, with a rogue druid and Kai's unconscious fiancée in tow. This would be *so* much fun.

18

AARON PULLED UP in front of the Crow and Hammer, parking at the curb instead of using the small rear lot. Squashed between Ezra and Zak in the back seat, I sat with my nose pinched between my finger and thumb.

"You guys stink," I declared. "Everyone stinks. It reeks of toxic smoke in here. Next time we enter a burning building, we're bringing a change of clothes."

"We didn't know it was burning until we got there," Ezra pointed out.

Aaron unbuckled his seat belt. "Next time, we'll just take our clothes off before we go in. I could've saved my vest and baldric."

Hmm. Stripping down for battle? It had my vote. I'd show a little skin to get an even better eyeful.

"Don't ever engage in combat while in the nude," Kai murmured from the front seat where he held Makiko. "Better to ruin clothes than ruin body parts."

Ezra made a thoughtful noise. "Speaking from experience?"

"I wasn't the naked one."

I leaned over the center console. "I have so many questions."

"Maybe later. Would someone open my door?"

Aaron and Ezra hastened out of the vehicle to help him. Zak, on my other side, was a bit slower; having been bowled over at least once by a magical tank on four legs, he was moving stiffly. I scooched out after him as Ezra got Kai's door, and he and Aaron lifted Makiko's limp form off his lap. She groaned faintly.

Zak stretched like every muscle hurt, then slid a vial off his belt. He pulled the cork and poured the gray liquid into his mouth.

"What's that?" I asked.

"Healing potion."

"You couldn't have given it to Makiko?"

"It reduces inflammation and pain. It doesn't fix concussions."

"You don't have a concussion potion?"

"I could make one, but it needs to simmer for about twelve hours."

"Never mind." I pointed at his face. "By the way, you can't go in the guild like that. We have witches."

They'd take one look at his freaky fae eyes and figure out all kinds of things about him that we didn't want anyone to know.

"I'm not going in your guild," he replied shortly.

"Yes, you are."

"No, he's not." Aaron tipped Makiko into Ezra's arms and pivoted to face us. "He can crawl back into whatever hole he came from."

I planted my hands on my hips. "He's already been seen, and it's way later now. There'll hardly be anyone left in the pub. Besides"—I raised my voice, speaking over their protests—"we need to combine our information about Varvara."

Zak scowled, which I took as agreement. Grumbling under his breath, he half turned away. Shadows swirled over him, then Lallakai's wings swept off his arms and her dark eagle form pulled out of his body. Her green stare raked me like blades before she faded from sight.

"Perfect." I rubbed my chilled hands together. "Let's get out of the cold!"

Ignoring Aaron's and Zak's matching scowls, Kai's eye roll, and Ezra's silent amusement, I marched to the guild door, threw it open, and breezed inside.

A wave of noise hit me like a slap to the face.

Pulling up short, I blinked. I blinked again. The guild hadn't emptied while we were gone. It had gotten busier. Thirty-five surprised faces turned my way, the noise level dying down—then those thirty-five pairs of eyes turned to the men coming in behind me.

I whirled around, intending to stop the guys from entering, but it was too late. They had walked in after me, and now we all stood on display for over half the guild—Ezra, smudged with soot and carrying an unconscious woman; Aaron, naked from the waist up with holes burned in his pants; Kai, blood down one side of his face and his arm blackened; and Zak, the bottom of his long coat shredded from golem teeth, still holding the potion vial he'd downed.

The nearest mythics swarmed us. A hundred jumbled questions flew our way, and I didn't know who was speaking.

"Whoa, shit! Are you hurt?"

"Who's the woman? Is she from the SeaDevils?"

"Where were you guys?"

"Do you need a healer? Sanjana is here."

"Did you come from the SeaDevils guild?"

Kai was saying something, his voice drowned out by others, then he swept into the crowd. Ezra followed right behind him with Makiko in his arms. Aaron started after them, waving at me and Zak to join him. Guild members hurriedly cleared a path for our rumpled, sooty group.

We traipsed upstairs to the large workroom, where we found the apprentice healer Sanjana, exactly where I'd last seen her: poring over medical textbooks for an upcoming test. On top of training in healing Arcana, she was a third-year med student. She instantly abandoned her work and had Kai lay Makiko across an empty table.

As Sanjana began her examination, her long, dark brown hair threatening to fall out of its loose bun, Sin stuck her head around the corner by the stairs.

"Hey," she called hesitantly. "Do you need help, Sanjana?"

The healer glanced up. "Do you have a burn salve? Can you apply it to Kai's arm? I'll get to him next, but it'll be a while." She squinted at us. "I assume there are no injuries beyond what I can see."

"Nope," Aaron confirmed. "We made it out relatively unscathed. Except for Makiko."

Sin heaved her alchemy case onto a free corner of the table, her curious gaze darting between Makiko and Zak. Kai turned away from his fiancée, and Sin blanched at the sight of the blood all over his face.

She recovered quickly. "Take off your shirt and I'll clean—"

"Cut it off him," Sanjana said without looking up. "You don't want to rupture any blisters. Aaron, can you get a healing kit from downstairs?"

"You got it."

Sin fetched scissors from the supply cupboard and snipped through Kai's shirt, revealing soot stains and pink burns all over his arm. Aaron returned a minute later with a huge medical kit. The guild always had supplies on hand for our healers so they didn't have to haul their personal kits around every day. Sanjana opened it and dug around.

Sitting Kai on a chair, Sin poured clear liquid on a white cloth and gently wiped the soot off his arm. "I was wondering where you'd all rushed off to earlier. How did you find out about the SeaDevils so fast?"

Me, Kai, Aaron, and Ezra gave her blank looks.

She frowned. "You *weren't* at the SeaDevils?"

"Why," I huffed, "does everyone keep bringing up the SeaDevils?"

"Because their guild was attacked an hour ago?"

We all stiffened.

"What?" Aaron demanded. "You mean like the Pandora Knights attack?"

Sin nodded as she uncapped a jar of white cream. "The SeaDevils' headquarters were destroyed. Lyndon said an Odin's Eye friend of his is claiming the building was completely leveled."

"Was anyone hurt?"

Her gaze dropped. "There were two mythics there and they … they were killed." She slathered cream over Kai's arm. "Some of our guys planned to go help, but the MPD issued a notice asking mythics to keep away for now because there were TV crews filming the fire."

I slumped in my chair. Another attack. Two mythics killed. Varvara wasn't messing around.

Silence fell over the room. As Sin wrapped gauze over Kai's arm, he watched his fiancée with a worried crease between his brows. Sanjana, biting her lip in concentration, was drawing directly on the table while Makiko lay prone on it like a beautiful, slightly scorched mannequin.

My gaze shifted to Zak. He sat on the edge of a nearby table, watching the healer with a "professional assessment" sort of air. His Arcana specialty was alchemy, but he dabbled in sorcery and healing, as I'd seen when he'd whipped up rattlesnake antivenin in thirty minutes. As a dedicated black-magic-wielding rogue with no social life, he probably had lots of free time to advance his skills.

My attention slid past Zak to a table even farther from the rest of us. Ezra leaned against it, his arms folded as he gazed absently at nothing. I remembered Kai's words on our flight to LA. *He's been quiet lately.*

Ezra *had* been quiet. Withdrawn. His deadpan humor had been noticeably absent, his smiles reserved, the sparkle in his eyes half-hearted at best. I couldn't imagine how he'd gone so long pretending everything was fine, but the future was weighing on him too heavily now for him to hide it—or maybe I was only now noticing the true weight he carried. Either way, his time was running out.

Pushing to my feet, I announced, "I need a shower. Later."

I felt my friends' attention on me, but I strode determinedly to the stairs. Rushing down them, I paused at the bottom to take in the number of guildeds filling the pub, drawn here by the attack on the SeaDevils. Over half our combat mythics, already in their gear, waited for the MPD's permission to get out there and start tracking down the culprits, and the rest were here because the company of their guildmates eased their disquiet over the attack.

How I wanted to slip in among them and let the conversation and camaraderie ease my discomfort too.

Instead, I wheeled around the corner to the door, hidden behind the upper staircase, that led into the basement. The lower level was abandoned, the exercise equipment waiting patiently for tomorrow's morning workout. Movie posters covered the walls, a glaring mishmash of colors that brightened the space.

I took a long shower, the falling water echoing off the tiled walls. As I massaged conditioner into my curls, my thoughts spun and anxiety poured into my poor stressed stomach. Kai and Makiko and his family. Zak and Lallakai and his stolen grimoire. Ezra and Eterran and the full moon only a few days away.

Then there was Varvara and her schemes. Two attacks in one night. Those terrifying golems. An unknown number of rogues. What exactly was her goal? A city-wide takeover? Did she want to run the guilds out so she could reign unopposed?

I splashed water over my face, eyes squeezed shut. A vision flashed in my head: the Death card, its dark reaper holding a bloody scythe, and Sabrina's quiet voice, her warning.

I think you need to tell him soon.

Shivering under the hot spray, I hurriedly finished my shower. I dried off and dressed in yoga pants and a sweatshirt from my locker, then dealt with my hair—back into a bun. Just before shutting my locker door, I touched the buckle of my combat belt. Hoshi's pouch was empty; she must've been off in fae land.

I'd come so far from the girl whose first weapon had been an umbrella, but I still wasn't strong enough. At this rate, I would lose all of them—Ezra, Kai, Zak. It'd just be me and Aaron left, and we'd both be miserable.

Rubbing a hand over my eyes, I shut my locker and wrinkled my nose at my smoky clothing, lying in a heap on the bench in front of the lockers. Yuck. I kicked them down to the end of the bench to deal with later. My pants fell onto the floor, and something colorful peeked out of the pocket.

Stooping, I picked up the small folded square. The deep purple fabric was soft, supple, and strangely heavy. The Carapace of Valdurna. Even at the cost of its user's magic, it seemed like a tool that could solve any problem. Invincibility! What mythic couldn't use that from time to time?

But I got why Zak didn't care for the Carapace. Invincible, but magic-less. Invincible, but useless. Invincibility couldn't save Ezra, Kai, or Zak. Keeping them alive wasn't strictly the problem. I needed to save Ezra's mind and soul, Kai's freedom, and Zak's … I wasn't sure what Zak needed, but he definitely needed some kind of help.

Sighing, I stuffed the Carapace in my pocket to return to Zak and pushed through the door into the workout room. The muffled clatter of a locker brought me up short. I paused, squinting at the door to the men's showers.

Another clatter, then Ezra appeared, his damp curls brushed back from his face as though he'd combed his fingers through them. He'd changed into a t-shirt and sweats, his baldric gone—which made sense, seeing as he no longer had a weapon for it to hold.

My stomach flip-flopped strangely. "Hey. Showered too?"

"Yeah." He smiled but it didn't reach his eyes. "Without you to babysit them, Aaron and Zak started a new glaring contest. It was getting on my nerves."

Since I wasn't all that eager to go give them shit for acting like twelve-year-olds, I dropped onto a weight-lifting bench, the leather giving off the faint smell of sanitizer.

"I don't know what to do about Zak," I muttered. "He's not a bad guy, but ..."

Ezra sank onto the bench beside me. "That's an ominous 'but.'"

I bit my lip. I hadn't told anyone what I'd witnessed on that rooftop, and I didn't know why. It wasn't that I was protecting Zak. I just couldn't seem to bring it up—but maybe I needed to.

"When we got back in town last night, he ran a rogue onto a rooftop, questioned the guy, then ..." I swallowed back my stomach, hearing the sound all over again. "Then dropped him off the building."

Ezra sucked in a sharp breath.

"I didn't think he'd do it." I wrung my hands together. "I mean, it crossed my mind, but I didn't believe he'd go that far. If I'd thought ... maybe I could've stopped him."

"It isn't your fault, Tori."

"But I was right there. I should've ... I should've realized ..."

He slid his warm arm around my waist and drew me against his side. "You couldn't have guessed what he was planning, and I don't think you could have stopped him even if you had."

My gut swooped in a sickening way. What would Zak have done if I *had* tried to save that man's life?

"He was annoyed ..." The words came slowly, the realization blossoming as I spoke. "When he realized I'd seen the whole thing, he was annoyed ... and when he noticed I was upset, he got angry at me."

Ezra studied the floor, his gaze distant. "When you take a life, which is worse? Feeling tormented over it, or being at peace with it because you believe it was the only option?"

A shudder ran through me. Twice I'd killed a person, and both times there'd been no other option. Aaron, Kai, and Ezra had all talked to me about it, checking every few weeks that I was okay. And I was, mostly. Nightmares were a thing, but not every night. Guilt was a thing, but not all the time.

I tried to imagine pushing that witch to his death and feeling only steady assurance that killing the man had been necessary.

"What do you feel?" I mumbled. "Are you at peace with the lives you've taken?"

His arm tightened around me. "No. Never."

How many times had he killed to protect his secrets? To prolong his life even though he believed he'd die in a few years anyway? I didn't know. He almost never talked about his past—just like me.

My mouth popped open. I stared sightlessly, mentally smacking myself in the forehead.

Just. Like. Me. I never talked about my past. I wanted to know Ezra's whole story, the nightmare tale about how he'd become a demon mage, what Enright was, and how'd he escaped the "extermination"—but aside from a few vague comments, I'd never told him anything about my own ugly history.

Sweat broke out on my forehead. I couldn't do it. I couldn't expose that part of me to anyone. I couldn't …

But this was Ezra.

"My dad was a drunk," I blurted.

His head snapped up, confusion and surprise scrunching his forehead. I took one panicked look at his face and squeezed my eyes shut.

"He was a drunk. He hit my mom. She couldn't take it and she left. She said … The last night, she said she couldn't do it anymore and she cried, and she told Justin to take care of me, and she said Dad would never hit his kids so we'd be okay. And she left."

"Tori …" Ezra whispered.

"A week later, he hit Justin for the first time. He—he just had to hit someone, I guess." My mouth trembled. "But Justin wasn't my mom. He was twelve then, almost thirteen, and he didn't take it lying down. So my dad hit him harder. By the time Justin turned fifteen, we—we were afraid he'd kill Justin. And Justin … it was the same as with Mom. He came to my room one night, and he said he had to go. And I told him to go. And we cried, and he left."

Ezra wrapped his arms around me, pulling me close. I struggled to breathe, eyes still closed.

"That …" I cleared my throat in a vain attempt to reset my voice from the hoarse quaver it had become. "That's all I've got for today."

A long pause. "I don't understand."

I opened my eyes, proud that they were tear-free, and offered him a wobbly smile. "It's really difficult for me to talk about, and I can't—if I talk about it for more than sixty seconds, it's like going back in time. I can't do it."

He pulled me onto his lap and banded his arms around my shoulders, holding me tight against his chest. I snaked my arms around his neck and buried my face in his chest.

"You don't have to tell me," he whispered into my hair. "You don't have to relive it for me."

"I know." I inhaled his calming scent. "I want to. It's just going to take me a while."

He gently caressed the back of my neck. "Okay. But Tori? Can I ask … why now?"

"It just seemed fair. You told me some stuff, but I haven't told you anything."

"Yes, but why *now*? This particular minute?"

I shrugged, face still buried in his chest. "Because I thought of it right now."

A moment of surprised silence, then a quiet chuckle. "Okay."

"Okay what?"

"That makes sense in a very Tori way."

"What does that mean?" I grumped.

He tightened his arms around me. "It's fine. I enjoy a bit of unpredictability to spice up my boring life."

I straightened—which put us nose to nose. I was sitting on his lap, my legs hanging off the back of the padded bench.

"You should put yourself out there more," I told him seriously. "Take more risks. Have more adventures."

"I do play it safe," he agreed so somberly I wasn't sure if he was serious or not.

"Live life to its fullest," I said in my best inspirational-speaker voice. "Take the bull by the horns. Seize the day. *Carpe diem!*"

The corner of his mouth twitched.

"You should be more like me," I decided loftily. "I know how to have a good time."

His lips pressed tight together.

"I mean, if you've never broken a mythic's face with an umbrella, are you even living?"

He made a strangled sound in his throat—then a snorting laugh broke through his control.

"Aha!" I crowed, throwing my hands into the air. "You laughed first! I win!"

He caught my waist before I could topple backward off his lap with my exuberant celebration.

Laughing, I looped my arms around his neck. "Admit it. I won."

His eyes met mine, strangely serious even as they sparkled with mirth. "You're too stubborn to lose."

My fingers tangled in his damp hair as I leaned in. "Damn right."

His gaze drifted to my mouth—and I was already closing the distance. Our lips met.

I kissed him slowly, savoring every feeling: his mouth, soft and firm; his scruff against my chin; the rush of his escaping breath; his heavenly scent, the nameless ambrosia I couldn't get enough of. Everything about him wrapped around me, a warm cocoon that blocked out the world.

My lips drifted across his, then I pulled back. Every atom of my being demanded I keep kissing him, but I shoved it all aside. This wasn't about me.

"Ezra, is this okay? You said you want to be friends, and if that's what you want, I can ..." My nose scrunched. "I can do that, I swear. I can just be your friend."

I ignored the ridiculousness of that statement while I was straddling his lap, hands tangled in his hair, moments after kissing him.

He brushed his thumb across my cheek as sorrow darkened his eyes. "I don't want to cause you more pain."

Telling him I'd find a way to save him wouldn't change his mind about anything, so I said, "I can handle it."

"Maybe … but I'm not sure I can."

My heart twisted. I blew out a long breath. "I understand. Do you want me to get off you?"

He stared at me, then shut his eyes with a muttered curse.

"Is that a … no?"

"I don't know."

He didn't open his eyes, probably hoping a lack of visual stimulation would bolster his willpower—though he hadn't moved his hand from my neck, which told me his strategy wasn't working in the slightest. Sympathy welled in me. This wasn't fair to him. He was trying to do the right thing for me, and I wasn't making it easy for him.

Besides, since I was going to save him anyway, I could wait. Patience was my middle name.

Actually, no, it wasn't. Not even close. But I could still be patient.

I dragged one leg off the bench, shifting backward so I could slide off his lap. His eyes flew open, and I smiled reassuringly as I withdrew my hands from his hair. I pushed to my feet—

His hand tightened on the back of my neck, and he pulled my mouth down onto his.

My stomach did a free-falling somersault. My hands were back on him in an instant, my lips crushed to his, lungs empty and heart racing. He grabbed my waistband and dragged me back onto his lap. I clamped my arms around him, erasing the space between our bodies. His hands found my hips, fingers digging in, holding me down in the absolute sexiest way possible.

"Goddamn it, Ezra," I groaned against his mouth.

"Sorry," he breathed. "I—"

I covered his mouth with mine before he could talk either of us into separating again. His tongue slipped between my lips and I moaned softly. Resisting him was a losing battle. Totally futile. What was the point?

I needed him so badly it hurt to breathe.

Pulling back, the air cold on my lips, I looked into his mismatched eyes. My mouth opened, terrifying words building up in my throat, fighting to escape, but I wasn't sure I could say them. I should. I needed to. But—

Ezra's brow scrunched—and his head jerked to the left. I looked in the same direction.

Oh shit.

Oh shit, oh shit, oh shiiiiit.

Kai stood three steps away, arms crossed over his bare chest, one dark eyebrow arched.

19

I SQUINTED CRITICALLY at my reflection. Combat belt over fitted leather pants. Snug-fitting top with a leather jacket over it, discreetly padded for extra protection. Heavy black hiking boots with steel toes. My red curls, gently tamed with hair product, fell around my shoulders, and I'd applied just enough makeup to not look like a pasty corpse with all the black I was wearing.

With a flash of silver, Hoshi swirled down from the ceiling, blinking her huge pink eyes.

"How do I look?" I asked her. "Would you believe I'm an experienced combat mythic on the trail of a dangerous rogue?"

She chuffed softly and bumped her nose into my shoulder. Colors flickered through my head, along with an image of my face. Was that a yes?

Dipping down, she pushed her head into the pouch on the back of my belt. She slid into the pocket, coiling her body into a tight orb with blue and pink ridges. Weird, but cool.

Relieved that she was coming with me, I grabbed my plain brown folder off the counter, pushed open the bathroom door, and walked into the pub. It was another busy evening, the Saturday dinner rush worse than usual. Everyone was buzzing over the inexplicable attack on the Pandora Knights two days ago, and the SeaDevils last night.

Cooper rushed around behind the bar, his greasy hair sticking to his face. Sliding a drink to Bryce, he spotted me on my way by.

"It's busy," he said accusingly, as though I'd invited all these people to make him work harder. I hadn't, but it was a good idea. I made a mental note to try that on his next shift.

"You're here," he added, slapping a cloth down on the bar. "You should take over. Saturdays are your night."

"But you wanted last Sunday off, remember? We traded shifts." I gave him my best shark smile. "So suck it up, buttercup."

"I covered for you last night too, and—"

"And I'll make it up to you, but not tonight. I have plans." I waved cheerily as I walked away, enjoying his hot glare on my back. Cooper took slacking to a whole new level, and I found perverse enjoyment in forcing him to work hard.

After way too much chaos in too short a time, last night had ended on a quiet note. Zak, Aaron, Ezra, and Kai had shared their thoughts on what had happened, but no one had a clear idea on what to do next. Finding Varvara was our top priority, but she was one hell of a slippery snake.

After agreeing to keep me in the loop on his tracking efforts, Zak had skulked off into the cold night. Shortly after, Kai—his arm healed of burns—had carried Makiko outside, where a black sedan had mysteriously appeared to pick them up. He'd promised to contact us within a day or two, once he found out what the Miura clan intended to do about Varvara.

I wished he was with us, but a teeny part of me was relieved he wasn't around. After catching me and Ezra making out, he walked into the showers without a word—but for the rest of the evening, he'd given us all sorts of looks, ranging from annoyed to thoughtful to concerned. It worried me that he hadn't said anything.

Pushing it out of my mind, I wove through the tables, calling hellos to everyone who greeted me and scanning for a less familiar face.

Robin had found the loneliest, most shadowy corner in the pub. Perched nervously on the edge of her chair, she stared into her glass of water like it held all the secrets of Demonica in its shallow depths.

"Hey," I said as I tucked in a chair someone had left two feet away from its table. Lazy butts messing up my pub. I needed to crack down on that shit.

Looking up at my greeting, Robin smiled weakly. She seemed pale. Or was she always pale? I didn't know.

Pursing my lips, I scanned her from head to toe, then grinned. "Nice jacket."

She tugged anxiously at a black sleeve. The leather hugged her petite body, the aggressive cut to the collar paired with bold silver buttons and a heavy zipper. She looked ready to jump on a motorcycle and tear off into the night.

Blushing, she nudged her glasses up her nose—the fussy gesture ruining her badass biker chick look entirely. "Do I look completely ridiculous? Zora said leather is better."

"Better for combat?" I slapped a hand against my leather-clad hip. "Yup, sure is. Not that I'm an expert. I only started training a couple months ago."

"You're new at this too?"

"Yeah, I'm a newb. Ready to go? Where are we going, by the way?"

Hopping to her feet and pushing her chair in—winning an extra point from me—she headed for the door. "It's not too far, but it'll be half an hour whether we bus or walk. Which do you prefer?"

"Walk," I decided as we walked out into the chilly evening breeze. "I hate standing around."

She navigated east to Main Street, checked her phone, then headed south. I matched her short stride, chafing at the pace. She wasn't exactly speedy.

"So," I began as we passed Victorian-style buildings in muted colors. Barren trees, interspersed with red lampposts, bordered the sidewalk. "Tell me about this infernus maker."

"I don't know much about him, to be honest. He was an accomplished summoner until he retired fifteen years ago. Now he makes infernus artifacts, but he's supposed to be well connected in the Demonica community."

We stopped at a crosswalk and waited for the light to change. The streetlamps glowed cheerily, relegating the darkness to alleyways.

"According to a rumor," Robin continued, lowering her voice as more pedestrians joined us to wait for the light, "he was ... cutting edge ... when he was a summoner, and he's still very interested in new summoning practices and unusual Demonica knowledge."

That sounded promising. I almost asked Robin what unusual knowledge she was hoping to gain, but then she'd ask me the same thing and that'd be awkward. Tucking my folder against my side, I asked instead, "If this guy doesn't pan out, who else might have useful information?"

"Um, well, Demonica isn't a common class to begin with, and summoners are even rarer. It requires a lot of study, and summoning demons is quite tedious ... and dangerous."

"Tedious *and* dangerous? Those two don't usually go together."

"It's dangerous when it goes wrong, and tedious when it goes right. Just setting up a summoning circle can take weeks, and you often have to wait weeks more for the demon to accept a contract."

"How did you become a contractor?" I asked curiously.

"I ... fell into it, I guess. Most of my family are Demonica mythics."

Her family? Demonica wasn't hereditary—you couldn't inherit a demon, as far as I knew—but if summoners preferred to pass their knowledge directly to an apprentice, like Zak had said, it made sense to turn it into a family business.

We continued down Main Street, the stores gradually morphing into the colorful shops of Chinatown. I glanced down the road where I'd once ordered sushi with Sin before Red Rum rogues attacked us and I sicced a sea fae on them. Fun times.

"We're halfway back to my place," I said dryly. "I should've asked where we were headed before meeting at the guild."

"Oh." Robin flushed. "I'm sorry. I thought this would be easier."

She led me across the street and away from the friendly shops. Blocky commercial buildings took over, and raised SkyTrain tracks on thick concrete pillars ran down the center of the wide road. Traffic diminished noticeably.

"Um, so ..." Robin's blue eyes flicked across my face. "How long have you been friends with Aaron and Kai and Ezra?"

"Since my first day at the guild, pretty much." I studied the self-conscious way her shoulders had hunched and smirked. "Aaron is single."

Her head jerked up. "What?"

"I know he's giving you the cold shoulder, but he's actually a really great guy."

She bristled like an angry cat. "I'm not interested. Why does everyone assume I want to date them? Just because they're good looking? Ridiculous."

Who was *everyone*? Had someone else tried to set her up with Aaron?

She continued for half a block in moody silence, then puffed out a breath. "I was wondering … about Ezra."

Now it was my turn to bristle. "What about him?"

"He seems nice."

"He *is* nice."

"He's an aeromage?"

"Yeah."

"Is he strong?"

I worked to keep my tone casual. "Not as strong as Aaron and Kai, but pretty tough."

"Hmm." She slowed as we came to an intersection and pulled out her phone to check the directions on the screen, then turned onto a narrow side street. "What happened to his eye?"

"Skiing accident. Ran into an unexpectedly aggressive pine tree."

Frowning, she let the subject drop.

At the end of the block, a wide set of train tracks behind a chain-link fence forced us to turn again. We headed farther east—and farther from the main road. I glanced uneasily from the fenced-off tracks to the dark, very closed car dealership opposite. No sign of life or movement disturbed the quiet rumble of traffic from busier streets I could no longer see, and the sparse light of the streetlamps offered little comfort.

"Hey," I muttered. "You sure this is the right way?"

She nodded. "Yes, very sure."

"Maybe we should've taken a cab," I grumbled.

"Oh, don't worry." She smiled with unexpected confidence. "We're safe."

I raised my eyebrows. "I could probably take on *one* mugger, but—"

"We don't have to take on any muggers. My demon can protect us."

Huh. When she put it that way …

We passed several blank-faced warehouses, a dirt yard with shipping containers and empty flatbeds, abandoned parking lots waiting for Monday morning's workers, and a recycling depot with semi-truck trailers docked at the loading bays.

"Here," she said breathlessly, her cheeks pink from the cold. "This is it."

At the very end of the street was a two-story building with a garish blue roof. Thick blinds covered the windows, but light shone through the frosted glass door. Looked like someone was working late tonight.

We passed a handful of cars in the small parking lot and approached the door. A symbol composed of three interlocking triangles with a stylized eye in the center was stamped across the glass in black, and underneath was the business's name.

ODIN'S EYE
PRIVATE SECURITY SERVICES

I stopped dead. "Whoa, whoa, whoa. Is this *Odin's Eye?* As in *the guild?*"

Robin looked over her shoulder, already reaching for the door. "Didn't I say that?"

"No."

"I thought I told you that the infernus maker is an Odin's Eye member? And his main role is Demonica consultation?"

"You did not mention that. At all."

"Oh. I … um … sorry."

I shook my head. "Well, we're here now. Let's do this."

We entered a warm lobby. Four plush leather chairs waited on either side of the door, guiding visitors toward a long reception desk with two monitors and a comfy-looking manager's chair, currently empty. A pair of doors led off each side of the room.

A white sign on the desk directed new arrivals to ring the bell. Robin minced up to the desk, peered at the button like it might bite her, then tapped it. Somewhere deeper in the building, an annoying buzzer sounded.

I glanced around, kind of impressed. The MPD required guilds to masquerade as legitimate businesses so the comings and goings of their members wouldn't draw suspicion, but I suspected Odin's Eye entertained actual clients here—mythic ones. Unlike the Crow and Hammer, which only dabbled in bounty hunting, Odin's Eye was a fully bounty-focused guild. No slackers allowed.

"Is anyone coming?" Robin mumbled, wringing her hands.

"Are they expecting us?"

"Well … no." Her small nose wrinkled. "I was worried that any advance warning would make it easier for him to avoid us."

"Fair point. Let's find out who's home, shall we?"

Grinning, I hammered on the button. The buzzer blared in short, ear-assaulting bursts. Six buzzes later, the door to my left flew open and a stocky man with short black hair and tawny skin stormed through, glaring furiously.

"Who the hell—" He broke off with a blink. "Tori?"

"Hey Mario. What's up?"

A grin replaced his scowl. "What brings you out here? I can't remember the last time a Hammer came 'round to our guild."

"Because my guild has a charming pub and the world's best bartender," I teased in a lofty tone. "What've you got?"

"Hey, we've got our own perks. You here to see Izzah? Their meeting already started, but I can take you back there."

"Uh, no, I'm actually here to see …" I trailed off with a significant look at Robin.

She was gazing between me and Mario with her mouth hanging open. At my look, she snapped to attention. "Is Naim Ashraf in?"

"Naim? Yeah, he's here." Eyebrows high with curiosity, Mario waved at us to follow him. "Come on."

Robin rushed to my side as I started after him through the door and into a hallway.

"You know people here?" she whispered in amazement.

"Yeah, they've been at the guild half a dozen times in the last few weeks." I nudged her with my elbow. "Hang out with us more and you'll get to meet people too."

Her shoulders drooped sadly—and I remembered Aaron's and Kai's cold glares when she'd tried to talk to me earlier this week. Maybe she didn't feel welcome enough to hang out at the guild. And maybe I should do something about that.

I'd add it to my to-do list for the week. Investigate guild bullying, save Ezra from his demon, end Kai's unwanted betrothal, defeat an evil sorceress before she destroyed the city while also recovering Zak's stolen grimoire, and order more limes because the last batch had gone off.

No problem at all.

The main level of Odin's Eye was set up like a typical small business, with a mixture of offices and a large central room with desks. Mario led us to the stairwell, and we headed up to the second floor.

"Oooh," I murmured as we walked through the door. "Nice."

Mario grinned.

Where the Crow and Hammer's second floor was all work and no play, Odin's Eye had combined the two. A huge wood-burning fireplace dominated a stone wall, and grouped around it were comfy leather chairs and low tables. Other clusters of furniture dotted the space—padded wooden chairs, stools, plush sofas, and lightweight worktables. A section of bookshelves and what looked like a self-serve bar and mini kitchen filled the back wall. One glass-fronted fridge held snacks and goodies with labels from several delicious Gastown cafes and bakeries, and a second one was stacked with every form of bottled or canned drink I could think of.

Two guild members were lounging by the fireplace, while three sat at a table, scrutinizing some papers. A sixth man was slouched in a recliner near the kitchen, a lamp glowing beside him and his nose buried in a leather-bound book thick enough to sink a boat. An air of "disreputable old man" hung around him like a cloud.

Of course, that was the guy Mario headed for.

Robin trailed after me as we swooped down on Naim Ashraf. His shaggy hair and frizzy beard were snowy white, a sharp contrast to his dark chestnut skin. Fine wrinkles around his eyes deepened as he glanced up from his book.

"Naim, you've got visitors." Mario clapped me on the shoulder. "Grab me when you're done and I'll make you a Caesar—my own recipe."

"Uh-oh. Not sure I like the sound of that."

Chuckling, he joined the three mythics at the table with all the papers and bent over their work.

"Who're you two?" Naim demanded in a sharp, vaguely nasal voice.

Wow, we had a polite one here.

"Can we ask you a few Demonica questions?" I inquired in my most professional voice. "We'll keep it quick."

He grunted. "Dunno what Mario told you, but I don't consult outside my guild."

"It won't take long."

"Doesn't matter." He lifted a rocks glass off the table beside his recliner and sipped the amber liquid filling the bottom third. "Go ask the Grand Grimoire if you need help."

"The Grand Grimoire has contractors." Robin's soft alto surprised me as she inched closer. "But MagiPol arrested their guild master and they don't have any other summoners—especially not ones with your experience and reputation for rare knowledge."

Ooh, the flattery approach. Nicely done, Robin. I'd been about to tell him he was an intractable buffoon who'd die alone.

Unfortunately, Naim didn't take the bait. "I'm not wasting my time explaining the basics of Demonica to little girls. My scotch is older than you two, now leave me to drink it in peace."

As he returned his attention to his monstrous book—which appeared to be written in Latin—I gritted my teeth. Cantankerous old geezer.

Robin slipped past me. Too short to tower over him—even though he was seated and she was standing—she got aggressively close. Liking this approach, I shifted closer as well.

"I don't need help with the basics." Tugging the zipper of her jacket down, she pulled out her infernus and settled it on her chest. "And if you're half the summoner I think you are, I shouldn't need to explain more than this."

Naim's jaw dropped. Gaze locked on her infernus, he shoved the super-tome onto the table, almost knocking his scotch off, and reached for her infernus. She stepped backward just before his fingers touched the silver disc.

I glanced curiously at her infernus. Runes edged the pendant, and in the center was a spiky, asymmetrical symbol. A vague sense of familiarity pinged in my head.

Sudden suspicion twitched Naim's beard. "It's a fake. No way a girl like you—"

Robin tapped her infernus. Deep red magic swirled across it, twisting over and around her fingers.

"Real?" he gasped. "Then you must be Robin Page! I heard rumors that a new House had finally appeared after all these years, but I couldn't believe it. Your demon can only be the lost First House. Unless—" Lustful hope burned in his face. "Unless it's the fabled Twelfth House?"

She sat on the coffee table in front of his recliner. "We can discuss my demon after Tori and I ask a few questions, if that's okay."

I blinked again. Her tone said all too clearly that he'd better be okay with it, because that was the only option. Damn. Aaron and Kai had been right. This girl wasn't the pushover I'd assumed.

Naim clasped his hands together, still greedily eyeing her infernus. "What would you like to know?"

Clutching my folder, I sat beside Robin. She glanced at me questioningly, and I nodded that she could go first. This was her party more than mine—but I was getting answers too.

"I'm researching an artifact." She slid a folded paper out of her pocket. "I believe it's an ancient infernus, and since you're an infernus maker ..."

He nodded, looking intrigued.

She unfolded the crisp white paper and carefully smoothed it, revealing a precise drawing of a round medallion. Runes formed a ring around the outer edge, similar to her infernus, but these ones were spiky and twisted. A second ring of larger shapes encircled a center symbol.

At the sight of that drawing, the floor dropped out from under me. My lungs locked, muscles going rigid, every atom of my being freezing in place so I didn't react.

Two things about that drawing had just blown my composure out of the water. First, the symbol in the center—it was the same as the one on Robin's infernus. That's why it had seemed familiar. Second, and the big reason I suddenly couldn't breathe: I'd seen that medallion before.

It was the demonic amulet.

The one I'd stolen from the winged demon's corpse after Robin's demon had killed it. The one I'd used to free Burke's demon from its contract. The one Eterran desperately wanted.

She was holding a drawing of the mysterious amulet I was currently attempting to research so I could use it to save Ezra's life and soul.

20

OH SHIT.

Those two words spun around and around in my head, and it was all I could do to sit still. A good half of my brain wanted me to leap to my feet with a shocked screech while pointing dramatically at her drawing.

Which, of course, I didn't do. But damn.

Robin was searching for the amulet I'd stolen. Her demon had killed the winged one who'd been carrying it. Was that why she'd shown up in the park? Had she been hunting that demon just to get the amulet? Did she know its power?

Were the answers I needed this close?

Oblivious to my internal freak-out, Naim frowned at the drawing. "These sigils"—he pointed to the middle ring—"are House emblems. I recognize most of them." His lips moved as he counted. "Eleven sigils … with a twelfth in the center. This represents *all twelve demon Houses*."

He snatched at the drawing but Robin lifted it out of reach. "Have you ever seen or heard of an infernus like this?"

"Is it an infernus?" he breathed, gaze darting between the drawing and her silver pendant. "Where did you learn about this? Where did you get your demon? Your demon *must* be the first House. The same sigil is in the center of the design."

"You haven't answered my question," she replied coolly.

"I've never seen an artifact like that before. But if you give me the drawing, I can certainly look into—"

She folded the paper and tucked it back into her pocket. "Tori? You had questions?"

I snapped out of my daze. "Uh. Questions. Right."

My brain whirred like a truck spinning its wheels. I was here to ask about the same thing as Robin, but how was I supposed to do that now? It would look damn suspicious.

Good thing I'd prepared a cover story—one that allowed me to tackle two birds with one stone. After my conversation with Zak about Ezra's fate, I'd decided that the demon amulet wasn't the only thing I needed more information on.

I flipped my folder open. "I'm investigating a series of unsolved bounties on demon mages."

Naim's expression turned sullen as he squinted at my stack of printouts from the MPD database—cold cases from across the west coast spanning the last twenty years. I'd printed everything that mentioned a demon summoner.

"Certain sources and witnesses," I went on, trying to sound pompous and official, "have suggested a summoner is creating demon mages using an artifact imbued with demon magic. What do you know about demonic artifacts?"

"I've never created a demon mage," Naim replied flatly. "I don't know how it's done, or if it requires artifacts."

"Yes, of course. I'm just looking for information." I shuffled through my papers in a purposeful way. Robin watched curiously as I flipped past several pages with black and white photos of blurry-faced men. "You don't know any—"

She inhaled sharply.

I glanced at her. She jerked her gaze up—away from my folder. "S-sorry," she stammered, her face white. "Go on."

The page she'd been looking at featured a grainy photo, taken with a zoom lens, of two men talking. One face was clear, the other in profile. I had no idea what the photo was; I'd just printed a bunch of cases.

Clearing my throat, I refocused on Naim. "You don't know *anything* about how demon mages are created? I thought you were a big-shot Demonica expert."

He rubbed his hands together nervously. "Demon-mage creation is so rare, and the summoners who engage in it are so secretive, that there's no standard procedure. Every demon-mage summoner has their own method. If you want to know anything about how a particular demon mage was made or if the summoner used an artifact, you'd have to ask the summoner directly."

"Like they'd talk to me."

"Precisely. That's why no one knows. I've heard MagiPol doesn't even know how it's done."

"What *can* you tell me?"

He studied me with dark, cold eyes. "In regular summoning, the demon is summoned into a circle, the boundary of which is impenetrable to the demon. In demon-mage creation, the demon is summoned into a human body."

Robin made a small, horrified sound.

"The human body—or, some say, their soul—is the cage that traps the demon. It will either assimilate into its host or keep fighting to escape until it kills the fool that offered himself up for the ritual. When the human dies, so does the demon."

"That's horrible," Robin whispered, pressing her fingers to her mouth.

"Wait." Chills ran down my limbs. "If the demon is summoned right into the human, is there even a contract? Or is the demon simply trapped and it just … goes along with everything so it doesn't die?"

"I assume there's a contract, or at least binding magic involved." He shrugged. "As I said, if you want specifics, you need the summoner. No two demon mages are exactly the same—though they all meet the same end."

Shuddering at the reminder, I snapped my folder shut. "'Kay, well, thanks for nothing."

His mouth twisted and he dismissed me with a jerk of his chin. His attention returned to Robin. "Now, girl, where did you get your demon?"

Robin rose to her feet. "If you learn anything about the artifact I'm interested in, or the demonic artifacts Tori asked about, let us know. You can reach us through the Crow and Hammer."

"Wait—you agreed to tell me if I answered your questions!"

"You didn't have any answers, did you? I expected more from a so-called expert."

Oh, burn. I mentally cheered her on as she gave him an even more coldly dismissive glance than he'd given me, then stepped around the coffee table. I hopped up and strode after her, leaving the ex-summoner spluttering in his recliner.

Robin marched across the room to the door and pushed it open. I followed her into the stairwell, bummed to see that Mario and his pals had left while we'd been talking to Naim. So much for my Mario-original Caesar.

The moment the stairwell door closed behind us, Robin deflated like a punctured balloon.

"Was I too rude?" she asked in a small voice. "I should've been nicer. He was sort of helpful. I shouldn't have—"

"That was perfect." I grinned. "He was a dick. You're one tough cookie, Robin."

She blinked. "Me?"

"You didn't let him intimidate you for a second."

She blinked again. "Was he intimidating?"

"Kind of, yeah. But still." My gaze flicked to the pocket where she'd tucked her drawing of the demonic artifact. I opened my mouth—then closed it again.

If she wanted the amulet, and I revealed I had it ... Aaron and Kai's warning repeated in my head. She wasn't a pushover, and she'd played that summoner no problem. Plus, her demon was a super-scary murder machine.

I couldn't reveal the amulet to her. It was my best chance at saving Ezra, and I wasn't about to risk it. She could take it from me—her and her demon. I had to keep it hidden.

But maybe I could find out more without revealing I had it.

"So, what's that ancient infernus thing you're researching?" I asked lightly as we headed down the stairs. "It looked interesting."

"I ran across it in an old grimoire," she replied, equally blasé. "What about your demon-mage case? What got you started on an investigation?"

"I'm just doing some legwork for Aaron and Kai," I answered evasively. "It's their job."

"Oh, I see."

We reached the bottom of the stairs and stopped. I gazed at her and she stared back, blue eyes unexpectedly piercing. Neither of us was willing to reveal anything about our "research," and I didn't know how to push her for more information without revealing why I needed to know.

Shrugging, I stepped into the hall—and almost crashed into a familiar mythic.

"Oh!" I forced a smile. "Hi, Izzah."

I had to hide my cringe, not because I didn't like Izzah—I thought she was awesome—but because I had no answers for her about Kai, and I didn't want to lie when she inevitably asked why he'd vanished.

"Tori?" Her brow furrowed. "*Wei*, what are you doing here?"

She'd traded her leather combat gear for a stylish blouse, tight black jeans, and tall boots. It wasn't quite business-professional wear, but close. My gaze flicked past her to three more Odin's Eye mythics, waiting politely while I blocked the hall—and behind them, almost unseen, was a bald head I recognized.

Shane Davila pushed his round glasses up his nose as he examined me like a scientist with a sample under his microscope. Now I knew who her "meeting" had been with—and clearly, she'd dressed to impress. What did Shane want with Odin's Eye?

Either way, the last thing I needed was more attention from the bounty hunter.

I gave the whole group a casual salute. "Nice to see ya. We're just heading out."

"What were you here for?" Izzah began. "Tori—"

Waving as though I hadn't heard her, I strode down the hall. Quick footsteps told me Robin was right behind me, and I made a beeline for the exit.

The petite contractor trotted to catch up. "Is something wrong?"

"Nope." I slowed my pace as we reached the lobby. Izzah hadn't followed us; she was probably saying her professional goodbyes to Shane. "It's just that guy—the short, bald one at the back—is a famous bounty hunter and he was a dick to me at the pub the other day."

"A famous bounty hunter? What's his name?"

"Shane Davila." Reaching for the front door, I glanced back at her. "Have you heard of—"

With an earsplitting crash, the entire building shook like a wrecking ball had hit it. I staggered into Robin, almost knocking her over. As shouts sounded from deeper in the building, I gawked at the front doors, terrified it might be an earthquake and equally terrified it wasn't.

For a moment, the door was dark, nothing showing beyond the frosted glass. Then amber light lit up the parking lot—and blazed brightly. Glowing orange burst across the glass.

I whipped out my Queen of Spades as the glass creaked, the frosting melting. Ripples ran across its surface. The pane bowed inward.

The door shattered.

"*Ori repercutio!*" I screamed.

A wall of flame exploded into the room, hit the shimmering reflection of my artifact, and rebounded. Fire burst across the walls.

As the flames died, Robin clutched my arm. "I thought you were a witch!"

"Yeah, well—"

Somewhere in the smoke haze, metal thunked and clattered, drawing closer. A shape appeared in the shattered window. Runes glowed across the familiar canine shape of a golem, its shark-like mouth ready to chomp down on squishy human flesh. It charged through the open threshold, glass crunching under its steel feet.

I grabbed Robin's arm and hauled her out of its path. It skidded on the slippery tiles and crashed into the desk, hundreds of pounds of steel crumpling the wood.

"Out!" I yelled. "Get outside!"

We needed room to maneuver if we were going to stand any chance against the golem. I raced for the door, Robin stumbling with me.

"What about the people inside?" she gasped. "They—"

"They're combat mythics! They can take care of themselves!"

I jumped over the broken glass and landed on the front stoop. Dragging Robin by the arm, I got three steps—and glimpsed something huge flying toward us.

All my recent training saved our lives. I threw us sideways and the massive projectile flashed by so close the wind of its passing whipped my hair across my face. We hit the ground—and a deafening crash shook my bones. Shattered concrete spilled out of the brand-new hole where the guild's front wall had stood seconds before.

Then I saw what had created the hole. It wasn't a projectile. It was a fist.

A huge steel fist attached to a huge steel arm connected to a huge steel shoulder.

The biggest hunk of metal I'd ever seen dragged its limb out of the wall and straightened to its full height. Twelve feet tall, broad and bulky, it looked like a cross between a steampunk Transformer and a medieval suit of armor. Giant runes glowed across it, their pinkish light competing with the firelight leaking from inside the guild.

The gargantuan golem turned its featureless helmet toward Robin and I, sprawled on our backs, and raised an arm above its head. Its basketball-sized fist plunged toward us, and with a wall on one side of me and Robin on the other, I couldn't even roll away as death whooshed down.

21

ROBIN'S TERRIFIED SCREAM rang out—and red light burst from her chest. Crimson power streaked upward and solidified into the shape of her demon. He stood over us, arms raised.

The golem's huge fist slammed into the demon's outstretched hands.

His muscles bunched with inhuman strength as he braced against the impact. The golem bore down with the weight of steel, the momentum of its swing, and whatever magical force powered its movements. The demon sank lower, then collapsed to one knee, his metal greave hitting the pavement with a crunch.

"Tori, move!" Robin yelled, scrambling backward.

I rolled over and threw myself away from the demon and golem. The moment we were clear, the demon shoved backward, letting the golem's fist smash into the ground.

"A golem," Robin panted wildly as her demon scooted after us on agile feet, staying between his contractor and the giant. "It's huge. How is it so huge?"

"Great question, but let's worry about it later!" I whirled, fully intending to run like hell across the parking lot, down the street, and all the way back to the Crow and Hammer. "We need to—"

I broke off, terror plunging through me.

Waiting at the edge of the parking lot were three more canine golems, and behind them was a line of men—dressed in black, some in combat gear, faces covered with masks, hats, or handkerchiefs.

"Take out the contractor first!" one of them yelled.

The canine golems charged toward us, and behind them came three rogues, two raising artifacts as the third conjured water out of thin air.

I unholstered my paintball gun. The CO_2 canister popped with my first shot, and I unloaded six of my seven potion balls. The sorcerers keeled over, too slow to counter, but the hydromage shaped water into a shield that blocked my paintballs.

Two out of three wasn't bad—except the golems were still pounding toward us, their steel footsteps so loud it was like listening to a cutlery factory falling down a mountain. And I had no magic to defend against them.

Robin's demon streaked past me.

He leaped over the golems like a champion pole vaulter, minus the pole, and slammed feet first into the hydromage's chest. The man keeled over backward, hitting the pavement with sickening force.

The demon leaped off his chest and straight into the nearest golem, ramming his bare fist into its side. With a gong-like boom, the steel panel caved in. Undeterred, the golem spun on the demon, metal teeth snapping. The demon sprang away.

Behind us, the super-golem smashed another hole in the Odin's Eye building.

"Knock it over!" I yelled desperately—then remembered the demon wasn't actually the one fighting. "Robin, use your demon to knock them on their sides! They have trouble getting up!"

"Right!"

Her demon launched at the golem again, twisted in midair, and landed on his back, skidding under the golem's belly. His body coiled, legs pulling in tight, then he kicked upward with explosive force. His feet hit the golem's underbelly and heaved it up and over. It crashed onto its side, limbs waving helplessly.

"Whoa," I breathed. "How'd you do th—shit!"

Grabbing Robin's arm, I pulled her backward—because while her demon had been distracting the golems, the remaining rogues had surrounded us. They spread out, magic sparking off them as they prepared their attacks.

"Hoshi!" I cried desperately.

The sylph burst from my belt pouch in a streak of silver. A gust of wind whipped across the parking lot, blowing debris into the mythics' faces. Dust billowed everywhere, thick as fog.

A furious shout—from behind us. I spun again.

Izzah appeared in the dusty haze, twin daggers in her hands. She leaped forward onto one foot, spinning in an elegant twist as her blades wove through the air. Water coalesced around the weapons, trailing after them like sparkling ribbons.

She spun like a dancer, her ponytail fanning out, and completed her move with crisscrossing slashes of her blades. A wide band of water shot outward, and it struck the cluster of rogues at knee height, blasting their legs out from under them. They howled in pain as they collapsed.

Behind Izzah, ten members of Odin's Eye streamed out of the burning building, diving past the hulking super-golem as it smashed another hole into the second floor. Fury burned in every face as they charged toward the rogues and remaining two canine golems. They met the rogues in a clash of magic and weapons, and it was immediately apparent why one group were feared bounty hunters and the other fugitive rogues.

The problem was the golems, and as I eyed the remaining two, the ground shook with a crashing footstep.

The super-golem had turned away from the building. Fire spread through the interior, and smoke poured from the holes. The golem took a lumbering step toward the battling mythics.

Oh hell. The waist-high wolfy ones were almost impossible to kill. How could anyone stop that giant? It wasn't very fast, but it was huge and deadly. I slapped my hands over my pouches, knowing I had nothing useful. Disabling it would require big, powerful, scary magic. Not my little trinkets. I needed something crazy, something—

My hand landed on my jean pocket, a square lump tucked inside.

Robin gasped. I jerked my head up—and saw the super-golem's arm whipping toward us.

Her demon shot out of the dust haze, grabbed us both, and sprang straight up. The swinging steel limb whipped underneath our feet. We plunged down. The demon hit the pavement and leaped again, propelling us out of reach. He landed in a skid and spun to face the golem, his arm crushing my ribcage.

The super-golem plodded after us. Upside: it was no longer advancing on the Odin's Eye mythics. Downside: we were screwed.

"Robin," I wheezed as her demon released us. Staggering for balance, I grabbed my belt buckle. "Can your demon get me up onto the golem's head?"

"Its head?" she squealed shrilly as the golem stomped closer. "Why—"

"Can you?" I pulled the buckle apart and lowered my belt to the ground. "Yes or no!"

Her frightened gaze flicked to her demon. "Yes, but—"

The golem drew its arm back. Robin jumped in front of us, and her demon grabbed her hand—simultaneously seizing me around the waist with his other arm.

"*Ori eruptum impello!*" Robin yelled.

Silver light burst out from her in an expanding dome. It whooshed gently over me and her demon—and hit the golem's oncoming fist. The force of her spell halted its attack, metal creaking and groaning from the sudden loss of momentum.

The demon swept me against his side and leaped. He landed on the golem's outstretched fist and sprinted up its arm to its shoulder. I jammed my hand in my pocket and pulled out the small square of purple fabric.

The golem lurched upright. Almost pitching off its shoulder, Robin's demon seized its helmet to stay in place, my legs swinging wildly with the motion. The golem's massive fingers shot for us.

The demon's arm loosened around my waist and I had just a moment to clutch the thick helmet. Releasing me, the demon caught the golem's fingers, knees bending as he coiled his body.

He launched off the golem's shoulder, forcing the arm back, metal groaning as the limb bent the wrong way. The golem teetered, thrown off balance. Gripping the helmet with my knees, I pulled on two corners of the folded fabric, yanking them apart.

The Carapace of Valdurna unfurled.

Shimmering purple cloth swept out. The fabric billowed—and magic poured from it. Streams of glittering purple and blue rippled off the Carapace, its edges softening into pure magic. Glowing indigo light bathed the parking lot, and a heavy, sweet tang filled the air, so thick it was hard to breathe.

I swept the fabric onto the golem's head. It settled over the steel in a swirl of light and magic. Power crawled up my arms, hot and cold, numbing all sensation.

The golem reached for me—but the glowing runes across its body were dimming. The luminescent markings darkened from bright pink to deep, burning red, then that too faded. In five seconds flat, it was inanimate steel once again.

Holy. Freaking. Shit.

I clutched the heavy fabric, wanting to let it go before the numbness spread even farther up my arms, but I was afraid to lift the artifact off the golem in case it returned to life. The Carapace had sucked out its magic, but would that magic return if—

Metal creaked—and the golem plummeted face-first toward the pavement.

Hoshi shimmered out of nowhere and her tiny paws seized the back of my jacket. Weightlessness washed through me and the golem fell away from my legs. It smashed down with a horrific bang, and I landed on its back, my feet touching down so softly they didn't make a sound on its hollow torso.

With a flick of her long tail, Hoshi let go. My limbs regained their usual weight as she faded away with a silver shimmer.

I looked down. Clutched in my hands was the purple fabric, magic rippling and sparkling off it in spectacular waves, its light washing over everything. As I raised it, the draping fabric fell into its proper shape: an ethereal purple cloak.

"Wow," I breathed.

"Tori?"

I looked around, belatedly realizing the cacophony of combat had quieted. The only sounds came from the golem limbs scraping on the pavement and the crackling flames spreading through the guild headquarters, the orange light competing with the Carapace's indigo radiance.

Cautiously approaching, Izzah sheathed her twin knives, her wide eyes on the Carapace. "*Celaka*, Tori. What *is* that?"

"Uh, this? It's ... on loan from a friend." Giving the cloak a shake, I folded it in half, then folded it again. It should've taken ages to gather it into a tiny square, but it shrank unnaturally with each fold, and before I knew it, it was an innocuous square again. Shoving it in my pocket, I jumped to the ground.

A faint splash accompanied my landing; dark liquid had leaked from the fallen golem's joints. Nose wrinkling, I hurried to Izzah. "Is everyone okay?"

"*Ya-lah*, we all got out of the building, and the rogues were no problem." She glanced over her shoulder at the final canine golems, lying on their sides, legs scrabbling uselessly for purchase. "It took a few guys to tip them, but we managed it."

"Good." I rubbed a hand over my face. The distant sound of sirens was growing louder. "Did someone call MagiPol?"

She nodded. "Agents are on the way. We also have ..."

As she trailed off, I followed her gaze. Shane Davila, who I hadn't glimpsed during the fight, was crouched beside the super-golem, his bare palm pressed to its head. After a long moment, he lifted his hand from the steel and touched the liquid pooled under its torso.

Shifting my weight nervously, I picked my combat belt off the ground. "Robin and I need to get back to our guild."

"I'll be in touch as soon as we're done with MagiPol." Izzah's cocoa eyes locked on mine. "We're the third guild now. You know what that means-*lah*, right."

Unease twisted through my gut, and I nodded before hurrying away.

Robin stood at the edge of the parking lot. Her demon was still out of her infernus, standing passively with a blank expression as she fussed over his hand. Her fingers were smeared with the dark blood leaking from his split knuckles.

"I don't think it's broken," she mumbled, gently prodding the back of his hand. "The bones seem solid."

Joining them, I frowned. I'd never seen a demon contractor show the slightest concern for their demon's wellbeing. Fenton, the Keys contractor, hadn't batted an eye when his demon had been gored half to death. He'd been angry that it couldn't get up.

"Can he feel pain?" I asked quietly, remembering the sound of him punching a golem in its steel side. "Demons look so blank all the time, like puppets ..."

She glanced at me, then back down at her demon's bleeding hand. "Yes, they all feel pain, contracted or not."

Not wanting to think too hard about that, I brushed the dust off my pants. "We need to go. We have to get back to the Crow and Hammer."

She released her demon's hand. "We do?"

"You should come with me. We might need you."

"Why?"

My anxious gaze flicked to the massive golem. "Because three combat guilds have been attacked in three days. That means the Crow and Hammer is probably next."

22

AN HOUR LATER, I stood behind the Crow and Hammer bar, not because I wanted to work a shift but because it's where I felt most in control. Aaron and Ezra sat on stools across from me, their backs to the counter as they watched the rest of the pub.

Voices buzzed in low, terse conversation. I counted over a dozen of our best combat mythics, from mages like Alistair and Laetitia, to sorcerers like Andrew and Gwen, to the telekinetic Drew and telepath Bryce. Another dozen members were non-combats, including Sin, Sabrina, Kaveri, and her boyfriend, Kier.

Tension clung to everyone, unease palpable in the air. With the attack on Odin's Eye, it didn't take a genius to figure out the pattern: the rogues were targeting combat guilds.

Our guild was in danger, and we all knew it.

The front door thumped, then swung inward with a jangle of the bell. Zak stepped inside, his villainous coat sweeping behind him, its hood drawn up and the leather shining with raindrops. Every mythic looked at him, but before anyone could freak out, I raised my hand.

"Over here," I called.

Pushing his hood off, he angled toward me. Dozens of eyes narrowed suspiciously, watching as he passed, but no one demanded to know who I kept inviting into the pub. They probably assumed he was with another guild.

"Well?" I demanded in a whisper as soon as he was close enough to hear it.

"She's preparing her next move." He leaned against the bar beside Ezra, "but I wasn't able to learn more than that. The rogues who've joined her have all vanished, and the few I found didn't know anything."

I rubbed my hand over my face. "Damn it. So you have no idea where to find her?"

"If I did, I wouldn't be here chatting about it." He glanced around. "What's everyone waiting for?"

"The meeting upstairs to finish." I braced my elbows on the bar top. "Since we don't know where to find Varvara, our options are either ditch the guild headquarters and let it get smashed to rubble, or gather everyone who wants to defend it and wait here until they attack."

He grunted expressively.

"By the way." I lowered my voice even more. "The Carapace came in pretty handy earlier, but a bunch of mythics saw me use it, including Shane, and I don't know if they can guess what it is. You should take it back now."

"Not here. I'll take it when no one is watching me."

Which wouldn't be happening anytime soon. Around half the present mythics were eyeing him, some surreptitiously and some with "I don't give a shit" boldness.

The conversation rumbling through the pub quieted, and a moment later, a group of mythics descended from the upper level: Darius, followed by Girard, Tabitha, and Felix, his three officers.

Last but not least came Kai and Makiko. After I'd broken the news of the Odin's Eye attack, Aaron had called Kai. It seemed Makiko was loosening up, as Kai had not only answered his phone, but also convinced her to join forces with the Crow and Hammer. Common enemies and all that.

As Kai and Makiko stopped at the far end of the bar, I scanned the room again. No sign of Robin. She'd gone upstairs nearly thirty minutes ago, and I was surprised she hadn't returned.

Darius moved to the center of the room, his officers flanking him. As he turned in a slow circle, surveying his guild with somber gray eyes, his gaze caught on my little group.

"I see we have a guest," he observed.

The guild's collective attention shifted from Darius to the druid. Zak tensed.

"This is Zak," I revealed. "He's a combat alchemist. Very useful."

Darius smiled pleasantly. "And how do you know Zak?"

His question's real meaning: Why is he here? Shit. How was I supposed to answer that? My head spun with wild theories, and only one made the slightest bit of sense to my scrambled logic.

"We dated," I blurted.

Ezra and Aaron jerked as if Kai had zapped them, while the electramage stared at me. Zak's mouth thinned but he refrained from shooting me any "you're an idiot" looks, which I probably deserved, considering he'd specifically told me this cover story didn't work.

"It was just a fling," I added hastily. "Like, two weeks." I'd spent two weeks at his farm, so it wasn't that much of a stretch? Okay, it was a stretch. "Anyway," I rushed on, flapping one hand, "he's got contacts around here that I asked him to check out."

"Did you learn anything interesting, Zak?"

Cool green eyes met equally cool gray ones.

"Nothing that can help your guild," the druid rumbled.

"Hmm." Darius's smile widened unexpectedly, then he turned to the rest of the room. "We're facing a dangerous situation."

A shiver prickled my spine as I stared at the GM. That knowing smile. What … *Oh*.

Zak's voice.

Those deep, distinctive raspy tones. After my kidnapping and abrupt return from the Ghost's clutches, Darius had briefly spoken to a mysterious stranger on the phone—a stranger who sounded just like Zak.

As I hyperventilated over what Darius might've figured out, he continued somberly, "Here's what we know. The dark-arts sorceress, Varvara Nikolaev, is currently active in the city. She's recruited a large group of unattached rogues and is striking at combat guilds in the downtown area. Last night, she also attacked MiraCo, which some of you may recognize as an offshoot of the Yamada Syndicate, an international guild."

Curious gazes darted to Kai and Makiko.

"The Yamada Syndicate is known for dabbling on both sides of the law, and to Varvara, they're competition." He tilted his head toward Kai and Makiko. "Miss Miura is the acting GM of MiraCo and has shared what she knows of Varvara's activities.

"We believe Varvara is destabilizing both her competition and the guilds that could oppose her while she takes control of Vancouver's criminal underground and black market. We also believe she'll attack the Crow and Hammer soon."

"Then let's find the sorceress!" Darren shouted from the back. "And stop her first!"

"Dark sorcerers do not advertise their location," Tabitha retorted coldly. "Finding her will take too long, require too much manpower, and leave our guild unprotected."

"Can we protect the guild?" Aaron asked, unusually grim. "It won't take many of those golems to tear the place apart. They spit acid, breathe fire, and are almost impossible to destroy."

"What do we know about golems?" Laetitia inquired to the room. "They're dark magic, aren't they?"

"Rare dark magic." Andrew drummed his fingers on the table where he sat with Gwen and Bryce. "They're difficult to make, from what I've heard, and aren't as useful as they seem. They have limited intelligence and—"

"They have no intelligence," Zak interrupted impatiently. "They perform basic sets of movements determined by simple stimuli. The better the sorcerer, the more complex the movements and the increased responsiveness to stimuli, but golems can't think."

Again, my guildmates eyed the stranger in their midst.

"What's the best way to counter them?" Darius asked.

"Destroy the animation array. Failing that, let the golem chase you until it runs out of juice. They aren't very fast." He folded his arms. "Golems are rare because they're so limited.

They take weeks to charge, but once they start moving, they burn through their stored magic within ten minutes."

"The golems that attacked MiraCo lasted longer than that," Kai reminded him. "At least one was still going after half an hour."

"And I told you then that it had to be a different golem."

"The ones we knocked over at Odin's Eye," I said. "They were still kicking when I left, and it'd been about twenty-five minutes at that point. Didn't you mention something about an alchemy component?"

"Alchemy?" Sin repeated, sitting at a table with Kaveri and Kier. "As part of a golem? That doesn't make any sense."

"That's what I said," Zak rumbled. "The liquid was probably blood, which makes even less sense. Golems use metallurgic ciphering fortified with astral conditioning, and blood alchemy has no overlap."

"So it couldn't be used to make the golems live longer?" I asked.

"They aren't *alive*. And no, human blood doesn't have any magical properties that could—"

He broke off, his green eyes losing focus. I blinked in confusion as he went completely still, staring at nothing.

Kaveri screamed.

Darkness burst through the ceiling as Zak launched away from the bar. Wings flaring wide, Lallakai swept down in a maelstrom of shadows. Her talons caught Zak's shoulders, her green eyes glowing from amidst the inky flames that danced from her feathers.

The guild door flew open, crashing into the wall. Two men burst through, decked in combat gear, weapons in hand.

Lallakai's wings closed around Zak. He and the eagle faded out of sight.

"Where is he?" one of the newcomers yelled.

Kaveri pointed at the staircase and shrieked, "That way!"

The saloon doors right behind me slammed and I almost jumped out of my skin. Two more combat mythics sprinted out of the kitchen and leaped over the bar like heavily armed gazelles, while the first two charged across the pub, shoving people out of their way. Everyone was shouting, on their feet, alarmed or angry—except for Darius, who looked mildly annoyed. Aaron was yelling something I couldn't make out over the racket.

But we all heard a window shatter upstairs.

The second pair of mythics changed direction in mid-stride and sprinted for the front door. The first ones continued up the stairs, weapons gleaming.

I slapped my hands down on the bar, vaulted over it, and ran for the door too. Aaron and Ezra were a step behind me as I burst out into the rain—and red light flared so brightly I couldn't see a damn thing.

My vision cleared, revealing four combat mythics positioned in the street. The two mythics who'd run upstairs jumped from the broken second-floor window. They landed in practiced rolls, sprang to their feet with weapons in hand, and took up positions in a triangle formation with the other four mythics—completing a team of six, which included Izzah and Mario.

The hydromage's twin knives were drawn and she stood in front of Mario. His demon stood a yard in front of her, tall and lanky with a black mane running down its back and empty magma eyes.

Trapped in the center of their formation, Zak stood with Lallakai's phantom wings arching off his back and yellow power coiling around his left arm. His hood was up, shadows hiding his face. He extended his right hand and summoned his scarlet saber. The colorful glow of his magic glinted off the wet pavement, joining the rippling reflections of the streetlamps and the glowing windows of the guild.

As rain poured down, quiet footsteps crunched on the concrete, drawing closer.

Shane Davila stopped beside Mario, safely behind Izzah and the hulking demon. He surveyed the druid and his terrifying shadow wings without emotion, then slid a sheet of paper from his pocket and unfolded it.

Clearing his throat, he read in a loud, steady tone, "'The rogue di-mythic dubbed "the Ghost," also known as the Crystal Druid, trained by the Wolfsbane Druid, confirmed to wield sorcery, alchemy, and fae magic, has been charged with three hundred and twenty-six felonies under MPD law. Due to the severity and violence of his crimes, the Ghost has been deemed a public danger and his capture is classified as DOA—dead or alive.'"

Pocketing his paper, the bounty hunter lifted his small eyes to Zak. "Zakariya Andrii, do you surrender?"

"Shit," Aaron whispered behind me—and his wasn't the only voice murmuring beneath the patter of rain. Most of the Crow and Hammer was crowded on the sidewalk to watch the showdown, Old West style.

"Is that really the Ghost?" someone muttered fearfully. "What's he doing here?"

"*The* Shane Davila is tagging a rogue at our guild!"

"I don't believe it," Kaveri breathed, half awed, half repulsed. "The Ghost and the Crystal Druid can't be the same person ..."

"Did Tori say she *dated* him?"

I winced.

Indigo magic swirled out from Zak's feet. It snaked across the pavement in an expanding circle—and the earth rumbled warningly.

"I'll give you one chance," the druid rasped in a voice like black ice, "to walk away."

"Six against one," Mario growled. "I like our odds."

"Do you?"

The air rippled—and five huge varg wolves appeared around him, their hackles raised and red eyes glowing as they bared their teeth at the mythics. Fear singed the air, palpable and intense.

As the Odin's Eye mythics hesitated, Zak pulled on a handful of leather cords hanging around his neck. Four colorful crystals lifted out of his jacket. With the murmur of his voice, the first one lit—then the second—then the third.

"If you won't move," he said, dangerously quiet, "which of you should I go through?"

The swordsman behind Zak flicked his short blade.

Zak pivoted as a fireball shot from the sword's tip. The yellow magic coiling over his arm flared outward into a shield and the flames burst harmlessly against it.

"You'll have to do a lot better than that," he said. The indigo magic snaking over the ground brightened and the earth rumbled again, the vibrations deepening.

A varg snarled, its teeth snapping at thin air. Zak turned again—and with his distraction, four combat mythics and Mario's demon launched forward.

My vision went black.

I gasped in fright, throwing my arms out. As fearful cries rang out around us, my elbows thumped against Aaron and Ezra, still behind me. The vargs were snarling, people were shouting, then—

"Everyone *stop!*"

I sucked in a sharp breath, barely recognizing that voice. None of Darius's usual humor touched the command in his tone.

The darkness slowly lifted, as though someone were sliding a dimmer switch for my vision. The revived streetlamps cast an orange glow over the Odin's Eye team, who'd closed half the distance to Zak, their weapons mere feet from the vargs.

Zak was still in the middle of the street—and Darius stood beside him, one hand gripping the back of Zak's neck, his hood pushed off. With his other hand, the GM held a shining silver dagger against Zak's throat, the blade resting just under his chin.

I blindly grabbed Aaron's and Ezra's arms, my fingers digging in as I tried to remember how to breathe. Maybe it was my imagination, but as everyone stood frozen in the sudden return of light—or vision, or whatever the hell the luminamage had done to blind us—I could've sworn I saw Darius's lips moving with fast, quiet words.

Zak's eyes, bright with Lallakai's power and burning with fury, flicked from the guild master to Shane.

"Now," Darius said, cool as a cucumber as he held a dagger to the druid's throat, "before damage is dealt and lives are lost, let's have a little discussion."

"Are you obstructing justice, Darius?" Shane asked, equally calm but nowhere near as cool. The total sum of his badassery couldn't fill Darius's left shoe. "That mythic is under arrest."

"Of course, Shane, of course. But unless I am very mistaken, you do not intend to arrest this mythic. Nor do you intend to kill him."

My eyebrows scrunched in confusion.

Shane wiped rain off his bald head with a gloved hand. "What makes you think that?"

"The Ghost is, by your standards, a rather small and local barracuda in a worldwide sea of sharks. Wouldn't you agree his list of crimes is trivial compared to your usual quarry?"

"Flattery will get you nowhere, Darius."

"My point is, Shane, that you didn't come to Vancouver for *this* mythic's bounty. So rather than risk the lives of this fine Odin's Eye team on an attempted capture, why don't you tell us what you really want from the Ghost?"

The famous bounty hunter adjusted his water-speckled glasses as he considered Darius's suggestion. "I want Varvara Nikolaev—and the Ghost will tell me everything he knows about her power."

23

"WAIT," I MUTTERED. "Shane isn't here for Zak?"

"He said he was investigating the Ghost," Aaron growled.

"But looking back," Ezra said quietly, "he hasn't been very focused on that. He spent more time investigating the guild attacks."

Which had been Varvara's doing.

In the center of the street, Shane and Darius were engaged in a staring match. Zak didn't move, seemingly unwilling to speak while Darius had a knife to his throat.

"In that case, Shane," the guild master said, "make your offer."

"I don't need to bargain. He'll answer my questions or suffer the 'dead' part of his DOA bounty. Unless you intend to help him escape, at which point we'll arrest you instead." Shane smiled coldly. "That would be a satisfying consolation prize, I'll admit."

"Helping him wasn't my plan, but you don't seem to realize how unlikely it is that you, I, or your team can stop him."

"You have a knife to his throat."

In response, Zak lifted his left hand—revealing an empty glass vial from his belt. As a silent, fearful rustle passed through the watching Crow and Hammer guildeds, he let the vial slip from his fingers. It shattered on the pavement.

My gaze followed its trajectory, and I spotted the black stain on Darius's knee where Zak had splashed the potion.

"Soon your arm will be too numb to hold that knife," the druid said. "You can slit my throat, but you'll die either way."

Darius sighed. "Unappealing, to say the least. Luckily, I'm a more flexible man than our dear friend Shane."

"Do not release him, Darius," Shane hissed. He clenched and unclenched his jaw. "Zakariya Andrii, assist me in capturing Varvara and you can walk free."

Gasps rang through the Crow and Hammer mythics.

"Why should I believe that?" the druid demanded.

"Your bounty is one-point-two million," Shane replied tersely, "encompassing eight years of criminal activity. Varvara Nikolaev's spans fifty-three years and is set at thirty-four million, with contributions from major guilds across Russia and Eastern Europe."

Whoa. The Ghost was a trivial rogue indeed.

"You," Shane added, "are a means to an end. Deliver on that end and you can go back to kidnapping children and selling cheap artifacts until a local guild finally catches up with you." A sharp smile. "Which won't take long now that your class, name, and face have been unveiled."

Zak studied the bounty hunter with his inhuman eyes, then Lallakai's huge shadow wings folded down his arms and faded away. The ten-foot-diameter indigo circle under his feet dissolved in sparkles that drifted skyward.

"Agreed," he said.

Darius lowered his knife, then slipped it out of sight under the back of his shirt. "Excellent. Shane, would you join us inside? We can pool our knowledge immediately."

Not waiting for a reply, Darius clapped his hand onto Zak's shoulder, splattering raindrops, and steered the druid toward the guild. His saber and yellow shield spell shimmered away as he walked with the GM, sparing not even a glance for the Odin's Eye mythics. His vargs faded into shadow, disappearing as swiftly as they'd joined the fight.

The Crow and Hammer mythics parted for their GM and the notorious rogue. I arched my eyebrows at Zak as he passed, then stepped after him. Aaron and Ezra followed.

"Were you planning to provide me with an antidote, Zak?" the guild master asked as we crossed the empty pub.

"No."

Darius stopped abruptly, pulling the druid to a halt.

"You don't need one," Zak added. "That vial was a burn-treatment potion with a full-body numbing effect. Though if I'd been carrying a lethal poison, I would've used it."

A short pause, then Darius threw his head back in a laugh. "Well played, alchemist. The sensation was distinctly alarming."

I rolled my eyes, half impressed by Zak's quick thinking but mostly annoyed by his penchant for pretending harmless potions were lethal. Sneaky cheat.

We gathered around a long worktable on the second level. Darius claimed the chair at the head of the table and Zak sat on the corner beside him. I took the next spot, and Aaron and Ezra followed suit. Kai, Makiko, Girard, Tabitha, and Felix—the third officer carrying a laptop—filled out the table's other side.

Tabitha glared arctic laser-beams at Zak, while Girard, sitting across from the druid, seemed cautiously curious.

"So," he said, "you're the one who stole our bartender for two weeks, eh?"

I propped my chin on my palm. "It was a lovely vacation. I enjoyed some hard manual labor, a battle with darkfae, and a dragon airshow. Oh, and he tricked me into thinking I'd die if I talked about him."

Girard pressed his lips together at his new understanding of why I hadn't revealed where I'd been or how I'd escaped.

"Don't forget the shower," Zak told me.

"Huh?"

"Showering together," he clarified. "Sleeping together. Waking up in bed together. It was so romantic."

My jaw hit the tabletop. Aaron's face was stamped with disbelieving horror and Ezra's had gone completely blank. Kai's suspicious gaze darted between me and the druid.

"After all," Zak added, a sneer slipping into his voice, "we *dated*, remember?"

I snapped my teeth together so hard my skull rattled. "I was covering for you, asshole."

"I told you that was an idiotic lie."

"You didn't suggest any alternatives, did you? You—"

Shane Davila swept into the room with two Odin's Eye mythics in tow—Izzah, plus a thickly muscled older man I assumed was their team leader. Shane sat opposite Darius, and Izzah and the Odin's Eye man sat flanking him.

Izzah glanced once at Kai, sitting beside Makiko, and looked away, her full lips squeezed into a pale line.

"Let's begin. Zakariya, you—"

"He prefers Zak," I barked aggressively, shifting my temper to an equally worthy target.

Shane glanced at me, then refocused on the druid. "You engaged in a direct altercation with Varvara last July. Is that correct?"

"Yes."

"And you fought her?"

"Yes."

Shane adjusted his glasses. "And you lost."

Temper flashed in Zak's face. "She had a hostage, which limited my options, but I held my own."

"Tell me everything about your fight with her."

"*That's* what you want from me?" He shook his head. "I'll keep it simple for you: she's lethal."

"I'm aware of her combat prowess," Shane said impatiently. "Shortly before she fled Russia last year, an elite bounty team cornered her in Moscow. She escaped—and killed most of the team. I can find her. What I need from you are details about her abilities so I can ensure she doesn't escape or slaughter another team."

"You're awfully confident that you can find her."

"I already have."

Zak's eyes narrowed to calculating slits. "Then tell me where she is and I'll take her down."

"Absolutely not."

"You can have the bounty. I want her head."

"I've told you what I require from you: her skills, strategies, and weaknesses."

The druid's upper lip curled as his gaze slashed across the people gathered around the table. "Haven't you seen enough black magic to know that a master practitioner could crush everyone in this room?"

"But *you* could defeat her?" Aaron snapped.

"Yes."

Aaron rolled his eyes in disgust.

"I'm not saying it would be easy. She thinks of everything, plans for everything. She has defenses in place for every kind of attack."

"How would you defeat her?" Shane asked Zak intently.

"In an ideal world, I'd crush her throat with my bare hands." His mouth twisted. "The only way to take her down is in close combat, but that puts you in range of her poisons. She's a highly adaptable strategist, and with fifty years of experience in the dark arts ... you can't plan for that."

"I'm quite certain I can. Tell me everything you saw in your confrontation with her."

Anger roughening his voice, Zak described the spells and alchemy Varvara had used against him, getting technical so quickly that my head spun from all the unfamiliar words. Felix typed rapidly on his laptop, his brow scrunched in concentration, while Girard and the Odin's Eye team leader nodded along. I couldn't tell if Shane was following or not.

"She carries far more magic than what I saw, so I doubt any of that will help you," Zak concluded. "That's assuming you can reach her when she has forty rogues to hide behind."

Tabitha leaned forward, her face paler than usual. "How do you know she has forty rogues?"

"I can count."

"Actually," Shane butted in with a pretentious air, "casualties from the Pandora Knights and Odin's Eye attacks have reduced her rogues to around thirty, though we don't yet know how many golems she has to supplement their numbers."

Zak grunted at the bounty hunter's correction. "Golems take a full moon cycle to charge, meaning she's been preparing for this for months."

"What's she preparing for?" Felix asked. "What's her end game?"

"Control of Vancouver's black market," Shane answered before Zak could. "Assuming she follows the same pattern as in St. Petersburg, Kiev, and Bucharest, she'll gain control of the artifact trade first, then expand into smuggling and human trafficking—mythic and not."

Zak thudded a gloved finger against the tabletop, drawing everyone's attention. His stare locked on the bounty hunter. "Tomorrow night, Varvara will animate a new batch of golems and send them and her rogues to level another guild. Are you planning to do something about that?"

Shane prodded his glasses up his nose. "Similar to Red Rum, Varvara favors sea travel on her yacht. She only comes to land when necessary. Otherwise, she's at sea and impossible to find. However, she needs a location to store her golems and hide thirty to forty rogues—and I've identified that location."

Almost everyone at the table leaned forward slightly.

"Over the last three nights, she's arrived at this secret location at seven p.m. and departed at seven-thirty. I assume the purpose of these visits was to animate the golems for the next attack."

"I thought golems only last ten minutes," I muttered to Zak.

He shrugged one shoulder. "If the golems are immobile, they could last a few hours."

"They transport the golems in a semi-trailer," Makiko added in a crisp tone. "We saw it on our security cameras. Once Varvara animates the golems, the rogues would need to load them and head to their attack location immediately."

"Then we strike before that," the Odin's Eye leader declared. "If Shane gives us the location, we can have teams in place well before seven tomorrow, and stop her next assault before it starts."

Shane shook his head. "It isn't that simple. If even a single enemy is detected, Varvara will flee. She needs to dock and come ashore before any combat teams move in."

"She can't be allowed to animate the golems," Darius countered. "Thirty rogues plus golems is more than we can safely handle, even with our combined forces. We can't count on help from the other guilds."

"Then what are we supposed to do?" Aaron slumped back in his chair. "If we attack the rogues first, we miss Varvara. But if we wait for Varvara, we'll have to fight her, all her rogues, and an unknown number of golems."

Silence fell over the table, and my heart sank.

"Battling the rogues will be loud and messy." Zak's vibrant eyes swept over the gathered mythics. "You can't engage them before Varvara is ashore, but the golems are a different matter. Until they're animated, they're vulnerable. Disabling them would be quick and quiet, and it could be done shortly before Varvara arrives."

"If we can remove her golems from the equation," Girard said, his eager smile showing through his beard, "then our combat teams can focus on the rogues and Varvara."

"The bitch is mine," Zak growled.

"We will *capture* Varvara," Shane cut in, "so she can be tried and convicted for her crimes before all the guilds and families she's harmed. She'll be executed without a doubt, but there are more and better mythics than you who deserve to see justice served."

Zak's jaw tightened.

"How are golems disabled?" Shane asked him.

"By damaging the animation array inside them."

"And how does one find and destroy the animation array?"

Zak arched a mocking eyebrow. "You can find them by studying dark Arcana and learning to decipher some of the most complex arrays in sorcery. Destroying them is straightforward, though, as long as you have a tool that can damage steel without making any noise."

Deep wrinkles settled into Shane's forehead. "In that case, you will be responsible for disabling the golems, since you have the required knowledge. That will be the extent of your role."

That arctic, burning hatred simmered in Zak's eyes as he stared Shane down.

Unflinching, the bounty hunter said, "Cooperate, and I'll forget I ever heard your name. Refuse, and you become my next tag. And this time, when you're arrested, I'll ensure you stay behind bars. There will be no miraculous rescues."

I shrank guiltily.

"Fine," Zak snarled. "I'll handle the golems."

Shane glanced at Darius. "Such a crucial part of our strategy shouldn't fall on one person—especially him."

The guild master nodded. "Aaron, Kai, Ezra? Zak needs a chaperone. Would any of you care to volunteer?"

As the three mages exchanged looks, Zak's green eyes turned to me. I blinked at him, confused by his attention.

He leaned forward to look around me. "Ezra?"

The aeromage paused thoughtfully, then shrugged. "I'm game."

It took me a moment to clue in. Zak was requesting Ezra's help because he was a demon mage, and his inhuman strength would come in handy against huge, heavy golems, even unanimated ones.

Shane turned his attention back to Darius, who nodded.

"Then it's agreed," the bounty hunter said. "Bring me a map of North Vancouver."

24

SLIDING MY HANDS ACROSS my combat belt, I took stock of my weapons.

Force-amplifying brass knuckles. Enemy-immobilizing fall-spell crystal. Interrogation crystal. Smoke and flashbang alchemy bombs. Paintball gun with an extra magazine of sleep potions. And my trusty Queen of Spades.

I supposed I could include the Carapace of Valdurna in my tally, seeing as I *still* hadn't returned it to Zak. The fae artifact was tucked in my front pocket.

Puffing out a breath, I gave myself a final check—black leather jacket, protective long-sleeved shirt, leather pants, heavy boots, hair pulled into a tight French braid, no makeup that could get in my eyes—then marched out of my bedroom.

The floor lamp cast warm light across the living room, and the TV flashed with color as a helicopter whooshed across the screen. Arnold Schwarzenegger hung out of the copter, reaching for a woman in a speeding car that was careening along a bridge. The scene appeared to involve a lot of shouting, but the movie's volume was too low to hear anything.

Twiggy sat on the sofa, his overly large feet sticking straight off the cushions, and for once, his chartreuse eyes weren't on the screen. He watched me with a worried crinkle in his waxy green forehead.

"Hoshi?" I called.

The sylph swirled out of nothingness. She undulated over to me, her insectile wings flared wide, and prodded my cheek with her cool nose. A rainbow of colors danced through my mind.

I rubbed her smooth neck. "Ready for this, girl?"

The colors solidified into a cheerful yellow. Affirmative.

"Tori?" Twiggy squeaked uncertainly. "You are going to fight the bad sorcerer woman?"

"Technically, no. That isn't my job." I held open the pouch at the back of my belt and Hoshi dove into it, curling into a tight ball. "But Odin's Eye and the Crow and Hammer combat guys are going to fight her."

I grabbed a keychain off the coffee table and bounced the keys on my palm, trying to think of anything I might have forgotten. Nerves danced in my gut, but my determination was stronger.

"Tori?"

I glanced down, surprised to find Twiggy standing at my feet.

"The Crystal Druid will protect you?"

No faith in my combat skills, huh? I shook my head. "He and Ezra have their own job to do."

Twiggy's face crumpled into a deeper frown. "The Crystal Druid is strong."

"Yep."

"Will you be alone?"

"Nope, I'll be with a team." I grinned. "Are you worried about me, Twiggy?"

He scrunched his small nose and muttered something too quiet for me to hear.

Laughing, I patted his twig hair. "I should be back by morning. Hold the fort while I'm gone, okay?"

He mumbled something else and glanced at the TV, where Arnie was now shooting holes in a skyscraper with a fighter jet. What'd happened to the helicopter? And why did he have a fighter jet in the middle of a city?

Leaving him to his movie, I trotted up the stairs and locked the door behind me. Why hadn't I started Twiggy on action flicks sooner? They were so far removed from real life that the impressionable faery hadn't found any human behaviors to mimic. Maybe I'd introduce him to Westerns next.

Aaron's SUV, on loan for the mission, was parked in front of my place, and my nerves increased exponentially as I hopped into the driver's seat. The engine rumbled to life, and I pushed the speed limit as I drove to the guild. I wasn't late, but my sense of urgency was growing.

I pulled up next to the guild's door. A black Mercedes idled in front of me, a cloud of exhaust hovering around it in the cold January air.

My heart raced as I walked into the guild. The pub's tables and chairs had been pushed up against the walls, and in the center of the room, more Crow and Hammer mythics in combat gear than I'd ever seen before milled together, casual but purposeful.

At one end of the room, Aaron and Tabitha waited with their teams of five. They were the ambushers; they, along with two Odin's Eye teams, would lie in wait for the rogues. Nearby, Kai spoke quietly with Makiko, while eight Japanese men with unreadable faces and all-black clothing stood silently beside them. Their stealth-focused team would flush the rogues out of their building and into Aaron's and Tabitha's waiting warriors.

The final and scariest of our main combat teams was composed of three mythics: Darius, Alistair, and Girard. Their one and only goal was Varvara—finding her, fighting her, and taking her down—but they wouldn't be challenging her alone. They'd be joining forces with the Odin's Eye guild's best team.

Before that could happen, a certain pair had an even more important job.

I scanned the room for them. Near the front door, Zak and Ezra had their heads bent together. Zak gestured as he spoke, and the light refracted off the crystals he carried—six hanging around his neck, six more in each leather bracer, and a dozen more hanging from his belt, loaded with potion vials. Knives were strapped to his thighs, and dark feather tattoos peeked up above the collar of his sleeveless shirt and swept down his arms.

Ezra was geared like usual, but his long steel-reinforced gloves weren't enough for this fight. He wore a short sword buckled at each hip, presumably borrowed since both his main pole-arm and his backup one had died premature deaths.

"You ready, Tori?"

Starting, I spun around to find Aaron behind me, eyebrows raised at my skittishness.

"Are *you* ready, Aaron?" Kai walked over, one hand on the hilt of his longer katana. "Your team will be taking the brunt of the rogue charge, assuming all goes to plan."

"Yeah, what he said." I glared warningly at the confident pyromage, my arms folded. "Don't forget your last fight with Varvara."

He winced at the reminder of how he'd gotten too close to the sorceress, been hit with a gooey substance that stuck an artifact to his face, and while under its influence, turned his sword on Ezra.

"You almost died that time too," I reminded Kai quietly. "We all need to be careful."

"Without her golems, Varvara won't know what hit her." Aaron glanced over my shoulder. "And Zak and Ezra won't be anywhere near her, which is the best for everyone."

Especially Ezra. A chaotic battlefield was the wrong place for a volatile demon mage who needed to hide his power and keep his emotions under tight control.

Tabitha called Aaron and Kai over, probably for a final check or something, so I headed toward the pair by the door.

Zak glanced up at my approach but didn't pause in his explanation. "As long as the lunar node is interrupted, the animation ritual will fail. Our only concern is getting at the arrays, which are inside the golems, but my saber can cut through steel."

"That shouldn't be a problem, then." Ezra's subdued smile lit his eyes as I joined them. "Is it time, Tori?"

"Yep. We're leaving in"—I checked my watch—"two minutes. You and Zak all set?"

"We're good to go."

I turned my gaze from his mismatched eyes, steady and calm as always, to Zak's green irises and the dark rage lurking behind their unnatural brightness.

"How about you, Zak?" I murmured, shifting closer to him.

His mouth twisted bitterly.

"The result will be the same," I whispered to him. "Even if you don't do it yourself, she'll still end up dead—and Shane's way, she'll have time to appreciate the full magnitude of her downfall before she bites the dust."

He grunted. "Your team starts at the north end of the terminal, right?"

"Yeah."

"Don't rush in when the fighting starts. It'll be easy to hem yourselves in, and you need the flexibility to shift positions or retreat."

"I'll be doing whatever Andrew tells me."

"He's one of our most experienced team leads," Ezra added. "Tori will be in good hands."

Zak nodded, tension in his jawline, and the cold pit of fear in my gut warmed as I realized he was worried about me.

"All right!" Darius called, striding through the pub. He was in combat gear, knives strapped to his hips, and older guy or not, *hot damn*. "We all know our roles. Team leads, the first check-in is at 6:50, and the final is at 6:58. We strike at 7:00."

The team leaders called affirmatives, several checking their earpieces. As my gaze passed over them, I spotted movement across the pub. In the corner, Robin had appeared, her tall, blond companion, Amalia, beside her. Both young women were dressed in black, and Robin's infernus glinted on her chest. Amalia didn't appear armed, but waiting beside them, and most definitely armed with a skull-splitting sword of doom, was petite sorceress Zora.

I frowned, wondering what their role was. Though I'd been around for most of the planning phase, no one had mentioned them.

Darius surveyed his guildeds. "Be careful, be safe, and be smart. Tonight, we set aside the first rule in favor of the third. This time, we hit first. See you on the battlefield!"

A deep-pitched cheer, almost a roar, rose from the waiting mythics, and all the hairs on my arms stood on end. The guild's first rule: *Don't hit first, but always hit back.* Tonight, however, we were the aggressors.

Darius strode for the door, Girard and Alistair following. The GM gestured to Zak as he passed. "Let's go."

Zak stepped after them. I watched him go, lower lip caught between my teeth. As he reached the door, he glanced back at me, his eyes dark and burning. Then he was gone, the door swinging shut with a cheerful jangle.

Three more mythics approached the door: Andrew, leading Bryce and Ramsey. My team.

We had two jobs: get Ezra in position, then ensure all teams stayed in contact. We'd be tracking the various fights, supporting where needed, and moving Bryce around the battlefield so he could telepathically connect all the team leaders, just in case electronic communication methods failed.

Taking Ezra's hand, I glanced over my shoulder. Aaron and Kai stood side by side, their teams behind them. The next time I saw them would be, if all went to plan, after the battle was over—rogues apprehended and Varvara either captured or dead.

Swallowing hard, I led the way to Aaron's SUV. Ezra got in, Bryce and Ramsey taking the backseat with him. Andrew slid into the passenger seat beside me.

"All right, Tori," he said in the careful, thoughtful voice that had made him a favorite among our team leaders. "Let's go."

I shifted into drive and pulled away from the curb.

"Right on schedule," he added, checking his watch. "Once we drop Ezra off, we'll have plenty of time to get in position. And Ezra should have no issues rendezvousing with … Zak."

He hesitated over the name, glancing at me.

"I can't believe we're working with *the Ghost*," Ramsey remarked. "Just the sight of him sends chills down my spine."

"Tori isn't afraid of him." In my rearview mirror, Bryce arched his eyebrows. "Neither is Ezra. Clearly, there's some familiarity there."

"Zak's reputation is greatly exaggerated … in some areas," I muttered, none too pleased that the telepath had picked up on my feelings. "Either way, he's taking care of the golems for us, so don't complain."

The plan was still for Zak and Ezra to deal with the golems together, but they were meeting on site instead of going in as a pair. It hadn't been Shane's preference, but a few security guards needed to be taken out, and as the first ones there, Zak and Ezra were the logical ones to do it.

The shivery nerves in my gut intensified. Taillights glared as I navigated away from the downtown core, last of the evening rush hour thinning. Any minute now, Kai's team would leave the guild. Ten minutes after that, Aaron's and Tabitha's teams.

A final traffic light marked the end of the residential neighborhood, and the street transformed into a wide freeway.

Streetlamps flashed by as we zoomed across a curving overpass and merged onto the highway. The miles zipped past, carrying us closer and closer.

I breathed hard through my nose, struggling with the looming dread building inside me.

With another easy curve, we sped onto the Second Narrows Bridge. The black water of the harbor reflected the city lights, and there, on the left, was our destination.

A maze of huge buildings and storage containers jutting into the harbor, endless stacks of steel piled on the expanses of concrete, blocky quays lined with monstrous equipment for unloading cargo ships. It was the largest stevedoring operation in the province, and the perfect place to source, build, and hide a small army of golems.

The arching bridge continued past the quays, and my heart sank into my gut as I realized how hopelessly, terrifyingly huge the facility was. The maps hadn't done it justice. It was a labyrinth of industrial buildings, equipment, and cargo spanning twenty city blocks. The eastern portion was dark, closed for the weekend, but on the western side, lights glowed where a long cargo ship was docked, a crane positioned above its deck.

Across the bridge, I exited the highway and drove onto a two-lane road bordered by rundown businesses and a few aged apartment buildings. Breathing deeply, I took the next left. Ahead, the road dipped beneath the train tracks that separated the stevedoring terminals from the rest of the neighborhood.

I turned left again. Passing a strip of small, industrial-type businesses, I steered onto the gravel-strewn alley beside a modest flooring warehouse, then stopped the SUV and shifted it into park. Dead ahead, raised train tracks blocked our path. A long line of black tankers chugged along, fifteen feet above the small lot behind the warehouse.

"This is my stop," Ezra said lightly, pushing his door open.

"Good luck," Andrew murmured. "Don't forget your mic."

Ezra climbed out, Bryce and Ramsey wishing him good luck too. My hands tightened on the steering wheel, my knuckles turning white as Ezra fiddled with his earpiece and checked the connection on his phone before sliding it into a pocket.

Fear swirled through my head as an internal voice screamed at me, but I didn't know what it was saying. I pressed the button for my window and it whirred down. Ezra stooped to look inside. My mouth opened, then closed.

"Be careful," I whispered hoarsely.

"I will." He gave my shoulder a quick, reassuring squeeze. "I'll see you soon."

As he strode away from the vehicle, my heart climbed into my throat. Pain spread through my fingers from their crushing grip on the wheel. Ezra was an experienced combat mythic, and he had unstoppable demon magic to back up his other skills. He could handle himself. I knew that.

So why couldn't I breathe? Why was panic ratcheting through me with each step he took?

"Wait!" The word burst from me. Unbuckling my seat belt, I flung my door open. "Ezra, wait!"

Halfway to the raised tracks and the slowly passing train, he looked back.

"What's wrong?" Andrew asked.

I didn't know. I couldn't answer. Clambering out of the vehicle, I waited with my heart hammering as Ezra jogged back to me, his eyebrows drawn with concern.

"What—" His gaze swept over my face, and his tone shifted to quietly questioning. "What is it, Tori?"

I sucked in a deep breath. Dread pulsed in the back of my throat, making me lightheaded. Something was wrong, something I couldn't put my finger on, but what …

A memory flashed behind my eyelids—Zak, his eyes burning with shadowy rage as he followed Darius out the guild door.

I gasped in realization. "I need to go with you."

Surprise flickered over his features.

"What?" Ramsey demanded from the back seat, his voice carrying through my open door. "I know you've been training, but you're still an amateur."

Andrew leaned across the driver's seat. "Tori, their job is too important for—"

"Zak isn't on board with our plan." I directed my words at Ezra. "Varvara destroyed everything that matters to him. The moment he's done with the golems, he's going for her throat, and I might be the only one who can talk him down."

Ezra absorbed that. "Change of plans, Andrew. She's coming with me."

"Wait." Bryce stuck his head over the console to peer out the door at me and Ezra. "Is it bad if he goes for Varvara? As long as she's defeated …"

"Did you see the footage of the LA precinct being destroyed?" I asked impatiently.

"Yeah, of course."

"*That's* why I need to make sure Zak keeps his head."

His eyes widened.

"That was *him*?" Ramsey whispered disbelievingly.

"One hundred and ten percent a pissed-off druid who doesn't care much about friendly fire." I looked at Andrew. "I'm going."

He unbuckled his seat belt. "You'll need to be extra cautious, then. You can't be detected before the golems are disabled."

"We'll get it done," Ezra said, his steadiness calming my jitters. "And we'll handle Zak."

He took my hand. As Andrew opened his door to switch to the driver's seat, Ezra pulled me across the lot, and I craned my neck back to watch the last tanker in the long train clatter past on the raised tracks.

I knew Zak was in a bad place, but with his steely composure, I'd assumed he could handle it. Now, I wasn't so sure. Had I underestimated the depth of his grief ... and his need for revenge? Either way, I needed to be beside him before he laid eyes on his enemy—and got himself, or anyone else, killed.

25

"I SHOULD'VE TALKED TO HIM," I berated myself as Ezra and I slid down the dirt bank on the far side of the train tracks. "*Really* talked to him."

Still holding my hand, Ezra led me into the deep shadows beside a long warehouse. The narrow road lacked streetlamps, but breaking from winter's usual pattern of nonstop cloud cover, the night sky was clear. The moon, nearly full, shone down.

"He's smart," Ezra murmured as we trekked along the grass that bordered the building. "He doesn't strike me as the type to fall victim to a sudden case of recklessness."

"I suppose," I muttered, a cold wind smelling of salt water and rotting seaweed blowing across my face. Zak was too wily to do something outrageously stupid.

We reached an intersection and Ezra slowed to a halt, his back against the wall. He scanned the street, then closed his eyes, stretching his senses for any hint of movement.

"Let's go," he breathed.

We darted into the shadows of the next building. Aside from overhead doors, the surrounding walls were blank, and everything was quiet. Farther west, light hazed the sky and the distant clatter of machinery reached my ears, almost too faint to hear.

Moving cautiously, we crept another half a block, then Ezra stopped in a shadowed nook. Across the street was a small parking lot that ended in a tall security fence covered in big warning signs. Beyond it were behemoth-sized cylindrical reservoirs, three stories high, with pipes and catwalks running around them.

Hesitating, he looked around. "I don't see him."

"Who?" I asked dumbly.

"Zak. This is the rendezvous point."

My stomach dropped. "He's late?"

"He should've beat us here, unless he had trouble with the other guard station."

Other guard station? I leaned out enough to look again at the parking lot and its tall fence. A security gate spanned the center, and tucked beside it was a small booth, lit up inside. Security for the facility.

"The other station was too exposed, so it was better he handle it with his shadow magic." Ezra puffed out a breath. "If he's been delayed—"

"Ezra." I squinted at the booth. "I don't see any guards."

"What?" He leaned out for a better look. "I can't see well enough to tell."

The bright windows were unobstructed by human shapes. Either the guards were napping on the floor, or nobody was home. "The booth is empty."

He hesitated. "Let's get closer."

Slinking into the open, he paused, then sprinted across the street. We cut along the fence line in a swift, half-crouching jog. Ezra stopped again, head canted as though listening, then he scooted under the window of the booth and peeked inside.

He swore under his breath. With no caution at all, he rose to his feet.

"What?" I demanded in a hiss. "What is it?"

He waved at the booth. Standing, I looked through the window.

I'd been partially right. The uniformed guards were on the floor—but they weren't napping. A shimmering silver potion splattered their unconscious faces. At least they weren't dead. Or … probably not dead? I wasn't sure.

"Zak *did* beat us here," Ezra said. "And he decided not to wait."

I groaned. Selfish, overly independent dickhead of a druid. He probably figured he could handle the golems himself. Why wait for his partner/backup/babysitter?

Ezra pressed his earpiece. "Andrew, do you copy? I'm at the rendezvous point. Zak was here, but it looks like he went ahead. Tori and I will try to catch up before he reaches the golems."

He listened for a moment. "Copy that." Lowering his hand, he said to me, "Andrew doesn't want us to rush. Zak can disable the golems without us. We just need to reach him before he finishes."

I clenched my jaw. Zak wanted to get the golems done fast—so he'd be free to go after Varvara. Growling under my breath, I faced the security fence, but my angry determination faltered at the sight of the barbed wire on top.

"Watch me first," Ezra suggested as he grabbed the thick metal post where two sections of fence joined. Pulling himself up, he used the top of the post as a hand and foot hold. He carefully swung one leg, then the other, over the barbed wire and dropped to the other side.

Gulping, I took hold of the fence and started to climb. It took me three times as long, but I made it over the barbed wire without tearing any skin or clothes. Ezra caught me, then we were moving again, this time at a quick jog.

Running alongside a set of train tracks, we crossed the facility. Scaling the fence at the far end went a lot faster, and we hopped yet another line of tracks. A steel yard stretched ahead. Ezra led me past stacks of I-beams and pipes, some shining and new, others rusting in the salty breeze. We jogged past two storage buildings with flimsy-looking roofs and open fronts.

Fifty yards away was the biggest warehouse yet—at least three stories with a single huge overhead door, dead center in the middle of its face. Train tracks ran across the back for easy loading of cargo directly onto the cars.

That was it. The set of warehouses where Varvara was storing her collection of golems.

A man-sized door, tucked at the edge of the building and miniscule compared to the overhead door, was a dark rectangle—but as we watched, a tiny orange light flared. A cigarette, its faint glow illuminating the shape of a man leaning in the open doorway. He was short, heavyset, and definitely not Zak.

Dread plunged through my center. "Is that one of Varvara's men?"

"Where's Zak?" Ezra muttered. "No way he didn't beat us here. No way."

But if he were here, he wouldn't have left that guard standing at the warehouse door.

"Did he run into trouble?" My hands clenched. "Was he captured or …"

"If he'd been spotted, I don't think that rogue would be casually smoking with the door open." Ezra raked his fingers through his hair, then touched his earpiece. "Andrew, do you copy? Andrew? … Anyone?"

He slid his phone from his pocket and tapped across the screen, then shook his head. "No signal. We're in a dead spot, and Bryce is too far."

I drew in a steadying breath, fighting back panic. Somewhere nearby, the combat teams were creeping into position: Kai and Makiko's team infiltrating the building where the rogues were staying; Aaron's and Tabitha's teams, as well as the Odin's Eye guild, encircling the building from the outside; and Darius's team positioning themselves halfway between our location and the dock where Varvara would arrive on her yacht.

Where was Zak? He'd been through here. Who else would've taken out the human security guards with a potion? But why, then, wasn't he *here*?

"He knows how important this is," I whispered hoarsely. "He knows we have to disable the golems before Varvara arrives. Where could he have wandered off to?"

Ezra looked up at me, his features frozen in disbelief. "He … shit."

"What?" I demanded.

"He told me how to disable the golems."

"He did? Wait—I thought it required obscure Arcana knowledge."

"That's what he told Shane, but at the guild, while we were waiting to leave, he described the symbols to look for. I thought he was explaining it so I could make myself useful, but ..." He bit off a curse. "Did he tell me because he wasn't planning to show up?"

The blood drained out of my head, leaving me dizzy. "He wouldn't. He ... he wouldn't do that."

Ezra woke his phone. The clock ticked from 6:38 to 6:39. Time was running out.

"We're going," he growled, uncharacteristic fury darkening his features. "Whether he intended to show or not doesn't matter. He isn't here, so it's up to us."

"But—" Meeting his determined stare, I straightened my spine. "You're right. He told you how to disable them, so we can do it ourselves. Then we're going to find that asshole. In fact ..."

I tapped the back pouch on my belt. Hoshi uncoiled in a swirl of glowing silver scales, and Ezra and I stepped shoulder to shoulder to block the faint light emanating from her.

"Hoshi," I whispered, laying my hand on the pink crystal in the center of her forehead, "can you find Zak? Find him, then come get me, okay?"

She bumped me with her nose, then faded out of sight.

"Okay," I said grimly, unholstering my paintball gun. "Let's go."

Ezra crept to the corner of the building we were using as shelter. "It's about to get a little cold."

"Huh?"

A faint red glow sparked in his left eye. The temperature plunged and the surrounding shadows thickened as though they were devouring the light. Aeromages couldn't create darkness, but demon mages could.

He darted into the open space, and I followed on his heels, scarcely able to discern his outline. My breath puffed white. We raced toward the waiting warehouse. Five more identical ones butted up against it, available to be rented by any client or criminal.

As soon as we were in range, I stopped, set my feet, and raised my gun. Taking aim, I fired two shots.

One hit the smoking rogue in the head, and the other burst against his shoulder. He yipped in pain, then pitched sideways, falling on the interior side of the threshold.

At the doorway, Ezra let the icy darkness around him fade. I joined him, and we peered into the warehouse. I couldn't see a thing—only unbroken black. He listened intently, then stepped over the downed rogue. I ducked in after him, swinging the door most of the way closed. It smacked against the sleeping man's foot.

"I can't sense any movement," Ezra whispered.

He activated the light on his vest, leaving it on the lowest setting to preserve our night vision. The pale glow swept across the empty floor, the ceiling obscured in shadows. A steel catwalk ran around the perimeter of the echoing space, the only accessory on the blank walls.

"What ..." he whispered with muted horror.

My limbs went numb, my brain buzzing with confusion.

The concrete floor, stretching over a hundred and fifty feet to the far wall, was marked with dozens of the most complex spell arrays I'd ever seen—not that I'd seen a ton of them. Each web of interconnecting geometric lines pierced a large hexagon, with three triangles pointing inward toward a small center circle. Hundreds of runes filled the arrays, and small bowls of spell ingredients sat in the inner circles.

But the arrays ... they were empty.

The golems were gone.

I grabbed Ezra's wrist, my fingers digging in. The golems had been here. What else could those spells be? But where were the steel beasts? Why weren't they here? How could we disable them *if they weren't here!*

He seized his vest light and snapped the button, switching it to full brightness. The white glare blazed across the warehouse interior.

My stomach dropped a second time. My hand ached from how tightly I was holding his wrist.

The golems weren't *all* gone. There was one left.

At the back of the warehouse, in the center of the largest array, was a steel monstrosity. Similar to the super-golem that had attacked the Odin's Eye guild, this one had gorilla-like arms and a thick bipedal body—but it was closer to twenty feet tall than twelve, and instead of fat fingers, its massive fists were solid blocks adorned with three sword-like claws, each one well over a foot long.

"Ezra," I choked out. "We have to disable that thing. It'll kill everyone."

"Yes. As soon as we're done with this one, we need to get back in signal range and warn the teams."

Nodding shakily, I holstered my gun and together we rushed forward—but three steps from the doorway, Ezra yanked his wrist from my grasp.

As I stumbled, thrown off balance, he pivoted with deadly grace and whipped his two short swords from their sheaths. He sliced them through the air, blades crossing. A blast of wind tore across the warehouse and hit the catwalk with so much force the steel rattled.

An answering swirl of pink magic danced above the catwalk, illuminating the silhouettes of three people.

As Ezra drew his swords back for another strike and I reached for my paintball gun, magic tingled over my feet. I looked down and saw what I hadn't noticed before, my attention on the new mega-golem.

A spell array on the floor under us, drawn in gray, almost invisible against the dingy concrete.

Its lines blazed with amber light. The radiant beam shot upward, and my body lifted off the ground. Gravity had vanished and I hung suspended in the glow, my feet kicking helplessly. The air felt thicker than mud and I could hardly move.

Caught in the spell with me, Ezra fought to raise his arms, sword blades shining in the spell's light.

A new color snaked through the amber array. Ugly blue lines lit up—a second array scribed inside the first. The dark magic twisted off the floor like dense smoke, then shot upward. Two bands coiled around Ezra's wrists, growing darker and denser, and more magic wrapped around his lower face. His hands snapped together as though drawn by magnets, and his swords fell from his grasp. They plunged to the floor, unaffected by the amber light.

The dark power flashed, and when the glow faded, black manacles bound his wrists together. A dark muzzle covered his lower face, a sizzling cord of power running from it to the manacles.

Red flashed in his pale left eye—then both eyes rolled up in his head.

"Ezra!" I screamed. My voice sounded wrong in my ears, muffled and deadened. I wasn't sure whether I was making any noise at all. "*Ezra!*"

Quiet footsteps tapped against metal stairs. Three figures descended from the catwalk and approached us. Terror and hatred fought for dominance as I looked into Varvara's deep-set eyes.

She smiled, lips painted a vivid red. Just like the last time I'd faced her, she looked ready for an exclusive dinner party with the world's most rich and powerful. Her silver hair was pulled into an elegant bun, a scarlet blouse and dark slacks clothing her slim figure, her chic coat hanging to her knees.

Strolling to the edge of the amber spell, she reached into the beam of light and caressed Ezra's cheek. His eyelids fluttered and focus briefly returned to his gaze, left eye still glowing, but he didn't otherwise react.

"More talented than I expected," she sighed in a thick Russian accent. "He sensed the shifting air as soon as I began an incantation. And it appears he is still conscious? I am rather impressed." She gestured to her companions—more henchman, these ones tall and muscular. "Pull him out."

The two men, their brutish faces impassive, stepped closer. Varvara moved aside for them—and turned to me.

"I was not expecting *you*," she mused. "How intriguing. I had assumed he liked you."

"What did you do to Ezra, you bitch!" I yelled, fighting against the spell as though I could swim through the thickened air and strangle her with my bare hands.

"You're wasting your breath, darling. I can't hear you—though I recognize one of those words."

The two brutes dragged Ezra out of the glowing beam. His knees hit the floor, head lolling forward then backward as he struggled to straighten. The men seized his arms and lifted him, his manacled wrists jerking taut. His unfocused gaze found me still trapped in the light—and I saw terror in his eyes.

Terror for me.

"Let me go!" I dragged my arm toward my belt of artifacts, but the farther my limb moved, the thicker the magic became. It was like trying to wade through hardening cement.

Varvara smiled, no doubt reading the words on my lips since she couldn't hear them. She raised her hands. Delicate metal claws and multiple rings adorned each finger. A fine net of chains connected the claws and rings to a disc on the back of her hand. According to Zak, each piece was a dark-magic artifact.

I expected her to utter an incantation. I expected magic to spear my body while I was caught helpless in her spell.

Her clawed fingers closed around my arms and she turned me to face the opposite direction, as easily as if I were suspended on invisible chains. I stared across the warehouse at the gargantuan golem, unable to look anywhere else—unable to see Ezra or the men who held him.

Varvara walked past the spell toward the monster golem. Stopping at the edge of the array, she glanced over her shoulder. "My other steel beasts are already animated and lying in wait for your guild friends. This one, however, was too large to hide—but it seems a shame to leave it here to rust."

She raised her arms and began to chant. I could do nothing but hang in her spell as she recited the incantation, each word of Latin flowing into the next with perfect rhythm. The array on the floor lit up with pale reddish light.

Her chant went on and on. I did nothing. I couldn't turn to see Ezra. Couldn't reach for a weapon. Couldn't even scream for help. No one would hear me.

Runes lit up across the golem's twenty-foot-tall body. With a final shouted phrase, Varvara lowered her arms. The golem creaked as it shifted its monstrous weight. Turning, she glided back to the amber spell and stopped in front of me a second time.

The fine lines around her eyes crinkled with her cruel smile. "I'd thought the druid a soft fool, but he is as pragmatic as his reputation suggests. Trading a demon mage for his grimoire's return, certainly, but sacrificing you as well? Not what I expected."

She stepped away, adding, "But he still thinks he can kill me once he's reclaimed his grimoire. I will enjoy telling him of your demise."

I wanted to scream at her, to call her every horrible insult I knew, but I couldn't find my voice. I couldn't even breathe through my spiking panic as she walked away, disappearing from my line of sight.

She murmured a command to her minions. Grunts of effort as they lifted a weight. Footsteps accompanied the scuff of limbs dragging on the floor as they hauled Ezra away.

Trading a demon mage for his grimoire's return.

Varvara knew our plan. She'd already animated her golems. She'd been waiting here for Ezra, and now she would escape with him on her yacht while her golem army ambushed all my friends and guildmates.

And I …

The floor shook as the twenty-foot mega-golem took a long stride on thick steel legs, its blank face pointed at me.

And I would die right here, crushed flat by the golem before it joined the desperate battle about to commence outside—and massacred everyone I cared about.

26

THE GOLEM ADVANCED ON ME. It wasn't fast, but its huge stride covered a lot of ground, and all I could do was watch it come. Despite Varvara's spell suspending my body in shimmering amber light, suffocating weight dragged at my lungs—frigid heaviness that had nothing to do with the magic.

It couldn't be true. Zak hadn't betrayed us to Varvara. He hadn't traded Ezra to the sorceress to get his grimoire back.

He couldn't have double-crossed us ...

But if he hadn't, why had Varvara been waiting for us, a trap already set? If he hadn't, why were her golems gone? If he hadn't, why wasn't he here?

I'm here to kill Varvara.

He'd shut down his farm because of her. He'd sent away all his wards—the only nonhostile company he had aside from fae, who treated him like a "feast." Then she'd destroyed his only refuge. Slaughtered his horses. Murdered the last loyal companion he had left. Killed the dryad and stole his grimoire.

I didn't come back to enact justice or some noble shit like that.

He'd returned to commit murder. He wouldn't *make a deal* with his nemesis, no matter how badly he wanted his grimoire back. And even if he *did* need the grimoire, he still wouldn't knowingly hand one of my best friends over to the enemy. He wouldn't disclose our entire plan to her, putting my entire guild in terrible danger.

What were you expecting, Tori?

Tears burned in my eyes as the golem stomped closer. I'd thought I more or less understood Zak, but how much did I really know about him? Could I be sure that the druid who'd unleashed a violent spell in a building full of people would care about the safety of a guild that had once hunted him? Could I be sure that the rogue who'd dropped a pleading, terrified man off a building would value the life of my demon-mage friend?

I didn't know anymore—what Zak was capable of, where he was now, whether Varvara was lying—and I would never find out.

Tears slid down my cheeks as I fought to get my arm down to my belt, but I could no longer move my limbs. The magic had thickened so much I could scarcely breathe. The golem took another lumbering step, its foot landing a yard from the spell's edge. The impact of steel on concrete reverberated through the warehouse.

The golem raised a gargantuan arm, its steel limbs shining gold in the light of the spell. My heart seized as its fist arced downward, blades sweeping for my torso.

The amber light of the spell blinked out.

I dropped to the ground in a heap. The blades whipped past, inches above my head, the wind of their passing turning the tears on my cheeks to ice.

All around me, small plants pushed up through the floor, breaking the lines of Varvara's spell. They'd destroyed the array just in time to save me—but where the hell had they come from?

"Tori!"

The squeaking voice, shaking with fear, had me on my feet in an instant. As I bolted away from the golem, I spotted a tiny figure hunkered in the shadows by the door where the sleeping goon had collapsed.

Less than three feet tall, thin branches sticking off his head, Twiggy had an oversized hand pressed to the floor, his spindly fingers glowing with faint green magic. His huge green eyes were wide and glassy, but pride lit his face despite his terror.

"Twiggy!" I shrieked.

"Watch out!" he gasped.

I flung myself down as the golem's fist swung over my head a second time. Its reach was insane. Scrambling up, I sprinted to Twiggy and scooped him off the floor, resisting the urge to crush him to my chest and weep incoherently. I had no idea why he was here but I wasn't complaining.

Ignoring the slumbering mythic on the floor, I whipped the building's door open—and hesitated. I glanced back, my heart hammering as a cowardly voice in the back of my head howled at me to *run run run*.

The golem stomped after me, shaking the ground with each step. Ezra's dropped swords were no more than shattered bits of steel, crushed under its foot. It could smash right through the flimsy overhead door, and once outside, it would find the battle between the smaller golems, the rogues, and my guildmates.

This thing alone would obliterate the already slim odds that my friends would survive the night.

And I was the only one who had a chance in hell of stopping it. Only I carried an artifact that could suck the animation magic right out of it.

The golem stomped closer, bringing me in reach of its swing. Instead of jumping through the door to relative safety, I sprang sideways and ran along the wall. The floor shook as the golem turned to follow me. The warehouse was a dark, echoing cavern, the only light coming from the pinkish runes glowing all over the golem's body.

When I reached the corner, I gulped back my panic and set Twiggy on the ground. "Thanks, bud. You saved my butt. Now I need to stop this thing."

"Stop it?" He straightened to his full, unimpressive height. "We will stop it!"

"No, you—"

"I saved you! I can help!"

The faery wasn't exactly a powerhouse, but my list of allies was so damn thin I could see through it.

I pulled the Queen of Spades card from its pouch, then unbuckled my belt and tossed it into the corner. Nothing else in it was of any use against a golem. This would all come down to me, Twiggy, and the Carapace of Valdurna—except this time, I didn't have an agile demon to get me on top of the golem's head. I'd have to find out how far the Carapace's power could stretch.

"Okay, Twiggy." I plucked the folded fabric from my pocket. "You distract it while I use my secret weapon."

Face lighting up, Twiggy charged straight for the approaching steel monstrosity. Eyes bugging with fear for the reckless twig-head, I dashed away at an angle so I could loop around the golem, Carapace in one hand and Queen in the other.

Twiggy closed half the distance, set his green feet, and threw his hands up. His body shimmered as he cast illusion magic over himself. Darkness rippled upward and solidified into a ten-foot-tall King Kong. Rearing back, he drummed his fists on his chest and loosed a surprisingly convincing roar.

I ran wide, then cut toward the golem's heels as I shook out the Carapace one-handed.

The golem took a thundering step toward King Kong Faery, then swung its huge fist. Its whole torso rotated in a way no human's could, and its bladed fist slashed toward me.

The angle of the swing—even if I dove for the floor, it wouldn't save me. I was mincemeat.

"*Ori repercutio!*" I screamed desperately.

The air rippled and the golem's steel fist bounced off nothing. As its arm was flung away, the momentum forced the mega-golem's whole torso to rotate 180 degrees, metal grinding loudly. It wobbled, off balance.

Holy *crap*. The golem was more magic than steel, so the Queen had deflected its blow. Damn, I loved this card.

Stuffing it in my back pocket to recharge, I pulled the Carapace open and prayed that the fae artifact's proximity wouldn't wipe the magic out of my card. As the sparkling, rippling fabric unfurled, I flipped it over the golem's lower leg—the only part I could reach.

The glowing runes under the fabric dimmed and faded. The runes just above the artifact faded too. The effect spread, the runes dying out one by one—but not fast enough.

"Tori!"

At Twiggy's shrieked cry, I dove for the floor and another deadly strike missed me by inches. The Carapace fluttered off its leg and the golem lifted its foot. A terrifying shadow fell over me. I rolled away, too slow to escape that crushing steel boot.

A cracking sound, followed by the creak of metal.

Thin, tough vines had erupted from the floor and wound around the golem's foot, holding it back. The steel beast pulled its leg forward and the vines snapped, but the few seconds allowed me to leap up and sprint away. Its foot stomped down, shattering bits of floor under it.

Twiggy, back to his twiggy self, darted in and snatched the Carapace. As I ran across the width of the warehouse, the golem stamping along in my wake, Twiggy rushed to join me with the cloak streaming after him like an amethyst banner.

He thrust the fabric at me. "Take it, take it!"

I pulled it from his hands, cringing as my fingers went numb from its power. I got why he didn't like it.

Breathing hard and aching from too many ungraceful dives to the floor, I watched the golem come, slow but unstoppable. The Carapace's magic wasn't fast enough to immobilize it, not from the feet upward. I needed to get the artifact on its head or torso.

My gaze slid to the catwalk that encircled the warehouse's perimeter. I gulped, taking stock of my options. Even assuming the Carapace's nearness wasn't hindering my artifact's magic, the Queen hadn't had time to recharge yet. I couldn't count on the reflector spell.

"Round two, Twiggy. Can you slow it down with vines again?"

"One more time only." He shivered where he stood. "I do not have much magic."

"What you don't have in magic you make up for by being the bravest fae I've ever met." As bashful delight lit his face, I measured the distance of the golem and the speed of its approach. "I'm going up on the catwalk, and the golem will come after me. When it's close enough to hit me, stop it with the vines."

He bobbed his head, and I raced away. The stairs onto the catwalk beckoned. Ignoring the monster's footfalls vibrating the floor, I sped up the steps and onto the platform.

The golem, oblivious to Twiggy, stomped after me, and I stared into its helmet-like face, the two eye sockets black and empty. The catwalk was level with its shoulders, which put my head higher than its hollow helmet. It plodded closer and closer, and I braced a hand on the railing.

"Now, Twiggy!" I bellowed.

Vines burst out of the concrete and spun around the golem's ankles. Its stride stuttered—and I vaulted over the railing, a move I'd practiced more than any combat skill so I could hop my bar without making a fool of myself.

Soaring over the railing, I landed on the golem's steel shoulder. Its body lurched as it tore free from the vines, and its bladed fists whipped up to impale me.

I jammed the Carapace into its empty eye socket and leaped off the back of its shoulder. Unforgiving concrete rushed up, and I tried to remember the fall-break techniques Aaron and Kai had taught me but my mind was blank and I was going to shatter my leg bones and oh god—

Wind burst around me, and a sinuous silver tail looped around my torso. I thumped gently to the floor, with Hoshi clinging to my middle, her paws clutching my jacket.

314 ◆ ANNETTE MARIE

"Hoshi!" I gasped, hugging her as I sprinted away. "You're back!"

"Tori, look!" Twiggy cried.

I spun around.

The golem stood unmoving, half the Carapace hanging from its helmet like a stream of purple tears. The runes on its head had vanished, and the Carapace's magic swept downward, dousing the runes all across its torso. Five seconds later, the last runes blinked out, and the only source of light came from the radiant cloak and Hoshi's faintly luminescent body.

With a groan of steel, the unanimated golem tipped over backward. I slapped my hands over my ears just before it hit the ground, and the thundering crash was so loud I felt the boom in my chest.

The echo rebounded off the walls, then finally, it was silent.

Uncoiling her tail from my waist, Hoshi touched her nose to my cheek. A vision filled my mind: Zak, geared for battle as I'd last seen him, leaning against a pillar in a dark space with the look of a man waiting for something.

Emotion twisted in my chest, painful and confusing. Was he waiting for Varvara? If she'd told the truth about him trading Ezra for his grimoire, she'd be meeting with him to complete the exchange.

What was Zak playing at? Did he have a plan? And if he did, why the hell had he left me in the dark!

"Goddamn you, Zak," I snarled as I pulled the Carapace out of the golem's helmet, folded the enchanted fabric into a square, and shoved it in my front pocket.

Twiggy trotted out of the darkness, carrying my combat belt. I reclaimed it and buckled the leather around my hips. If

Varvara was meeting with Zak before taking Ezra to her yacht, we still had time to stop her.

"You did great, Twiggy." I exhaled roughly. "I have one more job for you, then you need to hide because you used up all your magic."

He tilted his face up attentively.

"Find Aaron or Kai—they should be just north of this building—and tell them ... tell them we couldn't find the golems, and Varvara has Ezra. I'm going after her. Got that?"

He nodded.

"And ..." I swallowed hard. "Tell them Zak might've double-crossed us."

His huge eyes widened. "The Crystal Druid betrayed you?"

"I'm not sure."

"I will tell them. I'll go right now!" He scurried away, but at the warehouse door, he looked over his shoulder. Puffing his chest, he said in the deepest, growliest voice he could produce, "I'll be back."

He vanished out the door, and I blinked. Blinked again. "*Oh.*"

Action movies. Arnold Schwarzenegger. Fearless musclemen saving the day. Twiggy *had* picked up new "human" behaviors from his latest film binge. That's why he'd followed me on my dangerous, adrenaline-fueled mission—and thank god he had, or I'd be dead.

"It's you and me now, Hoshi," I whispered. "Let's find Zak—and hopefully Ezra."

She swirled around me in a quick, encouraging circle, then undulated toward the door. I ran after her, muscles trembling and joints aching, but there was no time to stop and whine about it.

I burst outside—and a cacophony of booms, bangs, clangs, shouts, and screams assaulted my ears.

Terror flooded my chest. When Varvara had said her animated golems were waiting for my "guild friends," I'd hoped she was wrong—that Zak had pulled the wool over her eyes and she only believed her golem army was ready to fight.

But even as I followed Hoshi, sprinting back the way Ezra and I had come, the dissonant roar of battle continued. At the train tracks that ran behind the warehouse, the sylph swung right—and somewhere on the other side of a long line of freight cars, a fireball erupted. Orange flames spewed into the sky, belching black smoke, and masculine shouts rang out in a nonstop clamor.

I burst into a mad sprint. Hoshi whirled, confused, as I jumped the first set of tracks. Grabbing a freight car, I hauled myself onto the back, then scaled the metal ladder attached to the butt end. I had to know. I had to see.

Scrambling onto the roof on my hands and knees, I squinted across the scene. A street. A parking lot. Then the building where the rogues had hidden during the day.

Now all three were a war zone.

Smoke billowed, fire burning everywhere. Shadowy figures darted in chaotic patterns, some wielding weapons, others glowing magic. I couldn't tell who was who, guildeds and rogues impossible to tell apart, but the canine golems were easy to spot as they stomped among the combatants, belching fire or acid and snapping their crushing jaws.

Varvara's golems were attacking my guildmates—along with no small number of rogues. All our strategizing to ensure our teams wouldn't face both the rogue and golem forces had failed, and now over half my guild was fighting for their lives.

Choking on dread, I slid back down the ladder and forced myself away from the train. Ezra needed me. I had to find him.

I rejoined Hoshi and she led me into the maze. As we approached the facility with the giant reservoirs, I wondered if we would follow my and Ezra's route in reverse, but she sped past the fence. I ran along another set of train tracks to a different fence—a taller one with much meaner barbed wire at the top.

As I started to climb, Hoshi grasped the collar of my jacket. With a tug from her, I flew up and over the fence. I dropped onto the grass, stumbled down the embankment, and trotted into a parking lot. Water sloshed loudly, city lights reflecting off its black surface. We'd reached the marina.

Passing a never-ending storage building, we cut through the narrow gap between buildings and came out in a boat … lot. Like a parking lot, but for boats. Lots of boats. I sprinted down a row and squeezed between two speedboats.

With a warning flick of her tail, Hoshi ducked behind a retaining wall. I followed suit, then cautiously peeked above it.

Yet another parking lot. Behind it was a low, wide building with several overhead doors, one open, and a dozen covered boats lined up in front. A repair business? That was my best guess.

Hoshi bumped me with her nose, and a vision appeared in my head—zooming across the parking lot, rushing between two covered boats, sweeping through the overhead door. A dark interior, interrupted by concrete pillars. Most of the bays were open, while yachts and equipment waited in the far bays for work to resume Monday morning. In the center, leaning against a pillar, Zak waited.

That's what Hoshi had seen before coming to get me. This was the place.

I was about to stand up but caught the faintest glimpse of movement—a dark figure shifting his weight. Two big, bulky men stood on either side of the open overhead door. I couldn't be sure from this distance, but they looked like Varvara's goons.

Varvara was in there. She had to be.

I could do this. Find Ezra, get him away from her, and run like hell. That was my plan. First, I had to get past the henchmen, and there was no way to approach without being seen.

I dug into my pouch. My brass knuckles went on one hand. I looped the strings of my fall spell and interrogation spell crystals around my other wrist, then unholstered my paintball gun. Lastly, I tugged the elastic hair tie from the end of my braid, slid it over my hand, and tucked my Queen of Spades under it, snug against my inner wrist.

"Hoshi," I whispered, "can you make me invisible long enough to get close?"

Her tail flicked nervously back and forth. She blinked her huge eyes and rustled her insect-like wings, then booped me with her nose. I interpreted that as, "I'll try."

I set my feet and Hoshi curled her tail around me, small paws holding my shoulders.

"Now," I breathed.

Cool magic rushed over me and the world faded to a phantom landscape of white and gray. The boats were dark, semi-transparent shapes, and Varvara's goons were even more transparent shadows.

I launched from behind the retaining wall and sprinted as fast as my legs could carry me. Stare locked on my shadowy targets, I raced toward them. Forty feet. Thirty feet. Twenty—

Shimmering color swept across my vision. With a faint hiss of dismay, Hoshi fell off me, her body shimmering out of my perception.

If the sight of a running woman appearing out of nowhere startled the goons, it didn't show. The nearer one pulled two blades from his thigh sheaths, and the other raised his hands.

But I already had my gun up, and my trigger finger was faster. I fired three paintballs into the upper chest of the nearer man, then dove. Goon Two shot a blast of ice shards over my head.

"*Ori*," I gasped as I hit the ground and rolled. I jumped to my feet, whirling. "*Deci—*"

A flash of silver. I threw up my arm and the knife sliced through my leather jacket and into my arm. My lungs locked.

Despite the yellow potion splattered all over his chest and neck, Goon One hadn't gone down. Grinning, he jerked the blade off my arm, tearing a hoarse sound from my throat.

Universal antidote. Varvara must've dosed her men to protect them.

So I fired my next shot into his eye.

He lurched back with a pained gasp, one dagger clattering from his hand.

"*Ori decidas!*" I cried as I slammed my hand into his potion-free shoulder, the fall spell under my palm. Magic flashed against my skin and the man pitched over backward. His head hit the pavement with a sickening crack.

I shoved up, the fall spell swinging from my wrist—and a barrage of ice shards slammed into me. I fell back into a covered boat on a trailer, agony lancing my torso. My leather jacket had deflected the smaller shards, but the larger ones had torn through the leather and embedded in my flesh. I slumped against the hull, muscles seizing with pain and shock.

Lips curled in a sneer, the kryomage held his hands up, the air around him sparkling with crystals. A shard coalesced between his palms, growing into a harpoon of ice. He drew it back.

I flung my hand up, blood dripping from my sleeve.

He hurled the ice harpoon.

"*Ori repercutio!*"

Air rippled out from the Queen, strapped to my wrist, and the harpoon hit the magical force. It shattered and hunks of ice whipped back at the mage. He winced from the onslaught.

Yanking a sphere from my belt, I threw it to the pavement. It shattered, releasing a thick cloud of peppery smoke. As the white haze expanded, I launched off the boat trailer toward the man—or where he'd last been standing. His shadow appeared in the fog, and I drew my fist back.

He spotted me and lifted an arm to block my obvious attack.

"*Ori amplifico!*"

My fist hit his forearm and force blasted out from the impact. The man flew backward and slammed down, barely keeping his head off the pavement. I pounced on his chest and slapped the fall spell, its magic still active, against his throat. He went limp with a furious snarl.

"*Ori ostende tuum pectus,*" I chanted.

The second crystal, hanging from my wrist and resting on his neck beside the ruby, flared with faint light. The mage's eyes glazed over.

"Where is Ezra?" I hissed.

"I don't know who—"

"Where is the demon mage Varvara took prisoner?"

The mage's eyelids fluttered. "Inside with Varvara."

"Is there anyone else with her?"

"Only the druid."

I inhaled roughly—then smashed the butt of my pistol into his temple. It hit with a crunch and I hoped I hadn't killed him. Standing on unsteady legs, I whimpered in pain. Bits of melting ice stuck out of my jacket. I didn't think any had pierced too deep, but it still hurt like hell, and my arm throbbed mercilessly. My hand was covered in blood.

Fumbling at the back of my belt, I slid a handful of vials from a pouch—gifts from Sin. Each one was labeled with glow-in-the-dark ink. As I shuffled through them, two fell from my shaking hands and bounced away. I found the one with "STP BLD" on it and pulled the cork. Nudging my sleeve up, I poured the watery liquid over the deep slice in my forearm.

The spot went completely numb. The wound didn't change, but blood stopped welling in the slice. Good enough. Tossing the vial away, I turned to the open doorway, filled with darkness.

Inside were Varvara, Ezra ... and Zak.

27

"OUR AGREEMENT WAS VERY SIMPLE."

In the middle of creeping behind a line of boats mounted on trailers, I froze in place.

"I deliver a demon mage for you to play with," Zak continued, his rumbling voice as frigid as I'd ever heard it, "and you return my grimoire."

"The spells you imbued into it are very clever," Varvara murmured in her heavy accent. "Try as I might, I could not make a copy."

"That's the idea. Now hand it over."

Moving in a half crouch, I continued past the boats. When I reached the last one, a thirty-foot cruiser suspended on a steel frame that held its keel a yard off the floor, I peeked around the bow.

The building's wide interior, interrupted by evenly spaced pillars, looked exactly as Hoshi had shown me. A soft blue glow emanated from a crystal hanging around Zak's neck as he leaned casually against a pillar, arms folded.

Varvara stood at the other end of the open space, her back to a line of large cardboard boxes on wooden pallets. She thoughtfully tapped one clawed finger against her painted lips as she studied the druid. Her other hand gripped Ezra's hair.

He was on his knees, listing to the side. The black-magic muzzle and manacles around his face and wrists sizzled with dark power. Varvara yanked on his hair, forcing him upright before he crumpled sideways. His head jerked—and his left eye glowed crimson. Whatever that spell was doing to him, he was only half conscious.

Eterran, however, was probably a lot more conscious. And that was a very bad thing.

"Let us be frank with each other," the sorceress crooned. "I am well aware that as soon as you can confirm I have your grimoire here, you'll attack me. We need not play these silly games."

I inched under the cruiser's hull, ignoring the sick feeling in my gut as I measured the distance between me and Ezra— which was a lot—and tried to plot an angle of approach where I wouldn't immediately die.

"If you know why I'm here," Zak rumbled, "why did you meet me?"

"Because I would much rather kill you now than endure your pathetic attempts at revenge later."

Zak pushed off the pillar, his arms falling to his sides. "Where is my grimoire, Varvara?"

"Right here, dearest druid." She dipped a hand into her coat and pulled out a small leather-bound book. Opening her hand, she let it fall to the floor like a worthless piece of trash.

Zak's face tightened. "Then we can proceed."

With dark shimmers, his five vargs materialized around him, and Lallakai's wings swept off his arms and unfurled to their full width.

Varvara snapped her fingers.

The cardboard boxes behind her tore apart. Four golems surged off the pallets, their feet clanging on the floor. They stomped forward to flank her, and I gritted my teeth. How was I supposed to reach Ezra now?

"Do you think those will help you?" Zak mocked, his scarlet saber swirling into existence in his hand.

"These are merely for defense." She sighed like a satisfied lover. "Ah, druid, it was an excellent plan. Offer me something I can't refuse to ensure I come ashore. Lie in wait for my return to my yacht. Kill me, free the demon mage, and reunite triumphantly with your pretty redhead friend."

He tensed, a subtle shift of limbs and shoulders.

"Overconfidence has always been your shortcoming, hasn't it, druid? You share that trait with your master. The Wolfsbane trained you well before you killed him." She tapped a claw against her chin. "I have wondered, were you so determined to protect my sweet Nadine because you saw so much of yourself in her?"

Zak went very, very still.

"How old were you," she whispered sweetly, "when he stole you from your parents? Have you ever tried to find them, or were you too young to remember their names?"

My gut twisted painfully.

"How very tragic." She made a mockingly sympathetic sound. "I encountered the Wolfsbane several times before he fled overseas, and he did leave an impression. I would have been far kinder to Nadine than he ever was to you, I am sure."

"What would you know of kindness?" Zak rasped, scarcely sounding human.

"Very little, I admit. Our sort cannot tolerate kindness. Your pretty redhead friend, though … she brimmed with it. I could see her simple, fragile heart breaking as I told her how you'd betrayed her."

Zak's scarlet saber twitched as though his hand had spasmed. "What?"

"Did it not occur to you that your pawns might deviate from your plan? You told me the demon mage would arrive alone, so imagine my surprise when your pretty friend walked in with him."

"No. She wasn't there."

"She was weeping as I left her trapped in the spell you suggested I use."

He hesitated. "You left her?"

"Yes." Varvara smiled. "In the gentle company of my last golem."

Zak jolted like she'd struck him—and so did Ezra. His shoulders hunched inward, a low sound growling in his throat, muffled by the spell over his face.

Black shadows swirled around Zak's feet, spreading outward. "You're a dead woman, Varvara. I'll watch you die choking on your own blood."

"Ah," she purred, "but you haven't yet realized your greatest oversight."

His jaw flexed, then he spat, "What?"

"The demon mage." She stroked her clawed fingers through Ezra's hair. "You never should have let me take the demon mage first."

She snapped her fingers a second time. The manacle spell around Ezra turned to black ink, which dropped to the floor with a splash. It was still falling from his face as he lunged for Varvara—but she was ready for his attack.

"*Ori tuum da mihi pectus*"—her hand slapped against his cheek—"*tuum iam meum est!*"

Ezra staggered backward, hands half raised and crimson magic sparking weakly over his fingers. He took another stumbling step away from her, and the light from Zak's crystal washed over his face. I choked on a gasp.

A dark splotch, radiating a sickly green glow, covered his cheek.

I'd seen that splotch before. Seen that exact spell. Seen it stuck to Aaron's face as he turned on Ezra and cut the aeromage down with a merciless stroke of his sword.

With her golems standing guard around her, the sorceress gestured at the druid. "Kill him."

Ezra lurched away, shaking his head back and forth. His left eye glowed more brightly and a ring of frost formed around his feet.

Varvara frowned. "Kill the druid *now*."

Arms falling to his side, Ezra stood unmoving, except for the rise and fall of his shoulders—and the crimson magic igniting over his hands.

With a bright flare, eight-inch talons of phantom power extended from his fingers. Veins twisted up his arms, and curved spines protruded from his shoulders. The temperature plunged below freezing.

He raised his head. Eerie light snaked up the left side of his face and over his glowing eye. Semi-transparent horns formed above his temples, and with a flare of red, the gel-like splat on his cheek burned away. The artifact fell off him and hit the floor with a clink.

"You cannot control me."

His words were a guttural rasp, and I had no idea if it was Ezra or Eterran speaking.

Zak threw his head back in a harsh laugh. "Who's the overconfident one, Varv—"

Ezra flung his hand up. Power surged down his arm and blasted out of his palm.

Zak sprang sideways and the spinning orb of demonic magic hit the pillar behind him. The concrete burst into shards. He reeled away, his vargs scattering as debris showered the floor.

"I'm not your tool," Ezra snarled, sounding nothing like himself. Magic blazed across his forearms and snapped outward into complex circles filled with jagged runes. He extended both palms toward Varvara, mere feet away from him.

Terror blanked her face.

"I won't be used!"

A beam of crimson exploded from his hands. Varvara threw herself onto the floor and the attack scarcely missed her as it screamed across the building, tearing through concrete pillars, thirty-foot boats, and heavy machinery like they were flimsy movie props. Crashes and booms pierced my ears like knives.

Shoving onto her hands and knees, Varvara shouted a command in Latin. Her golems charged the demon mage.

He raised his arms. Four spell circles appeared in the air, hovering above the golems—moving with them as they closed in. Four more circles appeared beneath them. Crimson power pulsed.

As the steel beasts leaped for him, he bared his teeth. *"Evashvā vīsh."*

Light blazed between each pair of circles, forming cylinders of solid crimson. The four spells shrank inward and disappeared with a hiss. Torn scraps of metal clattered to the floor, all that was left of the golems.

"This …" Varvara stammered, backing away with her hands raised defensively. Her trembling breath puffed white in the arctic air. "This is … the power of … a demon mage?"

Crouched amidst the rubble with his vargs around him, Zak watched Ezra, his face pale and tense.

"I am not *adh'vēthēs*," Ezra hissed, the words cracking and breaking. "*Eshanā nul adh'vēthēs … Eshanā … nul …*"

He jerked his head sideways, then lifted his hands again. As red circles ringed his arms, his left eye glowed even brighter—but his right eye was still dark. When Eterran was in control, both Ezra's eyes glowed. What was happening?

The circles around his arms flared.

A spell coalesced underneath Varvara, fifteen feet across. Another one flashed beneath Zak. More appeared beneath his vargs. The frigid air shuddered as intangible power suffused the atmosphere, heavy and violent.

The spells exploded.

I screamed, my voice lost in the detonation. Pillars shattered, the floor split, chunks of the ceiling collapsed. As red light filled my vision, I ducked behind the thick post of the rig suspending the cruiser. Stinging debris whipped across my shoulders, tearing my leather sleeves, and the steel rig shook. The boat fell to the concrete with a bang.

The glare faded, and I looked around the post to find … rubble. Nothing but rubble and the four walls of the building. Moonlight streamed down through gaping holes in the ceiling.

With a faint clatter, Zak stumbled out of a cloud of dust, Lallakai's wings curled around him. Blood ran down his face, his clothes half shredded from shrapnel.

Violet light gleamed, and a cube-shaped spell faded to reveal Varvara crouched inside it, unharmed. She clutched a pendant around her neck, breathing hard.

Ezra stood in the center of the destruction. Red magic surged over his body in writhing patterns. Horns rose from his head. Spines jutted from his shoulders. And … and …

And phantom red wings arched off his back, stiff ribs curving with deadly elegance. A long tail ending in barbs lashed behind him, semi-transparent—but solid enough to send bits of gravel rolling away from it. One eye glowed bright red, the other dark as night.

He thrust his hands out, mouth moving, unintelligible words snarling from his throat. Power flashed—spell circles. More spell circles. They popped into existence all around him, blazing, expanding. More. And more. A dozen circles, then two.

"Ezra!" Zak roared, staggering upright. "Stop it before you destroy everything!"

His demonic wings flared wide, mismatched eyes staring. "*I will not be used!*"

Zak's face blanked, and I knew he'd heard the same thing in those five words as I had.

Madness.

Ezra's face contorted with uncontrollable rage, with mindless fear, with soul-destroying torment. He stretched his arms out and his arsenal of spell circles swelled with building power.

Madness.

The word hammered in my skull.

Ezra's fear of what Varvara would do to him. Eterran's fury at her attempt to control him. Ezra's grief over my supposed death. Eterran's rage at being a tool trapped in a human body. Ezra's despair over his impending death.

Fear, fury, grief, rage, despair, terror, torment. Ezra's emotions feeding Eterran's feeding Ezra's. The feedback loop. The unstoppable spiral into madness and death.

I shoved away from my hiding spot and ran for him.

The spell circles were flaring brighter. Varvara was rushing away, but there was no escaping the spells—they were everywhere. Zak shouted my name but I didn't stop, my pain and fatigue forgotten.

"Ezra!" I screamed.

His head turned. Mismatched eyes fixed on me, one burning with manic power, one dark and empty. His lips peeled back.

Blind hatred and rage and anguish—and no sign of the man I loved.

He extended his hand toward me. Power blazed over his fingers, a final spell circle taking form across his palm and spreading outward, aimed square at my chest. The magic pulsed one more time, the tainted air poison in my lungs, my breath puffing white, the ground coated in ice.

I wrenched the Carapace of Valdurna from my pocket, and the demonic spells detonated.

The world turned to howling crimson. What remained of the ceiling tore away. The floor shattered into chasms. Water pipes burst, spouting liquid that instantly froze. Hunks of concrete and rebar slammed down like cannonballs.

And none of it touched me.

The Carapace clung to me in draping folds, the hood resting on my head. My whole body was numb, all sight and sound and sensation muted, but I could feel the quaking ground under my feet as I ran.

The magic spilling through the room melted out of my path. Ezra's hand was still stretched toward me, phantom wings spread, teeth bared. I didn't slow.

I dove for the floor and slid full tilt into his legs. He pitched forward, catching himself on his hands. As he shoved up onto his knees, I threw myself at his chest, knocking him over backward.

With a sweep of my arms, I pulled the Carapace over us both.

He thudded into the ground and the amethyst fabric, shimmering with unfathomable power, settled gently over us. His crimson wings and horns dissolved into glittering specks that swirled into the sparkling fabric. The veins crawling over him faded as they too were drawn into the Carapace. Last of all, the glow in his left eye dimmed from burning red to the palest pink, then finally to ice white.

"Ezra?"

He didn't react to my whisper, gazing blankly upward.

"Ezra?" I shook him gently, then with more force. "Ezra? Say something."

Reaching over my shoulder, I grabbed the Carapace and flung it away. The fabric soared three feet and pooled gracefully amidst the rubble. I shook him again, his stare terrifyingly empty.

"Ezra, please answer me!" My voice broke. "Say something. Anything!"

His eyelids flickered. The faintest gleam in his left eye, and the pale pupil contracted in the dim light. His gaze turned to my face, and I knew. I knew at a glance it wasn't Ezra looking at me.

He'd told me. Warned me. *Eterran might survive it, but I won't.*

"Where is Ezra?" I demanded shrilly. "Give him back, Eterran!"

His mouth twisted.

"Give him back!" Tears spilled down my cheeks. "Give Ezra back right now! He's there! You're suppressing him again, but he's still—he's still there."

For the first time in any of our interactions, Eterran broke eye contact with me. He looked away, but I'd already seen his pity.

"No!" I seized his face and forced his gaze back to mine. "If you want out of that body, Eterran, you'll bring Ezra back! Right now! Bring him back and I swear I'll free you!"

He considered me in silence, pain and exhaustion and things I couldn't name swirling in that pale eye.

"I want freedom," he whispered, a guttural accent tinging his words, "more than I want this body. I will try."

He closed his eyes. His jaw tightened, muscles tensing beneath me, and he drew in a deep breath. Released it. Breathed in again. I couldn't breathe at all, still holding his cheeks, his skin icy under my chilled fingers.

His chest rose again—and his eyes cracked open.

My fingers dug into his face. I didn't dare to hope. Couldn't stop myself from hoping anyway. "Ezra?"

A warm brown eye focused on my face, and his forehead wrinkled in confusion.

"Tori?" My name was a rough rasp in his throat, nothing like his usual silken voice—but it was him. *It was him.*

"*Ezra!*" A sob tore through me and I collapsed onto his chest, burying my face in his neck. "I thought you were gone. I thought you were gone!"

I clutched him, crying hoarsely and unable to stop. He wrapped his arms around me, his limbs trembling, devoid of strength.

"I thought you were dead," he muttered into my hair, the words as unsteady as his arms. "I thought she killed you. I thought …"

My hands tightened on his shoulders, my whole body shaking.

Gravel crunched nearby. I jerked up with a gasp and my hysterical relief went cold.

Varvara bent down and pinched the Carapace between two fingers. She lifted a corner of the enchanted fabric. "So, this … is the Carapace of Valdurna."

How? How had she survived that demonic unleashing? The ceiling was gone. All the yachts and equipment inside the building had been reduced to pebbles and scrap metal. Fissures zigzagged across the floor. Ezra's magic had destroyed *everything*.

She lifted her hooded gaze to us. "Impressive, my darling demon mage. Now that you've been so thoroughly disarmed, I can find a better way to control all that power."

Fury seared my innards—but my terror was stronger. I looked down at the hair elastic on my wrist where I'd tucked the Queen of Spades. The card was nestled exactly as I'd left it, but its rectangular face, where the regal Queen had sat with her scepter in hand and a mysterious smile on her lips … it was blank.

The Carapace had wiped it clean.

28

VARVARA POINTED her clawed fingers at me and Ezra. "*Egeirai—*"

The tiniest clink of a dislodged rock.

Her head snapped sideways, and she whipped her hand out, screaming, "*Impello!*"

Zak, leaping across the rubble with Lallakai's wings sweeping out on either side of him, thrust his arm out, a black rune marking his palm. "*Impello!*"

The identical cantrips met with a boom. Zak soared through the rippling air and slammed into Varvara, his scarlet saber just missing her side. She hurled a potion to the floor and it erupted into a cloud of pink smoke. He reeled back, three crystals glowing on his chest, then charged into the opaque mist.

A clang of metal, Varvara shrieking an incantation, Zak's furious snarl—but I wasn't watching.

"Tori?" Ezra whispered.

Sprawled half on his chest, I stared at my Queen of Spades card.

Gone.

The card's face was blank, the spell inside it gone, and I felt naked. The Queen had been my first artifact, my first ally in battle. She'd been with me for every fight, my ace in the hole, my literal trump card. She'd fended off mages, sorcerers, demons, golems. Every time I'd needed her, she'd been there to save my butt.

Now she was gone, erased by the Carapace's magic.

I'd had no time to remove my artifacts before donning the cloak. A single second's delay would've meant my death—and Ezra's. I'd known what I was sacrificing when I pulled the Carapace from my pocket, but seeing it …

The crystals hanging from my wrist clinked together, dull and mundane. The brass knuckles were no more than brass. Even the potions in my paintball gun had been rendered impotent.

For the first time since I'd picked up the Queen of Spades in that back alley across from my brother's apartment, I was magicless.

I wrapped my arms around Ezra and buried my face in his shoulder, shielding him as I hid from the bursts of power, the clang of weapons, the sizzle of magic. Strange odors singed my nose as Zak and Varvara unleashed spell after potion after spell. Their voices rang out with incantations.

Two dark-arts masters, nothing left to fight with but their own skills.

Varvara screamed, and I dragged my head up.

High above us, the full moon shone down through the shattered roof, silvery light streaking the smoke that hung over the battle arena. Colorful liquids splattered the broken floor and hunks of collapsed ceiling. One piece of concrete bubbled, the steam rising in bizarre corkscrews.

Still screaming, Varvara clutched her wrist to her chest—the bloody stump of her wrist, her hand gone. Scrabbling in the front of her coat, she flung a glittering artifact away from her, howling the incantation.

Zak braced his arm and his yellow fae shield popped outward, spanning his full height. Lances of shiny fuchsia power impaled his shield, their points inches from his body. He cast his arm out, banishing the shield and the spell it had halted, and leaped closer, blade swinging.

She spat an incantation, and a shimmer of darkness appeared in the path of his sword. The scarlet blade, able to cut through steel, bounced off. He recovered and slashed again, but more Latin fell from her lips. Over and over, as fast as he could strike, she called a spell to stop him.

As he lunged furiously, his blade skidded across a patch of dark magic and he took a step too close.

She surged toward him and raked her steel claws down his forearm—tearing through his druid tattoos. His saber burst into shards of light and he stumbled backward.

"*Ori tuum da mihi pectus,*" she screamed triumphantly as she reached for him, a dark disc in her grip, "*tuum iam—*"

He pulled a serrated dagger from the sheath on his thigh and rammed the blade into her chest.

The air behind the sorceress shimmered. In a swirl of raven hair, Lallakai appeared, her full red lips smiling—and only then did I realize the feather tattoos were missing from Zak's arms. She leaned over Varvara's shoulder as the sorceress gaped at Zak, shock in her eyes.

"You lose," the darkfae whispered into the silence.

Zak ripped the blade out of his enemy. As she fell back, he threw the dagger aside and grabbed her by the throat with both hands. Teeth bared, he lifted her, bringing her face close to his, her feet brushing the ground.

"I told you," he rasped, "I would watch you die while you choked on your own blood."

The muscles in his arms tautened, and a horrible crunch echoed through the demolished building. A spasm shook her body, a strangled whimper escaping her crushed throat.

"One death isn't enough." He stared into her eyes. "You could die a thousand times and it wouldn't be enough."

She scraped at his wrist with her remaining hand, wheezing with pain and terror, her legs thrashing. Zak didn't move, his arms steady as he held her by the throat, the seconds dragging. Her movements grew more frantic, then slowed. Her arms fell to her sides, and with a final hoarse gurgle, she went still.

Even then, he didn't move. Lallakai, standing a few steps away, smiled as she observed her druid.

A slow breath slid from him, then he opened his hands. The sorceress's body hit the floor in a graceless heap. He studied his defeated enemy for a moment more, then walked into the rubble. Stooping, he searched through the crumbling concrete. After a minute, he straightened, brushed the dust off his grimoire, and tucked it into a pocket.

His green eyes, human and exhausted, turned to mine.

Evidence of the violent struggle he'd survived was written all over him. Blood ran down his face from a cut across his cheek. More slices raked his torso, his shirt in tatters. Burns singed one shoulder. His belt was nearly empty of vials, his spelled crystals dark. Only one fae rune remained on his left forearm, and his right was a mess, blood obscuring the remaining tattoos.

Ignoring Lallakai, he started toward me.

I looked down. Ezra watched me, his fatigue a thousand times worse than Zak's—and made worse by the anguished despair lurking in the back of his gaze. Ezra knew he'd reached the precipice. Knew that, for a few minutes, he'd fallen into the madness he'd feared for almost a decade.

He had survived the night, but at what cost?

I touched his cheek. "Wait here."

He smiled. It was faint, shallow, tinged with sorrow, but somehow, he still smiled for me. "I don't think I can stand, so sure."

Two more tears leaked from my eyes as I brushed a gentle kiss across his lips. Then I pushed myself up, rubbed the tears from my cheeks, and faced the druid.

He stopped five long steps from me, subtle wariness in his expression. I peered into his eyes, searching for the one thing I needed to see.

"You killed her." I pointed at the sorceress's body. "With your own two hands, just like you wanted."

He flicked a glance at his slain foe, then looked back to me.

"Are you satisfied?" I fought to keep the words steady. "Was it worth it, Zak?"

"I avenged the lives I needed to avenge."

A tremor ran through me from head to toe, and I searched his eyes one more time, but no matter how hard I looked, I saw no regret. My jaw quivered but I fought back the sob.

He rolled his shoulders. "Don't give me that look. My plan all along was to kill Varvara before she could escape with Ezra. I had no idea he'd lose it like that."

"I told you he was almost out of time," I said hoarsely, the tremor condensing in my chest. "I told you he was losing control."

"I still didn't know that would happen."

"What about the others? Aaron and Kai? My guild?" My hands clenched into fists. "You told Varvara our whole plan and let them walk into a trap."

"I misled her about your numbers. She was expecting half their force. They could handle it."

"Handle it?" My composure broke, my voice rising. "*Handle it?* You have no idea! No idea what Varvara set up, what they had to fight! You said yourself she could anticipate anything! You have no idea whether they're still alive!"

His scowl deepened. "Tori—"

"*Was it worth it?*" The question burst out of me in a scream. "Was killing her with your bare hands worth everything you lost? Was avenging lives already gone worth destroying the ones still left? Was getting everything you wanted worth betraying me?"

"I told you—"

"*You put everyone I love at risk!*" My voice, my scream, was so loud it hurt my ears. "My guild, my friends, Aaron, Kai, Ezra! You lied to us and tricked us! You put us all in danger so you could kill someone who'd have died anyway when MagiPol executed her!"

"*If* they ex—"

"Aaron and Kai could be dead! Sin is out there too! Everyone—"

"If Aaron and Kai are dead, then they weren't half the mages they pretended to be."

His words hit me like blows, interrupting my burning fury. No regret. No apology. Was he that determined to feel no remorse? Was he that certain everything he'd done had been necessary ... or did he just not care about the lives he'd endangered?

I looked down at my wrist and the blank face of my Queen of Spades artifact. I'd run into an explosion of demonic power to save Ezra, sacrificing my only magic to reach him. I had put my life on the line again and again to save my friends, because that's what friends did.

"We were never friends," I whispered.

"I know."

Instead of the annoyance I'd expected, his words were quiet and bitter.

"We could've been friends. If you'd opened up even a little. If you'd trusted me."

He gazed at me, expressionless. Silence stretched between us.

Turning, I walked through the debris to the Carapace. I carefully folded the material, then returned to the druid. Taking his hand, his skin streaked with blood and dirt, I pressed the fabric square into his cantrip-marked palm and held it there.

His fingers closed tight around the artifact. "Tori—"

"I risked my life for you, Zak." I held on to his hand, unable to look up and see his remorseless eyes again. "I trusted you with everything that mattered to me, with everyone I love, and they trusted you because I did. I would've been your loyal friend, even if you're a mean dickhead and kind of scary sometimes."

Releasing his hand, I stepped back. "But you chose your revenge instead. I hope it was worth it."

His eyes widened at my tone. My fury was gone, and I'd whispered the words with miserable resignation.

It didn't matter if grief and fury had clouded his judgment. It didn't matter if he'd had a plan. It didn't matter if he'd thought everything would work out just fine in the end. I wouldn't allow someone in my life who was willing to risk my loved ones for his own goals. Someone who would hurt us, betray us, for selfish ambitions.

"Don't come back," I whispered, my voice breaking, "until … or unless … you decide it wasn't worth it."

As I turned away from him, my eyes met Lallakai's. Standing nearby, with her arms folded and a hip cocked, she ran the tip of her pink tongue across her lips.

My breath shuddered out as I walked back to Ezra. He'd managed to sit up, but his shoulders were hunched, his eyes closed and his normally bronze skin pale with exhaustion so deep it was closer to an illness. The Carapace had drained every iota of his magic—and his strength.

Kneeling beside him, I put my arm around his shoulders. His eyelids fluttered.

Silence. I could feel Zak's attention on me. Unable to stop myself, I looked back.

He stood where I'd left him, hands fisted at his sides. His chest heaved, his eyes burning—but not with rage. Behind him, Lallakai uncrossed her arms, her face hardening with displeasure.

Opening his mouth to speak, Zak took a step toward me.

Fire exploded out of the shadows.

Lallakai sprang forward. Her arms swept around Zak, and with a flick of her slender hand, she sent a wave of shadow crashing into the oncoming fire. Another flick of her fingers and the bolt of lightning leaping for Zak's chest burst apart, the branching electricity diving for the ground.

Shadowy wings unfurled from her back. Green eyes glowing, she looked straight into my face, mouthed a single word, and folded her wings around Zak. The last thing I saw before he disappeared in a shimmer of fading shadows was the intensity in his eyes dousing with bitter resignation. He and the fae vanished.

"No!" His shout echoing off the walls, Aaron charged out of the darkness. Fire sparked off his hands. "Where did he go? Damn it!"

A few steps behind him, Kai jogged into view. Twiggy hung from his shoulders, crystalline eyes wide. Katana in hand, the electramage turned in a circle, then gave his head a sharp shake. "They're gone."

Aaron swore furiously.

Sheathing his sword, Kai turned to me. So did Aaron. Smudged with soot. Torn, dirty clothes and scuffed gear. Splattered with blood, marred with scrapes.

But alive. Unhurt. Mostly unhurt. Good enough.

As I heaved myself to my feet, they rushed to meet me. Aaron scooped me against his chest, and Kai brushed a hand over my hair before kneeling beside Ezra. Arms banded around my shoulders, Aaron gave me a comforting squeeze—and I yelped as a truckload of pain hit me all at once, every part of my body in sudden agony.

"Sorry." Hands on my shoulders, Aaron took a step back. "Are you hurt? Where …" His gaze zoomed down me, and his face went white. "Holy shit! Kai!"

Kai was at our side in an instant. "What?"

"She's covered in blood!"

My eyebrows scrunched confusedly. Blood? Was I hurt?

Aaron tugged my zipper down and Kai peeled my jacket off. Punctures across my torso leaked blood all down my shirt.

Oh. Right.

"Do you have a blood replenisher?" Aaron demanded. "We need to get her to Elisabetta."

Kai pulled a vial with one of Sin's handwritten labels from a pocket in his vest. "Tori? Stay with us."

"I'm okay. I used a bleeding ... stopper ... potion thing on my arm."

"Your arm?" Aaron found my sliced limb and swore under his breath. "Drink the potion, Tori."

They dosed me with an icky brown liquid, bandaged my arm so tightly my hand went numb, then Aaron scooped me into his arms. Kai helped Ezra to his feet, then pulled the unsteady aeromage over his shoulder in a fireman carry.

"Why," he grunted breathlessly as he braced against Ezra's weight, "do you get the girl and I get a guy who's taller than me?"

"Luck of the draw."

"You're an ass."

A giggle scraped my throat—and the next thing I knew, I was crying. Aaron's arms tightened, and he whispered reassurances as he strode to the overhead door. Neither mage commented on the destruction—or on Varvara's body.

Through tear-blurred vision, I peered over Aaron's shoulder at the spot where Zak had disappeared. Lallakai's smug smile flashed in my mind, along with the single-word message she'd delivered to me alone.

One word.

Mine.

29

I TOSSED A KERNEL of popcorn in the air and caught it in my mouth. Score! Was I awesome or what?

Too bad no one was watching.

Beside me, Aaron's head was slumped back against the cushions, his bowl of popcorn sliding sideways off his lap and his mouth gaping as he snored. Scooping up his bowl, I set it on the coffee table and curled up again, munching through another handful of buttery deliciousness.

Dramatic music poured from the surround-sound speakers as our action hero—Jason Statham, this time—ran across the screen. Or what I could see of the screen. A spindly bush blocked a portion of my view.

"Twiggy," I called quietly. "Don't sit so close."

Not looking away from the flawless LCD before him, the faery backed up maybe three inches. Rolling my eyes, I let him enjoy it. His reaction to Aaron's monstrous flat screen had been priceless. The poor, sheltered fae hadn't realized TVs came that large, and he quivered with excitement as Jason punched his way through a pack of goons—losing his shirt in the process. I fully approved.

Silently laughing, I glanced at Aaron, wishing he was awake to see Twiggy's newfound love for his tech, but less than twenty-four hours had passed since he'd battled for his life—and the lives of his guildmates—and he was still exhausted. Elementaria took a heavy toll on the mage's body.

As he gargled through a snore, I got out my phone and opened the camera. Leaning close, I pulled a funny face, Aaron's sleeping countenance framed over my shoulder. The phone made a fake shutter noise as I snapped the pic.

Perfect. Maybe I'd print the photo and hang it above the bar.

Tucking my phone away, I settled down again. On my other side, a silver head lifted and fuchsia eyes blinked drowsily. Another sleepy survivor of last night's chaos. Hoshi yawned widely, flashing her scary little teeth, then tucked her nose under her tail.

I stroked her warm neck, missing the reassuring flickers of color she'd normally send me. Our connection, like my artifacts, was gone. I could no longer communicate with the fae.

My throat tried to close, and I hurriedly stuffed more popcorn in my mouth. I was determined not to wallow. It didn't matter how shitty everything was. My friends were alive and unharmed, and that's what mattered.

Finishing my popcorn, I started on Aaron's bowl as Jason Statham, fully clothed again, parachuted onto the back of a fast-moving semi-truck. Yeah, that was cool and all, but I knew three mages who were way more badass.

A quiet clatter brought my head around. Twiggy tore his stare off the TV and squinted toward the entryway.

The front door thudded and Aaron woke with a snort, his head lifting off the cushions. His bleary blue eyes scrunched with confusion.

A man stepped into the doorway between the living room and front hall.

"Kai!" I half shrieked, almost dumping popcorn all over the sofa as I leaped to my feet. I flew across the room and grabbed him in a crushing hug. He wrapped his arms around me, holding just as tight.

"Dude," Aaron exclaimed right behind me. He clapped his best friend on the shoulder. "Finally!"

Kai smiled wanly, paler than usual. "I can't stay long."

My exuberant relief crashed and burned. I pushed back from his hug, gripping his arms. "What do you mean? You ... aren't ..."

Of course he wasn't back for good.

Varvara was dead, her rogue army—the survivors—arrested and in MagiPol lockup. But defeating the sorceress hadn't magically changed Kai's fate. He was still under orders to rejoin his family, and disobedience still meant death.

Aaron swore quietly.

"I came to get my things, but I have a few minutes." Kai drew us toward the sofa again. "How are you doing, Tori?"

As I dropped onto the sofa, pulling Kai down with me, Hoshi raised her head. She flared her wings, then faded out of sight. With a quick glance at us, Twiggy muttered something, pressed pause on the remote, and vanished too. I frowned. Had he just taken a TV remote to faery land?

I scanned the floor for any sign of it. Huh.

"I'm fine," I told Kai as Aaron sat on my other side. "Elisabetta fixed me up last night, then I slept until, like, three this afternoon."

"How's Ezra?"

"He's sleeping upstairs. His aero magic is coming back, but he's still wiped. The Carapace did a number on him."

An anxious crease formed between his brows. "Have you talked to him?"

"A few times, but he hasn't been very talkative."

Aaron looked away, his jaw clenched. Kai rubbed a hand over his forehead, equally tense. In brief, whispered spurts last night, I'd told them how Varvara had tried to use her mind-control splat on Ezra, how he'd gone on a demon-magic rampage, and how I'd used the Carapace to stop him.

"We need to talk to him," Kai whispered. "This is … He's said all along …"

"That if he ever truly lost control," Aaron finished gruffly, "he didn't want to put others in danger."

"Darius promised to do it." Kai closed his eyes, haggard lines deepening around his mouth. "But I think … Aaron, I think we should do it. We should do that for him."

Aaron's hands balled into tight fists. "The demon may fight back. We'll have to plan—"

I grasped their arms. "No."

"Tori," Aaron said heavily, "I know it's hard, but this isn't about us. It's about Ezra and—"

"No." Nerves danced through my gut. "We're not giving up yet."

Neither of them met my eyes, despair rolling off them. I gritted my teeth, debating whether this was the time to bring them in on my secrets—but no. They were too raw and too hopeless to handle the knowledge that Eterran already had the upper hand over Ezra. I couldn't risk them taking drastic action.

Besides, I was due for an important discussion first.

"We all need to talk to Ezra," I said bracingly. "Don't jump the gun."

Aaron let out a shaky breath. "Right. You're right. We don't need to rush."

Kai nodded, not quite able to hide his relief. "How's everyone at the guild? Elisabetta and Miles were working overtime when I left last night."

"Left" was an awfully nice way of saying, "Makiko dragged me away while half my guildmates were still injured." Then again, half *their* team had been injured too and she'd needed help getting them to their own healers.

Aaron leaned back on the sofa. "Everyone who was critically injured is out of danger except Zora, but Elisabetta and Miles think she'll pull through."

"Zora?" Kai's expression darkened. "She was paired up with Robin Page."

The two mages exchanged meaningful looks.

"I'll have a word with her," Aaron said. "Find out what really happened."

Before I could ask if he meant he'd be having a word with Zora or with Robin, Kai slid his phone out of his pocket to check the time. "I need to go."

I'd grabbed his arm before I realized I was moving. "Don't leave. We need you here."

He covered my hand with his. "I know, Tori, but I have to."

"Kai …"

He lifted his gaze to Aaron, who stared back at him with blazing blue eyes.

"Are you running?" the pyromage asked. "Or are you fighting?"

"I'm done running."

"Good."

I frowned in anxious confusion.

Kai squeezed my hand, then rose to his feet. "I don't know what I can do or how I can fix this, but I'm going to try."

Nerves churned in my gut, but I smiled fiercely in answer to the determination in his face. Together, we traipsed upstairs, and Aaron and I helped—or rather, mostly got in the way—as Kai packed some clothes, gear, weapons, and electronics in a duffel bag. We waited in the hall as he ducked into Ezra's bedroom, then we descended the stairs.

Kai hooked the duffel bag's strap on his shoulder. "Take care of Ezra. I'll be back as soon as I can."

"You'd better." I threw my arms around him. "And you'll answer your phone?"

"Yes."

Good. Because very soon, I would need them both.

The guys embraced, then Kai left Aaron and I standing side by side behind the screen door as he crossed the front lawn to the black sedan idling at the curb. He slid into the backseat, his pale face turning toward us before he closed the door.

As the car pulled away, Aaron put his arm over my shoulder, holding me close. I slid an arm around his waist, my fingers gripping his shirt.

"He'll be back," Aaron whispered. "He'll figure it out."

If anyone could find a way out of that mess, Kai could. In the meantime, I had my own mess to figure out.

I shooed Aaron back to the sofa, knowing he'd drift off again within five minutes—and did a double take when I saw that Twiggy had reappeared in front of the TV, the movie playing again. Shaking my head, I ascended the stairs.

For a long moment, I stood outside Ezra's bedroom, staring at the door. Then I pushed it open. The room was dark, his guitar a silhouette in the corner. Ezra was an unmoving shape under the blankets, but as I approached the bed, the shadow of his head turned.

"Tori?" he murmured.

"Hey." I sat on the edge of the mattress. "How are you feeling?"

"Exhausted," he admitted. "I'm not sure I've ever been this tired in my life."

"The Carapace is pretty crazy, huh?"

A quiet pause. "Tori, you … What you did …"

I pulled my feet onto the bed and scooched closer. "I did what I did to keep you alive, Ezra. I don't regret a thing."

Again, he was silent, and I could guess what he was thinking. I'd known him long enough now to read his silences.

I'd kept him alive, but it was all futile. His time was up. He'd lost control, and he couldn't continue pretending to live a normal life while his emotions—and sanity—were so volatile. He was a danger to everyone around him. Soon, he would ask Aaron, Kai, or Darius to end his life before he hurt someone.

But he didn't say any of that, and I was glad.

I found his face in the darkness and slid my fingertips across his cheek. My thumb traced his lower lip, then I leaned down and kissed him softly. His hand ran across my shoulder, slid up my neck, and tangled in my hair.

Lifting my mouth, I let my lips brush across his. "Don't give up yet, Ezra."

"How can I fight this?" he whispered. "How can I stop it?"

"Trust me." I touched our foreheads together. "Hold on a bit longer."

He sighed tiredly. I settled beside him, our hands entwined. For a few minutes, I could feel his gaze on my face, though it was too dark to see much. Gradually, his breathing evened out, his chest rising and falling in the slow rhythm of sleep.

I stayed where I was, caressing the back of his hand, tracing each knuckle and finding the callouses from years of weapons training. My gaze lingered on the window, but I couldn't see the sky where, behind the thick winter cloud cover, the full moon glowed.

Ezra's chest rose in a deeper breath. The air slid from his lungs. His fingers tightened around mine, then relaxed.

Faint red sparked in the darkness.

I looked into those crimson eyes. "Eterran."

"Tori."

I tightened my grip on Ezra's hand. Eterran's hand. The difference between the two had shrunk, their fates bound, their time almost up.

Fear slid through me—but my determination was stronger.

"Eterran, we need to talk."

LOOKING AT THE BLANK FACE of my Queen of Spades card, yellowed with age and tattered at the edges, hurt like an open wound. Two days had done nothing to numb the sting.

My other artifacts lay across the table: the fall-spell ruby, the interrogation spell, the brass knuckles. Replacing the sleep potions and smoke bombs had been as simple as asking Sin for more, but these ... these were a different case.

At the table with me were four of my guildmates. Lim and Jia, bent with age and their hair snowy white, sat quietly. Weldon, wearing a greasy cowboy hat, frowned at the line of former artifacts. Ramsey, his black hair falling across one dark-lined eye, watched me with subdued sympathy.

"This one." Jia tapped her wrinkled forefinger against the poisonous green crystal. "Arcana that unduly influences the mind is illegal and harshly punished."

"You'll be lucky to find anyone who can make a spell like that," Weldon added in his rural drawl. "Though if you do ... worth a lot."

Ramsey shot the older sorcerer an irritated glare. "Tori doesn't want spells to sell on the black market. She wants to replace the magic she lost."

"I don't need that one," I said. "Even if you could do it, I won't ask anyone to make illegal magic." I slid the green crystal aside. "What about the fall spell?"

Weldon grunted. "I'm more familiar with the stronger version—*decidas in astris*—but I could try to find the baby one if that's what you want. Might not be exactly the same."

"It will *not* be the same," Lim decided. He lifted the ruby and laid it across his palm. "This is no mundane gemstone. It's a crystalized alchemic potion."

As Ramsey let out a low whistle, I blinked. "It's a potion?"

"Distilled into crystal form, yes. Using it as a spell receptacle would enhance or alter the spell in some way, but it's an obscure form of artifact engineering that I know little about."

"Where did you get it?" Ramsey asked me.

"From the Crystal Druid. You know … the Ghost."

His eyes widened. "You bought magic from him?"

"Nah. I stole it." Ignoring his shocked expression, I asked, "Can you put a new fall spell in it, or … not that simple?"

"Not that simple." Weldon pushed the brim of his hat up. "Spell would need to work with the alchemic receptacle and all that, but I can make you a new one in a standard talisman."

"Right," I said, squashing my disappointment. "Okay."

"I'm familiar with the amplifying spell," Lim murmured, picking up the brass knuckles. "I could replicate it without too much trouble."

My heart leaped. "That would be wonderful."

Nodding, he slid the brass knuckles into his pocket. We all looked at the last artifact on the table: the former Queen of Spades, now a blank card.

Ramsey lifted the card with quiet reverence. "Reflector spells aren't as rare as most abjuration, but this one was something else."

Lim adjusted his thick glasses. "A recharge of five minutes, you said? Extraordinary."

Weldon leaned closer to peer at the card. "The painting is gone. Y'all know what that means?"

The other three nodded, but I frowned blankly. "What's it mean?"

"The painting itself was part of the spell," Ramsey explained. "Maybe the engineer used special ink, or hid runes in the artwork. I can't be sure, but it was masterful work."

"So … so you're saying …"

Lim shook his head. "Jia and I have no skill in abjuration."

I looked pleadingly at Weldon.

"The one reflector spell I know," he grunted, "only works on astral sorcery, and it isn't meant for combat. Recharge is two weeks."

Two weeks? That was all but useless. Desperate, I turned to Ramsey.

He set the blank card on the table in front of me. "I'll ask around and see if anyone is selling something similar, but ... this was an exceptional artifact, Tori. It'll be difficult to replace."

I nodded mutely. The four mythics pushed their chairs back from the table.

"I'll begin preparing for the amplifying spell tomorrow," Lim assured me. "I'll let you know later this week when to expect it."

"Thank you."

Jia patted my shoulder as she passed, and the two elderly sorcerers crossed the workroom and descended the stairs. Weldon paused, grunted again, then followed them.

Ramsey leaned down and gave me a sideways, one-armed hug. "There are loads more artifacts out there, Tori. You'll find new ones that work for you, and I'll keep you posted on anything interesting I come across."

"Yeah," I mumbled. "Thanks, Ramsey."

He vanished down the stairs as well, leaving me alone in the huge room. Rumbling noise and bursts of laughter leaked up from the pub below, but the jubilant sounds held little appeal.

I touched a corner of the blank card, my eyes stinging. I'd suspected the Queen was irreplaceable. I'd known as soon as I saw the missing painting. Not for a minute did I think she was more valuable than Ezra, but I kept replaying her final moments in my head, wondering what I could have done differently. Had there been time to drop the card? If I'd acted sooner, could I have saved the Queen too?

Pointless questions with no answers.

Gathering my artifacts, I placed each one in its pocket or pouch in my combat belt. As I rose to my feet, I glanced at the front of the building, where afternoon sunlight shone through the windows—except for the one covered in a sheet of plywood.

I dried my cheeks before descending the steps. As I walked into the pub, warmth and light washed over me. Over half the guild was here, eating and drinking and celebrating the hard-fought victory on Sunday night.

My three favorite mages were noticeably absent from the gathering, but I tried not to think about that.

"Tori!" Cooper called desperately from behind the bar. "Take over for five minutes so I can have a break—"

"Nope." I flashed him a sharp grin. "Elisabetta's orders. I'm supposed to take it easy for a week."

"But—"

Clara burst through the saloon doors, balancing plates of spicy chicken wings on her arms. "Cooper, stop pestering Tori! She's still recovering!"

"But I need a break," he whined.

"You've only been working for two hours!" she yelled. "And this bar is a mess! Did you spill every drink you poured? Where's your towel? … *What?* How can you not find *the bar towels?*"

Chuckling, I walked by as Clara berated Cooper, the apprentice sorcerer shrinking with each angry word. In the basement, I deposited my combat belt and non-magical artifacts in my locker, then returned to the pub.

As I angled toward the stairs to the second floor, an ambush was sprung.

Sin grabbed one of my arms. Sabrina clamped down on the other. And Kaveri stepped in front of me, eyes blazing.

"Uh …" I looked between them. "Hi?"

"*You*," Sin declared, "have some explaining to do."

"I do?"

Kaveri poked me in the sternum. "The 'combat alchemist' who came to the guild for your phone number. The one you kept inviting back. The one who poisoned our GM!"

"Funny thing, he didn't actually—"

"You said you dated him!" Sabrina blurted, shaking my arm as though the truth might spill out of me. "You *dated* the *Ghost*? Did you know he was the Ghost? Did he—"

"The Crystal Druid! Every witch in the province has heard of him!" Kaveri poked me again. "And his familiar is the Night Eagle! Do you even know the legends about her? She's—"

"He kidnapped you," Sin cut in. "Last summer, you were gone for two weeks, then you showed up again and wouldn't talk about what happened." She leaned closer, her stare scarily intense. "Now you *have* to tell us. *Everything*."

My mouth opened, then closed. "Um. Well. I didn't date him, for starters. I just made that up to explain how I knew him. And I couldn't talk about last summer because … uh …"

"Have you been in contact with him since then?" Kaveri demanded. "How well do you know him? Everyone is saying he double-crossed us. Do you—"

I pulled my arms from Sin's and Sabrina's hold. "I need to go."

"Don't worm out of explaining—"

"I actually need to go," I snapped. "I have an appointment."

"What appointment?"

"With Darius."

Surprise washed over their faces, and Kaveri and Sabrina grudgingly backed away. I marched for the stairs.

"Tori."

I reluctantly paused.

Sin stepped onto the bottom stair with me, tucking a lock of silvery-purple hair behind her ear. "Are you okay?"

"Yeah."

"You don't want to talk about the Ghost," she guessed.

"No."

She nodded. "I'll tell the others. We won't bother you about it again." When I looked up uncertainly, she smiled. "But if you need to unload, let me know."

Eyes prickling with tears, I pulled her into a quick hug and mumbled, "Thanks."

As she rejoined the others, I continued up the stairs. Their questions weren't the only ones I'd be getting about the Ghost—nor would they be the only mention of his betrayal. My gut twisted. Why did I feel responsible for his actions? Why did I feel guilty, as though I'd let everyone down? Including him in our strategy had been Shane's call, not mine.

Halfway up the steps to the third floor, I slowed. A voice, raised in anger, echoed down from the offices. Speaking of Shane ...

I hurried forward and the voice grew clearer.

"... *denied* credit entirely."

Darius replied, too quiet for me to make out his words. I entered the large office where Girard's, Tabitha's, and Felix's desks were arranged, buried under paperwork but currently unmanned. At the far end, the door to Darius's smaller office hung open.

"Do you have any idea how long I spent on Varvara's case? Two years, Darius! I started two years ago!"

"I admire your dedication."

I crept across the room. Eavesdropping was a nasty habit, but … whatever.

"Though," Darius added, "if you hadn't crossed paths with the Ghost and realized he had encountered Varvara, the case may never have reached a satisfying conclusion."

"Satisfying?" Shane spat. "Am I satisfied that the MPD has denied me any credit for her bounty?"

"They *are* offering partial bounty payouts to you and the guilds involved," Darius pointed out. "A rather generous one million each, which—"

"I don't care about the money!" A loud smack, like palms striking a tabletop. "*You* told agents it was the Ghost who made the kill. You tipped them off, I know it."

A long, heavy pause.

"I delivered my report, in full, as required," Darius murmured. "How the MPD chooses to assign credit has nothing to do with me."

"You did this to spite me." Another slamming sound. "I will bring you down, Mage Assassin. I'll bring all your crimes down on your head and you'll—"

A chair rolled across the hardwood floor. "You will find a new bounty to chase, Shane. Interfere in my guild again …"

Gooseflesh prickled across my arms.

"Are you threatening me?" Shane asked in a low, hard tone.

"If that's how you'd like to interpret our final farewell," the GM replied pleasantly. "Have a nice day, Mr. Davila."

I stepped aside as footsteps stomped across the floor. Shane wheeled out of the office, his bald head pink with anger. Spotting me, he pressed his lips together and marched right past.

When he was almost at the door, I called, "Shane."

He glanced back, a muscle twitching in his cheek.

"Are you going after Zak now?"

His upper lip curled. "The Ghost isn't worth my time."

"Even though he betrayed you?"

"I expected him to betray me, but I didn't expect him to win." He stepped across the threshold. "Darius's report on her death did not mention the demonic magic all over the scene, but mine will."

He disappeared through the doorway, and his feet thumped on the steps, heading down.

Chilled inside and out, I rubbed my hands over my arms. Why had Shane made a point of telling me he'd identified demonic magic in the building where Varvara had died? If the bounty hunter's psychic abilities had revealed the source of that magic, he would already have arrested—or killed—Ezra.

Gulping, I stuck my head into Darius's office. The GM stood behind his desk and smiled at the sight of me.

"Right on time, Tori."

I stepped inside. "Did you really report that Zak killed Varvara just to spite Shane?"

"It wasn't my sole motivation." He lowered himself into his seat and gestured at the chair across from him. "Is Zak the reason you requested this meeting?"

"No." I closed the office door, then sat. "Zak is gone."

"Will he return?"

I looked down at my hands, a phantom feeling worming into my head—his skin under my fingers as I pressed the Carapace into his hand. "I don't know."

Darius leaned back. "In that case, what can I help you with?"

I squeezed my hands between my knees to banish the phantom sensation. "You know Ezra used his demon magic in that building." I forced my gaze up. "He lost control."

"That has happened, to some degree, before." A pause. "But this time was different?"

"Very different." I stopped, needing to breathe. "He's going to ask you to kill him. Maybe not right away, but soon."

Darius's expression smoothed, becoming unreadable. "I see. Do Aaron and Kai know this?"

"They ... they were talking about it."

"And they want to take this terrible burden on themselves, even though Ezra asked me years ago to do it instead." He considered me. "Are you here to make sure I act first?"

"No. I'm here to ask you not to kill Ezra when he asks you."

A flash of surprise. "Ending Ezra's life while his mind is still intact is a mercy, Tori."

"I know that, but saving his life is better than mercy. You told me anything Ezra's demon wants won't be good for Ezra, but maybe ... maybe that isn't the case."

I took a slow, shuddering breath, then told the guild master what had happened at Christmas—how Eterran had learned to control Ezra while he slept, that he'd snuck into my room, the agreement we'd made. I told Darius about my research, about my meeting with the infernus maker. I described Ezra and Eterran's breakdown at Varvara's hands, and Eterran's whispered words—*I want freedom more than I want this body.*

The only thing I didn't mention was Robin's simultaneous search for the demon amulet; that was a complication I hadn't thought through yet.

When I finished, Darius sat silently. My nerves wound tighter and tighter as he studied me with somber gray eyes.

"I'm afraid you've given me more reason to act quickly rather than any reason to wait."

I leaned forward, gripping my knees. "I told you everything so you'd understand why we *should* wait."

"And why is that?"

My artifacts, my magic, were no more. Zak was gone. Kai was caught in his family's control. Aaron was heartbroken, dreading what would come next. And Ezra's steely strength had finally worn thin, his will to fight cracked and crumbling.

But I wasn't ready to despair. I wasn't ready to give up.

"Eterran and I have a plan, and I need you to trust me."

TORI'S ADVENTURES CONTINUE IN

LOST TALISMANS AND A TEQUILA

THE GUILD CODEX: SPELLBOUND / SEVEN

You know that squirmy sensation in your gut when you have no idea what you're doing and you're about to screw everything up?

Yeah, that feeling.

I thought I was a good judge of character, but recent events proved me very wrong. Now, in a brilliant demonstration of my newfound caution, I'm putting all my faith in a demon—a demon who's tried to kill me before. The squirmy feeling is making sense, right?

Unfortunately, I don't have any other options. Ezra's time is almost up, which means I need answers and I need them fast. So it's time to toughen up, pack my gear, and find me one of the most illegal, reviled, and scarce mythics out there: a demon-mage summoner.

And all I have to do is follow a demon's instructions on where to look. How could *that* go wrong?

www.guildcodex.ca

ABOUT THE AUTHOR

Annette Marie is the author of YA urban fantasy series *Steel & Stone*, its prequel trilogy *Spell Weaver*, and romantic fantasy trilogy *Red Winter*.

Her first love is fantasy, but fast-paced adventures, bold heroines, and tantalizing forbidden romances are her guilty pleasures. She proudly admits she has a thing for dragons, and her editor has politely inquired as to whether she intends to include them in every book.

Annette lives in the frozen winter wasteland of Alberta, Canada (okay, it's not quite that bad) and shares her life with her husband and their furry minion of darkness—sorry, cat—Caesar. When not writing, she can be found elbow-deep in one art project or another while blissfully ignoring all adult responsibilities.

www.annettemarie.ca

SPECIAL THANKS

My thanks to Erich Merkel for sharing your exceptional expertise in Latin and Ancient Greek, to Umayal for helping bring Izzah to life, and to Perry for your Japanese translations. Any errors are mine.

THE
GUILD CODEX
SPELLBOUND

Tori may have lost her magic, but she's still a mythic at heart.
Artifacts or no artifacts, she has her sights set on the man who started
it all: the summoner who turned Ezra into a demon mage.

Welcome to the Crow and Hammer.

DISCOVER MORE BOOKS AT
www.guildcodex.ca

THE
GUILD CODEX
DEMONIZED

Robin Page: outcast sorceress, mythic history buff, unapologetic bookworm, and the last person you'd expect to command the rarest demon in the long history of summoning. Though she holds his leash, this demon can't be controlled.

But can he be tamed?

DISCOVER MORE BOOKS AT
www.guildcodex.ca

STEEL & STONE

When everyone wants you dead, good help is hard to find.

The first rule for an apprentice Consul is *don't trust daemons*. But when Piper is framed for the theft of the deadly Sahar Stone, she ends up with two troublesome daemons as her only allies: Lyre, a hotter-than-hell incubus who isn't as harmless as he seems, and Ash, a draconian mercenary with a seriously bad reputation. Trusting them might be her biggest mistake yet.

SPELL WEAVER

The only thing more dangerous than the denizens of the Underworld ... is stealing from them.

As a daemon living in exile among humans, Clio has picked up some unique skills. But pilfering magic from the Underworld's deadliest spell weavers? Not so much. Unfortunately, that's exactly what she has to do to earn a ticket home.

GET THE COMPLETE TRILOGY
www.annettemarie.ca/spellweaver

CPSIA information can be obtained
at www.ICGtesting.com
Printed in the USA
LVHW032013140220
647002LV00002B/262